MODERN HUMANITIES RESEARCH ASSOCIATION
CRITICAL TEXTS
Volume 78

EDITOR
STEFANO EVANGELISTA
(ENGLISH)

JEWELLED TORTOISE
Volume 10

EDITORS
STEFANO EVANGELISTA
CATHERINE MAXWELL

Decadent Writings of Aubrey Beardsley

EDITED WITH AN INTRODUCTION AND NOTES BY
SASHA DOVZHYK AND SIMON WILSON

Decadent Writings of Aubrey Beardsley

Edited with an Introduction and Notes by

Sasha Dovzhyk and Simon Wilson

Modern Humanities Research Association
2022

Published by

The Modern Humanities Research Association
Salisbury House
Station Road
Cambridge CB1 2LA
United Kingdom

First published 2022

ISBN 978-1-83954-108-7 (paperback)
ISBN 978-1-83954-109-4 (hardback)

Copies may be ordered from www.tortoise.mhra.org.uk

CONTENTS

LIST OF ILLUSTRATIONS

CR refers to a work's number in Linda Gertner Zatlin's *Aubrey Beardsley: A Catalogue Raisonné*, 2 vols (New Haven: Yale University Press, 2016).

ACKNOWLEDGEMENTS

The original manuscript of *Under the Hill* is held in the Rosenbach in Philadelphia, and we must therefore first thank that institution for its co-operation in this project. We would particularly like to thank the registrar Jobi Zink for her help. We discovered that as long ago as 1985 the Rosenbach established that the manuscript was too fragile to copy, and this book would therefore not have been possible without the high-quality photographic record of it made a few years earlier by a German scholar, the late Rüdiger Kampmann, in preparation for his remarkable exhibition *Aubrey Beardsley in den 'Yellow Nineties' 1891–1898: Dekadenz oder Modernität*, held at the Museum Villa Stuck in Munich in 1984. He shared these photographs with Linda Gertner Zatlin, the author of the Beardsley catalogue raisonné published by Yale University Press in 2016. She in turn shared them with us and we are deeply grateful to them both.

The book would have been much less likely to have seen print without the existence of Jewelled Tortoise, the MHRA series presciently set up by Stefano Evangelista and Catherine Maxwell in 2014 specifically to publish scholarly editions of key texts of Decadence, a then burgeoning area of scholarship that continues to expand. Beardsley's unfinished novel, poetry, and other writings fitted perfectly into that, and we thank the editors most warmly for their initial enthusiasm, their patience, and particularly for their meticulous editing which included many valuable suggestions that have enormously improved our texts. Equally meticulous has been Simon Davies's copy-editing of this complex document. We must also thank Gerard Lowe, Senior Publishing Manager at MHRA, for his role in accepting our book for publication. Martin Lohrer gave invaluable help in preparing for publication the digital files of the manuscript. We have thanked in footnotes a number of scholars who kindly helped with queries.

Finally, we would like to acknowledge the work of Ian Fletcher and Annette Lavers who, from the 1960s on, pioneered an appreciation and understanding of Beardsley's writing that established it as something to be taken seriously. In our transcription and annotation here of *Under the Hill* in particular, we have built on their insights and interpretations to offer both a reliable reading of the manuscript, and a fuller picture of the extraordinary complexities and range of reference of Beardsley's text. We hope and anticipate that it may become a springboard for future critique and commentary.

FOREWORD

Simon Wilson

They are not long, the days of wine and roses:
Out of a misty dream
Our path emerges for a while, then closes
Within a dream.
Ernest Dowson, *Verses* (1896)

In the autumn of 1960, I arrived aged eighteen as a student of French at the University of Reading, England. There I met Ian Fletcher, a lecturer in the Department of English, who showed me albums of prints of the work of an artist called Aubrey Beardsley.[1] 'I sat and looked and my soul leaped out upon the new thing.'[2] Beardsley has been central to my life ever since. In 1965, I became a postgraduate student of the history of art at what was then the Courtauld Institute of Art. At some point in my two years there, on a visit to Paris I obtained a copy of the 1959 Olympia Press edition of Beardsley's erotic novella *Under the Hill*, a handsome hardback, bound in green silk. It was based on Leonard Smithers's edition of the story, limited to 300 copies and clandestinely published in 1907. I fell into its warm enchanted world of guilt-free pan-sexual eroticism, and it became an iconic text for me.

At the same time, my interest in Beardsley was supercharged by the legendary 1966 retrospective exhibition of his work at the Victoria and Albert Museum, which incidentally included the original manuscript of *Under the Hill*. Sometime in the early 1990s I obtained a copy of that manuscript. Art has a passion for authenticity. It needs to know that every square millimetre is by the hand of the artist. I felt the same way about Beardsley's book. Reading *Under the Hill* in Beardsley's writing was a thrilling experience and I became aware of the deeply unsatisfactory nature of the published texts that we had. I conceived the idea, a dream then, of an edition such as the one presented here, which is indeed the final realization of that dream. I must add that it would not have been possible without the absolute commitment of Dr Sasha Dovzyk, a brilliant and passionate Beardsley scholar of a much younger generation. I instigated the project and have been a contributor, advisor, and guide, but this is her book and her dream too.

Since the easing of literary censorship in Britain and America in the 1960s, there have been numerous further reprints of Beardsley's little book, all based on Smithers, but until now no one has gone back to the manuscript, although it has been in the Rosenbach in Philadelphia since its foundation in 1954 and had been in its founder's collection since before 1926.[3] In our reading of the manuscript, Sasha Dovzhyk and I have discovered that the supposedly complete 1907 Smithers edition is riddled with his own edits of Beardsley's original words, including

[1] Dr Ian Fletcher (1920–1988) was a poet and academic with an encyclopaedic knowledge of the world of the 1890s. The albums were those published by John Lane after Beardsley's death, *The Early Work of Aubrey Beardsley* (1899) and *The Later Work of Aubrey Beardsley* (1900). See his iconographic study, Ian Fletcher, *Aubrey Beardsley* (Boston: Twayne Publishers, 1987).

[2] D. H. Lawrence, *The White Peacock* (London: Heinemann, 1911), p. 243. The quotation is the reaction of one of Lawrence's characters to discovering Beardsley's work in one of the same albums as I did. Beardsley appears twice in Lawrence's first novel, both times in an erotic context, the second of which is intensely homoerotic. The title may refer to the white peacocks of Herod in Oscar Wilde's play *Salome*, notorious for Beardsley's illustrations, which include many images of peacocks.

[3] The Rosenbach is a museum and library which holds a collection of nearly 400,000 rare books, manuscripts, and fine and decorative arts objects.

occasional misreadings; it even perpetuates some of the bowdlerizations of then unpublishable passages that had been made for the original heavily censored publication of an incomplete text in the magazine the *Savoy* in 1896. What is here presented for the first time therefore is the text as Beardsley originally wrote it.

Our desire to preserve the full flavour of his writing has led us to reproduce the eccentricities of his spelling and punctuation. Beardsley frequently omits commas and invariably uses an ampersand instead of 'and'. He almost never crosses his t's, although the cross sometimes appears as a dash further along the word. All these characteristics convey the urgency with which this dying man wrote, an urgency given added and powerful poignancy by the way the manuscript ends abruptly in mid-sentence at the end of a page, the result perhaps of a sudden tubercular attack. A 'Publisher's Note' at the end of the April 1896 issue of the *Savoy*, in which the second and last part of *Under the Hill* was published, states, 'owing to Mr. Beardsley's illness he has been unable to finish one of his full-page drawings to Chapter IV. of "Under the Hill"'.[4] He never did finish it, or the book.

We have additionally preserved therefore even his uncertain placing of accents in the myriad French words and phrases that occur in the text. Also, Beardsley never underlines these to indicate they should be placed in italics, as is conventional for foreign language words in an English text, and so they are not placed in italics in our transcription. As is well-known, Beardsley was absolutely steeped in French literature and culture and in our view the elements of French in the text of *Under the Hill* are entirely integral — to express himself in French was simply natural for him. But the whole atmosphere of *Under the Hill* is French, specifically evoking the royal courts of the eighteenth-century *ancien régime*, and their distinctive artistic style, rococo. The great artist of this world and style was Antoine Watteau, who created entirely novel, mysterious, and unforgettable images of beautiful, elegant people flirting, making music, and dancing, in paradisal pastoral surroundings. For this new kind of painting the French Academy had to invent a new category and named it *fête galante*.[5]

As Sasha Dovzhyk shows in her Introduction here, Beardsley's reputation as a writer, and as the author of *Under the Hill* in particular, had been trashed by his first biographer, Arthur Symons, who unforgivably dismissed *Under the Hill* as 'hardly more than a piece of nonsense'.[6] This judgement, added to its other difficult features, made it invisible to literary scholarship until 1967 when, in the collection *Romantic Mythologies*, the French-born Annette Lavers, in a ground-breaking essay, set out the parameters of a reappraisal. It is her insight that the book is itself a *fête galante*, that is, a literary equivalent to a Watteau painting.[7] In the introduction to *Romantic Mythologies* the editor, Ian Fletcher, writes of 'the figure of Beardsley, wavering between the literary and the visual'.[8]

There is one passage in *Under the Hill* where Beardsley describes the French rococo engravings decorating a room. Re-reading these descriptions in the preparation of this volume, I became aware of echoes of elements from his own work, and then it dawned on me that the engravings are effectively Beardsley drawings. It is relevant to add that whereas references to artists in *Under the Hill* are generally to real figures, in this case the named artist cannot be linked to any plausible painter of the period, although it is the name of a prominent writer. In fact, the entire book may be taken as a Beardsley drawing in word form, or rather a series of Beardsley drawings, and in this respect alone it is innovatory. As Sasha Dovzhyk notes, further twists to this startling elision of art and literature are the chapter he proposed entirely of drawings, and the chapter that would consist simply of a poem, neither of which were eventually included, although the poem survives.

On page 26 of the manuscript, Beardsley's account of part of a conversation at Venus's banquet reads: 'then a general criticism of the decorations, everyone finding their own peculiar meaning in the fall of a festoon, turn of twig, & twist of branch'. Against this Beardsley has written in the margin 'My own drawings'. The 'peculiar' meanings to be found in Beardsley's drawings, including outright but cleverly hidden erotic imagery, have been

---

[4] 'Publisher's Note', *Savoy*, April 1896, n.p.

[5] For *fête galante*, see our annotation on p. 35, note 16.

[6] Arthur Symons, 'Beardsley as a Man of Letters', *Saturday Review*, 9 January 1904, p. 41.

[7] Annette Lavers, '"Aubrey Beardsley, Man of Letters"', in *Romantic Mythologies*, ed. by Ian Fletcher (London: Routledge, 1967), pp. 243–70 (p. 245).

[8] Ian Fletcher, 'Foreword', in *Romantic Mythologies*, ed. by Ian Fletcher (London: Routledge, 1967), pp. vii–xiii (p. xii).

comprehensively noted in Linda Zatlin's 2016 catalogue raisonné of his work. This marginal note provides a vivid illustration of Beardsley's own awareness of the elision of the visual and the verbal in his text.[9]

Lavers points out the congruence of the rococo character of *Under the Hill* and the rococo style of drawing that Beardsley had developed at this time.[10] In his brief career of five years or so, Beardsley's art evolved through a dizzying sequence of styles. The most significant of these was the radical Art Nouveau and Symbolist, ultimately proto-modernist style that reached its apogee in his 1893 suite of drawings for Wilde's *Salome*. But by 1896 he had fallen in love with the eighteenth century and specifically with Watteau, the great painter of the French rococo movement, and his contemporaries, whose work Beardsley knew primarily through the intricate engravings, works of art in their own right, which brought them to a wider audience. Beardsley began acquiring engravings after Watteau as early as September 1893, later adding works after Jean François de Troy which he described as 'Dreadfully depraved things'.[11]

It is an irony that his outstanding works in this style were not his illustrations for *Under the Hill* but those he made in 1896 for Alexander Pope's quintessential piece of English literary rococo, the mock epic poem *The Rape of the Lock*. This became the fourth of the great illustrated books that form the cornerstones of the edifice of Beardsley's art. This is perhaps not so surprising given that the conjunction of Beardsley and Pope's glittering poem was a marriage made in heaven. Also, by the time Beardsley came to make drawings for the publication of *Under the Hill* in the *Savoy*, he was battered both by the destruction of his soaring career and celebrity status brought about by the arrest of Oscar Wilde in April 1895, and the destruction of his life itself by rapidly advancing tuberculosis.[12] The *Under the Hill* drawings do include one masterpiece, the picture of the protagonist, often seen as a slightly mocking self-portrait. The other four illustrations he managed to make are in varying degrees disappointing. Two of them are also inconsistent in style, not only from the three rococo ones but from each other, so even the five he made do not add up to a coherent suite.[13] However, given that, as suggested above, *Under the Hill* may itself be considered as an elision of the visual and verbal, it could also be that Beardsley realized that in attempting to illustrate it he was essentially perpetrating a tautology.

Previous editors of *Under the Hill* have occasionally picked out names and references for footnoting. Beardsley's text is in fact allusive to a quite extraordinary degree. As Sasha Dovzhyk says below, we found ourselves 'unpacking Beardsley's coded language with references ranging from French erotic slang to medieval chivalric poetry' and, I will add, taking in a great deal in between. This unpacking and codebreaking is reflected in the copiousness of our commentary in the annotated version of the text presented here. In Chapter II of the story Beardsley refers to 'Delvau's Dictionary'. This proved to be the *Dictionnaire érotique moderne* by Alfred Delvau, a series of successively enlarged editions of which were published clandestinely between 1864 and 1879. We soon realised that it provided a key to a hidden code in many words and expressions in the text. Delvau is not just a dictionary of sexual slang. Terms are amusingly defined, often with illustrative quotations from France's rich history of literary eroticism. Beardsley must have read it as the highly entertaining book it is and then drawn on it in his writing.

Beardsley's reference to Delvau is also formally fascinating. It concludes a passage in which Beardsley recounts the erotic responses of Venus's courtiers to her appearance at the end of the long toilette she has undergone in preparation for the great banquet that follows. For one group of courtiers, instead of describing their behaviour, Beardsley simply writes that they 'illustrated pages seventy two & seventy three of Delvau's Dictionary'. This seems an extraordinary if not unprecedented literary device. To appropriate part of a text is one thing, to send the reader to find it, in furthermore a highly arcane source, rather than writing it into one's own text, is quite

---

[9] See our note on p. 27, note 26.

[10] Lavers, '"Aubrey Beardsley, Man of Letters"', p. 256.

[11] *The Letters of Aubrey Beardsley*, ed. by Henry Maas, J. L. Duncan, and W. G. Good (London: Cassell, 1970), pp. 54, 309. Some of Jean François de Troy's 'galantes' scenes have a salacious edge, as Beardsley notes.

[12] On 5 April 1895, Oscar Wilde was arrested on charges of gross indecency and subsequently condemned to two years in prison, from which he never recovered.

[13] This edition nevertheless includes the illustrations, in an attempt to supply the reader with an extensive frame of references.

another. Beardsley's choice of the term 'illustrated' is also arresting. The courtiers are acting out Delvau's descriptions and the reader is invited to form their own mental picture of the scene — an illustration. Beardsley thus co-opts the reader as the creator of an illustration that he himself could not make.

There is a French saying, whose origin I know not, *bête comme un peintre* — stupid as a painter. Highly literate visual artists are indeed a rarity. Despite his short life, Beardsley may well be the best-read artist in the Western canon. In a British context particularly, Beardsley's only real ancestor as an artist-writer is William Blake. Of course, Beardsley's text is a mere scrap compared with Blake's magisterial illuminated books. But as I have tried to show, Beardsley's *Under the Hill* does not need illustrations. Its gripping paradox is that it blurs the distinction between visual art and literature to become something seriously other.

INTRODUCTION

Under the Hill: Aubrey Beardsley's Cabinet of Decadent Curiosities

Sasha Dovzhyk

> The essence of the English decadent school is contained in the forty-odd pages of Aubrey Beardsley's Under the Hill.
>
> Mario Praz, *The Romantic Agony*[1]

Aubrey Beardsley (1872–1898) is predominantly recognized as an emblem of the late-Victorian Decadence, a graphic artist whose fluid line became a bedrock of the international Art Nouveau style and who 'carried the art of Black and White further than any man since Albert Dürer'.[2] He defined the visual language of the two avant-garde journals of the 1890s, the *Yellow Book* and the *Savoy*, and illustrated one of the decade-defining volumes, the English edition of Oscar Wilde's drama *Salome* (1894). Less well-known to this day is Beardsley's authorship of some extraordinary examples of Decadent prose and verse. This scholarly edition aims to bring Beardsley's writing from the margins of literary history and establish his reputation as a major figure in Decadent letters.

Compared to his over eleven hundred original drawings, Beardsley's literary oeuvre seems slight: three poems, a translation of Catullus, and an unfinished erotic novel which, nevertheless, suggested to contemporaries such as W. B. Yeats 'a literary genius as great maybe as his artistic genius'.[3] The Decadent quality of the work was likewise realized early. In his study *The Eighteen Nineties* (1913), Holbrook Jackson observes that Decadence in England 'began by accident with Walter Pater's *The Renaissance*' and 'ended with Oscar Wilde's *Picture of Dorian Gray* and Aubrey Beardsley's romance, *Under the Hill*, which were nothing if not decadent'.[4] While the works of Wilde (1854–1900) and Walter Pater (1839–1894) have generated entire libraries of critical scholarship, Beardsley's 'romance' has received little academic scrutiny so far. With the exceptions of Emma Sutton, who provides an in-depth discussion of *Under the Hill* in relation to music and, particularly, turn-of-the-century British Wagnerism, and Matthew Potolsky, who dedicates a section of *The Decadent Republic of Letters* to an insightful reading of Beardsley's erotic novel, modern scholarship on Decadence tends to address Beardsley's visual rather than literary art.[5] In addition, the Beardsleyesque is often brought up as a specific Decadent

---

[1] Mario Praz, *The Romantic Agony*, trans. by Angus Davidson, 2nd edn (New York: Meridian Books, 1956), p. 342. Originally published in 1930.

[2] John Lane, 'Publisher's Note', in *Under the Hill and Other Essays in Prose and Verse* (London: Bodley Head, 1904), p. x.

[3] W. B. Yeats, *Autobiographies: Reveries over Childhood and Youth and The Trembling of the Veil* (London: Macmillan, 1926), p. 398.

[4] Holbrook Jackson, 'Aubrey Beardsley', in *The Eighteen Nineties: A Review of Art and Ideas at the Close of the Nineteenth Century* (London: G. Richards, 1913), pp. 109–25 (p. 70).

[5] Emma Sutton, *Aubrey Beardsley and British Wagnerism in the 1890s* (Oxford: Oxford University Press, 2002); Matthew Potolsky, *The Decadent Republic of Letters: Taste, Politics, and Cosmopolitan Community from Baudelaire to Beardsley* (Philadelphia: University of Pennsylvania, 2013), pp. 153–63. For the recent discussion of the afterlives of Beardsley's visual works as forgeries, see also Gregory Mackie, 'Aubrey Beardsley, H. S. Nichols, and the Decadent Archive', *Volupté: Interdisciplinary Journal of Decadence Studies*, 3.1 (2020), 49–74.

sensibility with an impact on such phenomena as cinema or the emergence of camp.[6] Beardsley's writing, however, is yet to be situated and analysed within the Decadent literary tradition.

The reason for the obscurity of *Under the Hill* during and shortly after Beardsley's lifetime lies in the combination of this work's overtly sexual subject matter and its convoluted history of censorship, fragmentation, and clandestine circulation. Our edition aims to make this work more visible by reproducing for the first time the text as it was written, from the original manuscript, while simultaneously unpacking Beardsley's coded language with its references ranging from French erotic slang to medieval chivalric poetry.

Under the Hill: Publication History

In April 1894, the first issue of the avant-garde journal the *Yellow Book* was published by John Lane (1854–1925) with Beardsley as its Art Editor. He was quickly becoming a household name, with spoofs and interviews appearing regularly in the press. Neither Beardsley's ambition nor his talent was exclusively devoted to the *Yellow Book* job. He was working on other commissions, socializing, and attending music halls and 'a season of German Opera at Drury Lane' with his sister Mabel (1871–1916). '[N]ever', according to their mother, 'was German Opera enjoyed more'.[7] A fervent Wagnerite, he saw Richard Wagner's (1813–1883) opera *Tannhäuser* on 26 June 1894.[8] The next day, he mentioned for the first time working on his own version of the ancient legend, 'a big long thing of the revels in act I of *Tannhäuser*' which would 'simply astonish everyone'.[9] He titled it *The Story of Venus and Tannhäuser* and offered it to Lane, who advertised it as 'in preparation' in volumes III and IV of the *Yellow Book*.

However, the spring of 1895 was marked by the trials of Oscar Wilde for 'gross indecency' which tainted Beardsley by association: the illustrations for *Salome* tied the artist to the writer in the public mind. In May 1895, Lane took the decision to sack his Art Editor from the *Yellow Book* to save the reputation of his publishing house. Beardsley moved to his last publisher and close friend Leonard Smithers (1861–1907), taking with him the manuscript of what at that point was still titled *The Story of Venus and Tannhäuser*. To publish the story in the new periodical that Beardsley and Smithers planned, the *Savoy*, but without running the risk that Lane might recognize it as the story that had been promised to him, the two disguised it under the alternative title of *Under the Hill*. For the same purpose, the main characters' names were altered: Tannhäuser became Fanfreluche, and Venus was given the pseudonym of Helen, alluding to the mythical femme fatale Helen of Troy.

Since Beardsley's pen turned the Wagnerian tale of sin and redemption into a Decadent dream of erotic excess, a general readership could only be exposed to a heavily expurgated version of his 'romantic novel'. Four abridged, partially rewritten chapters appeared in the first and second issues of the *Savoy* in 1896. 'The Ballad of a Barber', which had been intended as Chapter IX of *Under the Hill*, was published as a standalone poem in the third issue of the *Savoy*; its connection to the novel was not acknowledged.[10] Beardsley meant Chapter X to 'consist of pictures', but this radical media-blending idea was never realized.[11] The novel remained unfinished, either because of the author's declining health or his predilection for a decidedly open-ended exploration of

---

[6] David Weir, 'Decadence and Cinema', in *Decadence and Literature*, ed. by David Weir and Jane Desmarais, Cambridge Critical Concepts (Cambridge: Cambridge University Press, 2019), pp. 300–15 (p. 304); Kate Hext, 'Rethinking the Origins of Camp: The Queer Correspondence of Carl Van Vechten and Ronald Firbank', *Modernism/Modernity*, 27.1 (2020), 165–83 (p. 166).

[7] Ellen Agnus Beardsley, 'Aubrey Beardsley', in *A Beardsley Miscellany*, ed. by R. A. Walker (London: Bodley Head, 1949), pp. 75–83 (p. 77).

[8] *Tannhäuser* is an opera in three acts by Wagner to his own libretto, performed for the first time in Dresden on 19 October 1845. Wagner kept revising the work, and the full score was published in 1888. See Barry Millington, 'Tannhäuser', in *The Grove Book of Operas* (Oxford University Press, 2008), in *Oxford Reference* <https://www.oxfordreference.com/view/10.1093/acref/9780195309072.001.0001/acref-9780195309072-e-245> [accessed 5 January 2021].

[9] *Letters of Aubrey Beardsley*, p. 72.

[10] A facsimile of the poem's manuscript is reproduced in *A Beardsley Miscellany*, ed. by R. A. Walker (London: Bodley Head, 1949), pp. 109–10. It is titled 'Under the Hill. Chap. IX. "The ballad of a barber"'.

[11] Beardsley to Smithers, *c.* 27 March 1896, in *Letters of Aubrey Beardsley*, p. 120.

the erotic realm 'under the hill' and its Decadent pleasures. On Smithers's bankruptcy in 1900, Lane purchased all his Beardsley material and printed the *Savoy* chapters in a posthumous collection of Beardsley's writings titled *Under the Hill and Other Essays in Prose and Verse* (1904). Although Lane preferred the bowdlerized version of the story from the *Savoy*, his collection includes 'The Woods of Auffray', a previously unpublished fragment of the manuscript, as part of Beardsley's 'Table Talk'.[12] Three years later, Smithers published a near-complete, yet edited version of the novel under Beardsley's original title *The Story of Venus and Tannhäuser* in a pirated clandestine edition of 300 copies. This publication divided the five extensive chapters from the manuscript into ten shorter ones and supplied them with titles, probably invented by Smithers. It also preserved some of the bowdlerizations made for the *Savoy* version. Subsequent publications would either use the Smithers edition (1907) or a compilation of all existing versions. On two occasions, concluding chapters were appended to Beardsley's text by other authors, namely Franz Blei (1871–1942) and John Glassco (1909–1981).[13]

The present volume untangles the convoluted publication history of *Under the Hill* by reproducing the 'romantic novel' from the original manuscript, which is housed in the Rosenbach, Philadelphia.[14] Although the editions which appeared after Smithers's publication in 1907 have used the title *The Story of Venus and Tannhäuser*, we adhere to the manuscript, in which the first pages of the opening chapter appear to have been rewritten by Beardsley with a view to publication in the *Savoy*. In the rewritten first page, the title appears as *Under the Hill*. Beardsley's text is here presented in two forms. A faithful transcription of the novel as originally written is fully annotated to enable readers to contextualize the work and grasp the extraordinary wealth of its hitherto underexplored references to the fields of aesthetics, literature, cultural history, and the history of sexuality. This annotated text of *Under the Hill* is followed by a full diplomatic transcription which also indicates the multiple bowdlerizations, deletions, and insertions handwritten by the author, editor, and publisher for the *Savoy*. Our footnotes in the diplomatic version track the changes and expurgations introduced by Smithers and Lane in the foundational editions of 1896, 1904, and 1907, as well as textual variations across two manuscript versions of the first chapter of the novel. Our commentary aims to shed light on multiple kinds of interference with the text during the transmission from handwritten medium to print, and to reveal the differing priorities of the parties involved. In addition, we include 'Chapter IV' from the *Savoy*, which was substantially rewritten to make the open publication possible, with our annotations; and a checklist of Beardsley's letters which mention his 'romantic novel'.

By way of introducing readers to other forms of his writing, this book also reproduces and annotates Beardsley's poems ('The Three Musicians' and 'The Ballad of a Barber', his translation of Catullus's 'Carmen CI', and the unfinished lyric fragment 'The Ivory Piece') and two examples of his essayistic prose ('The Art of the Hoarding' and the introductory notes in Leonard Smithers's Prospectus for *Volpone*). To provide easy access to contextual and critical material, we reprint, in order of first publication, Beardsley's interview for *The Idler* and two contrasting appraisals of his writing by Arthur Symons (1865–1945) and E. F. Benson (1867–1940).

---

[12] Aubrey Beardsley, *Under the Hill and Other Essays in Prose and Verse* (London: Bodley Head, 1904), p. 65. See note 83 to the diplomatic transcription, p. *88*.

[13] The German edition of 1920 contains 'Chapter 1 to 10 by Beardsley; 11 to 18 and epilogue by Franz Blei'; see Aubrey Beardsley and Franz Blei, *Venus und Tannhäuser, eine romantische Novelle*, trans. by Prokop Templin (Hannover: Steegemann, 1920). John Glassco completes chapter 10 and provides his own versions of chapters 11 to 19 in Aubrey Beardsley and John Glassco, *Under the Hill; or, The Story of Venus and Tannhäuser* [...] *Now Completed by John Glassco* (Paris: Olympia Press, 1959).

[14] The complete original manuscript is held at the Rosenbach, Philadelphia EL4.B368u MS. Several opening sheets are also housed at Yale University; see Beinecke Rare Book and Manuscript Library MSS MISC Box: 156 (Broadside), Folder: GROUP 22, F-3; *'Under the Hill' and 'The Ballad of a Barber' – AMs, 4 pp.* The diplomatic transcription in the present edition traces textual variations across the available manuscripts.

Beardsley as a Man of Letters

While *Under the Hill* has in recent years been anthologized as a work of Decadent fiction, Beardsley's relation to Decadent literature remained contested throughout his lifetime and most of the twentieth century.[15] Firstly, Beardsley's view of the term 'decadence' itself was ambivalent (this issue is addressed further on in this introduction). Secondly, his very claim to the status of *littérateur* was dismissed by contemporaries and early critics. As Robert Ross (1869–1918), a key figure in the Decadent milieu of the 1890s, observes, Beardsley 'was ambitious of literary success, but any aspirations were wisely discouraged by his admirers' so that the artist would not diverge from the path of his 'true genius', which supposedly rested in the pictorial realm.[16]

The one contemporary who defined Beardsley's literary reputation more than anyone else was the poet and critic Arthur Symons, the author of the manifesto 'The Decadent Movement in Literature'.[17] As editor of the *Savoy*, Symons found himself engaging with the bulk of Beardsley's writing: besides the bowdlerized chapters of *Under the Hill*, the poems 'The Three Musicians' and 'The Ballad of a Barber', as well as the translation from Latin of 'Carmen CI', were also published in the *Savoy*.[18] Symons's obituary, re-issued in quarto form with illustrations in 1898, became a cornerstone of Beardsley's reception.[19] It is through Symons that we know that 'Beardsley would rather have been a great writer than a great artist' and that he referred to himself as a 'man of letters' on a library admission form.[20] The same essay ensured that Beardsley's literary work was perceived as nothing more than the painstaking exercises of a diligent amateur. Symons continued to polish his critical verdict in a review of Lane's edition of *Under the Hill and Other Essays* (1904), unwinding a string of dubious compliments: 'Beardsley was very anxious to be a writer, and his force of mind, his energy and persistence were so great that he could not have failed to write something remarkable'; 'he wrote and he saw, unimaginatively, and without passion, but with a fierce sensitive precision'. A synecdoche for his prose style, Beardsley's very handwriting was characterized as 'neat' and 'clerk-like', and his unfinished novel brushed away as 'hardly more than a piece of nonsense' which 'was hardly meant to be more than that'.[21]

However, Beardsley did mean his unfinished novel 'to be more than that'. Besides the highly wrought style of his prose, the richness of his sources and allusions are proof enough of his serious approach. The basis of the story of Venus and Tannhäuser is found in a folk legend, recorded for the first time in the sixteenth-century ballad *Tannhäuserlied* (1515).[22] It is a tale about a medieval knight who comes to the grotto of Venus. He spends seven years in the underworld with the goddess of love, exiled from the upper realm by the advent of Christianity. The knight then repents, flees, and seeks the pope's forgiveness. Besides Wagner's opera, the nineteenth-century retellings of the story encompass Charles Baudelaire's article 'Richard Wagner et Tannhäuser à Paris' (1861), Algernon Charles Swinburne's poem 'Laus Veneris' (1866), and William Morris's 'The Hill of Venus' (1870, part of his epic poem *The Earthly Paradise*). By contributing his version, Beardsley partakes in a decades-long Decadent tradition of rewriting the legend.

---

[15] Aubrey Beardsley, 'The Story of Venus and Tannhäuser', in Karl Beckson, *Aesthetes and Decadents of the 1890s: An Anthology of British Poetry and Prose* (Chicago: Chicago Review Press, 2005), pp. 9–46; Aubrey Beardsley, 'The Story of Venus and Tannhäuser', in *Decadence: An Annotated Anthology*, ed. by Jane Desmarais and Chris Baldick (Manchester: Manchester University Press, 2012), pp. 210–32.

[16] Robert Ross, *Aubrey Beardsley* (London: John Lane, 1909), p. 21.

[17] Arthur Symons, 'The Decadent Movement in Literature', *Harper's Magazine*, 87.522 (November 1893), 858–67.

[18] Aubrey Beardsley, 'The Three Musicians', *Savoy*, January 1896, pp. 65–66; Aubrey Beardsley, 'The Ballad of a Barber', *Savoy*, July 1896, pp. 91–93; Catullus, 'Carmen CI', trans. by Aubrey Beardsley, *Savoy*, November 1896, p. 52.

[19] Arthur Symons, 'Aubrey Beardsley', *Fortnightly Review*, 63 (May 1898), 752–61. Symons added a short introduction to the obituary when it was reprinted in the illustrated quarto *Aubrey Beardsley* under the imprint of Unicorn Press. Subsequent references are to the later, enlarged version of the essay.

[20] Arthur Symons, *Aubrey Beardsley* (London: At the Sign of the Unicorn, 1898), p. 10.

[21] Arthur Symons, 'Beardsley as a Man of Letters', *Saturday Review*, 9 January 1904, pp. 41–42 (p. 41).

[22] The legend involves a real historical figure, the German Minnesinger (lyric poet) Tannhäuser, who in 1228–1229 was involved in a crusade. The prototype's wanderings in an exotic land apparently inspired the disappearance of the legend's Tannhäuser in the grotto of Venus. It is unlikely that Beardsley knew of the Minnesinger, whose poems were only edited in 1934.

Unlike Wagner's opera, which remains the key source for *Under the Hill*, Beardsley's unfinished narrative does not reach the point of redemption. Instead, it focuses on the hero's revelries in the realm of heterogeneous eroticism, unfolding an imaginative apology of pleasure and desire. Beardsley's other crucial source is *Le Roman de la Rose*, the medieval French poem of chivalric love translated into Middle English by Geoffrey Chaucer.[23] Taken from the *Roman de la Rose*, Beardsley's epigraph for his story, 'La chaleur du brandon Venus' ('the heat of Venus's torch') directs the reader towards the theme of erotic love. As if predicting the critical dismissal of his novel on these grounds, Beardsley writes in the burlesque dedication of *Under the Hill* that, '[i]n the judgment of many the amorous passion is accounted a shameful thing & ridiculous' — and proceeds to emphasize that his book will, nonetheless, 'be found to contain matter of deeper import'.[24]

In addition to his radical revision of the classic plot, Beardsley's literary accomplishment relates to the intertextual qualities of his book. Having once unabashedly proclaimed that his 'favourite authors [were] Balzac, Voltaire and Beardsley', the author of *Under the Hill* certainly establishes, as our annotations show, a dialogue with these canonical writers — and with many others.[25] The belief, held by several esteemed critics, that most of the names and toponyms in the novel 'are pure inventions' also proves incorrect.[26] Next to bogus references — which more often than not reveal surprising connotations if examined through the lens of Alfred Delvau's dictionary of French erotic slang — deliberate allusions to real places and historical characters are included and form a component of significance in the text.[27] Regularly forced by his illness to spend prolonged periods of time in bed, Beardsley indeed seems to 'have read everything', from the lives of saints to eighteenth-century pornography, and he allowed his bookishness to seep into the novel.[28] As one example among many, the names of the servants of Venus in the second chapter exemplify Beardsley's intertextual range, overlooked or intentionally downplayed by the early critics.

The author of the Beardsley catalogue raisonné, Linda Gertner Zatlin, argues that Symons's dismissive attitude was rooted in his envy for the precocious artist's literary talent and annoyance at his interference with the literary matters of the *Savoy*.[29] The fact that the periodical was regarded by critics as 'the decadent journal in which the one and only Aubrey Beardsley officiates' must have added fuel to the fire.[30] Whatever his exact motivation, Symons is not the only contemporary source on the matter.[31] His account of Beardsley's working process differs greatly from the one left by the artist William Rothenstein (1872–1945). Both memoirists recall an instance of Beardsley composing his poem 'The Three Musicians'. In Symons's recollection, the aspiring poet — who had 'no natural impulse whatever' for writing verse — is said to have 'laboured' at it 'from early morning to sunset, forcing his brain to think in metre'.[32] By contrast, Rothenstein remembers that Beardsley 'wrote with astonishing ease and command of language. [...] One day he began scribbling some verses about three musicians; shortly afterwards he sent me the whole poem'.[33]

---

[23] Beardsley read the *Roman* in the original but was also familiar with Chaucer's translation. For details, see our commentary on the epigraph to the annotated version.

[24] See Dedication, p. 25.

[25] Arthur H. Lawrence, 'Mr. Aubrey Beardsley and His Work', *Idler*, March 1897, pp. 188–202 (p. 200). Included in this edition on p. 194.

[26] Walker, p. 36.

[27] Alfred Delvau, *Dictionnaire érotique moderne* (Bale: Karl Schmidt, 1864). Beardsley left a textual clue about his favoured dictionary in the main text of the novel. For details, see note 24 in the annotated version.

[28] Symons, *Aubrey Beardsley*, p. 14.

[29] Linda Gertner Zatlin, *Aubrey Beardsley: A Catalogue Raisonné*, 2 vols (New Haven: Yale University Press, 2016), II, p. 233; hereafter referred to as *CR*.

[30] 'Books and Authors. Review of the *Savoy*, Vol. 2', *Globe and Mail*, July 1896.

[31] For a discussion of Symons's myth of Beardsley, see Chris Snodgrass, 'Decadent Mythmaking: Arthur Symons on Aubrey Beardsley and *Salome*', *Victorian Poetry*, 28.3/4 (1990), 61–109.

[32] Symons, 'Beardsley as a Man of Letters', p. 197.

[33] William Rothenstein, *Men and Memories: Recollections of William Rothenstein, 1872–1900*, 2 vols (London: Faber and Faber, 1931), I, pp. 185–86.

While belittling the significance of Beardsley's literary work, Symons does not question its Decadent quality. Describing the original idea behind *Under the Hill*, he assures the readers that the author 'decided on one point: that it was to be quite the most "decadent" thing that had ever been written'.[34] Coming from 'the chief spokesman of Decadence in England', as Jane Desmarais and Chris Baldick rightfully name Symons, the characterization does not necessarily read as a condemnation.[35] Moreover, it invites us to consider how Decadence was understood by Beardsley's contemporaries and by Beardsley himself.

Beardsley as a Decadent

The exact meaning of the term 'decadence' is notoriously difficult to pin down. It is traditionally associated with certain landmarks in the nineteenth-century culture of France, Beardsley's spiritual homeland: with the decline of the Roman Empire and the perceived deviance of post-Augustan Latin literature, as explicated by the classical historian Désiré Nisard; with a constellation of writers, including Charles Baudelaire, Théophile Gautier, and Joris-Karl Huysmans, who professed to admire those late Latin works, thus 'declaring [themselves] citizen[s] of a bankrupt or doomed civilisation';[36] with Anatole Baju's unsuccessful attempt to formalize Decadence as a movement in Paris through his short-lived literary journal *Le Décadent* (1886–1889). These historical references are insufficient when one considers the significance 'decadence' acquires internationally at the *fin de siècle*, both as an expression of anxiety for declining moral and cultural standards and as an umbrella term for the experimental tendencies now largely associated with the late-Victorian avant-garde.

As Kate Hext and Alex Murray note, 'conservative cultural critics' used the term 'in a wholly pejorative fashion to attack all things "new" (the New Woman, the New Art, the New Journalism, etc.)'.[37] Reactions to Beardsley's work are illustrative of this tendency. One of the opponents of the new art currents associated with the French Decadence, Margaret Armour, pronounced in 1897:

> Mr. Beardsley might adapt the *mot* of Louis XIV, and say, almost without arrogance, '*L'art decadent, c'est moi*'. In his work we have most complete expression of what is typical of the movement — disdain of classical traditions in art and of clean traditions in ethics; the *fin de siècle* outlook on the husk of life, and brilliant dexterity in portraying it.[38]

Armour's diatribe 'Aubrey Beardsley and the Decadents' channels some of the preoccupations with national purity and the sanctity of class segregation which often characterize the critics' rejection of the artist. She objects to the 'Cockney soul' and foreign spirit of Beardsley's Decadent transgressions. Evoking the decline of the Roman Empire, Armour links Decadence to the idea of national decay: 'The nations ripe and ripe, and when they rot and rot, decadence is the tale that hangs thereby'.[39] She proceeds to reaffirm the 'wonderful recuperative powers' of England and suggests a solution to the problem posed by the Decadents: one should expel to France those 'that lodge the Gallic germs in our [English] lungs'.[40] Beardsley certainly felt more at home in France, where he died from tuberculosis of the lungs a mere fourteen months after the publication of Armour's article.

Considering the negative connotations attached to Decadence, Beardsley's ambiguity towards it is unsurprising. He was not the only author who was simultaneously considered an epitome of Decadence and

[34] Symons, 'Beardsley as a Man of Letters', p. 196.
[35] Desmarais and Baldick, *Decadence*, p. 8.
[36] Desmarais and Baldick, *Decadence*, p. 3.
[37] *Decadence in the Age of Modernism*, ed. by Kate Hext and Alex Murray (Baltimore: Johns Hopkins University Press, 2019), p. 10.
[38] The French *L'art decadent, c'est moi* ('Decadent art, it's me') paraphrases the expression attributed to Louis XIV, *L'état, c'est moi* ('The state, it's me'); Margaret Armour, 'Aubrey Beardsley and the Decadents', *Magazine of Art*, January 1897, pp. 9–12 (p. 9).
[39] Armour, pp. 10, 11.
[40] Armour, pp. 11, 12.

hesitant to adopt Decadence as a self-description (Baudelaire, Huysmans, and Wilde, to name but a few, were of the same disposition). In the interview for *The Idler*, which he stated to have written himself, Beardsley comments on Armour's identification of him with the art of Decadence: '"*L'art decadent, c'est moi*" is somewhere stated to have been Mr. Beardsley's own idea on the matter; whether that utterance is to be taken as a proud boast, or a humble confession, there is no evidence to show'.[41] The rest of the interview is interlarded with Decadent tropes, including the artist's penchant for Wagner's music, for urban living, for working by candlelight in daytime, for possessing rare and expensive things. It is worth bearing in mind Beardsley's aptitude for cultivating a public image that facilitated the resonance, and ultimately the sales, of his books. Playing with the aura of Decadence could successfully function as a marketing strategy, aimed at maintaining his *succès de scandale*.

To add a final and yet crucial facet to the discussion of Beardsley's relation to Decadence, one must pay attention to the close alignment of his literary technique with that famous definition of the Decadent style by Paul Bourget:

> A style of decadence is one in which the unity of the book is decomposed to give place to the independence of the page, in which the page is decomposed to give place to the independence of the phrase, and the phrase to give place to the independence of the word.[42]

Symons refers to the same tendency towards fragmentation when observing that Beardsley's 'every sentence was meditated over, written for its own sake, and left to find its way in its own paragraph'.[43] In Osbert Burdett's critical reassessment of the 1890s, titled *The Beardsley Period* (1925), a tribute to *Under the Hill* paraphrases Bourget's formula: the novel 'perfects a manner of writing in which the parts are more important than the whole, the details than the subject, the sentence than the paragraph, the epithet than the phrase'.[44] Annette Lavers, the first scholar to study Beardsley's unfinished novel with the seriousness it deserves, also singles out the author's emphasis on 'the flavour of isolated words and phrases, on the rhythm of sentences'.[45]

Beardsley is indeed a connoisseur of words: he accumulates archaisms and neologisms, ecclesiastical names, and erotic slang, liberally embedding Gallicisms in the mix. In the description of a tray on which lie the shoes of Venus, he prefers 'pantoufles' to 'slippers', picks the Chaucerian term 'sarsinesshe' to describe a specific dye, and chooses the French '*maréchale*' scent for 'delicate leathers'.[46] Each paragraph of *Under the Hill* opens a verbal cabinet of curiosities. One quickly identifies ubiquitous catalogues as Beardsley's preferred literary technique. The lists of precious objects, amusing characters, and nuanced sexual practices describe each item as interesting in its own right while at the same time producing an effect of encyclopaedic, infinite multiplicity. Numerous mock-encyclopaedic notes and digressions also destroy the unity of Beardsley's text with respect to genre. As Elisa Bizzotto observes, *Under the Hill* 'conforms to *fin-de-siècle* canons of genre hybridisation, alternating diegetic and argumentative passages following Pater and Wilde in the identification of criticism as the finest art'.[47]

---

[41] Lawrence, p. 189. See Beardsley's letter to Marc-André Raffalovich, 20 December 1896, in *Letters of Aubrey Beardsley*, p. 229. This edition uses Raffalovich's baptismal name Marc-André, although he himself used different spellings and was addressed by others as Mark André, Marc André, and simply André.

[42] Havelock Ellis, 'A Note on Paul Bourget', in *Views and Reviews: A Selection of Uncollected Articles, 1884–1932. First Series: 1884–1919* (London: Desmond Harmsworth, 1932), pp. 48–60 (p. 52). For John R. Reed, all Decadent art 'resembles a Beardsley drawing', in which individual parts become significant 'in themselves', inviting the viewer to assemble the details into a meaningful whole; John R. Reed, *Decadent Style* (Athens, OH: Ohio University Press, 1985), p. 11.

[43] Symons, *Aubrey Beardsley*, pp. 9–10.

[44] Osbert Burdett, *The Beardsley Period: An Essay in Perspective* (London: John Lane, 1925), p. 194.

[45] Lavers, '"Aubrey Beardsley, Man of Letters"', p. 244.

[46] See p. 33.

[47] Elisa Bizzotto, 'Blurring the Confines of Art and Gender: Aubrey Beardsley's *Legend of Venus and Tannhäuser*, "The Fragment of a Story"', in *Strange Sisters: Literature and Aesthetics in the Nineteenth Century*, ed. by Francesca Orestano and Francesca Frigerio (Bern: Peter Lang, 2009), pp. 213–32 (p. 217).

Beardsley's is, as Emma Sutton points out, a 'paratactic prose'.[48] Rather than gluing the text with a plot, he disassembles novelistic conventions and exposes the reader to the languid drift of over-elaborate tableaux. Roland Barthes writes about the peculiar delights that such 'drift' may grant to the reader in *The Pleasure of the Text*:

> *Drifting* occurs whenever *I do not respect the whole*, and whenever, by dint of seeming driven about by language's illusions, seductions, and intimidations, like a cork on the waves, I remain motionless, pivoting on the *intractable* bliss that binds me to the text (to the world).[49]

Beardsley is a master of shocks and seductions which re-orient the reader towards his allusive, wrought, artificial language. Illustrative of this effect is the only passage of *Under the Hill* which explicitly mentions Decadence. It is the scene in which Venus and Tannhäuser attend a performance of Gioachino Rossini's *Stabat Mater* (composed between 1831 and 1841):

> This afternoon the piêce de resistance was a performance of Rossini's Stabat Mater & adorable masterpiece. It was given in the beautiful Salle des printemps parfumés. Ah! what a stunning rendering of the delicious demodé piece of decadence. There is a subtle quality about the music, like the unhealthy bloom upon wax fruit, that both orchestra & singer contrived to emphasize with consummate delicacy.[50]

Smithers's edition of *The Story of Venus and Tannhäuser* gives the full phrase in French: '*demodé* [*sic!*] *pièce de décadence*'.[51] As the manuscript shows, Beardsley prefers the incongruity of the Anglo-French mix which evades the contemporary idea of Decadence as a Gallic influence, entirely foreign to English culture. He then deploys the full arsenal of Decadent imagery in his description of the music: it bears the mark of corruption, which is a quality only to be highlighted by the artistic skill of the performers. He offers us a 'delicious' but poisoned meal. Beardsley's 'unhealthy bloom' brings to mind the Baudelairean 'flowers of evil' while also echoing Symons's famous definition of Decadence as 'a new and beautiful and interesting disease'.[52] Tapping into the Decadent obsession with intense multisensory experiences, the passage conjures olfactory, visual, gustatory, and aural impressions. It oscillates between the excesses of aesthetic appeal and revulsion.

And then Beardsley adds irony to the mix. What distinguishes his approach is his ability to skilfully employ Decadent techniques while at the same time undermining the gravitas of his Decadent performance. The tone he adopts is a playful one, interspersed with jovial exclamations and mannerisms.[53] As Linda Dowling observes, 'it is his rattling chatter, the gushing confidences alternating with coy reticence, and his peculiarly campy patois which deflate the pretensions of Decadence'.[54] Beardsley's treatment of sexuality is at the heart of the subversive effect of his text.

Under the Hill as a Queer Decadent Utopia

In his influential book *Decadence and Catholicism*, Ellis Hanson points out that

> Wagner is a touchstone for the peculiar dialectic of shame and grace that is the foundation for decadent Catholicism. [...] As is well known, the decadents were much seduced by the Christian discourse of sin, but they were also drawn to the more poetic flights of shame, remorse, and piety.[55]

---

48 Sutton, p. 132.

49 Roland Barthes, *The Pleasure of the Text*, trans. by Richard Miller (New York: Hill and Wang, 1975), p. 18. The correlation between Barthes's definition of 'drift' and Decadent style has been pointed out by Ellis Hanson, 'The Queer Drift of Firbank', in *Decadence in the Age of Modernism*, ed. by Hext and Murray, pp. 118–34 (pp. 126–27).

50 See p. 52. *Pièce de résistance* is 'main dish' in French and means the best and most exciting thing. *Salle des printemps parfumés* means 'hall of perfumed springs'. For the defamiliarization of Rossini's opera, see Sutton, pp. 159–60.

51 Aubrey Beardsley, *The Story of Venus and Tannhäuser* (London: [Smithers], 1907), p. 85.

52 Symons, 'The Decadent Movement in Literature', p. 859.

53 These features are exaggerated by Smithers: his 1907 edition adds numerous exclamation marks and interjections to Beardsley's prose.

54 Linda Dowling, '"Venus and Tannhäuser": Beardsley's Satire of Decadence', *Journal of Narrative Technique*, 8.1 (1978), 26–41 (p. 36).

55 Ellis Hanson, *Decadence and Catholicism* (Cambridge, MA: Harvard University, 1997), p. 29.

At first sight, Beardsley's life seems illustrative of this argument. He was obsessed with Wagner and produced 'more than twenty drawings on Wagnerian subjects', not to mention *Under the Hill* and a projected but unrealized narrative reworking of Wagner's opera *Das Rheingold*.[56] Moreover, Beardsley did convert to Catholicism in March 1897. A year later, in his 'death agony', he begged Smithers to destroy all his 'obscene' works as a final demonstration of his Catholic repentance.[57] And yet, composed between 1894 and 1896, the text of *Under the Hill* lacks any evocation of such 'flights of shame, remorse, and piety'. On the contrary, the realm of Venus sustains all forms of desire without dispensing moral judgement, often in ways that many readers may find troubling today.[58]

The central character is perhaps the chief example of Beardsley's light touch when it comes to the sexual attitudes at the Venusberg. Tannhäuser is an autobiographical character. The manuscript of Chapter I demonstrates that, before assuming the pseudonym of Fanfreluche, Tannhäuser briefly featured as the Abbé Aubrey. The self-referentiality was underscored therefore not only through the author's first name but also his initials. As many commentators have noted, 'Abbé' is 'a homophone of Beardsley's initials pronounced in French, and his frequent signature in his later drawings'.[59] Lavers also observes that the worldly abbé, a fashionable character in French literature, who is neither entirely ecclesiastical nor secular, 'is for many people the actual symbol of the eighteenth century' — Beardsley's beloved epoch.[60] The in-between state of this figure perfectly fits the situation of Tannhäuser, whom the reader meets at the Venusberg's portal, the literal border between two worlds, just as he readies himself 'to slip into exile'.[61]

Nothing is quite determined about the Chevalier. His sexual interests are diverse and non-aggressive. He is equally pleased by sexual encounters with Venus and with his boy attendants and most eager to adopt both active and passive sexual roles. However, he lacks the 'Gargantuan facility' which allows the heroes of pornography to 'give a lady proof of their valliance at least twenty times a night'.[62] He is curious about the sexual pursuits of others and invested in the erotic potential of clothes. Cross-dressing features prominently among his tools of self-fashioning. In the words of Nicole Fluhr, Tannhäuser's costumes 'move from dandified elegance as he enters the Venusberg [...] to the novel's final image of him departing for a dinner party "dressed as a woman and look[ing] like a goddess"'.[63] In an ironic reversal of gender conventions, the chivalric knight of medieval romance and traditional ideal of heroic masculinity is turned into a mirror image of Venus, the novel's universal object of desire.

Under the Hill could signify, as Lavers suggests, the invention of a genre of 'the erotic pastoral', if only it had any interest in nature.[64] When Susan Sontag famously explicated camp sensibility in 1964 ('the essence of Camp is its love of the unnatural: of artifice and exaggeration'), she included Beardsley's drawings in her list of canonical camp items.[65] As befits an emblem of Decadence and camp, Beardsley's art discards the belief in the natural as an organizing principle of productive society and reproductive sexuality. Imagining 'petticoats cut like artificial flowers' and 'stockings clocked with *fêtes galantes*', Beardsley reduces nature to a decorative pattern and installs an alternative dictate: that of style, of artifice, of art.[66] Queer eroticism is not confined to the sexual

---

[56] Sutton, p. 5. *Das Rheingold* (composed in 1853–4; performed in London in 1889) is Wagner's Prologue (*Vorabend*) to his operatic tetralogy *Der Ring des Nibelungen*. In a letter to Smithers on 16 September 1896, Beardsley mentions 'writing an elaborate version of *Das Rheingold*, called *The Comedy of the Rhinegold*'; see *Letters of Aubrey Beardsley*, p. 164.
[57] *Letters of Aubrey Beardsley*, p. 439.
[58] The story includes several paedophilic episodes and descriptions of sexual violence.
[59] Zatlin, *CR*, II, p. 256.
[60] Lavers, '"Aubrey Beardsley, Man of Letters"', p. 246.
[61] See p. 237.
[62] See p. 44.
[63] Nicole Fluhr, '"Queer Reverence": Aubrey Beardsley's Venus and Tannhäuser', *Cahiers Victoriens et Édouardiens*, 90, 2019 <https://doi.org/10.4000/cve.6482>, para. 16.
[64] Annette Lavers, '*L'eau Savante*: Aspects of Erotic Writing in Aubrey Beardsley: Part II' [1998], in *AB 2020: The Aubrey Beardsley Society* <https://ab2020.org/leau-savante-aspects-of-erotic-writing-in-aubrey-beardsley-2/> [accessed 15 September 2021].
[65] Susan Sontag, 'Notes on "Camp"', in *Against Interpretation and Other Essays* (London: Vintage, 2009), pp. 275–92 (p. 275).
[66] See p. 35.

sphere and consistently saturates the descriptions of garments. In this vein, Venus's shoes have 'buttons so beautiful that the button-holes might have no pleasure till they closed upon them'.[67] In an account of the courtly appearances at Venus's supper, Beardsley blurs the distinction between the human and the bestial, between obscenity and art, as well as the very foundation on which such a binary could rest: 'There were masks of green velvet that make the face look trebly powdered; masks of the heads of birds, of apes, of serpents, of dolphins, of men & women, of little embryos & of cats; masks like the faces of gods; masks of coloured glass, and masks of thin talc and of india-rubber'.[68] Through its camp-like cultivation of artificiality on the levels of form and content as well as through its rejection of binary logic, the novel truly represents a queer Decadent utopia rather than a pastoral.

The queer is generally understood as being in direct opposition to the notion of the normative. Jackson's oft-quoted statement that 'there are passages [in *Under the Hill*] which read like romanticised excerpts from the *Psychopathia Sexualis* of Krafft-Ebing' misrepresents Beardsley's novelistic world, which remains unaware of the incentive or tendency to pathologize.[69] In *Under the Hill*, sexual fantasies and tastes constitute a matter of public knowledge, while sexual acts often take place on a genuine theatrical stage.[70] The most notable examples of this include a ballet turning into an orgy in the course of some courtly entertainment in Chapter III and a scene in Chapter V featuring excited members of the audience who go on to ravish the Spiridion of 'whorish thighs' ('a type of Oscar Wilde', according to Dowling), after his 'miraculous' performance of the Virgin's part in *Stabat Mater*.[71] Fluhr refers to Matthew Potolsky's *Decadent Republic of Letters* and to a core text of queer theory, 'Sex in Public' by Michael Warner and Lauren Berlant, when describing the queer arrangement of the Venusberg: 'the land "under the hill" is constituted as a genuinely alternative paradise, a counterpublic of perverts who communally flout the dictates of heteronormativity, together constructing a world that does not simply exclude shame, guilt, and sin but disavows them entirely'.[72]

Likewise, the realm of Venus disavows the sense of belonging to any one national body. By interspersing his English prose with French sexual slang, Beardsley perverts the very language in which he writes, as it were. The values of his 'beloved Venusberg' exclude linguistic, sexual, or national purity.[73] Its sexual practices are non-reproductive and not designed to support the biological renewal of an industrious society. In this sense, the non-conforming queer life of the Venusberg is 'quite useless' — like 'all art'.[74]

Writing the novel after his dismissal from the *Yellow Book*, in the aftershock of Wilde's queer scandal, Beardsley must have felt a kinship with Venus and her subterranean court of outcasts. This affinity would have been strengthened by the fact that his sexually explicit work relied on clandestine publishing and circulation among the minority audiences of Smithers: connoisseurs of rare books, erotica, and facetiae (a booksellers' term implying pornography).[75] When mentioning his novel to Smithers for the first time in their preserved correspondence, Beardsley suggests: 'Might not my little book be called *The Queen in Exile*?',[76] alluding to the German poet and writer Heinrich Heine's 'Gods in Exile' (written in 1853). Heine's account elaborates on the

---

67 See p. 33.

68 See p. 35.

69 Jackson, 'Aubrey Beardsley', p. 122. The reference is to the influential work on forensic psychiatry and sexual perversion, which was published in German in 1886 and translated into English in 1892, by the Viennese professor of psychiatry Richard von Krafft-Ebing, *Psychopathia Sexualis*, trans. by Charles Gilbert Chaddock (Philadelphia: F. A. Davis, 1892).

70 For a discussion of sex as a public ritual in the Venusberg, see Potolsky, pp. 160–62.

71 Dowling, '"Venus and Tannhäuser"', p. 29.

72 Fluhr, para. 6. See also Potolsky, p. 18; Lauren Berlant and Michael Warner, 'Sex in Public', *Critical Inquiry*, 24.2 (1998), 547–66.

73 *Letters of Aubrey Beardsley*, p. 79.

74 'All art is quite useless' is the final line of Wilde's 'Preface' for *The Picture of Dorian Gray*; see Oscar Wilde, *The Complete Works of Oscar Wilde, Vol. 3: The Picture of Dorian Gray: The 1890 and 1891 Texts*, ed. by Joseph Bristow (Oxford: Oxford University Press, 2005), p. 168.

75 For a discussion of the exclusive readerships cultivated by Smithers, see James G. Nelson, *Publisher to the Decadents: Leonard Smithers in the Careers of Beardsley, Wilde, Dowson* (University Park: Pennsylvania State University Press, 2000).

76 *Letters of Aubrey Beardsley*, p. 97.

lamentable fate of Greek and Roman gods under Christianity, when the classical deities 'were compelled to flee ignominiously and conceal themselves under various disguises on earth'.[77] The *fin-de-siècle* edition of Heine's prose in English included 'Gods in Exile' alongside 'Religion and Philosophy', the work described by the sexologist Havelock Ellis in the introduction as the finest apology of the 'harmony of flesh and spirit'.[78] In 'Religion and Philosophy', Heine comments on the afterlife of the goddess of love: 'The gloomy fanaticism of the monks alighted with special severity on poor Venus: she was considered a daughter of Beelzebub, and the good knight Tannhäuser tells her to her face — "O Venus, lovely wife of mine, You are but a she-devil!".'[79] As Lene Østermark-Johansen observes, 'the basic idea behind' Heine's 'Gods in Exile', 'that the pagan gods had assumed new and often much debased forms in the Christian world', as well as 'the compound literary genre employed by Heine, part mythology, part essay, part fiction', influenced Walter Pater. Some of Pater's 'imaginary portraits', such as 'Apollo in Picardy' (published in *Harper's New Monthly Magazine* in November 1893), participated in queer revisionist myth-making concerning the lives of gods in exile.[80] Beardsley's account of the 'Queen in Exile' is therefore part of the nineteenth-century tradition of reimagining the faith of pagan gods after the advent of Christendom.

The exiled world he creates in the novel is open, mutable, and accepting of diverse sexual as well as literary and artistic cultures. In the words of Potolsky, 'Venusberg is a mirror of decadent cosmopolitanism, a literally underground society composed from a dizzying variety of national, linguistic, and historical traditions'.[81] *Under the Hill* is populated by characters from Molière and Aristophanes, medieval saints and eighteenth-century libertines, and decorated with real and imagined artworks encompassing, in the words of Robert Ross, 'all the delightful manias' of Decadence and its famously transnational tastes.[82] It is no wonder that Beardsley's work was enthusiastically received at the turn of the century and translated into a number of European languages by the transnational networks of his admirers.

The European Reception of Beardsley's Writing

By the time Lane issued the collection *Under the Hill and Other Essays*, Beardsley had already gained extraordinary popularity in Europe as an artist who was 'indispensable' for understanding modernity. In 1904, Julius Meier-Graefe, the German writer, art dealer, and founder of the Berlin Jugendstil (Art Nouveau) magazine *Pan*, wrote about Beardsley:

> Of a hundred important artists born within so many years, a certain number are indispensable, not because they produce this or that effect upon the mind, but because they affect their age and because they are symbolical of ourselves, and to know them is to have a true knowledge of our own life. [...] These men, in one word, give us knowledge; they are themselves concentrated knowledge. Beardsley is one of them, and to have seen every one of his fragments is a more urgent necessity than to know a single picture by Burne-Jones or Watts, even were the works of these artists ten times more beautiful than they are.[83]

---

77 Heinrich Heine, *The Prose Writings of Heinrich Heine*, ed. by Havelock Ellis (London: Walter Scott, 1887), p. 269. Beardsley was aware of Heine's work and the writer's complicated relationship with faith. His late letter (1897) to his Catholic patron Marc-André Raffalovich comments on Heine's religious stance, calling it 'the great warning' to all artists; see *Letters of Aubrey Beardsley* p. 249.

78 *The Prose Writings of Heinrich Heine*, p. viii.

79 *The Prose Writings of Heinrich Heine*, p. 152.

80 See Walter Pater, *Imaginary Portraits*, ed. by Lene Østermark-Johansen (London: Modern Humanities Research Association, 2014), p. 293. There is epistolary evidence that Beardsley knew and appreciated Pater's writing; see *Letters of Aubrey Beardsley*, p. 188. He might have first come across the discussion and English translation of Heine's 'Gods in Exile' via Pater's essay 'Pico della Mirandola' (1872), included in Walter H. Pater, *Studies in the History of the Renaissance* (London: Macmillan, 1873).

81 Potolsky, p. 155.

82 Ross, *Aubrey Beardsley*, p. 53.

83 Julius Meier-Graefe, *Modern Art: A Contribution to a New System of Aesthetics*, trans. by Florence Simmonds and George William Chrystal, 3 vols (London: W. Heinemann, 1908), II, p. 253. For the original German publication, see Julius Meier-Graefe, *Entwickelungsgeschichte der modernen Kunst*, 3 vols (Stuttgart: J. Hoffmann, 1904), II.

Beardsley's reputation abroad was shaped by the circulation of his designs and critical appraisals of his work in key art periodicals of the *fin de siècle*, including *Pan* and *Jugend* in Germany, *Ver Sacrum* in Austria, *Mir iskusstva* and *Vesy* in Russia, *Joventut* in Spain, and *Courrier français*, *L'Ermitage*, and *La Plume* in France, to name but a few. Those chief English magazines that published Beardsley's work — *The Studio*, the *Yellow Book*, and the *Savoy* — were also disseminated among art lovers beyond Britain.[84] Attuned to new international trends, these Decadent networks of cultural mediators encompassed critics, translators, collectors, and publishers, as well as those cosmopolitan contemporaries who outlived Beardsley and kept his name in the pages of the international press. Thus, John Gray (1866–1934), the Decadent poet-turned-Catholic priest and editor of Beardsley's *Last Letters* (1904), wrote an obituary in French for the important Symbolist periodical *La Revue blanche*.[85] Symons's obituary was translated into French by Jack Cohen and Edouard and Louis Thomas in 1905;[86] while the translation into German by Anna Muthesius (1870–1961) was printed as a separate issue of *Ver Sacrum* in 1903.[87]

According to Nathan J. Timpano, the publication of Symons's essay became an influential source for German-language critics such as Meier-Graefe and Rudolf Klein who, in their turn, went on to write extensively on Beardsley.[88] Since these publications drew attention not only to his drawings but also to the artist's wit, self-fashioning, and tragic early death, readers were prepared to engage with the literary side of Beardsley's talent once it became possible. The reissue of his literary remains by Lane was followed a year later by the translation of the expurgated chapters of *Under the Hill* as well as 'The Three Musicians' and 'The Ballad of a Barber' into German by Rudolf Alexander Schröder.[89] Another key figure in the popularization of Beardsley in the German-speaking countries was Fritz Wärndorfer, the Viennese textile industrialist, art collector, and financial backer of the Wiener Werkstätte (Viennese workshops which realized the vision of the Secession in the applied arts).[90] Wärndorfer admired and collected Beardsley's work. In 1908, he published Beardsley's correspondence with Smithers in German, stimulating the pan-European fascination with the Decadent artist's life and personality. Featuring their frivolous jokes and discussions of erotica, these letters concluded with a reproduction of the artist's last epistle in which he begged the publisher to destroy 'all obscene drawings'.[91] Beardsley's public image was further complicated when his more pious letters to his friend and benefactor Marc-André Raffalovich (1864–1934), the Catholic convert and 'sexual invert', were issued in German.[92]

Yet another significant German-language Beardsleyite was the writer, editor, and connoisseur of erotica Franz Blei. As early as 1899, he published an essay which discussed, in the manner of Symons, the correlation of sin and beauty in Beardsley's art and compared his rendering of the body to that of the Belgian Symbolist artist

---

[84] This impressive and polymorphous body of commentary is analysed in Jane Desmarais, *The Beardsley Industry: The Critical Reception in England and France 1893 to 1914* (Aldershot: Ashgate, 1998).

[85] Aubrey Beardsley, *Last Letters of Aubrey Beardsley*, ed. by John Gray (London: Longmans, Green, 1904); John Gray, 'Aubrey Beardsley', *La Revue Blanche*, May 1898, pp. 68–70. The letters were addressed to Marc-André Raffalovich, Beardsley's benefactor and Gray's intimate friend.

[86] A. W. Symons, *Aubrey Beardsley* (Paris: Floury, 1906), quoted in Desmarais, *Beardsley Industry*, p. 144.

[87] Arthur Symons, 'Aubrey Beardsley', trans. by Anna Muthesius, *Ver Sacrum*, 6.6 (1903), 117–38.

[88] Nathan J. Timpano, '"His Wretched Hand": Aubrey Beardsley, the Grotesque Body, and Viennese Modern Art', *Art History*, 40.3 (2016), 554–81 (p. 559).

[89] Aubrey Beardsley, *Unter dem Hügel: Eine Romantische Novelle*, trans. by R. A. Schröder (Leipzig: W. Drugulin, 1905). See also Rudolf Klein, *Aubrey Beardsley*, ed. by Richard Muther, Die Kunst (Berlin: J. Bard, 1902), v.

[90] The name Secession (Sezession) was applied to German and Austrian art groups that opposed official academies at the turn of the century. The most important among them was the Vienna Secession, spearheaded by the painter Gustav Klimt, architect Josef Maria Olbrich, and designer Koloman Moser. They pursued the ideal of a unity of architecture, decorative arts, and design, and developed a distinct version of the Art Nouveau style.

[91] Aubrey Beardsley, *Briefe [an Leonard Smithers]: Kalendernotizen u. die vier Zeichnungen zu E. A. Poe* (Munich: Hans von Weber, 1908), p. 181.

[92] Raffalovich was a student of 'sexual inversion', a term for homosexuality at the turn of the century; see 'Uranism, Congenital Sexual Inversion', *Journal of Comparative Neurology*, 5.1 (1895), 33–65. For the German publication of *Last Letters*, see Aubrey Beardsley, *Aubrey Beardsleys letzte Briefe*, trans. by Karl Moorburg (Leipzig: Insel-Verlag, 1910).

Félicien Rops.[93] Blei reproduced Beardsley's sexually overt illustrations for Juvenal and Aristophanes in his periodicals *Die Opale* (1906) and *Der Amethyst* (1907), disseminating the imagery among the early twentieth-century readers who would go on to push the boundaries of art, including Franz Kafka and André Gide.[94] As we have mentioned above, Blei also supplied the concluding chapters to an edition of *Venus und Tannhäuser* in 1920.

In Russia, a special Beardsley issue of the Decadent journal *Vesy* was published in 1905, containing the bowdlerized chapters of *Under the Hill* from Lane's collection alongside a set of Beardsley's aphorisms, from the same publication.[95] In 1908, promptly following Smithers's pirated publication of *The Story of Venus and Tannhäuser*, some of the newly available fragments of the novel appeared in the Moscow periodical.[96] Beardsley's high profile in *Vesy* was mainly due to the efforts of the journal's secretary, the critic and translator Mikhail Likiardopulo, who cooperated with Robert Ross to bring Wilde's and Beardsley's work to Russia. In 1912, Likiardopulo published a Beardsley miscellany which contained a nearly complete version of the Venus and Tannhäuser story.[97] Like the German and Austrian readerships, Russians were interested in Beardsley the man and enthusiastically consumed his selected letters, also translated by Likiardopulo.

Beardsley's poetry acquired exceptional significance in the Russian context thanks to the translations by Mikhail Kuzmin.[98] Kuzmin was not only a leading modernist poet of his generation but also an open homosexual and the author of the pioneering 'coming out' story *Wings* (*Kryl'ia*, 1906).[99] He knew of the unique pathways leading to the emerging queer public in Russia and helped Beardsley's writing become prominent in those circles.

In France, another acquaintance of Beardsley who contributed to the posthumous international circulation of his writing was the painter Jacques-Émile Blanche. The creator of a beautiful portrait of Beardsley as a dandy (1895, National Portrait Gallery, London), Blanche was at the core of the Anglo-French artistic coterie that gathered in the mid-1890s in Dieppe.[100] Beardsley was an active participant in this milieu. In 1907, Blanche wrote an essay titled 'Aubrey Beardsley', filled with reminiscences of their friendship, for the journal *Antée*.[101] Here he pronounced *Under the Hill* 'an *À Rebours* of sexuality'.[102] A year later, this text was turned into the preface of a French edition of Beardsley's writing which included the expurgated version of *Under the Hill*, the poems 'The Three Musicians' and 'The Ballad of a Barber', the translation of 'Carmen CI', and 'table talk'.[103]

---

93 Franz Blei, 'Aubrey Beardsley', *Pan*, 5.4 (1899), 256–60 (p. 259).

94 Kafka's letters and diaries show that he enjoyed reading *Der Amethyst* and *Die Opale*; see Anna Katharina Schaffner, 'Seasick in the Land of Sexuality: Kafka and the Erotic', in *Modernist Eroticisms: European Literature after Sexology*, ed. by Shane Weller and Anna Katharina Schaffner (Basingstoke: Palgrave Macmillan, 2012), pp. 80–104 (p. 83).

95 Obri Berdslei, 'Pod Kholmom', *Vesy*, 11 (1905), 30–49; Obri Berdslei, 'Zastol′naia boltovnia', *Vesy*, 11 (1905), 50–52.

96 Obri Berdslei, 'Istoriia Venery i Tangeizera: Romanticheskaia novella', trans. by M. Likiardopulo, *Vesy*, 1 (1908), 61–69.

97 *Obri Berdslei: Risunki, povesti, stikhi, aforizmy, pis′ma, monografii i stat′i o Berdslee*, ed. by M. Likiardopulo, trans. by M. Likiardopulo and M. Kuzmin (Moscow: Skorpion, 1912).

98 Obri Berdslei, 'Tri muzykanta', in *Obri Berdslei: Risunki, povesti, stikhi, aforizmy, pis′ma, monografii i stat′i o Berdslee*, ed. by Mikhail Likiardopulo, trans. by Mikhail Kuzmin (Moscow: Skorpion, 1912), pp. 117–18; Obri Berdslei, 'Ballada o Tsiriul′nike', in *Obri Berdslei: Risunki, povesti, stikhi, aforizmy, pis′ma, monografii i stat′i o Berdslee*, ed. by Mikhail Likiardopulo, trans. by Mikhail Kuzmin (Moscow: Skorpion, 1912), pp. 119–24.

99 Mikhail Kuzmin, 'Kryl′ia', *Vesy*, 11 (1906), 1–81. For the English translation, see Mikhail Kuzmin, *Wings: Prose and Poetry*, trans. by Neil Granoien and Michael Green (Ann Arbor: Ardis, 1972).

100 See Emily Eells, 'Du Côté de Dieppe: Jacques-Émile Blanche and the "Not Quite Conventional" English', *Forum for Modern Language Studies*, 53.3 (2017), 291–302.

101 Jacques-Émile Blanche, 'Aubrey Beardsley', *Antée*, 1 April 1907, 1103–22.

102 Quoted in Desmarais, *Beardsley Industry*, p. 34.

103 Aubrey Beardsley, *Sous la colline et d'autres essais en prose et en vers: précédé d'une préface par Jacques-E. Blanche*, trans. by A.-H. Cornette (Paris: H. Floury, 1908). According to Desmarais, the first French publication of *Under the Hill* was in the periodical *Antée* (November 1906); see *Beardsley Industry*, p. 117.

The first edition of Beardsley's novel in the Czech language came out in 1930. Proving the text's enduring subversiveness, it had to be published privately, in a limited edition for subscribers.[104] The most remarkable feature of the volume is the visual interpretation by the surrealist artist and queer icon Toyen, who produced three explicit erotic illustrations. The economical linear style of Toyen's drawings is also an homage to Beardsley's graphic technique.

As a result of the wide dissemination of Beardsley's writing, allusions to his prose and verse crop up in the European literatures of the avant-garde throughout the early decades of the twentieth century. The French Symbolist author Alfred Jarry referred to him as 'the king of Lace' in a chapter of his novel *Exploits and Opinions of Doctor Faustroll, Pataphysician* (*Gestes et opinions du docteur Faustroll, pataphysicien*, 1898), dedicated to Beardsley.[105] The Russian poet Nikolai Gumilev based his so-called fictionalized 'manifesto', the short story 'Cards' ('Karty', 1907), on *Under the Hill*, while Franz Blei infused the German tradition of erotic literature with Beardsleyesque motifs.[106] Decades after the author's death, the cosmopolitan underworld of Beardsley's imagination kept inspiring curious literary hybrids across the continent. Far from attempting a comprehensive history of Beardsley's reception, this list of fruitful encounters with his literary work presents a preliminary sketch for the much bigger picture which is yet to be drawn.

Stephen Calloway, who co-edited a collection of Beardsley's 'literary remains' in 1998, has observed with respect to *Under the Hill* that '[n]ot even Huysmans in his seminal novel of the decadence, *À Rebours*, could sustain such a level of fantastic invention and minute description in the pursuit of perverse effect'.[107] It is only fitting that this new, fully-annotated edition comes out at a time when queer theory and transnational approaches to literature and art have become an integral part of the humanities, and Decadence has enjoyed an upsurge of academic interest, promoted by the British Association for Decadence Studies. Complemented with other examples of his writing, this first faithful reproduction of Beardsley's novel in its unbowdlerized glory restores it to its place among the key texts of the Decadent literary canon.

---

[104] Aubrey Beardsley, *Venuše a Tannhäuser*, trans. by Arnošt Vaněček (Prague: M. D. N., 1930).

[105] Alfred Jarry, *Selected Works of Alfred Jarry*, ed. by Roger Shattuck and Simon Watson Taylor (London: Methuen, 1965), pp. 101–02.

[106] Nikolai Gumilev, 'Karty', in *Polnoe sobranie sochinenii*, ed. by M. Basker and others, 10 vols (Moscow: Voskresen´e, 2005), VI, 17–19.

[107] Stephen Calloway, *Aubrey Beardsley* (London: V & A Publications, 1998), p. 140. See also Aubrey Beardsley, *In Black and White: The Literary Remains of Aubrey Beardsley*, ed. by Stephen Calloway and David Colvin (London: Cypher, 1998).

AUBREY BEARDSLEY: AN EXPANDED CHRONOLOGY

1872
Aubrey Vincent Beardsley is born in Brighton, on the south coast of England, on 21 August to Ellen Agnus Beardsley (née Pitt) and Vincent Paul Beardsley. He is an artistic and musical prodigy from a young age.

1879
Beardsley is diagnosed with tuberculosis in the summer and is sent to board at Hamilton Lodge School, Hurstpierpoint, Sussex, in the autumn.

1883
Aged eleven, through a family friend, he gains three drawing commissions, earning £30 (about £4,000 at 2020 prices). The drawings reveal the influence of Kate Greenaway, a significant figure in the development of book illustration and design at that time.

1885
Beardsley attends Brighton Grammar School where he acts, sings, learns French and Latin, reads fiction, and writes poetry and a play entitled *A Brown Study*, marking his beginnings as a writer. He continues to draw. During his time at the school, he makes 29 drawings for Book II of Virgil's *Aeneid* and, in his last term, makes illustrations for the programme of a Brighton Grammar School production of the comic opera *The Pay of the Pied Piper*. Beardsley's juvenilia reveal a rapidly developing, witty, and accomplished illustrator, and a budding writer.

1889–90
On 1 January 1889, Beardsley starts work as a clerk in London. In December, he suffers severe episodes of tubercular lung haemorrhages and is off work for about eighteen months, during which time he reads prodigiously in English and French literature, but draws little. This lays the foundation for a later reputation for being formidably literate and, as his friend the artist William Rothenstein put it, knowing 'his Balzac from cover to cover'. A proof of this exceptional literacy lies in the extraordinary range and richness of reference in *Under the Hill*. Beardsley considers a literary career. In January 1890, he succeeds in publishing a short story, 'The Story of a Confession Album', in the magazine *Tit-Bits*, for which he was paid one pound and ten shillings (equivalent to about £160 in 2020).

1891
In July, Beardsley resumes his job, which has been kept open. With his sister Mabel, he visits the studio of the painter Edward Burne-Jones, at that time both famous in Britain and much admired abroad, who recommends Beardsley to the Westminster School of Art and becomes his mentor. Beardsley writes: 'The drawings I showed Burne-Jones were those done within the last few weeks, as prior to that I don't think I put pencil to paper for a good year. In vain I tried to crush it out of me but that drawing faculty would come uppermost'. Nevertheless, he remained a writer too.

At the Westminster School of Art, Beardsley is taught by the Impressionist Frederick Brown, who encourages him to develop his own natural talent. His drawings increasingly reflect the late Pre-Raphaelitism of Burne-Jones but also the much more modern influence of James McNeill Whistler.

1892
Beardsley meets the prominent designer and close associate of William Morris, Aymer Vallance, who acquires a drawing, and at a reception at his house on 14 February introduces Beardsley to an artistic circle that includes Robert Ross, Oscar Wilde's close friend and sometime lover. Ross later recorded how profoundly struck he and

the company had been by both Beardsley's personality and his 'marvellous drawings', and how everyone was 'astonished by his knowledge of Balzac'. This marks Beardsley's entry into the London world of art and literature. In May, he spends a week in Paris, where he shows his work to the celebrated and revered painter Puvis de Chavannes who, according to Beardsley, gave him 'the greatest encouragement' and introduced him to friends as 'un jeune artiste anglais qui fait des choses étonnantes' ('a young English artist who makes astonishing things').

In the summer, he meets the London publisher J. M. Dent and is commissioned to make illustrations for a new edition of *Le Morte Darthur*, Thomas Malory's 1485 translation from the original French versions of the legends of King Arthur. Beardsley is able to leave his job. Eventually, he makes 353 drawings for it (many of them small), to produce a masterpiece of book illustration. Created between autumn 1892 and June 1894, they reveal the rapid development of a completely personal style under the added influence of Japanese art. Late in the year, in response to reading Oscar Wilde's Decadent play *Salome*, written in French, Beardsley produces a drawing of its climactic moment when Salome seizes the head of John the Baptist.

1893

In April, the first issue of what proves to be an important new art magazine, the *Studio*, includes a major article, 'A New Illustrator: Aubrey Beardsley', reproducing eight drawings by him, the one for *Salome* among them. This brings Beardsley to a wider public and, seen by Wilde, that drawing secures him the commission to illustrate the English edition of the play. When the translation by Wilde's lover, Lord Alfred Douglas, is rejected by Wilde, Beardsley, deploying his literary skills, produces a fresh translation, which in turn is rejected when Wilde takes back Douglas's for diplomatic reasons, and which sadly has disappeared. Between June and November, Beardsley then produces a total of eighteen drawings for the play in a style which is now an entirely original synthesis of his early influences. With their extraordinary blend of abstraction and vivid representation, and their emphasis on the themes of sexuality and death in the play, they constitute a major contribution to the new forms of art that were being forged at that moment.

1894

In February, the publication of *Salome* in English creates a sensation. Beardsley is by now famous and hugely in demand. Notably, he designs twenty-two covers for the publisher John Lane's important Keynotes series of modern novels, many by so-called New Woman writers, who are setting out to dismantle the prevailing Victorian view of women as sexually pure, intellectually incapable, and politically immature. In the public eye, this radical revision marks these authors as Decadent.

Beardsley is appointed art editor of a new periodical, the *Yellow Book*, also published by Lane, Wilde's publisher. Its appearance from April creates further sensation, largely because of Beardsley's contributions of his own drawings, in a new style in which he casts a sinister, sensual, and satirical eye on the contemporary world. With Beardsley's unconventional depictions of women between and on the yellow covers, the periodical not only helps to visualize the New Woman trope but also disseminates work by the New Woman writers, including George Egerton, Charlotte Mew, Netta Syrrett, and Ella D'Arcy (whom the literary editor Henry Harland pays from his own pocket to act as a sub-editor). Despite the absence of Wilde from the list of contributors, the assumption that the new Decadent magazine is linked with Lane's notorious author surfaces in a review in the American journal *The Critic*, where the *Yellow Book* is called 'the Oscar Wilde of periodicals'.

In June, Beardsley sees and is entranced by Richard Wagner's opera *Tannhäuser*. The next day, he mentions in a letter that he is writing his own version of the story 'that will simply astonish everyone' — the first mention of the novel he titled *The Story of Venus and Tannhäuser* but that would see its only publication in his lifetime as *Under the Hill*. In July, he publishes in the magazine *New Revue* a sparkling essay 'The Art of the Hoarding', which deals with that novel phenomenon of the 1890s, the pictorial advertising poster, an art form to which Beardsley added his own significant contribution. In October, in the third volume of the *Yellow Book*, Lane announces that *The Story of Venus and Tannhäuser* is 'in preparation' for publication as a book. Regular mentions of Beardsley's progress with the story, as well as with drawings for it, occur in his letters through the rest of 1894. By November, he is 'worrying about [his] beloved Venusberg' and mentions 'a picture of Venus feeding her pet unicorns', suggesting he had advanced as far as Chapter IV; he was to write only one further chapter.

1895

In April, Oscar Wilde is arrested on charges of committing indecent acts and subsequently convicted of 'gross indecency' and imprisoned for two years. With the fifth issue about to appear, Beardsley is fired from the *Yellow Book* due to his association with Wilde through his illustrations for *Salome*. Beardsley's world falls apart. He briefly takes refuge in Paris. He meets the publisher Leonard Smithers, who is heroically to support both him and Wilde in their remaining years. In the summer, with Smithers, he begins to plan the *Savoy* magazine, a rival to the *Yellow Book*, which has continued publication.

1896

The first issue of the *Savoy*, edited by Arthur Symons, is published in January with a striking cover by Beardsley in another new style, inspired by the great seventeenth-century French landscapist Claude Lorrain, and by French eighteenth-century Rococo engravings. The literary contents signal a much more cosmopolitan and genuinely Decadent and subversive tone than the *Yellow Book*. However, unlike its rival, Smithers's publication centred on male authors and catered for male readers, a tactic which eventually undermined its commercial success. The literary contributions notably include an opening article by George Bernard Shaw attacking both the Christian Church and society's dependence on caffeine, alcohol, and meat; a defence, by the pioneer British sexologist Havelock Ellis, of the French writer Émile Zola, whose novels were then execrated in Britain, and whose London publisher, Henry Vizetelly, had been imprisoned for 'obscene libel' in 1889 for persisting in publishing them; an essay by the editor provocatively celebrating the pleasures of the casino and the voyeuristic delights of the beach at the French seaside resort of Dieppe; and, in a concluding flourish of Decadence, the first part of Beardsley's *The Story of Venus and Tannhäuser*. For this open publication, it is heavily rewritten and censored. Through the life of the *Savoy* until its demise in December, Beardsley also contributes three poems, one of which, 'The Ballad of a Barber' was originally intended to be part of *Under the Hill*, as well as numerous striking drawings.

At the same time, Beardsley completes a set of illustrations for Alexander Pope's satire in verse *The Rape of the Lock* that encapsulates his French rococo style and represents one of his key bodies of work. In yet another stylistic development, he creates a set of illustrations for the ancient Greek comedy *Lysistrata*, inspired by Greek vase painting. Deploying pure line and startling expanses of open space, these drawings are technically brilliant, extremely beautiful, and highly sexually explicit. The book is published clandestinely by Smithers in October. *The Rape of the Lock* and *Lysistrata*, added to the earlier *Le Morte Darthur* and *Salome*, complete a quartet of great illustrated books, each radically different, that constitute the cornerstones of the edifice of Beardsley's art. His achievement in this miracle year of intense activity is all the more remarkable since in March his tuberculosis had seriously reasserted itself. In December, he writes an interview with himself which is published as 'Mr Aubrey Beardsley and his Work' in the magazine the *Idler* in March 1897.

1897

Continues to struggle with tuberculosis. Book illustration projects with Smithers are begun and not completed. Produces six illustrations for the gender-bending novel *Mademoiselle de Maupin* (1835) by Théophile Gautier, whose preface with its vindication of amoral aesthetics has become a foundational text of Decadence. In March, he is told to move to Menton in the South of France for his health. Before leaving England, he is received into the Catholic Church. Eventually arrives in Menton with his mother in late November and settles into the Hotel Cosmopolitain. Starts planning his last project, a richly decorated and illustrated edition of Ben Jonson's *Volpone*, which he does not live long enough to realize in full.

1898

On 7 March, Beardsley writes to Smithers imploring him to 'destroy *all* copies of Lysistrata' and '*all* obscene drawings', signing off the letter 'in my death agony'. He dies at the Hotel Cosmopolitain in Menton in the early hours of 16 March. In his obituary of Beardsley, Arthur Symons reveals that he described himself as 'a man of letters' on a library admission form. His literary works here presented are evidence of the core of truth in this observation.

1900

Death of Oscar Wilde in Paris. From then on, he and Beardsley are increasingly seen as the two key figures in the art and literature of the Decadent 1890s in Britain. Both will gain international reputation and influence.

A NOTE ON THE TEXTS AND EDITORIAL DECISIONS

The original manuscript of *Under the Hill* is a highly complex document since it bears the traces of the editing process carried out by Beardsley and Leonard Smithers to adapt it for publication in the *Savoy*, as well as Beardsley's own authorial changes.[1] Sexual passages were lightly scored through so as to remain legible for potential later publication, nevertheless adding to the difficulties of transcription. For Chapter IV Beardsley also wrote some entirely fresh material that only appears in the *Savoy*. An additional layer of difficulty arises from the relationship of the manuscript and the *Savoy* text to the supposedly uncensored edition published clandestinely by Smithers after Beardsley's death. We have dealt with all this by creating, in addition to the annotated continuous transcription of the manuscript, what is known as a 'diplomatic' transcription, that is, a page-by-page typographic version of the manuscript, tracking all the changes made and the variations between the three texts, as well as various marks and comments by its editors.

The annotated and diplomatic transcriptions of *Under the Hill* retain the original grammar and spelling as well as the peculiarities of Beardsley's use of French. The original punctuation is also preserved with one exception: while Beardsley uses double quotation marks, we adhere to the MHRA Style Guide and use single quotation marks. We discuss the history of the manuscript and the early editions of *Under the Hill*, and our approach to the transcription, in the Foreword and Introduction. Those discussions are essential reading before embarking on the texts which follow here. The annotated version of the manuscript is followed by what appeared as Chapter IV of *Under the Hill* in the *Savoy*: Aubrey Beardsley, 'Under the Hill', *Savoy*, April 1896, pp. 187–96. Annotations for the names and terms which appear in the manuscript, for example *Le Romaunt de la Rose*, are not repeated.

Additional texts included in Appendix A are taken from their first published versions: 'The Three Musicians', *Savoy*, January 1896, pp. 65–66; 'The Ballad of a Barber', *Savoy*, July 1896, pp. 91–93; Catullus, 'Carmen CI', trans. by Aubrey Beardsley, *Savoy*, November 1896, p. 52; Aubrey Beardsley, 'The Art of the Hoarding', *New Review*, 11.62 (1894), 47–55 (pp. 53–55). The fragment of a poem 'The Ivory Piece' and the unfinished notes for 'Volpone Prospectus' are taken from R. A. Walker's *A Beardsley Miscellany* (London: Bodley Head, 1949), which contains facsimiles of Beardsley's manuscripts for both pieces: 'The Ivory Piece', p. 116; 'Volpone Prospectus', pp. 87–88. Critical materials included in Appendix B are taken from their original publications: Arthur H. Lawrence, 'Mr. Aubrey Beardsley and His Work', *The Idler*, March 1897, pp. 188–202; Arthur Symons, 'Aubrey Beardsley as a Man of Letters', *Saturday Review*, 9 January 1904, pp. 41–42; E. F. Benson, *As We Were: A Victorian Peep-Show* (London: Longmans, Green, 1930), pp. 268–73.

[1] The pages of the manuscript of *Under the Hill* are reproduced here (figs 6–85). Beardsley wrote the story in what appears to be a pre-ruled blank accounts book approximately 11 × 9 inches (28 × 23 cm). He wrote on the right-hand (recto) page only, but on a number of occasions wrote additional material on the verso of a page and then marked the place on the recto where the new text was to be inserted. After Beardsley's death in 1898 the manuscript remained with Leonard Smithers until he got into financial difficulties in 1900 and sold all his holdings of Beardsley material to John Lane. Presumably Lane later sold it to the American dealer and collector A. S. W. Rosenbach, who is mentioned as already its owner in the catalogue of the sale at auction of John Lane's Beardsley collection in New York in 1926. It then became part of the library and museum in Philadelphia, the Rosenbach, founded in 1954 by A. S. W. Rosenbach and his brother Philip. The manuscript is sumptuously bound in full vellum, stamped in gold with Beardsley's original but unused peacock feather design for the cover of the 1894 edition of Oscar Wilde's play *Salome*. This binding is identical to that of the de luxe issue of Lane's 1904 edition of *Under the Hill*, except for the addition of the words 'Original Manuscript' below the peacock feather design, and the use of cream-coloured cloth for the Lane book, rather than vellum. It seems likely that it was bound thus by Lane rather than Rosenbach. (See also Introduction, p. 3 and note 14.)

Under the Hill

Annotated Version

ABBREVIATIONS

BE Manuscript fragment from Beinecke Rare Book and Manuscript Library MSS MISC Box: 156 (Broadside), Folder: GROUP 22, F-3; *'Under the Hill' and 'The Ballad of a Barber' – AMs, 4 pp.*

CR Linda Gertner Zatlin, *Aubrey Beardsley: A Catalogue Raisonné*, 2 vols (New Haven: Yale University Press, 2016)

JL Aubrey Beardsley, *Under the Hill and Other Essays in Prose and Verse* (London: Bodley Head, 1904).

LS Aubrey Beardsley, *The Story of Venus and Tannhäuser* (London: [Smithers], 1907).

SV The initial publication of the novella in the *Savoy*: Aubrey Beardsley, 'Under the Hill', *Savoy*, January 1896, pp. 151–70; and Aubrey Beardsley, 'Under the Hill', *Savoy*, April 1896, pp. 187–96.

Under the Hill
A romantic novel

By
Aubrey Beardsley

with his illustrations & ornaments
Chaps I II III IV V

'La chaleur du brandon Venus'
Le Roman de la Rose, v. 22051[1]

---

[1] *Le Roman de la Rose* is an allegorical poem of chivalric love and a landmark of French medieval literature. The first part was written in 1236 by Guillaume de Lorris to illustrate 'the whole art of love'. It centres on the protagonist's dreamlike voyage in pursuit of the rose which stands for the love of his Lady and presents an obvious sexual metaphor. Like Beardsley's Tannhäuser, the Lover, the leading protagonist of the *Roman*, arrives at a luxuriant garden of pleasure containing behind its walls a set of allegorical characters; the allegories embody various virtues of the Lady as well as darker forces of seduction. The *Roman* was completed around 1275 by Jean de Meun. Moving 'from the courtly to the philosophical' tradition, the continuation of the story reflects, as Christine McWebb points out, 'the interests of late thirteenth-century scholasticism' (*Debating the Roman de La Rose: A Critical Anthology*, ed. by Christine McWebb (New York: Routledge, 2007), p. xii). Beardsley's epigraph is taken from very near the end of the *Roman*. The Lover has battled through many enemies to reach the rose and embraces it. Immediately more enemies, including Shame and Fear, raise a high-walled castle between him and the rose. Eventually, the Lover calls on his Lord for help. This is Cupid, who with Venus attacks the castle. It is Venus who takes command, beginning with a long speech of blood-curdling threats, calling on Shame and Fear to surrender, and then delivering the crucial blow by setting fire to the castle with her *brandon*, her flaming torch. This is summarized at the head of this section of the poem in a quatrain from which Beardsley has taken the third line: 'Comment ceulx du chastel yssirent | Hors, aussi-tost comme ilz sentirent | La chaleur du brandon [de] Venus, | Dont aucuns jousterent tous nudz'. This translates as: 'How those within the castle | Issued forth as they felt | The heat of Venus's torch | Which some were fighting naked' (translated by Wilson; see original Guillaume de Lorris and Jean de Meun, *Le Roman de la rose*, ed. by Pierre Marteau, 5 vols (Paris: Paul Daffis, 1878), IV, p. 340). The enemies flee and the Lover at last gains access again to the rose, which he plucks from its bush. He then awakes from what has been a dream. The line 'the heat of Venus's torch' foregrounds the eroticism of Beardsley's 'romantic novel'.

To the most Eminent & Revered Prince
Giulio Poldo Pizzoli
Cardinal of the Holy Roman Church
Titular Bishop of S. Maria in Trastavere
Archbishop of Ostia & Velletri
Nuncio to The Holy See
in
Nicaragua & Patagonia
A father to the poor
A reformer of Ecclesiastical Discipline
A pattern of Learning
Wisdom & Holiness of life,
This book is dedicated with due reverence
by his humble servitor
a scrivener & limner of worldly things[2]
who made this book
Aubrey Beardsley[3]

---

[2] 'Scrivener' and 'limner' are archaic terms for writer and painter. Beardsley's self-descriptions here are interesting not least for the order in which he puts them. It is a commonplace of Beardsley commentary that he aspired to be a man of letters, then a more prestigious profession than that of painter and even more so than that of illustrator. 'Limning' originated as a term for illuminating manuscripts and by the sixteenth century had come to refer specifically to miniature painting. That meaning is enshrined in the celebrated *Treatise Concerning the Art of Limning* (*c.* 1600) by one of the greatest of all miniaturists, Nicholas Hilliard. Beardsley would have been well aware of Hilliard and his treatise, and art historical parallels can be drawn between them, including the fact that they both left a brief literary monument that encapsulated their art.

[3] The dedicatee is fictional. However, Linda Dowling persuasively argues that Beardsley dedicates the novella to his patron and friend Marc-André Raffalovich. He was a wealthy Jewish émigré, an aesthete, and a devoted partner of the Decadent poet turned Catholic priest John Gray. Raffalovich converted to Catholicism in 1896 and played a key role in Beardsley's conversion a year later. The mixture of religiosity, unorthodox sexuality, and inside knowledge of 1890s literary and erotic discourses makes Raffalovich a plausible real-life referent of the dedication. See Linda Dowling, '"Venus and Tannhäuser": Beardsley's Satire of Decadence', *Journal of Narrative Technique*, 8.1 (1978), 26–41 (pp. 32–34). It is just possible that Beardsley took the name of his imaginary cardinal Pizzoli from the great Italian art collector Count Gian Giacomo Poldi Pezzoli, founder of the Poldi Pezzoli Museum in Milan. Pezzoli's collection notably included works by Sandro Botticelli and Andrea Mantegna, both important early influences for Beardsley. In the famous photograph of Beardsley in his hotel room in Menton (1897), where he died, his group of prints after Mantegna is prominent on the wall. Santa Maria in Trastevere is one of Rome's most ancient and most beautiful churches, whose incumbent priests are traditionally both cardinals and bishops. The incumbency is honorary or 'titular', so Beardsley is entirely accurate in his description, as he is equally plausible in making Pizzoli archbishop of Ostia and Velletri, which was one of the episcopal sees of Rome. Note, however, that Beardsley here misspells Trastevere as 'Trastavere'. In the ecclesiastical context, 'See' means seat, but the term 'Holy See' usually refers to the government of the Catholic Church, housed in the Vatican, as well as to the Vatican itself. A nuncio is a papal ambassador. The Catholic Church established formal diplomatic relations with Argentina, which Patagonia is part of, in 1877, and eventually with Nicaragua in 1908.

Most Eminent Prince,[4]

I know not by what mischance the writing of epistles dedicatory has fallen into disuse, whether through the vanity of authors or the humility of patrons. But the practice seems to me so very beautiful & becoming that I have ventured to make an essay in the modest art & lay with formalities my first book at your feet. I have it must be confessed many fears lest I shall be arraigned of presumption in choosing so exalted a name as your own to place at the beginning of this history, but I hope that such a censure will not be too lightly passed upon me for if I am guilty, 'tis but of a most natural pride that the accidents of my life should allow me to sail the little pinnace of my wit under your protection.

But though I can clear myself of such a charge I am still minded to use the tongue of apology, for with what face can I offer you a book treating of so vain & fantastical a thing as love? I know that in the judgment of many the amorous passion is accounted a shameful thing & ridiculous, indeed it must be confessed that more blushes have risen for love's sake than for any other cause, & that lovers are an eternal laughing-stock. Still as the book will be found to contain matter of deeper import than mere venery, inasmuch as it treats of the great contrition of its chiefest character & of canonical things in certain pages I am not without hopes that your Eminence will pardon my writing of the Hill of Venus, for which exposition let my youth excuse me.

Then I must crave your forgiveness for addressing you in a language other than the Roman, but my small freedom in Latinity forbids me to wander beyond the idiom of my vernacular. I would not for the world that your delicate Southern ear should be offended by a barbarous assault of rude & Gothic words,[5] but methinks no language is rude that can boast polite writers, & not a few have flourished in this country in times past, bringing our common speech to very great perfection. In the present age, alas! our pens are ravished by unlettered authors & unmannered critics, that make a havoc rather than a building, a wilderness rather than a garden. But alack what boots it to drop tears upon the preterit?[6]

T'is not of our own shortcomings though, but of your own great merits that I should speak, else I should be forgetful of the duties I have drawn upon myself in electing to address you in a dedication. T'is of your noble virtues (though all the world know of 'em), your taste & wit, your care for letters & very real regard for the arts, that I must be the proclaimer.

Though it be true that all men have sufficient wit to pass a judgment on this or that, & not a few sufficient impudence to print the same (these last being commonly accounted critics), I have ever held that the critical faculty is more rare than the inventive. T'is a faculty your Eminence possesses in so great a degree that your praise or blame is something oracular, your utterance infallible as great genius or as a beautiful woman. Your mind, I know, rejoicing in fine distinctions & subtle procedures of thought, beautifully discursive rather than hastily conclusive, has found in criticism its happiest exercise. T'is pity that so perfect a Maecenas should have no Horace to befriend, no Georgics to accept; for the offices & function of patron or critic must of necessity be lessened in an age of little men & little work.[7] In times past t'was nothing derogatory for great princes & men of State to extend their loves & favour to poets, for thereby they received as much honour as they conferred.

---

[4] This reverential address presents another clue identifying Raffalovich as the novella's addressee. In his letter to Leonard Smithers (postmark 19 February 1897), Beardsley refers to Raffalovich as '[t]he Russian prince'; see *Letters of Aubrey Beardsley*, p. 254.

[5] Goths were a Germanic tribe who invaded both the Eastern and Western empires between the third and fifth centuries, and founded kingdoms in Italy, France, and Spain. The word is used to characterize an uncivilized person who behaves like a barbarian, neglecting or ruining works of art. In architecture, the term 'gothic' was originally applied to that style because it appeared barbaric compared to the Greek and Roman tradition. It came to represent an alternative concept of beauty from the classical, and is the origin of the dichotomy in western aesthetics between the classic and romantic.

[6] 'Preterit' means 'the past' in Middle English; in this sentence, Beardsley alludes to lines 5009–10 from Chaucer's *Romaunt of the Rose*, 'She wepeth the tyme that she hath wasted | Compleyning of the preterit'; Geoffrey Chaucer, *The Complete Works of Geoffrey Chaucer*, ed. by Walter W. Skeat, 6 vols (Oxford: Clarendon Press, 1894), VI, p. 217. Skeat's edition of Chaucer was the one Beardsley used, as his letter to F. H. Evans (early October 1894) proves; see *Letters of Aubrey Beardsley*, p. 75.

[7] Gaius Maecenas was a Roman politician under the rule of Octavian (Augustus) who became most famous for his support of Augustan poets, including Horace. The mention of Maecenas is one of the details underpinning the identification of the dedicatee as Raffalovich; see Dowling, p. 33.

Did not Prince Festus with pride take the master-work of Julian into his protection, & was not the Aeneis a pretty thing to offer Caesar?[8]

Learning without appreciation is a thing of nought, but I know not which is greatest in you, your love of the arts or your knowledge of 'em. What wonder, then, that I am studious to please you & desirous of your protection? How deeply thankful I am for your past affections, you know well, your great kindness & liberality having far outgone my slight merits & small accomplishment that seemed scarce to warrant any favour. Alas! T'is a slight offering I make you now, but, if after glancing into its pages (say of an evening upon your terrace) you should deem it worthy of the most remotest place in your princely library, the knowledge that it rested there would be reward sufficient for my labours & a crowning happiness to my pleasure in the writing of this slender book.

The humble & obedient servant of Your Eminence,
Aubrey Beardsley.

[8] Beardsley could refer to the fourth-century Latin historian Festus, the author of *Breviarium rerum gestarum populi Romani*, a history of Rome. Festus's dates are not known precisely but the history was completed about 370 AD. Julian could be the Emperor Julian, a fascinating figure who tried to restore the pagan gods and abolish Christianity. Beardsley might have considered Julian's masterwork to be his *Hymn to the Mother of the Gods*. Beardsley would have known Swinburne's great *Hymn to Proserpine* (1866), the epigraph of which is Julian's supposed last words *Vicisti, Galilaee* — you have won, Galilean (i.e. Christ). Festus's history goes up to the reign of Julian, which makes him a plausible candidate. Alternatively, Beardsley might have been thinking of the Christian martyr St Julian of Antioch who died *c.* 305, which could also fit with Festus. Since Beardsley is here probably addressing Raffalovich, his patron and a devout Christian, the saint is a possibility (see note 3 above). *Aeneis* is a form of the classical Latin *Aenēidos*, more commonly known as the *Aeneid*, a Latin epic poem by Virgil written 29–19 BC.

UNDER THE HILL

Chapter I

The Abbé Aubrey having lighted off his horse, stood doubtfully for a moment beneath the ombre[9] gateway of the Hill of Venus, troubled with an exquisite fear lest a day's travel should have too cruelly undone the laboured niceness of his dress.[10] His hand slim & gracious as La Marquise du Deffand's in the drawing by Carmontelle, played nervously about the gold hair that fell upon his shoulders like a finely curled peruke, & from point to point of a precise toilet the fingers wandered, quelling the little mutinies of cravat & ruffle.[11]

It was taper time; when the tired earth puts on its cloak of mists & shadows, when the enchanted woods are stirred with light footfalls & slender voices of the fairies, when all the air is full of delicate influences, & even the beaux, seated at their dressing tables, dream a little.[12]

A delicious moment, thought Aubrey, to slip into exile.[13] The place where he stood waved drowsily with strange flowers, heavy with perfume, dripping with odours.[14] Gloomy & nameless weeds, not to be found in Mentzelius.[15] Huge moths so richly winged they must have banqueted upon tapestries & royal stuffs, slept on the pillars that flanked either side of the gateway, & the eyes of all the moths remained open, & were burning &

---

[9] From French *ombre*, meaning shadow or shade. Here Beardsley uses this noun adjectivally to mean the shaded or shady gateway.

[10] For publication in the *Savoy* Beardsley had to disguise the story that he had promised to John Lane as *Venus and Tannhäuser* by changing both its title and the names of the two protagonists. He rewrote the first page of Chapter I, changing the title to *Under the Hill* and Tannhäuser to 'the Abbé Aubrey'. He and Smithers then seem to have realized this was too obvious. In the manuscript, the eponymous and telling name 'Aubrey' is crossed out; 'Fanfreluche', overwritten in mauve ink, is then adopted in SV. After rewriting the first chapter, Beardsley gave up, and the manuscript thereafter is his original draft in which the name is Tannhäuser. This means that in this transcription of the Rosenbach manuscript the protagonist appears as 'Abbé Aubrey' on the first page only. After that, we revert to what Beardsley wrote in the first draft. Occasionally, Beardsley refers to Tannhäuser as 'the Knight' or 'the Chevalier' (French for knight). The editorial process is also visible with regard to the novel's key toponym. The initial 'Hill of Venus' of the manuscript, which becomes simply 'a mysterious Hill' in SV, offers an exemplary Beardsleyesque pun on *mons Veneris* (Latin: mount of Venus), the mons pubis of a woman. The phrase had been in use since the seventeenth century (for example, 'Some worshipped *Nymphae* and *Hymen*, and Mons Veneris, which words signifie the secret parts of womens bodies', in Benjamin Spencer, *Chrysomison, a Golden Meane; or, Middle Way for Christians to Walk By* (London, 1659), p. 15.). In the manuscript, 'of Venus' is underlined and marked with an X in the margin. In SV, it is substituted with 'the mysterious Hill', which is transformed into 'Venusberg' in LS. It is interesting to note that from the first mentions of the story in Beardsley's letters, he alludes to his 'beloved Venusberg', thus proving that the toponym was the author's construction, not Smithers's uncalled-for change; see the letter to F. H. Evans (November 1894) in *Letters of Aubrey Beardsley*, p. 79.

[11] Marie de Vichy-Charmond, Marquise Du Deffand, was a woman of letters and a cornerstone of French salon society. Known portraits, including those by the court artist Louis Carmontelle, often depict Marie Du Deffand with half-closed eyes, evoking her late-life blindness, and instead draw attention to her elegant hands, posed as if conducting a polite conversation. An engraving after Carmontelle was reproduced as a frontispiece in the nineteenth-century edition of her letters. See M. de Lescure, *Correspondance complète de la marquise Du Deffand avec ses amis* (Paris: Henri Plon, 1865).

[12] 'Taper time' was Beardsley's cherished phrase. He uses it in a letter to Ada Leverson (April 1895): 'If I can possibly manage it I will turn up at taper time or rather earlier this afternoon', *Letters of Aubrey Beardsley*, p. 82.

[13] In an early letter to Smithers, Beardsley asked, discussing the publication (postmark 19 August 1895): 'Might not my little book be called *The Queen in Exile*?'; see *Letters of Aubrey Beardsley*, p. 97.

[14] As Maxwell notes, this sentence echoes the 'strange flowers' and 'curious odours' which feature in Walter Pater's Conclusion to *Studies in the History of the Renaissance* (1873); see Catherine Maxwell, *Scents & Sensibility: Perfume in Victorian Literary Culture* (Oxford: Oxford University Press, 2017), pp. 61–62.

[15] Mentzelius, or Christian Mentzel, was a German scholar and pioneering botanist who introduced binominal taxonomy into

bursting with a mesh of veins. The pillars were fashioned in some pale stone & rose up like hymns in the praise of Venus, for from cap to base, each one was carved with loving sculptures, showing such a cunning invention & such a curious knowledge that Tannhäuser lingered not a little in reviewing them. They surpassed all that Japan has ever pictured from her maisons vertes, all that was ever painted on the infamous bath rooms of Cardinal La Motte & even outdid the astonishing illustrations to Jones' *Sidelights on child life.*[16]

'A pretty portal,' murmured the Knight, correcting his sash.[17]

As he spoke, a faint sound of singing was breathed out from the mountain, faint music as strange & distant as sea-legends that are heard in shells.

'The Vespers of Venus, I take it', said Tannhäuser & struck a few chords of accompaniment ever so lightly upon his little lute.[18] Softly across the spell-bound threshold the song floated & wreathed itself about the subtle columns till the moths were touched with passion & moved quaintly in their sleep. One of them was awakened by the intenser notes of the Chevalier's lute-strings & fluttered into his cave. Tannhäuser felt it was his cue for entry.

---

botany; see Christian Mentzel, *Pinax botanonymos polyglottos katholikos = Index nominum plantarum universalis* (Berlin: Christoph Runge, 1682).

[16] *Maisons vertes* (French for 'green houses') refers to seirō, luxury pleasure quarters in Edo, often depicted in ukiyo-e prints which famously influenced Beardsley's style. Cardinal La Motte presents a hybrid of two historical figures involved in the so-called Affair of the Diamond Necklace: Jeanne de Valois, Comtesse de la Motte, and Louis de Rohan, Cardinal-Archbishop of Strasbourg. Alexandre Dumas *fils*, one of Beardsley's favourite writers, based his novel *The Queen's Necklace* (*Le Collier de la reine*, 1848) on this historical event. Comtesse de la Motte and her accomplices convinced Cardinal de Rohan, who was in the bad graces of Marie-Antoinette, that the restoration of the queen's favour was dependant on his clandestine purchase of a necklace consisting of 579 large diamonds. The scheme involved the fabrication of Marie-Antoinette's signature and arrangement of a midnight date in the gardens of Versailles with a prostitute disguised as the queen. In reality, Comtesse de la Motte was procuring the necklace for herself and her partners in crime. When the incident was made public, the reputation of Marie-Antoinette, in this case innocent of squander, was severely damaged. Having come to signify the decadence of the *ancien régime*, this case tapped into Beardsley's penchant for the eighteenth century; the criminal mastermind of the entire scheme, Jeanne de Valois, would have fascinated him. An offspring of an illegitimate but recognized son of Henri II, she grew up as a destitute orphan but, 'taken in hand by a court lady', she started her adventurous career, married a guardsman, La Motte, with the fabricated title of count, and, as John Hardman notes, 'probably became [a] lover' of Cardinal de Rohan (see John Hardman, 'The Diamond Necklace Affair 1785–1786', in *Marie-Antoinette: The Making of a French Queen* (New Haven: Yale University Press, 2019), pp. 97–121 (p. 100)). Combining the cardinal and the Comtesse under the name 'Cardinal La Motte', Beardsley uses one of his favourite art devices and creates a linguistic hermaphrodite. Like Hermaphroditus, a progeny of the love goddess Aphrodite and the patron of thieves, Hermes, 'Cardinal La Motte' is a character that knowledgeable readers would have instantly associated with eroticism and criminality. An additional sexual connotation is added by 'motte', meaning woman's pubis in French erotic slang, according to the dictionary favoured and cited by Beardsley: Delvau, p. 268. The mention of bathrooms evokes Roman bath houses, decorated with erotic frescoes, as well as 'bath' used in the meaning of 'bagnio' or brothel.

Sidelights on child life is an allusion to the tradition of literature on erotic initiation taking place in the nursery. In a passage of his notorious sexual autobiography, Frank Harris recalls that during a stroll in Hyde Park with Aubrey and Mabel Beardsley, the artist alluded to an incestuous relationship with his sister. The remark 'it is usually a fellow's sister who gives him his first lessons in sex' is attributed by Harris to Beardsley. See Frank Harris, *My Life and Loves*, 4 vols (Paris: privately printed, 1922), I, pp. 9–10. During the 1960s and 1970s, critics speculated about whether the relationship between Mabel and Aubrey ever became sexual. See, for example, Malcolm Easton, *Aubrey and the Dying Lady: A Beardsley Riddle* (Boston: Godine, 1972).

[17] Earlier in the section of *Le Roman de la Rose* from which Beardsley took his epigraph is a description of a window in the castle which is: 'Between two pillars placed. | These pillars were of ivory, Most pleasing, and bearing in silver | The image of a hunt [...] | All modelled in proportion | Arms, shoulders and hands [...] | Most pleasing were the other limbs, | And more scented than pomander of ambergris: | Within was a sanctuary' (trans. by Simon Wilson; see original Lorris and Meun, IV, p. 306). In the sanctuary, we are given to understand, is an image of a woman of surpassing beauty. It seems plausible that Beardsley had this passage in mind when describing the twin pillars of the gateway of the Hill of Venus.

[18] 'Vesper' is an evensong; in poetic use, it also means Venus as the evening star (Hesper), while 'vespers' can mean evening prayers or devotions. According to Fletcher, 'the lute in "underground" language' alludes to 'the female pudendum', and the choice of the instrument draws attention, 'along with the drawing for the episode, [... to] the ambiguous sexuality of the hero'; see Ian Fletcher, 'Inventions for the Left Hand: Beardsley in Verse and Prose', in *Reconsidering Aubrey Beardsley*, ed. by Robert Langenfeld (Ann Arbor: UMI Research Press, 1989), p. 234.

'Adieu' he exclaimed with an inclusive gesture, & 'Good-bye Madonna,' as the cold circle of the moon began to show, beautiful & full of enchantments. There was a shadow of sentiment in his voice as he spoke the words.

'Would to heaven' he sighed, 'I might receive the assurance of a looking-glass before I make my début! However as she is a goddess I doubt not her eyes are a little sated with perfection & may not be displeased to see it crowned with a tiny fault.'

A wild rose had caught upon the trimmings of his muff, & in the first flush of displeasure he would have struck it brusquely away, & most severely punished the offending flower.[19] But the ruffled mood lasted only a moment, for there was something so deliciously incongruous in the hardy petal's invasion of so delicate a thing, that Tannhäuser withheld the finger of resentment & vowed that the wild rose should stay where it had clung, a passport, as it were, from the upper to the underworld.

'The very excess & violence of the fault' he said 'will be its excuse', & undoing a tangle in the tassel of his stick, stepped into the shadowy corridor that ran into the bosom of the wan hill. Stepped with the admirable aplomb & unwrinkled suavity of Don John.[20]

---

[19] Beardsley's 'muff' is a sexual pun: 'muff' was used as a slang term for the 'private parts of a woman'; see *Lexicon Balatronicum: A Dictionary of Buckish Slang, University Wit, and Pickpocket Eloquence*, ed. by Francis Grose (London: Printed for C. Chappel, 1811). Beardsley revisits the joke in his illustration *The Abbé* (Fig. 1). Tannhäuser is depicted with his left hand emerging from a luxuriant muff, which is indeed enwreathed by the 'offending flower'. With one crooked, bent finger, the hero is holding a phallic walking stick. The amalgamation of sexual signifiers can be read as another comment on Tannhäuser's gender ambivalence.

[20] An allusion to *Don Juan*, a legendary Spanish nobleman famous for his seductions. The legend saw various adaptations, including Molière's *Don Juan* (1665), Mozart's opera *Don Giovanni* (1787), and Byron's poem *Don Juan* (1819). In 1896, Beardsley made a drawing *Don Juan, Sganarelle and the Beggar* which illustrates Molière's version (see Zatlin, *CR* II, pp. 293–94). The treatment of Don Juan in the design foregrounds autobiographical connotations: Beardsley dresses the hero in the costume of Pierrot. Beardsley's identification with this commedia dell'arte character has been established by numerous critics as well as the artist himself (see, for example, Milly Heyd, *Aubrey Beardsley: Symbol, Mask, and Self-Irony* (New York: Peter Lang, 1986), pp. 44–48; Zatlin, *CR* II, p. 286; *Letters of Aubrey Beardsley*, p. 51).

~

II

Before a toilet that shone like the altar of Nôtre Dame des Victoires, Venus was seated in a little dressing gown of black & heliotrope.[1] The coiffeur Cosmé[2] was caring for her scented chevelure, & with tiny silver tongs, warm from the caresses of the flame, made delicious intelligent curls that fell as lightly as a breath about her forehead & over her eyebrows, & clustered like tendrils about her neck. Her three favourite girls, Pappelarde, Blanchemains & Loreyne waited immediately upon her with perfume & powder in delicate flacons & frail cassolettes,[3] & held in porcelain jars the ravishing paints prepared by Chateline for those cheeks & lips that had grown a little pale with anguish of exile.[4] Her three favourite boys Claude, Clair, & Sarrasine stood amorously about with salver, fan & napkin. Millamant held a slight tray of slippers, Minette some tender gloves, La Popelinière, mistress of the robes, was ready with a frock of yellow & yellow, La Zambinella bore the jewels, Florizel some flowers, Amadour a box of various pins & Vadius a box of sweets.[5]

---

[1] Nôtre Dame des Victoires is a Parisian basilica, completed in the mid-eighteenth century. The altar in the East transept containing the crowned statue of Virgin and Child is decorated with a lustrous golden mosaic. Heliotrope is a shade of purple derived from the scented flower of the same name, and a recently fashionable colour (the first use of this sense of the word recorded by the *OED* was in 1882).

[2] The name Cosmé appears to be a shortening of the French word *cosmétologue*, a cosmetics expert or beautician, although here Beardsley gives it to a hairdresser. Another connotation is 'cosmos', meaning universe as an ordered and harmonious system.

[3] A 'flacon' is a flask, here a perfume bottle. A cassolette is a ceramic dish; 'frail' suggests that it might be of delicate porcelain.

[4] See note 76 to the Introduction.

[5] The names of Venus's servants represent a *locus classicus* of the destabilization of the opposition between high and low cultures that characterizes Beardsley's text, in which literary and religious allusions are often thrown into the mix with French sexual slang. To begin with literary evocations, Beardsley mentions two characters of Honoré de Balzac's novella 'Sarrasine' (1830): the eponymous young sculptor Ernest-Jean Sarrasine of 'the impetuous character and the wild genius', and La Zambinella, the prima donna of Roman opera with whom Sarrasine falls passionately in love (see Honoré de Balzac, 'Sarrasine', in *Parisian Life*, trans. by William Walton, 11 vols (Philadelphia: George Barrie & Son, 1896), IX, 203–60 (p. 231). It has been noted by friends that Beardsley 'knew his Balzac from cover to cover' (see, for instance, William Rothenstein, *Men and Memories: Recollections of William Rothenstein, 1872–1900* (London: Faber and Faber, 1931), p. 236). The description of Sarrasine, who even in church left behind him 'gross sketches, the licentious character of which filled with horror the younger fathers' (Balzac, p. 230), would have resonated with Beardsley, and so would have the central enigma of the story, tied to La Zambinella's ambiguous gender. Sarrasine's passion cannot be consummated since the object of his desire, instead of an ideal woman, turns out to be a castrato. The shifting of gender signifiers upon which Balzac bases his narrative is also central to Beardsley's work. Besides Sarrasine, Venus's three 'favourite boys' include Claude and Clair, and while the significance of Clair is unclear, Claude might be a reference to *Juliette* (published 1797–1801) by the Marquis de Sade. As Wilson explains, one of the characters of this 'scathing' attack 'on the eighteenth-century Catholic Church' is a Carmelite monk Claude, whom Juliette and her companion are trying to seduce; see Simon Wilson, *'Rose et Noir': An Erotic Metaphor. From Bataille to Baudelaire and Back Again* (London: The Sign of Nine, 2015), p. 57. Among Venus's 'favourite girls', we encounter Blanchemains, meaning 'white hands' in French. This character may be an allusion to Isoud la Blanche Mains, the second heroine named Isoud in Thomas Malory's *Le Morte Darthur* (Beardsley's first major commission as an illustrator, published in 1893–4 by J. M. Dent). She is wedded to Sir Tristram but their marriage remains unconsummated because of the knight's love for La Beale Isoud. Another literary character among the servants is Millamant, who bears the name of the charming heroine of William Congreve's restoration comedy *The Way of the World* (1700). She is an heiress and a witty coquette who insists on preserving her freedom after marriage. Beardsley also mentions Florizel, a character in Shakespeare's *The Winter's Tale* (and a name adopted by George IV in his correspondence with the actress Mary Robinson). A Bohemian prince, Florizel falls in love with rustic Perdita. Their storyline brings to mind the Decadent

Her doves[6] ever in attendance walked about the room that was panelled with the gallant paintings of Paul Chatouilleur De La Pine, & some dwarfs & doubtful creatures sat here & there lolling out their tongues & behaving monstrously wise.[7] Sometimes Venus gave them little smiles.

As the toilet was in progress, Priapusa, the fat manicure & farded,[8] strode in & seated herself by the side of the dressing table, greeting Venus with an intimate nod.[9] She wore a gown of white watered silk with gold lace trimmings, & a velvet necklet of vermilion.[10] Her hair hung in bandeaux[11] over her ears passing into a huge chignon at the back of her head; & the hat, wide-brimmed & hung with a vallance of pink muslin, was floral with red roses.

Priapusa's voice was full of salacious unction; she had terrible little gestures with the hands, strange movements with the shoulders, a short respiration that made surprising wrinkles in her bodice, a corrupt skin, large horny eyes, a parrot's nose, a small loose mouth, great flaccid cheeks, & chin after chin. She was a wise person, & Venus loved her more than any of her other servants, & had a hundred pet names for her, such as, Dear Toad, Pretty Pol, cock robin, dearest lip, Touchstone, figs faute de mieux, bijou, buttons, astiquelle, dear heart, dick-dock, tête-bêche, Mrs Manly, little nipper, cochon de lait, naughty-naughty, blessèd thing, & tup.[12]

---

tension between barbarism and nobility which Beardsley explores further in the Bacchanals of Fanfreluche (renamed Sporion in SV). As for the paragraph's one straightforward Catholic reference, Amadour may be linked to the fifth-century St Amadour who, after the death of his wife St Veronica, became a legendary hermit and built a shrine to the Blessed Virgin Mary, called Rocamadour. This string of literary and religious allusions is punctuated with deliberate obscenities, such as Minette (French for oral sex), and coded erotic references, such as La Popelinière, which stands for Alexandre La Riche de la Popelinière, or Pouplinière, a great eighteenth-century patron of music. He is also cited sixty-six times as an author of erotica in Delvau's dictionary of erotic slang. Finally, this Decadent assemblage includes a figure of order, Chateline, from French *chatelaine*: the female castellan, the mistress of a castle or country house.

[6] Doves are birds associated with love, hence 'attributes' of the goddess Venus, that is, they accompany and identify her.

[7] In SV, JL, LS, 'their tongues' is followed by the phrase 'pinching each other, and behaving oddly enough'. The addition closely corresponds with the depiction of dwarfs in the illustration *Toilet of Helen*. This suggests that the phrase, although absent from the original manuscript, was added by Beardsley at the editorial stage. In the name of the painter, Chatouilleur comes from the verb *chatouiller* meaning to tickle or titillate, while *pine* means penis or 'the male tool' (*l'outil masculine*), according to Delvau (p. 299). The name Beardsley came up with can therefore be translated as Paul Tickler of the Tool.

[8] Until well into the twentieth century, the term 'manicure' meant equally the person performing a hand treatment and the treatment itself. The term manicurist has now entirely taken over for the operative. The word 'farded' derives from the French 'fard' meaning makeup and is an example of Beardsley's practice of adapting French words into English. In the *Savoy* text this appears as 'fardeuse' — makeup artist — and it is unclear whether this might have been with Beardsley's approval. Here 'farded' means rouged.

[9] Priapusa was turned into Mrs Marsuple for the SV publication. The transformation of Priapusa (the female incarnation of Priapus) into Mrs Marsuple was one of the unfortunate name changes Beardsley implemented to disguise his work from Lane. 'Marsuple' relates to 'marsupial', the zoological term indicating the abdominal pouch within which certain mammals nurse their immature young. The name thus underscores Mrs Marsuple's maternal functions and correlates with the woman's physique, described further in the text. She was clearly an important character for Beardsley. In a letter to Smithers on 26 April 1896 he reports to have written 'a little for "Chronicles"' (presumably, a continuation of *Under the Hill*) which he conceived of as 'a story to be told by Mrs Marsuple'; see *Letters of Aubrey Beardsley*, p. 126.

[10] Vermilion is a brilliant, light-red pigment made from mercury sulphide. It is expensive and poisonous. Smithers added 'false' to Beardsley's vermilion, apparently referring to the cheaper synthetic version of the pigment (see Diplomatic transcription, p. 72).

[11] A French word meaning a style of hair in which it is parted in the middle and pulled back at the sides, either covering, as here, or behind the ears.

[12] The list of names bestowed upon Priapusa consists for the most part of sexual slang found in Delvau's dictionary. Thus, 'bijou' ('jewel') designates both male and female sexual organs; 'astiquelle' derives from *astiquer* ('to polish'), meaning to make love, and Delvau also gives the slang meaning 'to masturbate' (p. 14); 'tête-bêche' ('head-to-tail') describes a sex position in which each person's mouth is near the other's genitals; 'cochon de lait' stands for suckling pig, while *cochon* can also acquire a sexual meaning of talking obscenities to arouse one's partner (see Delvau, pp. 99–100). To 'tup' means to copulate. Mrs Manly may refer to Delarivier 'Delia' Manley, who wrote several plays and novels, including a roman à clef *The New Atlantis* (1709) which saw her arrested. She also had several illustrious love affairs, including one with the warden of the Fleet Prison. Jonathan Swift's (1667–1745) characterization of Mrs Manley in *Journal to Stella* (1814) is, in a way, reminiscent of Priapusa: 'she has very

The talk that passed between Priapusa and her mistress was of that excellent kind that passes between old friends, a perfect understanding giving to scraps of phrases their full meaning, & to the merest reference, a point.[13] Naturally Tannhäuser the new comer was discussed a little. Venus had not seen him yet, & asked a score of questions on his account that were delightfully to the point.

Priapusa told the story of his sudden arrival, his curious wandering in the gardens & calm satisfaction with all he saw there, his impromptu affection for a slender girl upon the first terrace & of the crowd of frocks that gathered round & pelted him with roses, of the graceful way he defended himself with his mask, & of the queer reverence he made to the statue of Priapus; kissing the huge emblem with a pilgrim's devotion.[14] Just now he was at the baths & was creating a most favourable impression.

The report & the coiffing were completed at the same moment.

'Cosmé' said Venus 'you have been quite sweet & quite brilliant, you have surpassed yourself to-night.'

'Madam flatters me' replied the antique old thing with a girlish giggle under his black satin mask, 'Gad[15] Madam sometimes I believe I have no talent in the world, but tonight I must confess to a touch of the vain mood.'

It would pain me horribly to tell you about the painting of her face, suffice it that the sorrowful work was accomplished, frankly, magnificently, & without a shadow of deception.

Venus slipped away the dressing gown & rose before the mirror in a flutter of frilled things. She was adorably tall & slender. Her neck & shoulders were so wonderfully drawn & the little malicious breasts were full of the irritation of loveliness that can never be entirely comprehended, or ever enjoyed to the utmost. Her arms & hands were loosely but delicately articulated & her legs were divinely long. From the hip to the knee twenty-two inches from the knee to the heel twenty-two inches as befitted a goddess.[16] I should like to speak more particularly about her, for generalities are not of the slightest service in a description. But I am afraid that an enforced silence upon many points would leave such numerous gaps in the picture that it had better not be begun at all than be left unfinished.

Priapusa grew quite lyric over the dear little lady & pecked at her arms with kisses.

'Dear Tongue, you must really behave yourself' said Venus, & called Millamant to bring her the slippers.

The tray was freighted with the most exquisite & shapely pantoufles, sufficient to make Cluny a place of

---

generous principles for one of her sort, and a great deal of good sense and invention: she is about forty, very homely, and very fat'. Edited by Walter Scott, Swift's *Journal* also cites Mrs Manley's novel *The Adventures of Rivella* (1714), in which the autobiographical protagonist is described as follows: 'from her youth she was inclined to fat; whence I have often heard her flatterers liken her to the Grecian Venus. It is certain, considering that disadvantage, she has the most easy air that one can have. [...] I have heard several wives and mistresses accuse her of fascination: they would neither trust their husbands, lovers, sons, nor brothers, with her acquaintance'; see Jonathan Swift, *The Works of Jonathan Swift: Journal to Stella*, ed. by Walter Scott, 19 vols (Edinburgh: Printed for A. Constable, 1814), III, p. 26.

[13] The description of the special intimate language adopted by Priapusa and her mistress can be applied to those groups in Beardsley's milieu who were used to communicating in code, including connoisseurs of erotica and homosexuals.

[14] At the time of writing, the word 'queer' had already come to designate 'homosexual'. This can be exemplified by the line from the Marquess of Queensbury's letter to Oscar Wilde (1 November 1894): 'I write to tell you that it is a judgement on the whole lot of you. Montgomerys, The Snob Queers like Roseberry & certainly Christian hypocrite Gladstone the whole lot of you' (reproduced in Richard Ellmann, *Oscar Wilde* (London: Penguin Books, 1988), p. 402). Priapus is the ancient god of fertility, usually depicted with a large phallus. As Fluhr notes (para. 14), Tannhäuser's 'devotional "kiss" clearly suggests fellatio' and marks the hero 'as a pagan pilgrim in a distinctively queer Venusberg'.

[15] A now archaic euphemism for God used as an expletive, common in the seventeenth and eighteenth centuries, so appropriate to this context.

[16] Beardsley here refers to the obsession that artists have had since the Renaissance with finding a perfect proportion for the human body. In a famous drawing known as *Vitruvian Man* (Venice, Accademia) Leonardo da Vinci picked up on the theory of the ancient architect Vitruvius that a perfect human body with arms and legs extended could fit into a circle or a square. Leonardo's drawing, of a male figure, has the proportions of hip to knee and knee to heel as equal. This equality may be seen too in ancient sculptures of Venus. The measurements given by Beardsley suggest that she was at least six feet tall.

naught.[17] There were shoes of grey & black & brown suède, of white silk & rose satin & velvet of sarsinesshe, there were some of sea green sewn with cherry blossoms, some of red with willow & some of grey with bright winged birds.[18] There were heels of silver of ivory & of gilt, there were buckles of very precious stones set in most strange & esoteric devices, there were ribbands tied & twisted into cunning[19] forms, there were buttons so beautiful that the button-holes might have no pleasure till they closed upon them, there were soles of delicate leathers scented with *maréchale*, & linings of soft stuffs scented with the juice of July flowers.[20]

But Venus finding none of them to her mind called for a discarded pair of blood red maroquin diapered with pearls.[21] These looked very distinguished over her white silk stockings. As the tray was being carried away Florizel snatched as usual a slipper from it & fitted the foot over his penis, & made the necessary movements. That was Florizel's little caprice.

Meantime La Popelinière stepped forward with the frock.

'I shan't wear one tonight' said Venus. Then she slipped on her gloves.

When the toilet was at an end all her doves clustered round her feet, loving to frôler her ankles with their plumes, & the dwarfs clapped their hands & put their fingers between their lips & whistled.[22] Never had Venus been so beautiful before. Claude & Clair pale with pleasure stroked & touched her with their delicate hands, & wrinkled her stockings with their nervous lips, & smoothed them with their thin fingers; & Sarrasine undid her garters & kissed them inside & put them on again pressing her thighs with his mouth.

There was almost a mêlée.[23]

The dwarfs grew very daring & illustrated pages seventy two & seventy three of Delvau's Dictionary.[24]

In the middle of it all, Pranzmungel announced that supper was ready upon the fifth terrace.[25]

'Ah' cried Venus 'I'm famished!'

---

[17] As Sutton observes (p. 140), the mention of Cluny here evokes the Musée de Cluny in Paris with its famous collection of medieval art (in particular tapestries) as well as 'Cluny net or bobbin lace', fashionable in England from the 1870s onwards. The reference thus mixes the evocations of 'artisanal' and industrial production and mocks the hierarchy of high and low culture. 'Pantoufles' is a borrowing from French and means slippers.

[18] 'Sarsinesshe' is a Middle English term for 'Saracenic', derived from the Old French *sar(r)asinois*, feminine *sar(r)asinesche*, adjective of nationality, Saracen, i.e., 'a name for the nomadic peoples of the Syro-Arabian desert' among the later Greeks and Romans (*OED*). Beardsley probably took the word from Chaucer: 'Largesse hadde on a robe fresh | Of riche purpur Sarsinesshe' (line 1118). As Skeat explains, *Sarsinesshe* means 'Saracenic, or coloured by an Eastern dye'; see Chaucer, VI, p. 426.

[19] Beardsley is here using this word in its now archaic meaning of cleverly or intricately made, also adding a sexual connotation. The cunning forms may therefore have been vulval.

[20] *Maréchale* is a scented powder made of dried herbs, including souchet, orange flowers, and others.

[21] Maroquin means goatskin leather originally produced in Morocco. To diaper means to decorate a surface with a diamond-shaped pattern.

[22] *Frôler* (French) means to lightly brush against.

[23] *Mêlée* (French) means a confused struggle, especially involving many participants.

[24] 'Delvau's Dictionary' refers to the *Dictionnaire érotique moderne* by Alfred Delvau (1825–1867). Named here for the first and only time in Beardsley's text, it in fact provided an indispensable source for him. Published by Jules Gay, the first edition of 1864 was condemned to destruction by the 'tribunal de correction de la Seine' (a Paris court). Three further, progressively enlarged editions of the *Dictionnaire érotique* were published clandestinely and anonymously under a variety of imaginative fake imprints by Gay in 1874, 1875, and 1879 (see Patrick J. Kearney, *A Catalogue of the Publications of Jules Gay, Jean-Jules Gay and Gay et Doucé* (Santa Rosa, CA: Scissors and Paste Bibliographies, 2019). Many thanks also to Peter Mendes for invaluable help and advice). It is not possible to be entirely certain which edition Beardsley was using and therefore what his page numbers refer to. However, a combination of bibliographical probability and a judgement of the appositeness to the scene being described by Beardsley of the Delvau text on those pages in the two editions we have been able to access, strongly suggests that it was the fourth and final edition of 1879. Here the two pages constitute a spread occupied by entries for five variations of the verb *branler*, to masturbate, together with two related nouns. In four examples of the verb, it is transitive, describing different forms of one person giving pleasure to another by means of friction of the sexual parts. One is the simple reflexive form *se branler*, to pleasure oneself. Armed with Delvau, the reader is enabled to construct in their own imagination the behaviour of Venus's attendants that Beardsley has chosen thus to evoke.

[25] According to Walker (p. 51), Pranzmungel 'was the real name of a butler in a friend's house'. *Pranzo* also means 'lunch' in Italian.

~

III

She was quite delighted with Tannhäuser & of course he sat next her at supper. The terrace, made beautiful with a thousand vain & fantastical things, & set with a hundred tables & four hundred couches presented a truly splendid appearance. In the middle was a huge bronze fountain with three basins. From the first rose a many-breasted dragon, & four little loves mounted upon swans, & each love was furnished with a bow & arrow.[1] Two of them that faced the monster seemed to recoil in fear, two that were behind made bold enough to aim their shafts at him. From the verge of the second sprang a circle of slim golden columns that supported silver doves with tails & wings spread out. The third, held by a group of grotesquely attenuated satyrs[2] was centred with a thin pipe hung with masks & roses, & capped with children's heads.

From the mouths of the dragon & the loves, from the swan's eyes, from the breasts of the doves, from the satyrs' horns & lips, from the masks at many points, & from the childrens' curls, the water played profusely, cutting strange arabesques[3] & subtle figures.

The terrace was lit entirely by candles. There were four thousand of them not numbering those upon the tables. The candlesticks were of a countless variety & smiled with moulded cochonneries.[4] Some were twenty feet high & bore single candles that flared like fragrant torches over the feast, & guttered till the wax stood round the tops in tall lances. Some hung with dainty petticoats of shining lustres, had a whole bevy of tapers upon them, devised in circles, in pyramids, in squares, in cuneiforms,[5] in single lines regimentally & in crescents.

Then on quaint pedestals & terminal gods & gracious pilasters of every sort were shell-like vases of excessive fruits & flowers that hung about & burst over the edges & could never be restrained. The orange trees & myrtles looped with vermilion sashes stood in frail porcelain pots & the rose-trees were wound & twisted with superb invention over trellis & standard. Upon one side of the terrace, a long gilded stage for the comedians was curtained off with amphytrien tapestries, & in front of it the music stands were placed.[6] The tables arranged

---

[1] The 'many-breasted dragon' has a visual counterpart in Beardsley's oeuvre. The illustration *How King Arthur Saw the Questing Beast, and Thereof Had Great Marvel* for *Le Morte Darthur* (1893) features a grotesque dragon with breast-like pouches on its neck and under its eyes. 'Loves' here refers to the mythological personification of romantic affection or passion, identified with Amor, Eros, or Cupid.

[2] Mythical creatures associated with woodlands; in classical mythology, believed to be attendants of the Greek god of wine and fertility Dionysus (identified with Bacchus in Roman mythology). Satyrs are distinguished by their lasciviousness and partly human, partly bestial (goat-like) form. Since the sixteenth century, the word satyr has also been used to describe a man with strong sexual appetites.

[3] Arabesque refers to a decorative pattern consisting of flowing and interlacing lines (particularly, branches, flowers, tendrils), that are arranged geometrically and exclude bestial or human figures.

[4] The French *cochônneries* stands for obscenities. The candlesticks with 'moulded' obscenities bring to mind Beardsley's illustration *Enter Herodias* for *Salome* (1894) which features three phallic candlesticks placed candidly in the foreground.

[5] Cuneiform (from the Latin *cuneus*, 'wedge') denotes wedge-shaped characters used in the ancient writing systems of Persia, Mesopotamia, and Ugarit, which survive mainly impressed upon clay tablets. *Cunnus* also means vulva in Latin.

[6] Beardsley had a struggle with the spelling of this adjectival form of the noun amphytrion, inserting then deleting a 't'. We have left it in since it is obviously correct. *OED* gives 'amphitryon' as 'a host — a dinner giver' and cites Molière's play *Amphitryon* as a source. The relevant lines read: 'Le véritable Amphitryon | Est L'Amphitryon où l'on dine' ('the true Amphitryon is the Amphitryon where one dines'). Beardsley's illustration to Molière's *Don Juan* appeared in the *Savoy* in December 1896. The tapestries are, therefore, ones suitable as decoration for a grand dinner. Comedians simply means actors.

between the fountain & the flight of steps to the sixth terrace were all circular, covered with white damask & strewn with irises, roses, king-cups, colombines, daffodils, carnations & lilies, & the couches, high with soft cushions & spread with more stuffs than could be named,[7] had fans thrown upon them & little erotic surprise packets.

Beyond the escalier stretched the venereal gardens,[8] which were designed so elaborately & with so much splendour that the architect of the Fêtes d'Armailhacq could have found in them no matter for cavil, & the still lakes strewn with profuse barges full of gay flowers & wax marionettes, the alleys of tall trees, the arcades & cascades, the pavilions the grottos, & the garden-gods[9] all took a strange tinge of revelry from the glare of the light that fell upon them from the feast.[10]

The frockless Venus & Tannhäuser, with Priapusa & Claude & Clair & Farcy[11] the chief comedian sat at the same table. Tannhäuser who had doffed his travelling suit wore nothing but long black silk stockings, a pair of pretty garters, a very elegant chemise, slippers & a wonderful dressing-gown. Claude & Clair wore nothing at all, delicious privilege of immaturity, & Farcy was in ordinary evening clothes. As for the rest of the company it boasted some very noticeable dresses & whole tables of quite delightful coiffures. There were spotted veils that seemed to stain the skin with some exquisite & august disease,[12] fans with eye-slits in them through which their bearers peeped & peered, fans painted with postures & covered with the sonnets of Sporion[13] & the short stories of Scaramouche, & fans of big living moths stuck upon mounts of silver sticks;[14] there were masks of green velvet that make the face look trebly powdered; masks of the heads of birds, of apes, of serpents, of dolphins, of men & women, of little embryos[15] & of cats, masks like the faces of gods masks of coloured glass, & masks of thin talc & of india-rubber. There were wigs of black & scarlet wools, of peacocks' feathers, of gold & silver threads, of swansdown, of the tendrils of the vine, & of human hairs; huge collars of stiff muslin rising high above the head; whole dresses of ostrich feathers curling inwards, tunics of panthers' skins that looked beautiful over pink tights, capotes of crimson satin trimmed with the wings of owls, sleeves cut into the shapes of apocryphal animals, drawers flounced down to the ankles & flecked with tiny, red roses, that seemed like flecks of blood, stockings clocked with fêtes galantes & curious designs, & petticoats cut like artificial flowers.[16]

---

[7] Stuffs refers to fabrics.

[8] Escalier means the flight of steps mentioned above. If Beardsley wanted to refer to the gardens of Venus, 'venerean' should have been written. Either from ignorance or deliberately, he chose the word which had been loaded with sexual connotations since at least the fifteenth century.

[9] In Greek mythology, the god of gardens and fertility is Priapus, usually portrayed as a human figure with a grotesquely exaggerated phallus.

[10] Château Mouton-d'Armailhacq is the historic name of a family estate and a winery in the Bordeaux region of France. A famous treatise *Culture de Vignes* was published by the offspring of the family, Armand d'Armailhacq, in 1857. As Upstone mentions, the 'Fêtes d'Armailhacq' could have been 'an in-joke connected with wine, of which Beardsley was extremely knowledgeable'; Robert Upstone, 'Sado-Masochism and Synaesthesia: Aubrey Beardsley's "Frontispiece to Chopin's Third Ballade"', *The Burlington Magazine*, 145.1204 (2003), 510–15 (p. 512). However, it is not the only time Beardsley used the name: in 1895, he exhibited a drawing of 'a lady on a horse' under the title *Comtesse d'Armailhacq* at the Royal Society of Portrait Painters (see Zatlin, *CR* II, p. 139). The drawing is known to us today as *Chopin's Third Ballade*.

[11] Beardsley describes Farcy as a 'comedian', almost certainly in the French meaning of that word as simply an actor. However, his name relates to the English word 'farce' for a certain genre of comedy, so he might specialize in that. The French word '*farcie*' is a homophone of Farcy and means stuffed, in the culinary sense, but in English 'stuffed' is also a euphemism for 'fucked'.

[12] In his important essay 'The Decadent Movement in Literature' (*Fortnightly Review*, May 1893), Arthur Symons, Beardsley's editor at the *Savoy*, described decadence as 'a new and beautiful and interesting disease' (p. 859).

[13] Beardsley might have been thinking of spores, the means by which fungi propagate themselves. In '*L'eau Savante*' (part II), Lavers notes that 'Sporion's name may come from Sporus, the young Roman whom Nero "married", as recounted by Suetonius'.

[14] Scaramouche is a stock character in commedia dell'arte, usually an unscrupulous and foolish servant.

[15] Beardsley scholars have noted the recurrence of images of embryos in his art and this mild obsession is apparent here. The image first appears in a key early drawing, *Incipit Vita Nova* (1892). For an account of its significance, see Zatlin, *CR* I, p. 139.

[16] Capote is used here in its meaning of a cape; *capote anglaise* is also French for a condom. A clocked sock or stocking is one with a decorative design on the outer side. *Fête galante* ('courtship party' in French) is a type of painting in which costumed figures participate in amorous outdoor entertainment; the term was introduced by the French Academy in 1717 in relation to

Some of the women had put on delightful little moustaches dyed in purples & bright greens, twisted & waxed with absolute skill, & some wore great white beards after the manner of S[te] Wilgeforte.[17] Then De La Pine had painted extraordinary grotesques & vignettes over their bodies here & there.[18] Upon a cheek, an old man scratching his horned head, upon a forehead, an old woman teased by an impudent amor,[19] upon a shoulder, an amorous singerie,[20] round a breast, a circlet of satyrs, about a wrist, a wreath of babes, upon an elbow, a bouquet of spring flowers, across a back, some surprising scenes of adventure, at the corners of a mouth, tiny red spots, & upon a neck, a flight of birds, a caged parrot, a branch of fruit, a butterfly, a spider, a drunken dwarf or simply the bearer's initials. But most wonderful of all were the black silhouettes painted upon the legs, & which showed through a white silk stocking like a sumptuous bruise.

The supper provided by the ingenious Rambouillet was quite beyond parallel.[21] Never had he created a more exquisite menu. The consommé impromptu alone would have been sufficient to establish the immortal reputation of any chef, what, then, can I say of the Dorade bouillie sauce fouteuse, the ragoût aux langues de carpes, the ramereaux à la charnière, the ciboulette de gibier à l'espagnole, the poussins aux accidents féminins, the paté de cuisses d'oie aux pois de Monsalvie, the dindon de la menagerie à la peau de vièrge, the queues d'agneau au clair de lune, the vits de boeufs sauce naturelle, the rissolettes à la pine magistrale, the artichauts à la Grecque, the asperges sauce Lesbienne, the charlotte de Pommes à la Périnée, the bombes à la marée, and the glaces aux rayons d'or? A veritable tour de cuisine that surpassed even the famous little suppers given by the Marquis de Réchale at Passy, & which the Abbé Mirliton pronounced 'impeccable, and too good to be eaten'.[22]

---

the works of one of Beardsley's favourite artists, Antoine Watteau. See also *Fêtes galantes* (1869), a poetry collection by Paul Verlaine, whom Beardsley met in 1893 in London (see *Letters of Aubrey Beardsley*, p. 58).

[17] '[A]fter the manner of Ste Wilgeforte' is inserted in pencil in the margins and thus could have been Smithers's addition. Saint Wilgefortis of Uncumber was a Christian daughter of a pagan king of Portugal. To avoid a marriage devised for her by her father, she prayed to become unattractive, which resulted in a beard growing on her face. There is a statue of Wilgefortis in the Henry VII Chapel, Westminster Abbey. As Fluhr observes (para. 27), Wilgefortis uses her 'faith to sanction [her] non-(hetero)normative desire'; *Under the Hill* alludes to her legend in order to 'queer Catholicism and bring it under the aegis of the Venusberg's pagan polytheism'.

[18] *Pine* is an idiomatic French word for penis.

[19] *Amor* is Latin term for a Cupid or putto. In classical Latin, *amor* denotes sexual passion, illicit love, love affair; a more widespread form of the term as used to refer to a Cupid or putto is 'amour', a borrowing from French which means love, as well as a paramour, a person's lover.

[20] A singerie is a depiction of monkeys playfully impersonating humans. This decorative genre is associated with French rococo, beloved by Beardsley.

[21] Beardsley appears to have invented the name of the chef, but he may have been thinking of the famous Paris literary hostess La Marquise de Rambouillet. Her Château de Rambouillet is now the summer residence of Presidents of France.

[22] This menu is highly provocative, a number of items being either bizarre, or both bizarre and obscene, recalling Trimalchio's feast in Petronius's *Satyricon*, the most famous decadent novel of classical antiquity. Beardsley's menu appears to be a gleeful and occasionally schoolboyish parody of the classic gourmet French restaurant menu. It begins with soup, then two fish dishes, then a selection of eight meat dishes, two accompanying vegetable dishes, and three desserts. We are indebted to Robert Booth who brought both his knowledge of Beardsley and of matters both culinary and French for help with the translations.

In the manuscript, of the sixteen dishes, five are entirely lightly crossed through and two others have single words lightly crossed through. These deletions and changes were made for the SV version, but perhaps surprisingly were retained by Smithers in his supposedly unexpurgated 1907 edition. In some cases, new versions of dishes were created for the SV version. The dishes that appear in the manuscript are glossed below in the order they appear in the text.

Consommé impromptu: a *consommé* is simple meat, poultry, or fish stock served as starter; *impromptu* should mean whatever the kitchen had on the go.

Dorade bouillie sauce fouteuse: *dorade bouilli* is boiled sea bream; Delvau defines *fouteuse*' as 'Femme qui aime bien à être baisé' — a woman who loves to be fucked. For the SV this dish became *Dorade bouilli sauce Maréchale*. A *maréchale* is a rich herb and butter sauce.

Ragoût aux langues de carpes: carp tongue stew. A ragout is a stew made from meat, poultry, game, fish, or vegetables. That many hundreds of carp would be needed to make this dish gives it a Decadent touch.

Ramereaux à la charnière: ramereaux are the young of the ramier, a type of pigeon. Strictly speaking *charnière* means hinge or turning point, so the dish could translate literally as 'young pigeons at turning point'. Gastronomically this could refer to

Ah! Pierre Antoine Berquin de Rambouillet, you are worthy of your divine mistress![23]

Mere hunger quickly gave place to those finer instincts of the pure gourmet, & the strange wines cooled in buckets of snow, unloosed all the décolleté[24] spirits of astonishing conversation & atrocious laughter. At first there was the fun with the surprise packets that contained myriads of unmentionable things, then a general criticism of the decorations, everyone finding their own peculiar meaning in the fall of festoon, turn of twig, & twist of branch. Suculex as usual bore the palm[25] for insight & invention, & tonight he was more brilliant than ever. He leant across the table and explained to the young page, Macfils de Martaga, what was intended by a certain arrangement of roses.[26] The young page smiled & hummed the refrain of 'La petite

---

pigeonneaux or, in English, squabs. These are baby pigeons taken at the point just before they fly, when they are exceptionally plump and tender; such birds are an expensive treat. However, Beardsley might have been confusing *charnière* with *charnier*, which means charnel house, and might be making some kind of macabre play on words.

Ciboulette de gibier à l'espagnole: ciboulette is the chive plant and seems to have no other meaning, but Beardsley has used the word as if it were a term for a type of dish. However, *à l'espagnole* usually means with tomatoes and *gibier* is game. So game cooked with tomatoes and perhaps chives.

Poussins aux accidents féminins: baby chicken with feminine accidents. Delvau defines *accidents feminins* as *avoir ses règles* — to have one's period.

Paté de cuisses d'oie aux pois de Monsalvie: pâté of goose legs with Monsalvie peas. A pâté of goose legs is entirely feasible and might just be accompanied by a dish of peas done in the classic French way, cooked with butter, cream, onion, and lettuce. There is no place called Monsalvie in France, although Montsalvy is a commune in south-central France. If it was once famous for its peas, it no longer seems to be.

Dindon de la menagerie à la peau de vièrge: turkey from the zoo with virgin's skin; 'from the zoo' seems to be satirising restaurant menu language about the origins of their produce; *à la peau de vièrge* could mean that the turkey itself had virgin's skin, thus implying particular tenderness of the bird. Or it could mean virgin's skin as an accompaniment.

Queues d'agneau au clair de lune: lambs' tails by the light of the moon. Lambs' tails are docked in the spring and traditionally eaten by shepherds grilled on a fire in the field, probably at the end of the day and by moonlight. For urban sophisticates, lambs' tails, like carp tongues, might be considered a somewhat Decadent delicacy. However, in French *queue* commonly means penis as well as tail, so Beardsley is also possibly proposing an even more Decadent delicacy.

Vits de boeufs sauce naturelle: *vit* is a slang word for penis, so 'bull's pricks in natural sauce'. Presumably, bull semen.

Rissolettes à la pine magistrale: *pine* is an idiomatic French word for penis and, like *vit*, is best rendered in English as 'prick'. So this might be a dish of prick rissoles in a masterly manner.

Artichauts à la Grecque: the *artichauts* would be the delicious base or 'fond' of the globe artichoke, cooked in 'the Greek manner' in an olive oil, vinegar, garlic, and onion sauce. Beardsley might have been thinking that 'Greek' love was a euphemism for homosexuality.

Asperges sauce Lesbienne: asparagus with Lesbian sauce.

Charlotte de Pommes à la Périnée: a charlotte is a type of pudding made by lining a mould with finger biscuits and filling the centre with a fruit mix. In this case apples. *Périnée* is perineum, the area between the anus and the vulva in women and the anus and scrotum in men. Beardsley returns to the perineum a little later (see Chapter IV, the description of Tannhäuser's erotic encounter with his boy attendant in the basin, p. 46). In the SV this became *Charlotte de pommes à la Lucy Waters*. The most probable contender for the Lucy Waters referred to here would be the Welsh mistress of the English king Charles II. A fictitious portrait of her, called *Lucy Waters*, engraved by Ignatius Joseph van der Berghe, after a drawing by Silvester Harding, was published in 1793. Provocatively baring one breast, she is allegorically depicted as Venus. It is tempting to suggest that Beardsley knew the engraving and chose to refer to her here for this reason.

Bombes à la marée: a *bombe* is a frozen pudding made in a hemispherical mould, hence the name. The mould is filled with layers of different ice cream mixes. There are many recipes; *marée* is tide, so the dish translates as 'bombe in the manner of the tide'. Clearly another Beardsley fantasy, but with a possible link to the moon reference in his lamb's tails dish.

Glaces aux rayons d'or: ice cream with golden rays. The rays might be drizzled honey. But given the context here they could be of real gold leaf, which is perfectly edible. The Marquis de Réchale seems to be invented. Likewise, the Abbé Merliton; a *merliton* in French is a reed pipe. It is also a type of edible squash, so there is a food connection.

[23] Berquin is probably a reference to Louis de Berquin, a Protestant reformer who was burned at the stake for his views.

[24] *Décolleté* is a French term describing a low-cut neckline on a woman's dress, that to a greater or lesser extent reveals the breasts. Beardsley here adapts it to mean unbuttoned, uninhibited behaviour.

[25] A palm leaf is a symbolic prize, as in the Palme d'Or at the Cannes Film Festival.

[26] In the lower right margin of the manuscript page Beardsley has written 'My own drawing' against the lines that include 'everyone finding their own peculiar meaning'. The author is being self-referential: his tendency to charge 'the fall of festoon' (a garland of flowers) or 'twist of a branch' with sexual suggestions is well known. Roses, the curious arrangement of which Suculex

burette.'[27] Sporion too, had delicate perceptions. It was the disposition of the candelabra that amused him most, & suddenly noticing that the change of one of them would produce an entirely new and amazing effect he sprang from his seat and made the improvement. All the tables round about raised a shout of delight.

As the courses advanced the conversation became more personal. The infidelities of Cérise, Sarmean's caprices that morning in the lily garden, Thorilliere's declining strength, Vulva's affection for Roseola, Falix's impossible member, Cathelin's passion for Sulpilia's poodle, Sola's passion for herself, the nasty bite that Marisca gave Chloe, the epilation of Pulex, Cyril's diseases, and a thousand amatory follies of the day were discussed.[28]

From harsh & shrill & claimant, the voices grew blurred & inarticulate. Bad sentences were helped out by worse gestures, & at one table, Scabius[29] could only express himself with his napkin, after the manner of Sir Jolly Jumble in the 'Soldier's Fortune' of Otway.[30] Basalissa & Lysistrata tried to pronounce each other's names & became very affectionate in the attempt, & Tala the tragedian robed in purple & wearing plume & buskin,[31] rose to his feet & with swaying gestures began to recite one of his favourite parts.[32] He got no further than the first line but repeated it again & again with fresh accents & intonations each time, & was only silenced by the approach of the asparagus that was being served by satyrs costumed in white muslin.[33]

Clitor & Sodon had a violent struggle over the beautiful Pella & nearly upset a chandelier, Sophie became very intimate with an empty champagne bottle, swore it had made her enceinte, & ended by having a mock accouchement on the top of the table, & Bellmour pretended to be a dog & pranced from couch to couch on all fours biting & barking & licking, Mellefont crept about dropping aphrodisiacs into glasses, Juventus and Ruella

---

interprets for the benefit of the young page, signify passion in Victorian flower dictionaries. In the *Salome* illustrations, Beardsley made use of this floral symbolism to insinuate Salome's 'sexual awakening' as well as the blooming desire of the young page for the Syrian captain (Zatlin, *CR* II, p. 5).

[27] Delvau (p. 77) states that *burette (petite)* is the 'membre viril qui contient l'huile essentielle de l'amour', that is, the virile member that contains the essential oil of love. This also references the fact that in Catholic liturgy a 'burette' is a container for holy oil. *Burette* can also mean testicle in French — again a container of the essential oil of love.

[28] The names of the conversing friends offer a peculiar mixture of medical, botanical, zoological, sexual, mythological, and religious references. Sulpilia is close to 'Sulpician', which applies to a member of a congregation of Roman Catholic priests devoted to the education of new priests, founded in 1642 at St Sulpice, Paris. Cyril provides another religious allusion, being the name of several Christian saints. While Vulva unambiguously signifies female genitals, the name Falix phonetically evokes the words 'phallic' and 'phallus'. Sola alludes to onanism or the 'solitary vice' that haunted Victorian imagination. Chloe also carries an erotic connotation, recalling the Greek pastoral romance *Daphnis and Chloe* (second century AD) by Longus, which shows the two main characters in pursuit of sexual education. In addition, Chloe is one of the titles of Demeter as the goddess of young green crops. This meaning is thematically connected to Cerise or 'cherry' in French. To lose your cherry or to take someone's cherry are slang expressions for losing or taking virginity. Roseola is a rose-coloured rash in young children which is usually a sign of an infectious illness, and Marisca is Latin for haemorrhoids. Pulex is the Latin word for flea.

[29] Scabius is a blue flower so named because it was thought to be a cure for the unpleasant skin disease scabies. See p. 8, note 52 above for Arthur Symons's description of Decadence as a disease. The combination of beauty and disease is highly decadent.

[30] Sir Jolly Jumble is a pimp in Thomas Otway's comedy *The Soldier's Fortune* (1680) who always talks 'filthily to a lady' and 'mak[es] nasty figures in the napkins'; see Thomas Otway and Havelock Ellis, *The Best Plays of the Old Dramatists: Thomas Otway. With an Introduction and Notes by Hon. Noel Roden*, The Mermaid Series (London: Vizetelly, 1888), p. 196. Potolsky (p. 161) notes that Beardsley's 'use of the word "express" in the passage is also suggestive, signifying both a linguistic and a sexual performance (ejaculation)'.

[31] A buskin is a calf- or knee-length boot, dating back to ancient times and denoting tragedy, as a high-heeled version was worn by actors in ancient Greek tragedy to make them look taller. The use of the word is evidence of Beardsley's knowledge of the history of theatre.

[32] Lysistrata is the eponymous character of a comedy by Aristophanes, illustrations for which became one of Beardsley's most remarkable projects; see *The Lysistrata of Aristophanes* (London: [Smithers], 1896). Beardsley began the illustrations while still working on *Under the Hill*: see his letter to Smithers on 20 April 1896, *Letters of Aubrey Beardsley*, p. 125. Tala is an Indian musical term for a 'cyclical rhythmic period', which can be 'indicated by hand gestures, drum or hand beats'; Tala the tragedian's actions seem to illustrate this concept. See Kenneth Chalmers, 'Tāla', in *The Oxford Companion to Music* (Oxford: Oxford University Press, 2011) in *Oxford Reference* <https://www.oxfordreference.com/view/10.1093/acref/9780199579037.001.0001/acref-9780199579037-e-6635> [accessed 30 June 2020].

[33] Beardsley depicts a satyr 'costumed in white muslin' in his illustration *The Fruit Bearers* (Fig. 3). In addition to being highly suggestive in appearance, asparagus is often considered an aphrodisiac.

put on each other's things, Spelto offered a prize for whoever should come first, & Spelto won it, and Aubrey, just a little grisé, lay down on the cushions & let Julia do whatever she liked.[34]

I wish I could be allowed to tell you what occurred round table 15 just at this moment, it would amuse you very much & would give you a capital idea of the habits of Venus' retinue. Indeed, for deplorable reasons, by far the greater part of what was said & done at this supper must remain unrecorded & even unsuggested.

Venus allowed most of the dishes to pass untasted, she was so engaged with the beauty of Tannhäuser. She hid her head many times under his robe kissing him passionately, & his skin at once firm & yielding seemed to those exquisite little teeth of hers, the most incomparable pasture. Her upper lip curled & trembled with excitement, showing the gums. Tannhäuser on his side was no less devoted. He adored her all over & all the things she had on, & buried his face in the folds & flounces of her linen, & ravished away a score of frills in his excess. He found her exasperating & crushed her in his arms & slaked his parched lips at her mouth. He caressed her eyelids softly with his finger tips & pushed aside the curls from her forehead & did a thousand gracious things, tuning her body as a violinist tunes his instrument before he plays upon it.

Priapusa snorted like an old war horse at the sniff of powder & tickled Tannhäuser & Venus by turns & slipped her tongue down their throats & refused to be quiet at all until she had had a mouthful of the Chevalier. Claude seizing his chance dived under the table & came up the other side just under the queen's couch & before she could say one! he was taking his coffee aux deux colonnes.[35] Clair was furious at his friend's success & sulked for the rest of the evening.

After the fruits & fresh wines had been brought in by a troop of woodland creatures decked with green leaves & all sorts of spring flowers, the candles in the orchestra were lit, & in another moment the musicians bustled into their places.[36] The wonderful Titurel de Schenteflur was the chef d'orchestre, & the most insidious of conductors. His bâton dived into a phrase & brought out the most magical & magnificent things, & seemed rather to play every instrument than to lead it. He could add a grace even to Scarlatti & a wonder to Beethoven. A delicate thin little man with thick lips & a nez retroussé, with long black hair & curled moustache, in the manner of Molière. What were his amatory tastes, no one in the Venusberg could tell; he generally passed for a virgin, and Cathos had nicknamed him the Solitaire.[37]

---

[34] The name Clitor derives from 'clitoris'; Sodon evokes the biblical city of Sodom, destroyed by God for its depravity (Genesis 18. 16–19. 29), and the etymologically related term 'sodomy'. *Enceinte* means pregnant in French. Bellmour, from French *bel* for fair and *amour* for love, is now obsolete and means a loved one. Mellefont is a rake character in William Congreve's Restoration comedy *The Double Dealer* (1794). Ruella derives from *ruelle*, the seventeenth- and eighteenth-century ritual of a morning social gathering in the bedroom of a lady of fashion; in the nineteenth century, the *ruelle* was replaced with the *salon* (*OED*). Julia recalls the daughter of the Roman emperor Augustus and wife of Tiberius, sent into exile for adultery. The *grisé* (disoriented, intoxicated) Aubrey was turned into Tannhäuser in LS. Here it must have been overlooked when making the change from the initial Abbé Aubrey for the protagonist, to the Abbé Fanfreluche, for the *Savoy* version.

[35] Literally 'at the two columns'. This is a pun on French café names such as the famous Deux Magots (the two apes) in Paris. To have *café aux deux colonnes* means to perform cunnilingus; the two 'columns' indicate legs in this expression; see Delvau, p. 78.

[36] Two of the woodland creatures are portrayed in Beardsley's illustration *The Fruit Bearers* (Fig. 3). While the leading satyr's plate is indeed 'decked' with provisions, his human companion ironically carries an empty bowl and seems preoccupied with appreciatively eyeing the satyr's behind. The empty bowl is either for the debris from the fruit or is a finger bowl. If so, the joke is having an evidently high-ranking servant to carry it. As Zatlin notes (*CR* II, p. 262), the servant's attire seems similar to the clothes depicted in *The Abbé*. The boy or girl waiter overall resembles a younger version of the Chevalier.

[37] Titurel de Schentefl[e]ur is an invented musician, although he bears the first name of a character in Wagner's opera *Parsifal* (1882), where Titurel is the first ruler of the Kingdom of the Grail. Through reference to Molière, Beardsley establishes a link to the character's pictorial representation: a slim long-haired man with a *nez retroussé* ('upturned nose') and moustache à la Molière appears in Beardsley's *The Mysterious Rose Garden* (1894). This drawing presents, in Beardsley's words, 'nothing more or less than the Annunciation' (quoted in Zatlin, *CR* II, p. 115) in which the thin man is the messenger. While Titurel de Schentefleur 'passe[s] for a virgin', his lookalike from the drawing brings the news to the Virgin Mary. In both cases, the innocence is paired with a hint of corruption. The messenger in *The Mysterious Rose Garden* wears the winged shoes of Hermes, the god of liars; Titurel de Schentefleur only 'passes' for a virgin, his sexual tastes are a mystery, and his nickname Solitaire evokes the 'solitary sin' of masturbation. Cathos is one of the two heroines in Molière's *Les Précieuses ridicules* (literally 'the ridiculous precious ones'), known in English as *The Affected Ladies* (1659), a satire about over-refined pretentious ladies.

Tonight he appeared in a court suit of white silk, brilliant with decorations, his hair was curled into resplendent ringlets that trembled like springs at the merest gesture of his arm, & in his ears swung the diamonds given him by Venus. The orchestra was as usual in its uniform of red vest & breeches trimmed with gold lace, white stockings & red shoes. Titurel had written a ballet for the evening's divertissement founded upon De Bergerac's comedy of 'Les Bacchanales de Fanfreluche', in which the action & dances were designed by him as well as the music.[38]

The curtain rose upon a scene of rare beauty, a remote arcadian valley, a delicious scrap of Tempe, gracious with cool woods & watered with a dear river as fresh & pastoral as a perfect fifth.[39] It was early morning, & the re-arisen sun, like the prince in the Sleeping Beauty, woke all the earth with his lips. In that golden embrace the night dews were caught up & made splendid, the trees were awakened from their obscure dreams, the slumber of the birds was broken & all the flowers of the valley rejoiced forgetting their fear of the darkness.

Suddenly to the music of pipe & horn, a troop of satyrs stepped out from the recesses of the woods, bearing in their hands nuts & green boughs & flowers & roots & whatsoever the forest yielded, to heap upon the altar of the mysterious Pan that stood in the middle of the stage;[40] & from the hills came down the shepherds & shepherdesses leading their flocks & carrying garlands upon their crooks. Then a rustic priest, white-robed & venerable, came slowly across the valley followed by a choir of radiant children whose delectable limbs so tender and so [illegible] utterly transported Tannhäuser. The scene was admirably stage managed & nothing could have been more varied yet harmonious than this arcadian group. The service was quaint & simple, but with sufficient ritual to give the corps de ballet[41] an opportunity of showing its dainty skill. The dancing of the satyrs was received with huge favour & when the priest raised his hand in final blessing, the whole troop of worshippers made such an intricate & elegant exit that it was generally agreed that Titurel had never before shown so fine an invention.

Scarcely had the stage been empty for a moment, when Fanfreluche entered followed by a brilliant rout of dandies & smart women. Fanfreluche was a tall slim depraved young man with a slight stoop, a troubled walk, an oval impassable face with its olive skin drawn tightly over the bone, strong, scarlet painted lips, long Japanese eyes, & a great gilt toupet.[42] Round his shoulders hung a high-collared satin cape of salmon pink with long black

---

[38] Beardsley alludes to the French playwright and duellist Savinien de Cyrano de Bergerac, with whose play *Le Pédant joué* (1654) he was familiar. Its opening line 'Par les dieux jumeaux tous les monstres ne sont pas en Afrique' ('by the twin Gods, not all monsters are in Africa') is inscribed on Beardsley's *Portrait of Himself* (1894). The title of the ballet marks the original appearance in Beardsley's manuscript of the name Fanfreluche, adopted instead of Tannhäuser for the SV version, where the name of the ballet is changed to The Bacchanals of Sporion. In French *fanfreluche* means frill or frilly thing, and Beardsley's drawing of Fanfreluche shows him decked in frills. It also means light erotic or bawdy verse, as for example in the collection *Les Fanfreluches*, published by Gay et Doucé in Brussels in 1879.

[39] Tempe is a narrow valley near Mount Olympus dedicated to the cult of Apollo; in close proximity to the home of the Greek gods, it was described by the ancient poets as 'the most delightful spot on the earth' (Lempriere's *Classical Dictionary*, 1788). Describing the scene as 'arcadian', Beardsley refers to the idyllic Arcadia (a mountainous area in the Greek Peloponnese, believed to be the birthplace of the god Pan and the site of unspoilt rural simplicity), and saturates it with homosexual allusions. As Cook explains, 'arcadia' was associated during the period with a pure and 'natural' comradeship of men; for Beardsley's homosexual contemporaries, immersing themselves in rural contentment presented a way to escape the stigma of urban 'degenerates' and to redeem same-sex relationships; see Matt Cook, '"A New City of Friends": London and Homosexuality in the 1890s', *History Workshop Journal*, 56.1 (2003), 33–58 (p. 34).

A perfect fifth is a technical term in music describing a specific, peculiarly satisfying relationship between a series of notes of different pitch, that is, higher or lower. We are reminded that Beardsley was an accomplished musician.

[40] Pan is the god of the countryside, particularly associated with Arcadia; he is half-man half-goat and represents fertility. Satyrs are his creatures and look like him.

[41] In ballet the 'corps', or 'body', is the group of dancers who are not soloists or principals, but form a backdrop to them, often dancing in synchrony.

[42] Dowling (pp. 31–32) links the character to the *fin-de-siècle* poet, critic, designer, and erudite Herbert Horne, whose striking looks and predatory sexual behaviour made a lasting impression on contemporaries, including Arthur Symons and Ernest Dowson. Fletcher notes another source for Fanfreluche, this 'chief artefact in this natural paradise': 'Beardsley himself'; see Fletcher, 'Inventions for the Left Hand', p. 238. The later adoption of the name Fanfreluche for the autobiographical character

ribands untied & floating about his body. His coat of sea-green spotted muslin was caught in at the waist by a scarlet sash with scalloped edges & frilled out over the hips for about six inches. His trousers, loose & wrinkled, reached to the end of the calf, & were brocaded down the sides & ruched magnificently at the ankles. The stockings were of white kid with stalls for the toes, & had delicate red sandals strapped over them. But his little hands, peeping out from their frills seemed quite the most insinuating things, such supple fingers tapering to the point with tiny nails stained pink, such unquenchable palms, lined & mounted like Lord Fanny's in 'Love at all Hazards',[43] & such blue-veined hairless backs! In his left hand he carried a small lace handkerchief broidered with a coronet.[44]

As for his friends & followers they made the most superb & insolent crowd imaginable, but to catalogue the clothes they had on would require a chapter as long as the famous tenth in Pénillière's history of underlinen.[45]

On the whole they looked a very distinguished chorus.

Fanfreluche stepped forward & explained with swift & various gesture that he & his friends were tired of the amusements, wearied with the poor pleasures offered by the civil world, & had invaded the arcadian valley hoping to experience a new frisson in the destruction of some shepherd's or some satyr's naïveté, & the infusion of their venom among the dwellers of the woods.[46]

The chorus assented with languid but expressive movements.

Curious & not a little frightened at the arrival of the worldly company, the sylvans began to peep nervously at those subtle souls through the branches of the trees & one or two fauns & a shepherd or so crept out warily.[47] Fanfreluche & all the ladies & gentlemen made enticing sounds & invited the rustic creatures with all the grace in the world to come & join them. By little batches they came lured by the strange looks, by the scents & the drugs, & by the brilliant clothes & some ventured quite near timorously fingering the delicious textures of the stuffs. Then Fanfreluche & each of his friends took a satyr or a shepherd or something by the hand & made the preliminary steps of a courtly measure for which the most admirable combinations had been invented & the most charming music written. The pastoral folk were entirely bewildered when they saw such restrained & graceful movements, & made the most grotesque & futile efforts to imitate them. To the huge & suppressed pleasure of Franfreluche, the satyrs grew very warm in the attempt & cantered about the stage looking like the unappeased husbands of the Lysistrata of Aristophanes, though they were as innocent of offence as the very horses in Nanan's 'Amours catholiques.'[48] Dio mio, a pretty sight! A charming effect too, was obtained by the

---

of Tannhäuser makes Fletcher's interpretation plausible. The attention paid to Fanfreluche's hands later in the paragraph also evokes the 'slim & gracious' hand of Tannhäuser described in Chapter 1. Toupet is a large tuft or quiff of hair.

[43] Beardsley seems to have invented this title; hazard means chance but also implies risk or even peril. Lord Fanny was, according to Desmarais and Baldick (*Decadence*, p. 239), 'a nickname applied by Alexander Pope in the first of his Horatian Imitations (1733) to the politician Lord Hervey, who was bisexual and effeminate in appearance'.

[44] A parodic concentration of the *fin-de-siècle* Decadent traits, Fanfreluche's image is punctuated with this milieu's marks of distinction. Thus, the 'coronet' may hint at the Wildean circle's haunt, the Café Royal, as well as Smithers's premises at the Royal Arcade.

[45] *Pénillière* refers to women's pubic hair, according to Delvau (p. 291), so might be an appropriate name for the author of a history of underlinen.

[46] The 'infusion of their venom' echoes Charles Baudelaire's poem 'À celle qui est trop gaie', which uses similar language to fantasize about the destruction of the embodiment of health and natural gaiety: 'À travers ces lèvres nouvelles, | Plus éclatantes et plus belles, | T'infuser mon venin, ma soeur!' (Charles Baudelaire, *Les Fleurs du mal* (Paris: Calmann-Levy, 1860), p. 278). Roy Campbell's translation (1952) reads: 'Into those lips, so freshly striking | And daily lovelier to my liking — | Infuse the venom of my sprite'. By 'sprite', Campbell means spirit, and the 'venom' is Baudelaire's terrible sense of melancholy. Here however, Beardsley may have meant the depraved spirit of Fanfreluche and his friends.

[47] Sylvans are inhabitants of woods and forests. The dandified crowd evokes the 1890s' aesthetes and decadents. Calling the gathering 'those subtle souls', Beardsley links Fanfreluche's circle to that of Wilde, in which the idea of the soul was much valued: 'Your slim gilt soul walks between passion and poetry', wrote Wilde in a well-known letter to Alfred Douglas, publicized during the trial in April 1895; see *The Trials of Oscar Wilde: Transcript Excerpts from the Trials at the Old Bailey, London, during April and May 1895*, ed. by Tim Coates (London: The Stationery Office, 2001), pp. 26–27. Beardsley discussed the proceedings in correspondence with Ada Leverson and André Raffalovich; see *Letters of Aubrey Beardsley*, pp. 82, 88.

[48] Crossed-out in the manuscript and omitted in SV, JL, and LS, this sentence refers, for the second time in this chapter, to

intermixture of stockinged calf & hairy leg, of rich brocaded bodice & plain blouse, of tortured head dress & loose untutored locks.

When the dance was ended, the servants of Fanfreluche brought on champagne, and, with many pirouettes, poured it magnificently into slender glasses, & tripped about plying those Arcadian mouths that had never before tasted such a royal drink.

'Twas not long before the invaders began to enjoy the first fruits of their expedition plucking them in the most seductive manner with their smooth fingers, & feasting lip & tongue & tooth, whilst the shepherds & satyrs & shepherdesses fairly gasped under the new joys, for the pleasure they experienced was almost too keen & too profound for their simple & untilled natures.[49] Fanfreluche & the rest of the rips[50] & ladies tingled with excitement & frolicked like young lambs in a fresh meadow. Again & again the wine was danced round & the valley grew as busy as a market day. Attracted by the noise & merrymaking all those sweet infants I told you of, skipped suddenly on to the stage & began clapping their hands, & laughing immoderately at the passion & the disorder & commotion, & mimicking the nervous staccato[51] movements they saw in their pretty childish way. In a flash Fanfreluche disentangled & sprang to his feet gesticulating as if he would say 'Ah, the little dears' 'Ah, the little ducks!' 'Ah the rorty little things!',[52] for he was so fond of children. Scarcely had he caught one by the thigh than a quick rush was made by everybody for the succulent limbs; & how they tousled them & mousled them![53] The children cried out I can tell you. Of course there were not enough for everybody, so some had to share, & some had simply to go on with what they were doing before. I must not by the way forget to mention the independent attitude taken by six or seven of the party, who sat & stood about with half-closed eyes inflated nostrils clenched teeth, & painful, parted lips, behaving like the Duc de Broglio when he watched the amours of the Regent Orléans.[54]

Now as Fanfreluche & his friends began to grow tired & exhausted with the new debauch, they cared no longer to take the initiative, but, relaxing every muscle abandoned themselves to passive joys yielding utterly to the ardent embraces of the intoxicated satyrs who waxed fast & furious & seemed as if they would never come to the end of their strength. Full of the new tricks they had learnt that morning they played them passionately & roughly, making havoc of the cultured flesh, & tearing the splendid frocks & dresses into ribands. Duchesses & Maréchales,[55] Marquises & Princesses, Dukes & Marshalls, Marquesses & Princes, were ravished & stretched & rumpled & crushed beneath the interminable vigour & hairy breasts of the inflamed woodlanders. They bit at the white thighs & nozzled wildly in the crevices, they sat astride the women's chests & consummated frantically with their bosoms, they caught their prey by the hips & held it over their heads, irrumating with

---

Lysistrata. In the play by Aristophanes, the husbands' 'unappeased' desire is the result of the Athenian women's refusal to have sex with the men while they continue perpetrating military bloodshed. The husbands' gargantuan erections are in the spotlight of Beardsley's illustrations *The Lacedemonian Ambassadors* and *Cynesias Entreating Myrrhina to Coition*. In French erotic slang, *nanan* means 'the venereal act and the pleasure which is the result of it — the most exquisite of delicacies, the most delicious of all pleasures'; see Delvau, p. 272. The term 'catholic' means universal; therefore, the book, the title of which translates as 'catholic loves', may be a catalogue of the whole spectrum of love, or it might be an exposure of the alleged sexual behaviour of Catholic priests.

49 Tilling is an agricultural term describing the process of preparation of the earth for the sowing of seed. Here, untilled therefore implies innocence, particularly, perhaps, sexual.

50 Rips are rowdy young men.

51 In this context, staccato implies jerky movements. In music, staccato means to play with breaks between the notes, which is what the highly musical Beardsley may have been thinking of.

52 Rorty is a slang word meaning splendid or jolly.

53 Tousle is to make untidy; mousle is to pull about roughly. The terms are usually used together, as Beardsley does here.

54 Philippe d'Orleans, Regent of France between 1715 and 1723, was infamous for his licentious and depraved behaviour. Broglio was a participant in the Regent's debaucheries; according to the popular history by William Cooke Taylor, it is not known how he became introduced to the intimacy of the Regent, but 'so far as vice was a qualification, his claim was indisputable'; W. Cooke Taylor, *Memoirs of the House of Orleans*, 3 vols (London: Richard Bentley, 1849), I, p. 399.

55 A Maréchale is the wife of a Marshall — a high military rank in France.

prodigious gusto.[56] It was the triumph of the valley. High up in the heavens the sun had mounted & filled all the air with generous warmth, whilst shadows grew shorter & sharper. Little light-winged papillons flitted across the stage, the bees made music on their flowery way, the birds were very gay & kept up a jargoning& refraining,[57] the lambs were bleating upon the hill side, & the orchestra kept playing, playing the uncanny tunes of Titurel.

Venus & Tannhäuser had retired to the exquisite little boudoir or pavilion Le Con had designed for the queen on the first terrace, & which commanded the most delicious view of the parks & gardens.[58] It was a sweet little place, all silk curtains & soft cushions. There were eight sides to it, bright with mirrors & candelabra, & rich with pictured panels, & the ceiling, dome shaped & some thirty feet above the head, shone obscurely with gilt mouldings, through the warm haze of candle light below. Tiny wax statuettes dressed theatrically & smiling with plump cheeks, quaint magots that looked as cruel as foreign gods,[59] gilded monticules,[60] pale celadon vases,[61] clocks that said nothing, ivory boxes full of secrets, china figures playing whole scenes of plays, & a world of strange preciousness crowded the curious cabinets that stood against the walls. On one side of the room there were six perfect little card tables, with quite the daintiest & most elegant chairs set primly round them; so, after all, there may be some truth in that line of Mr Theodore Watts, 'I played at piquet with the Queen of Love'.[62]

Nothing in the pavilion was more beautiful than the folding screens painted by De La Pine with Claudian landscapes, the sort of things that fairly make one melt, things one can lie & look at for hours together & forget the country can ever be dull & tiresome.[63] There were four of them, delicate walls that hem in an amour so cosily & make room within room. The place was scented with huge branches of red roses, & with a faint amatory perfume breathed out from the couches & cushions, a perfume Chateline distilled in secret & had called *L'Eau Savante*.[64]

Those who have only seen Venus at the Louvre or the British Museum, at Florence, at Naples, or at Rome, can have not the faintest idea how sweet & enticing & gracious, how really exquisitely beautiful she looked lying with Tannhäuser, upon rose silk, in that pretty boudoir. Cosmé's precise curls & artful waves had been finely disarranged at supper, & strayed ringlets of the black hair fell loosely over her soft, delicious, tired, swollen eyelids.[65] Her frail chemise & dear little drawers were torn & moist & clung transparently about her, & all the body

---

[56] The term 'irrumation' comes from Latin *irrumāre* and relates to the Roman practice of active penetration of the mouth by the penis. It appears for the first time in English language in Forberg's *Manual of Classical Erotology*, published by Smithers in 1887 (*OED*). Beardsley seems here to be misunderstanding its meaning, since the satyrs appear to be doing the opposite — mouth to genitals activity.

[57] To jargon is to warble or chatter.

[58] The name Le Con, as Lavers points out, means the 'female organ', as well as being 'an obvious graphic and phonetic reminder of that of Le Vau, the famous seventeenth-century architect who built Fouquet's palace, the prototype of Versailles'; see Lavers, '*L'eau Savante*' (part I).

[59] *Magot* means an ape in French.

[60] *Monticule* is French for a small mound or hill. It is not clear what Beardsley was thinking of here. Possibly a purely decorative object in the form of a gilded cone.

[61] Celadon is a beautiful pale blue glaze found on Chinese porcelain.

[62] Theodore Watts, later Watts-Dunton, was a poet and critic as well as the legal adviser, friend, and caregiver of Swinburne. No evidence for his authorship of this pentameter, a standard metre of English poetry, has been found, so this is most likely Beardsley's satirical invention.

[63] The character of De La Pine evokes, according to Dowling (p. 32), the *fin-de-siècle* artist Charles Conder, with whom Beardsley often passed time at Dieppe at the time of the composition of *Under the Hill*. Conder was famous for his exquisite neo-rococo paintings on textiles and fans. *La pine* is French slang for penis. 'Claudian landscapes' means done in the manner of the great seventeenth-century French landscapist Claude Lorrain, much admired by Beardsley. The suggestion that looking at them would be more rewarding than the 'dull and tiresome' nature they represent is a pure expression of the fundamental Decadent doctrine that art is superior to nature, an idea exhaustively explored in *À Rebours* by J.-K. Huysmans, a key text of Decadence, and taken up by Oscar Wilde.

[64] *L'Eau Savante* means 'wise water'.

[65] Beardsley here plays on the fraught artistic issue of the relationship between art and reality, adding a further twist since his 'real' Venus is of course his invention. As Fletcher notes, the description of Venus with her 'tired, swollen' eyelids evokes

was nervous & responsive. Her closed thighs seemed like a vast replica of the little bijou she held between them; the beautiful tétons du derrière were as firm as a plump virgin's & promised a joy as profound as the mystery of the Rue Vendôme, & the minor chevelure, just profuse enough, curled as prettily as the hair upon a cherub's head.[66]

Tannhäuser pale & speechless with excitement passed his gem-girt fingers brutally over the divine limbs tearing away smock & pantalon & stocking, & then stripping himself of his own few things, fell upon the splendid lady with a deep-drawn breath.

It is I know the custom of all romancers to paint heroes who can give a lady proof of their valliance at least twenty times a night. Now Tannhäuser had no such gargantuan facility, & was rather relieved when an hour later Priapusa & Doricourt & some others burst drunkenly into the room & claimed Venus for themselves.[67] The pavilion soon filled with a noisy crowd that could scarcely keep its feet. Several of the actors were there, & Lesfesses[68] who had played Fanfreluche so brilliantly & was still in his make-up, paid tremendous attention to Tannhäuser. But the Chevalier found him quite uninteresting off the stage & rose & crossed the room to where Venus & the manicure were seated.

'How tired the dear baby looks', said Priapusa, 'shall I put him in his little cot?'

'Well, if he's as sleepy as I am' yawned Venus, 'you can't do better.'

Priapusa lifted her mistress off the pillows & carried her in her arms in a nice motherly way.

'Come along, children', said the fat old thing, 'come along, it's time you were both in bed.'

Swinburne's Tannhäuserean variation, 'Laus Veneris' (1866); the child-like image of the goddess brings to mind 'a naughty Kate Greenaway girl' and the 'child cult of the 1890s'; see Fletcher, 'Inventions for the Left Hand', p. 241.

[66] *Tétons du derrière* means buttocks — literally, 'the breasts of the bottom'; the Rue Vendôme, 'mentioned in some of Balzac's novels, had already been renamed the rue Béranger in 1864'; see Desmarais and Baldick, *Decadence*, p. 239.

[67] Critics agree that Tannhäuser's ironically unexaggerated sexual performance as well as his submission to the members of Venus's retinue present a parody of conventional pornography; see Dowling, p. 29; Fletcher, 'Inventions for the Left Hand', pp. 241–42. Doricourt is a character in the eighteenth-century comedy of manners *The Belle's Strategem* (1780) by Hannah Cowley. The term gargantuan refers to the famously bawdy works of the French writer François Rabelais, published in five volumes from 1532, recounting the adventures of the giant Gargantua and his son Pantagruel. Beardsley owned a set; see *Letters of Aubrey Beardsley*, p. 432.

[68] The name Lesfesses literally translates as 'the buttocks' — *fesses* is a colloquial term for them in French.

~

IV

It is always delightful to wake up in a new bedroom. The fresh wallpaper, the strange pictures, the positions of doors & windows, imperfectly grasped the night before, are revealed with all the charm of surprise when we open our eyes the next morning.

It was about eleven o'clock when Tannhäuser awoke & stretched himself deliciously in his great plumed four post bed, & nursed his waking thoughts & stared at the curious patterned canopy above him.[1] He was very pleased with the room which certainly was chic & fascinating & recalled the voluptuous interiors of the elegant amorous Baudouin.[2] Through the tiny parting of the long flowered window curtains the Chevalier caught a peep of the sun lit lawns outside, the silver fountains, the bright flowers, & the gardeners at work.

'Quite sweet', he murmured, & turned round to freshen the frilled silk pillows behind him, '& what delightful pictures,' he continued, wandering with his eyes from print to print that hung upon the rose striped walls. Within the delicate curved frames lived the corrupt & gracious creatures of Dorat & his school;[3] slim children in masque & domino[4] smiling horribly, exquisite letchers[5] leaning over the shoulders of smooth doll-like ladies & doing nothing particular, terrible little Pierrots posing as mulierasts, or pointing at something outside the picture,[6] & unearthly fops & strange women mingling in some rococo room lighted mysteriously by the flicker

---

[1] This looks like another cross-arts, self-referential nod to Beardsley's *Portrait of Himself*, which was published in the third volume of the *Yellow Book* (October 1894). The image is centred on a sumptuous four-poster canopy bed in which the artist's tiny smirking face is buried. Critics described the picture as 'impudent' (*Daily Chronicle*) and 'impertinent' (*Chicago Times-Herald*), perhaps due to the insinuating intimacy of such self-representation; see Zatlin, *CR* II, p. 104. The term 'curious' in this context is a euphemism for erotic; rare book sellers used to list erotica as 'curiosa'.

[2] Pierre Antoine Baudouin was a French rococo artist who studied under François Boucher and shared a studio with Jean-Honoré Fragonard. Baudouin specialized in idyllic subjects as well as erotica, often set in rich rococo boudoirs. For instance, his popular drawing *Le Matin* ('morning') portrays a voyeuristic scene in which two men gaze at a sleeping woman on a canopy bed; her rolled-up dress exposes her genitalia. Beardsley would have known Baudouin's works through popular engravings. Desmarais and Baldick link the allusion to Pavillon Carré de Baudouin, 'a grand eighteenth-century pleasure-villa overlooking Paris', where the Goncourt brothers were raised; Desmarais and Baldick, *Decadence*, p. 239.

[3] There appears to be no such artist of the rococo as Dorat. Beardsley may have taken the name from the well-known writer of the genre of mildly erotic French literature known as 'galante', Claude-Joseph Dorat. His most famous illustrator was the highly accomplished artist Charles Eisen, who while providing suggestive but publishable illustrations for Dorat also produced highly explicit ones for other authors. Except for the last, Beardsley's descriptions evoke the former. They also evoke his own work.

[4] A domino is a cloak worn, together with a half-mask, at masquerades; of Venetian origin.

[5] Beardsley misspells 'lecher'.

[6] The word 'mulierast' was coined within Oscar Wilde's circle to designate a heterosexual man. It was formed by the addition of '-erast' (as in 'pederast') to the Latin *mulier* (woman). The term was probably invented by Robert Ross, as Wilde's letter to Reginald Turner (June 1897) suggests: 'He is simply a manly simple fellow, with the nicest smile and the pleasantest eyes, and I have no doubt a confirmed "mulierast", to use Robbie's immortal phrase' (*The Complete Letters of Oscar Wilde*, ed. by Merlin Holland and Rupert Hart-Davis (New York: Henry Holt, 2000), p. 887). The word also appears earlier in Max Beerbohm's letter to Ross (November 1894): 'Mrs Leverson is delighted at your saying that she almost persuadeth you to become a mulierast' (Max Beerbohm, *Letters of Max Beerbohm, 1892–1956*, ed. by Rupert Hart-Davis (Oxford: Oxford University Press, 1989), p. 6). In Beardsley's graphic works, one often encounters Pierrots 'posing as mulierasts'. For instance, in *Two Women Golfers and Pierrot as a Caddie* (1894) and *Bookplate of John Lumsden Propert* (1893), Pierrots are depicted attending to dominant and imposing women characters. Beardsley's self-identification with the figure of Pierrot is documented in his letters; see *Letters of Aubrey Beardsley*, p. 51.

of a dying fire that throws huge shadows upon wall & ceiling.[7] One of the prints showing how an old marquis practised the five finger exercise whilst in front of him, his mistress offered her warm fesses to a panting poodle, made the Chevalier stroke himself a little.[8]

After a while he got up & slipping off his dainty night-dress postured elegantly before a long mirror & made much of his body. Now he would bend forward & admire the creases of his stomach, now he would stand upright & adore the contour of his loins & hips, now he would rest upon one leg & let the other hang loosely till he looked as if he might have been drawn by some early Italian master,[9] & now he would lie upon the floor with his back to the glass & glance amorously over his shoulder. Then with a white silk sash he draped himself in a hundred charming ways. So engrossed was he with his mirrored shape that he had not noticed the entrance of a troop of serving boys, who stood admiringly but respectfully at a distance ready to receive his waking orders. As soon as the chevalier observed them he smiled sweetly & bade them prepare the bath.

His bathroom was the largest & perhaps the most beautiful apartment in his splendid suite. The well-known engraving by Lorette that forms the frontispiece to Millevoye's 'Architecture du XVIIIme siècle' will give you a better idea than any words of mine of the construction & decoration of the room.[10] Only in Lorette's engraving the bath sunk into the middle of the floor is a little too small.

Tannhäuser stood for a moment like Narcissus gazing at his reflection in the still scented water & then just ruffling its smooth surface with one foot, stepped elegantly into the cool basin & swam round it twice, very gracefully.[11]

'Won't you join me?' he said turning to those beautiful boys who stood ready with warm towels & perfume. In a moment they were free of their light morning dress, & jumped into the water & joined hands & surrounded the Chevalier with a laughing chain.

'Splash me a little' he cried, & the boys teased him with water & quite excited him. He chased the prettiest of them & bit his fesses & kissed him upon the perineum till the dear fellow banded as freely [as] a Carmelite, & its little bald top-knot looked like a great pink pearl under the water.[12] As the boy seemed anxious to take up

---

[7] Rococo (from French *rocaille*, 'rockwork', and possibly *coquille*, 'shellwork') is the playful and decorative style in eighteenth-century art which flourished in France during the Regency (1715–1730) and the reign of Louis XV (1730–1774). Literary examples include Alexandre Pope's *The Rape of the Lock* (1712–1714), illustrated by Beardsley.

[8] The 'five finger exercise' usually means a piece of piano music written to exercise all the fingers, such as several etudes by Beardsley's beloved composer Chopin. Here, the exercise might also allude to masturbation.

[9] Beardsley is here referring to a pose known to art history as *déhanchement*. It was described by Kenneth Clark in his pioneering 1956 study: 'The pose was invented for the male figure but [...] the female figure has drawn from it more lasting profit; for this disposition of balance has automatically created a contrast between the arc of one hip, sweeping up till it approaches the sphere of the breast, and the long, gentle undulation of the side that is relaxed. [...] It is almost a geometric curve; and yet [...] it is a vivid symbol of desire'; Kenneth Clark, *The Nude: A Study in Ideal Form* (Princeton: Princeton University Press, 1984), pp. 79–81.

[10] The term 'lorette' originated in the mid-nineteenth century and referred to courtesans who lived and saw their clients near the Church of Notre Dame de Lorette in Paris. The architectural treatise by Millevoye is Beardsley's invention. However, the author's surname might evoke the right-wing French politician Lucien Millevoye. He was a lover of Maud Gonne, a famous Irish nationalist and suffragette and the muse of W. B. Yeats, whom Beardsley knew. He may also have had in mind Lucien Millevoye's grandfather the French Romantic poet Charles Millevoye. The title of the book may be an allusion to the famous study of rococo art by the Goncourts, *L'Art du XVIIIme siecle.*

[11] The culturally resonant myth of Narcissus as told by the Roman poet Ovid in *Metamorphoses* (8 AD) depicts a beautiful youth who scorned all his admirers, be it spirits of the woods, lustful men, or the nymph Echo. Narcissus was punished for his coldness by being made to fall in love with his own reflection in the pool. 'Unwittingly, he desired himself, and was himself the object of his own approval, at once seeking and sought, himself kindling the flame with which he burned'; Ovid, *Metamorphoses*, trans. by Mary M. Innes (London: Penguin, 1955), p. 85. Spellbound by his reflection in the water, Narcissus faded away; his body was transformed into a flower. The most influential Decadent retelling of the myth is Wilde's *The Picture of Dorian Gray.*

[12] Beardsley had terrible trouble with this sentence (see Diplomatic Transcription, p. 85). Parts have been heavily crossed out, corrections written in and then crossed out again in favour of the final version, in which the vital 'as' is missing. It still only makes sense if it is assumed that 'the dear fellow' is the perineum and if perineum is assumed to mean penis, as Beardsley mistakenly seems to think. It is in fact the area between the genitals and the anus. Beardsley also uses the equivalent French

the active attitude Tannhäuser graciously descended to the passive, a generous trait that won him the complete affections of his valets de bain, or pretty fish, as he called them, because they loved to swim between his legs.[13]

However it is not so much at the very bath itself, as in the drying & delicious frictions that a bather finds his chiefest pleasures, & Tannhäuser was more than satisfied with the skill his attendants displayed in the performance of those quasi amorous functions. The delicate attention they paid his loving parts aroused feelings within him that almost amounted to gratitude, & when the rites were ended, any touch of homesickness he might have felt before was utterly dispelled.

After he had rested a little & sipped his chocolate, he wandered into the dressing-room. Daucourt, his valet de chambre,[14] Chenille, the perruquier & barber,[15] & two charming young dressers, were awaiting him & ready with suggestions for the morning toilet. The shaving over, Daucourt commanded his underlings to step forward with the suite of suits from which he proposed Tannhäuser should make a choice. The final selection was a happy one. A dear little coat of pigeon rose[16] silk that hung loosely about his hips & showed off the jut of his behind to perfection, trousers of black lace in flounces, falling almost like a petticoat as far as the knee, & a delicate chemise of white muslin, spangled with gold, & profusely pleated.[17]

The two dressers, under Daucourt's direction, did their work superbly, beautifully, leisurely, with an exquisite deference for the nude, & a really sensitive appreciation of Tannhäuser's scrumptious torso.[18]

When all was said & done the Chevalier tripped off to bid good morning to Venus. He found her wandering, in a sweet white muslin frock, upon the lawn outside, plucking flowers to deck her little déjeuner.[19] He kissed her lightly upon the neck.

'I'm just going to feed Adolphe', she said, pointing to a little reticule of buns that hung from her arm.[20]

Adolphe was her pet unicorn.[21]

---

word in his fantasy menu for Venus's supper (see p. 36, note 22 to Chapter III). Beardsley has invented the word 'banded' to mean a state of erection; in fact he has simply adapted into English the French verb *bander*, which has that meaning and for which there is no English equivalent. A Carmelite is a monk of the monastic order of that name. Beardsley's citing of Carmelites as exemplary in the matter of erections reveals his familiarity with the work of the Marquis de Sade. In the latter's novel *Juliette* (published 1797–1801) the heroine and her companion set out to seduce a Carmelite monk, one Claude, who has taken their fancy. They do this by getting him to hear their confession, in which they admit to uncontrollable lust. The result, Sade remarks, is that, beneath his habit, 'Claude bandait comme un homme de son ordre' ('Claude had an erection like a man of his order'). A little later Juliette unveils this erection and exclaims, 'Oh! mes amis, qu'on a raison de citer un carme, quand on veut offrir un modèle de vit et d'érection' ('Oh my friends, how right to cite a Carmelite when wishing to offer a model of a cock and of erection'); see Wilson, *'Rose et Noir'*, p. 57. Beardsley may have named Venus's attendant, Claude, after this monk (see note 5 (p. 29) to Chapter II).

[13] *Valets de bain* means bath attendants. In using the phrase 'pretty fish' here Beardsley recalls the Roman historian Suetonius's account of how the Emperor Tiberius 'trained little boys whom he termed "fishes" to crawl between his thighs when he went swimming and tease him with their licks and nibbles'; see Wilson, *'Rose et Noir'*, p. 58.

[14] Claude Godard d'Aucourt was an eighteenth-century French writer and librettist, best known for an orientalist libertine novel *Les Mémoires turcs* (1745).

[15] In French *chenille* is a caterpillar and a *perruquier* is a wigmaker.

[16] This is a reference to the very pretty, pale, dusty pink colour of the breast of a wood pigeon (*columba palumbus*).

[17] This morning toilet continues the feminization of Tannhäuser: his trousers already resemble a petticoat.

[18] 'Scrumptious' means marvellous, enjoyable, delicious, or exceptionally attractive. As Dowling notes (p. 36), the word is 'expressive of childish appetites'.

[19] The phrase 'little déjeuner' is half English, half French for 'petit déjeuner', the French term for breakfast.

[20] A reticule is a handbag, tied with a drawstring.

[21] The name of the unicorn may contain a reference to Benjamin Constant's *Adolphe* (1816), which mixes traits of a *roman d'analyse*, or psychological novel, and *roman libertin*, novel of seduction. The title character is a melancholic and cultured youth who attaches himself to the court of an enlightened German prince. There, he falls in love with the beautiful Polish aristocrat Ellénore who is slightly older than him. Ellénore evokes Beardsley's Helen-Venus not only with her name but also with her status as refugee. In Constant's novel, the affair becomes all-consuming and culminates in Ellénore's death, which leaves Adolphe in a state of existential despair. See Benjamin Constant, *Adolphe* (Paris: Trottel et Wurtz, 1816). It is worth noting that, in the manuscript, Beardsley first named the unicorn Arthur, doubtless a reference to the *Morte Darthur* and its medieval world of mythical beasts. The name, however, would have jarred in the rococo world of *Under the Hill*.

'He is such a dear' she continued, 'milk-white all over excepting his black eyes, rose mouth & nostrils, & scarlet john. This way.'[22]

The unicorn had a very pretty palace of its own, made of green foliage & golden bars, a fitting home for such a delicate & dainty beast. Ah it was indeed a splendid thing to watch the white creature roaming in its artful cage, proud & beautiful & knowing no mate except the Queen herself.[23]

As Venus & Tannhäuser approached the wicket Adolphe began prancing & curvetting, pawing the soft turf with his ivory hoofs, & flaunting his tail like a gonfalon.[24] Venus raised the latch & entered.

'You mustn't come in with me, Adolphe is so jealous' she said turning to the Chevalier who was following her. 'But you can stand outside & look on; Adolphe likes an audience.' Then in her delicious fingers she broke the spicy buns & with affectionate niceness breakfasted her ardent pet.[25] When the last crumbs had been scattered Venus brushed her hands together & pretended to leave the cage without taking any more notice of Adolphe. Every morning she went through this piece of play & every morning the amorous unicorn was cheated into a distressing agony lest that day should have proved the last of Venus's love. Not for long though would she leave him in that doubtful piteous state but running back passionately to where he stood make adorable amends for her unkindness. Poor Adolphe! how happy he was touching the Queen's breasts with his quick tongue-tip. I have no doubt that the keener scent of animals must make women much more attractive to them than to men, for the gorgeous odour that but faintly fills our nostrils must be revealed to the brute creation in divine fulness. Anyhow Adolphe sniffed as never a man did — around the skirts of Venus. After the first charming interchange of affectionate delicacies was over, the unicorn lay down upon his side, and, closing his eyes, beat his stomach wildly with the mark of manhood.[26]

Venus caught that stunning member in her hands & lay her cheek along it. But few touches were wanted to consummate the creature's pleasure. The Queen bared her left arm to the elbow & with the soft underneath of it made amazing movements horizontally upon the tight-strung instrument. When the melody began to flow, the unicorn offered up an astonishing vocal accompaniment. Tannhäuser was amused to learn that the etiquette of the Venusberg compelled everybody to wait the outburst of these venereal sounds before they could sit down to déjeuner.[27]

Adolphe had been quite profuse that morning.

Venus knelt where it had fallen & lapped her little aperitif.

---

[22] John (sometimes John Thomas) is a slang word for the penis.

[23] Beardsley's description of Venus's relationship with the white unicorn may be inspired by the myth of Pasiphaë, the wife of the Cretan king Minos. Pasiphaë lusted after a beautiful white bull and was able to satisfy her desire by slipping inside a hollow wooden cow, which the white bull mounted. As a result, she gave birth to the Minotaur, a monster combining a human head with a bull's body. In medieval lore, a unicorn could only be captured by a virgin. Thus, Beardsley obviously subverts the traditional connotations of a unicorn as a symbol of grace and purity.

[24] A gonfalon is a banner.

[25] Beardsley planned to illustrate the scene, as his letter to F. H. Evans in November 1894 testifies: 'I am just doing a picture of Venus feeding her pet unicorns which have garlands of roses round their necks'; *Letters of Aubrey Beardsley*, p. 79. There is no record of this drawing.

[26] Readers may wonder how he did this. Assuming that unicorns have a comparable anatomy in this area to humans he would have used his pelvic floor muscles, specifically the ischiocavernosus. Several scholars have linked the character of Adolphe to the author. Lavers sees 'the symbol of the artist' in Adolphe, 'the only character in the novel whose behaviour expresses feelings and not the physiological whim of the minute'; see Lavers, '"Aubrey Beardsley, Man of Letters"', p. 263; see also Fletcher, 'Inventions for the Left Hand', p. 242.

[27] Beardsley's use of musical metaphors here reminds us that he was a musician as well as an artist and a writer.

~

V

The breakfasters were scattered over the gardens in têtes-à-têtes & tiny parties. Venus & Tannhäuser sat together upon the lawn that lay in front of the Casino, & made havoc of a ravishing déjeuner. The Chevalier was feeling very happy. Everything around him seemed so white & light & matinal,[1] the floating frocks of the ladies, the scarce robed boys & satyrs stepping hither & thither elegantly, with meats & wines & fruits, the damask tablecloths, the delicate talk & laughter that rose everywhere; the flowers' colour & the flowers' scent, the shady trees, the wind's cool voice, & the sky above that was as fresh & pastoral as a perfect fifth.[2] And Venus looked so beautiful. Not at all like the lady in Lempriere.[3]

'You're such a dear' murmured Tannhäuser holding her hand.

At the further end of the lawn & a little hidden by a rose-tree a young man was breakfasting alone. He toyed nervously with his food now & then but for the most part leant back in his chair with unemployed hands, & gazed stupidly at Venus.

'That's Felix', said the goddess, in answer to an enquiry from the Chevalier, & she went on to explain his attitude. Felix always attended Venus upon her little latrinal excursions holding her serving her & making much of all she did. To undo her things, to lift her skirts, to wait & watch the coming, to dip a lip or finger in the royal output, to stain himself deliciously with it, to lie beneath her as the favours fell, to carry off the crumpled crotted paper these were the pleasures of that young man's life.[4]

Truly there never was a Queen so beloved by her subjects as Venus. Everything she wore had its lover. Heavens how her handkerchiefs were filched, her stockings stolen! Daily, what intrigues, what countless ruses to possess her merest frippery! Every scrap of her body was adored. Never for Savaral could her ear yield sufficient wax! Never for Pradon could she spit prodigally enough! And Saphius found a month an interminable time.[5]

After breakfast was over & Felix's fears lest Tannhäuser should have robbed him of his capricious rights had been dispelled, Venus invited the Chevalier to take a more extensive view of the gardens, parks, pavilions, & ornamental waters. The carriage was ordered. It was a delicate shell-like affair with billowy cushions & a light canopy, & was drawn by ten satyrs, dressed as finely as the coachmen of the Empress Pauline the First.[6]

The drive proved interesting & various, & Tännhauser was quite delighted with almost everything he saw.

And who is not pleased, when on either side of him rich lawns are spread with lovely frocks & white limbs,

---

[1] Matinal (also matutinal) relates to the morning, especially just after awakening.

[2] Beardsley used the same phrase earlier in Chapter III. See p. 40 and note 39.

[3] Beardsley refers to an influential and entertaining reference book, John Lempriere, *Bibliotheca Classica: Or, a Classical Dictionary, Containing a Full Account of All the Proper Names Mentioned in Antient Authors* (Reading: T. Cadell, 1788). The primary definitions of Venus given by Lempriere are 'the goddess of beauty, the mother of love, the queen of laughter' (p. 773).

[4] Felix's role at the court corresponds with that of Groom of the Stool, the title of a high officer of a king's household (also in the household of a prince), responsible for assisting the king with excretions and hygiene. Beardsley adds a gender twist, since in the household of a queen or a princess, the office and title were held by a lady. Since the reign of Queen Victoria, the officer has not been appointed. 'Crotted' is a word of Beardsley's coinage, derived from the French *crotte* (*excrement*).

[5] Fletcher aptly summarizes, 'Venus's is the Body of Love. [...] All the functions of her body have the one teleology — giving pleasure to others'; Fletcher, 'Inventions for the Left Hand', p. 241.

[6] Beardsley was probably thinking of Napoleon's sister Pauline, an imperial princess who remains famous as the subject of the life-size, semi-nude marble portrait of her as Venus by Antonio Canova in the Galleria Borghese in Rome.

& upon flower beds the dearest ladies are implicated in a glory of underclothing, when he can see in the deep cool shadows of the trees, warm boys entwined, here at the base, there in the branch, when in the fountain's wave Love holds his court & the insistent water burrows in every delicious crease & crevice?

A pretty sight too was little Rosalie perched like a postillion upon the painted phallus of the god of all gardens. Her eyes were closed & she was smiling as the carriage passed. Round her neck & slender girlish shoulders there was a cloud of complex dress over which bulged her wig-like flaxen tresses, her legs & feet were bare & the toes twisted in an amorous style. At the foot of the statue lay her shoes & stockings & a few other things.[7]

Tannhäuser was singularly moved & rose out of all proportion. Venus slipped the fingers of comfort under the lace flounces of his trousers saying 'Is it all mine? Is it all mine?' & doing fascinating things. In the end, the carriage was only prevented from being overturned by the happy interposition of Priapusa who stepped out from somewhere or other just in time to preserve its balance.

How the old lady's eye glistened as Tannhäuser withdrew his panting blade, & in her sincere admiration for fine things she quite forgot & forgave the shock she had received from the falling of the gay equipage.[8] Venus & Tannhäuser were profuse with apology & thanks & quite a crowd of loving courtiers gathered round consoling & congratulating in a breath. The chevalier vowed he would never go in the carriage again, & was really quite upset about it. However after he had had a little support from the smelling salts, he recovered his self-possession, & consented to drive on further.

The landscape grew rather mysterious. The park, no longer troubled & adorned with figures was full of grey echoes, & mysterious sounds, the leaves whispered a little sadly, & there was a grotto that murmured like the voice that haunts the silence of a deserted oracle. Tannhäuser became a little triste.[9] In the distance through the trees gleamed a still argent lake, a reticent, romantic water, that must have held the subtlest fish that ever were.[10] Around its marge the trees & flags & fleurs de luce were unbreakably asleep.[11]

The Chevalier fell into a strange mood as he looked at the lake, it seemed to him that the thing would speak, reveal some curious secret, say some beautiful word, if he should dare wrinkle its pale face with a pebble.

'I should be frightened to do that though' he said to himself.

Then he wondered what there might be upon the other side; other gardens, other gods? A thousand drowsy fancies passed through his brain. Sometimes the lake took fantastic shapes, or grew to twenty times its size or shrunk into a miniature of itself, without ever once losing its unruffled calm, its deathly reserve. When the water increased the chevalier was very frightened, for he thought how huge the frogs must have become, he thought of their big eyes & monstrous wet feet, but when the water lessened he laughed to himself for the thought how tiny the frogs must have grown, he thought of their legs that must look thinner than spiders', & of their dwindled

---

[7] The 'god of all gardens' is Priapus, the ancient god of fertility, often depicted with a large phallus. 'Rosalie' evokes the rose as a metaphor for female genitalia and the *Roman de la Rose* of the epigraph; it derives from the Latin name Rosalia. St Rosalia was a twelfth-century Sicilian virgin. The scene may allude to the numerous depictions of phallic worship by the Belgian artist Félicien Rops. Beardsley knew Rops's work and considered buying a piece in 1896; see *Letters of Aubrey Beardsley*, p. 223. Rops's *L'Idole* from the series *Les Sataniques* (1882) shows a woman with blank eyes, naked apart from her shoes, mounting a statue of Priapus flanked by a menacing pair of gigantic phalluses. Zatlin notes that, 'as in Rops's other pictures with the same motif, the phallus is masochistically celebrated by woman. Its outlandish size [...] threatens to split the female's body even as she accepts it'. Linda Gertner Zatlin, 'Félicien Rops and Aubrey Beardsley: The Naked and the Nude', in *Reconsidering Aubrey Beardsley*, ed. by Robert Langenfeld (Ann Arbor: UMI Research Press, 1989), pp. 167–205 (p. 173). The same series by Rops includes an even more disturbing and blasphemous image, *Le Calvaire*, in which a figure of Satan, sexually aroused while being nailed to a cross, is depicted strangling a woman with the tresses of her own hair. Beardsley's strikingly different treatment of the same theme accentuates pastoral qualities rather than violence and satanism. While the girl's name has religious connotations, Rosalie is individualized, her toilette like that of others in Venusberg is described in detail, and her pleasure is highlighted.

[8] Equipage means a carriage and horses, with the attendant servants.

[9] *Triste* is French for 'sad'. Given the preceding episode in the carriage, Beardsley might have had in mind the well-known Latin proverb 'post coitum omne animal triste est' — 'after coition all creatures are sad'.

[10] *Argent* means silver in French. Of an animal, 'subtle' means wily, devious, and sly (now rare).

[11] In the stylized heraldic version, fleurs-de-luce (iris flowers) are conspicuously phallic. Flags are a kind of wild iris, contrasting with the more stylized fleurs-de-luce.

croaking that never could be heard. Perhaps the lake was only painted after all, he had seen things like it at the theatre. Anyhow it was a wonderful lake, a beautiful lake, & he would love to bathe in it, but he was sure he would be drowned if he did…[12]

When he woke up from his day-dream he noticed that the carriage was on its way back to the palace. They stopped at the Casino first & stepped out to join the players at petits chevaux.[13] Tannhäuser preferred to watch the game rather than play himself & stood behind Venus who slipped into a vacant chair & cast gold pieces upon lucky numbers. The first thing that Tannhäuser noticed was the grace & charm, the gaiety & beauty of the croupiers.[14] They were quite adorable even when they raked in one's little losings. Dressed in black silk & wearing white kid gloves, loose yellow wigs, & feathered toques:[15] with faces oval & young, bodies lithe & quick, voices silvery & affectionate, they made amends for all the hateful arrogance, disgusting aplomb, & shameful ugliness of the rest of their kind.

The dear fellow who proclaimed the winner was really quite delightful. He took a passionate interest in the horses & had licked all the paint off their balls. You will ask me no doubt 'Is that all he did'? I will answer, 'Not quite', as the merest glance at their little posteriors would prove.

In the afternoon light that came through the great silken blinded windows of the Casino, all the gilded decorations, all the gilded décor, the chandeliers, the mirrors, the polished floor, the painted ceiling, the horses galloping round their green meadow, the fat rouleaux of gold & silver,[16] the ivory rakes,[17] the fanned & strange frocked crowd of dandy gamesters looked magnificently rich & warm. Tea was being served. It was so pretty to see some flushed little lady sipping nervously, & keeping her eyes over the cup's edge intently upon the slackening horses. The more indifferent left the tables & took their tea in parties here & there.

Tannhäuser found a great deal to amuse him at the Casino. Ponchon was the manager, & a person of extraordinary invention. Never a day but he was ready with a new show a novel attraction. A glance through the old Casino programmes would give you a very considerable idea of his talent. What countless ballets, comedies, comedy-ballets, concerts, masques, charades, proverbs, pantomimes, tableaux-magiques, ombres fantastiques, & peep-shows excentriques, what troupes of marionettes, what burlesques![18] Ponchon had an astonishing flair for new talent, & many of the principal comedians & singers at the Queen's theatre and opera house had made their first appearance & reputation at the Casino.[19]

---

[12] According to Lavers, the dark waters of the lake symbolize sexuality 'conceived here as a fountainhead not of pleasure but of meaning […]. The size of the lake, now huge and full of frightening and repelling frogs, now puny and comical, can be explained both anatomically and as a representation of Beardsley's fluctuating attitude to a problem which loomed large in his mind'; Lavers, '"Aubrey Beardsley, Man of Letters"', p. 270. Lavers also compares the lake to 'a kind of hymen' which Tannhäuser hesitates to 'break with a pebble'; see '*L'eau Savante*' (part I).

[13] *Petits chevaux* (French for 'little horses') is a gambling game in which bets are placed on mechanical horses that rotate around a flag at the centre of a table. According to the *OED*, the phrase was first used in this sense in relation to the French resort preferred by English Decadents: 'Some of the most naughty of us will go and tempt fortune with the "petit[s] chevaux" — at Dieppe' (*Clown*, 9 June 1891, p. 13). Symons reminisced that *Under the Hill* was written in 1895 at Dieppe, where Beardsley fell under the spell of the local grand Casino: 'at night he was almost always to be seen watching the gamblers at *petits chevaux*, studying them with a sort of hypnotized attention for that picture of *The Little Horses* which was never done'; see Symons, *Aubrey Beardsley*, p. 8.

[14] French *croupier*, originally a person who rides behind on a horse's croup; hence, a person who stands behind a gambler providing advice, and now a person who rakes in and pays out the money or tokens at a gaming table.

[15] A *toque* (French) is a small hat with a full pouched crown and a narrow, closely turned-up brim, fashionable among both sexes in the sixteenth century; after *c.* 1880s, it denotes a small hat without a projecting brim, or with a very small or closely turned-up brim.

[16] A rouleau is a stack of coins wrapped in paper to form a roll (now rare).

[17] A rake is a tool used by a croupier for moving money or tokens staked at a gaming table.

[18] *Tableaux-magiques* literally means 'magic pictures' in French, but here has the meaning of a theatrical scene and probably means a conjuring show; *ombres fantastiques* means 'fantastic shadows' but, equally, here probably means shadow theatre.

[19] The following description of the concert in Venusberg is inspired by the scenes Beardsley witnessed in Dieppe. According to Symons, 'the benches of the concert-room when there was a band' was among Beardsley's favourite spots at the Casino in Dieppe, where he wrote most of his novel; Symons, 'Beardsley as a Man of Letters', p. 41. Beardsley 'rarely missed a concert, and would

This afternoon the piêce de resistance was a performance of Rossini's Stabat Mater & adorable masterpiece.[20] It was given in the beautiful Salle des printemps parfumés.[21] Ah! what a stunning rendering of the delicious demodé piece of decadence. There is a subtle quality about the music, like the unhealthy bloom upon wax fruit, that both orchestra & singer contrived to emphasize with consummate delicacy.[22]

The Virgin was sung by Spiridion that soft incomparable alto. A miraculous virgin too he made of her. To begin with he dressed the rôle most effectively. His plump legs up to the feminine hips of him were in very white stockings clocked with a false pink, he wore brown kid boots buttoned to mid-calf, & his whorish thighs had thin scarlet garters round them. His jacket was cut like a jockey's, only the sleeves ended in manifold frills & round the neck & just upon the shoulders there was a black cape. His hair, dyed green, was curled into ringlets such as the smooth Madonnas of Morales are made lovely with, & fell over his high egg-shaped creamy forehead & about his ears & cheeks & back.[23] The alto's face was fearful & wonderful. A dream face. The eyes were full & black with puffy blue rimmed hemispheres beneath them, the cheeks inclining to fatness were powdered & dimpled, the mouth was purple & curved painfully, the chin tiny & exquisitely modelled the expression cruel & womanish.[24]

Heavens how splendid he looked & sounded. An exquisite piece of phrasing was accompanied with some

---

glide in every afternoon, and sit on the high benches at the side'; Symons, *Aubrey Beardsley*, p. 9. As Fletcher notes, 'Venus's casino [...] is devoted to art as much as to hazard'; Fletcher, 'Inventions for the Left Hand', p. 243.

[20] *Pièce de résistance* is 'main dish' in French, but means 'most important or remarkable feature'.

[21] Literally, 'Room of scented springs'.

[22] *Stabat mater* is an ancient Christian hymn in Latin. Its opening line 'Stabat mater dolorosa' translates as 'Stood the sorrowful mother' — the place being at the foot of the cross where Christ is crucified. It has been set to music by at least fifty composers since the sixteenth century. Sutton argues that Beardsley wilfully misreads the operatic version of 1841 by Gioachino Rossini, a pillar of nineteenth-century operatic art and a counterpart to Richard Wagner, by 'making the music into something alien, morbid, and disturbing — something "Wagnerian" in its effects'; see Sutton, *Aubrey Beardsley and British Wagnerism*, pp. 159–60. *Démodé* (Beardsley omits the first accent) means outmoded or out of fashion. His comment may be taken to mean that Rossini's music is unsuited to the modern materialistic world of his own time and sheds interesting light on his attitude, here apparently positive, to the idea of Decadence as it emerged in the art and literature of the late nineteenth century.

[23] The sixteenth-century Spanish artist Luis de Morales gained such wide popularity in Spain for his religious paintings that he became known as El Divino. In 1887, the National Gallery in London acquired an example of a type of Madonna and child that Morales seems to have invented, in which the Christ child reaches a hand into his mother's dress for the breast he craves (*Virgin and Child*, *c.* 1565–1570). Beardsley would certainly have known this work, which prominently features a ringlet of the kind he mentions. It seems likely that he would also have been arrested by the gesture of the child's hand, as well as by the sophisticated 'smooth' beauty of the painting. Beardsley here identifies the highly refined style of the sixteenth century, Mannerism, of which Morales was an accomplished if provincial practitioner. As John Shearman notes in his authoritative reappraisal of the style, which had come to be considered marginal, Mannerism had been characterized as 'perverse and decadent'; see Shearman, *Mannerism* (London: Penguin, 1967), p. 16. He stresses however its emphasis on pure stylishness, on the artificiality of art, on 'works of art that are rarefied and idealized away from the natural: hothouse plants, cultured most carefully' (p. 19). All this refers us to the world of Huysmans, Wilde, and Beardsley. In Beardsley's time the National Gallery in London also already held what is now acknowledged as one of the most significant of all Mannerist paintings, *An Allegory with Venus and Cupid* (*c.* 1545) by Angelo Bronzino. Direct influence on Beardsley of this mysterious masterpiece of refined eroticism can be seen in the gesture of the hand of the musician in his *Toilette of Salome* (1893) and the figure of Cupid in the *Toilet of Lampito* (1895–1896), both among Beardsley's most sexually suggestive drawings. In art historical terms more generally, Beardsley may be said to be extending the tradition of Mannerism in both style and approach.

[24] Dowling (pp. 29–30) argues that Spiridion's appearance parodies Oscar Wilde, from the use of make-up to the symbolism of colours (green for the notorious green carnation) and popular caricatures of his overweight, decaying physique. If Dowling is right, then Beardsley has added to the insult by making Spiridion an alto; this can only mean that he was a castrato. Beardsley then goes even further to make Spiridion the passive focus of an extraordinary homosexual orgy. Fluhr points out the similarities between the images of Spiridion and Priapusa, equally marked by 'exaggerated embodiment'; see Fluhr, '"Queer Reverence"', paras 21–22. Beardsley's portrayal of Spiridion also evokes the appearance of the castrato Zaffirino in Vernon Lee's short story 'A Wicked Voice' (1887), which was based on the eighteenth-century castrato singer Farinelli (Carlo Broschi): 'That effeminate, fat face of his is almost beautiful, with an odd smile, brazen and cruel. I have seen faces like this, if not in real life, at least in my boyish romantic dreams, when I read Swinburne and Baudelaire, the faces of wicked, vindictive women'; see Vernon Lee, 'A Wicked Voice', in *Hauntings: Fantastic Stories* (London: W. Heinemann, 1890), pp. 193–237 (p. 206).

curly gesture of the hand, some delightful undulation of the stomach, some nervous movement of the thigh or glorious rising of the bosom. The performance provoked enthusiasm, thunders of applause. Claude & Clair pelted the thing with roses & carried him off in triumph to the tables. His costume was declared ravishing. The men almost pulled him to bits, & mouthed at his great quivering bottom. The little horses were quite forgotten for the moment. Sup the penetrating, burst through his silk fleshings, & thrust in bravely up to the hilt whilst the alto's legs were feasted upon by Pudex, Cyril, Anquetin, & some others. Ballice, Corvo, Quadra, Senillé, Mellefont, Theodore, Levit, Le Vit, & Matta, all of the egoistic cult, stood & crouched round saturating the lovers with warm douches.[25]

Later in the afternoon Venus & Tannhäuser paid a little visit to De La Pine's studio, as the Chevalier was very anxious to have his portrait painted. De La Pine's glory as a painter was hugely increased by his reputation as a fouteur, for ladies that had pleasant memories of him looked with a biassed eye upon his fêtes galantes, merveilleuses, portraits & folies bergères. Yes he was a bawdy creature & the workshop a regular brothel. However his great talent stood in no need of such meretricious & phallic support, & he was every whit as strong & facile with his brush as with his tool.[26]

When Venus & the Chevalier entered his studio, he was standing amid a group of friends & connoisseurs who were liking his latest picture.[27] It was a small canvas, one of his delightful morning pieces. Upon an Italian balcony stood a lady in a white frock, reading a letter. She wore brown stockings, straw-coloured petticoats, white shoes, and a Leghorn hat.[28] Her hair was red & in a chignon. At her feet lay a tiny Japanese dog, painted from the Queen's favourite 'Fanny', & upon the balustrade stood an open empty bird cage.[29] The background

---

[25] *Vit* is penis in French. Corvo is an evocation of 'Baron Corvo', the pseudonym of Frederick William Rolfe (1860–1913), a writer, artist, and Roman Catholic convert, whose 'literary sensibility', according to Hanson, presented 'a decadent mixture of the aesthetic, the pederastic, and the Catholic' (see Hanson, *Decadence and Catholicism*, p. 330). Baron Corvo's earliest tales were published in the *Yellow Book*; see Baron Corvo, 'Stories Toto Told Me', *Yellow Book*, 7 (1895), 209–24; Baron Corvo, 'Stories That Toto Told Me', *Yellow Book*, 11 (1896), 143–62. Dissident sexuality is especially prominent in the second instalment, in which the peasant boy Toto describes his personal experiences, for example a naked visit to a peach orchard: 'I ran away and enjoyed myself enough with the peaches. [...] When I came home I dried myself with a cloth, took my shirt from under the seat in the porch, and went to bed' ('Stories That Toto Told Me', p. 158). Evoked in this passage by Baron Corvo, masturbation is also implied by Beardsley's mention of the 'egoistic cult'.

[26] The French *pine* is synonymous with *vit* and means penis. Dowling (p. 32) identifies De La Pine's prototype as the artist Charles Conder, with whom Beardsley spent a lot of time in Dieppe in 1895, when he actively worked on his novel. Not only was Conder notorious for his 'sexual conquests', he was also a painter of fashionable *fêtes galantes* and a key artistic force behind the neo-rococo vogue at the *fin de siècle* (alongside Beardsley himself). The French *fouteur*, applied to De La Pine, translates literally as 'fucker', but carries the meaning of one who consistently and energetically pursues sexual intercourse and is skilled at it. Delvau defines the term as 'homme qui satisfait les femmes' ('a man who satisfies women'). The two other subjects of De La Pine's work are *merveilleuses*, that is, depictions of flamboyantly dressed aristocratic Frenchwomen of the Directory period, and *folies bergères*, a genre of Beardsley's invention which evokes the Parisian music hall Folies Bergère. Beardsley's punning association of the painter's brush (the tool of his trade) with the painter's tool (slang for penis) was probably not a new idea. Not long after Beardsley's death in 1898, it was to be crystallized in a famous comment by the Impressionist painter Pierre-Auguste Renoir, who towards the end of his life (he died in 1919) developed severe arthritis in his hands. When a journalist asked him how, with such hands, did he paint, Renoir replied 'Avec ma queue' ('with my prick'). This story is recorded by his son, the filmmaker Jean Renoir, in his biography of his father first published in 1962, but no doubt the journalist put it into circulation immediately. It appears in D. H. Lawrence's notorious, long banned or censored novel, *Lady Chatterley's Lover*, first published clandestinely in 1928. In a discussion about the nature of intelligence, a man remarks, 'The penis rouses his head and says: how do you do? — to any really intelligent person. Renoir said he painted his pictures with his penis'; see D. H. Lawrence, *Lady Chatterley's Lover* (London: Penguin Books, 1960), p. 41. Jean Renoir also comments in connection with this incident 'sa volupté d'homme devenait une volupté de peintre' ('his sensuality as a man became a sensuality of the painter'); Jean Renoir, *Pierre-Auguste Renoir Mon Père* (Paris: Editions Gallimard, 1981), p. 220. 'Meretricious' is derived from the Latin *meretrix*, meaning a prostitute.

[27] The remark embodies the attitude of artists that the sole function of the critic is positive appreciation of their work.

[28] 'Leghorn hat' refers to a wide-brimmed, flat-topped straw hat from Livorno (Leghorn in English) in Italy.

[29] Beardsley's description of the painting evokes the work of Conder. From Dutch seventeenth-century art to Jean-Batiste Greuze (*Girl with a Dead Canary*, 1765) and the Pre-Raphaelites (William Holman Hunt's *The Awakening Conscience*, 1853), the image

was a stretch of Gallic country. Clusters of trees cresting the ridges of low hills, a bit of river, a chateau, & the morning sky.

De La Pine hastened to kiss the moist & scented hand of Venus. Tannhäuser bowed profoundly & begged to have some pictures shown him. The gracious painter took him round his studio.

Cosmé was one of the party, for De La Pine just then was painting his portrait, a portrait by the way which promised to be a veritable chef d'oeuvre.[30] Cosmé was loved & admired by everybody. To begin with, he was past master in his art, that fine relevant art of coiffing, then he was really modest & obliging & was only seen & heard when he was wanted.[31] He was useful, he was decorative in his white apron, black mask, & silver suit, he was discreet.

The painter was giving Venus & Tannhäuser a little dinner that evening & he insisted on Cosmé joining them. The Barber vowed he would be de trop & required a world of pressing before he would accept the invitation.[32] Venus added her voice & he consented.

Ah I what a delightful little partie carré it turned out.[33] The painter was in purple & full dress, all tassels & grand folds. His hair magnificently curled, his heavy eye-lids painted, his gestures large & romantic, he reminded one a little of Maurel playing Wolfram in the second act of the opera of Wagner.[34] Venus was in a ravishing toilet, a confection of Camilles, & looked like Kxxxxx.[35] Tannhäuser was dressed as a woman & looked like a goddess. Cosmé sparkled with gold, bristled with ruffs, glittered with bright buttons, was painted, powdered, gorgeously bewigged, & looked like a marquis in a comic opera. The salle á manger at de La Pine's was quite the prettiest that ever was.[36] Upon

[Here the manuscript ends.]

---

of a caged bird has stood in a symbolic relation to the vision of female sexuality. The bird escaping from the cage, as depicted by De La Pine, often coded the loss of innocence; see Elaine Shefer, 'The "Bird in the Cage" in the History of Sexuality: Sir John Everett Millais and William Holman Hunt', *Journal of the History of Sexuality*, 1.3 (1991), 446–80. 'Fanny' was the adopted name of a notorious Victorian cross-dresser Frederick William Park, who was arrested with his accomplice Ernest Boulton (aka 'Stella') for wearing women's clothes in public at the Strand Theatre on 28 April 1870. In a widely publicized trial, which became a national scandal, Fanny and Stella were charged with 'conspiracy [...] to persuade persons unknown to commit buggery'; see Neil McKenna, *Fanny and Stella: The Young Men Who Shocked Victorian England* (London: Faber, 2013), p. 288. Another possible source for 'Fanny' is John Cleland's erotic novel *Fanny Hill*, first published in 1748–1749 as *Memoirs of a Woman of Pleasure*. The novel provides a detailed account of the life of a London prostitute and, condemned as pornography, was circulated clandestinely. Queen Victoria was portrayed with her dog, named Fanny, in Richard Westall's painting of 1830 *Queen Victoria as a Girl*. The subject's straw hat also features in the picture. The portrait was reproduced on the front page of *Illustrated London News* on 13 February 1892. In addition, 'fanny' has been used as a slang term for female genitals since the nineteenth century.

30 *Chef d'oeuvre* is a masterpiece in French.

31 Cosmé mirrors another literary character created by Beardsley, Carrousel from 'The Ballad of the Barber', who 'cut, and coiffed, and shaved so well | That all the world was at his feet'.

32 *De trop* means unwanted, unnecessary.

33 The French *partie carré* means a party of four or a foursome.

34 Victor Maurel was the French baritone who performed regularly in London in the early 1890s. Beardsley refers to his role as Tannhäuser's friend Wolfram and his song in praise of Platonic love in the second act of Wagner's opera, thus producing a paradoxical contrast with the depraved character of De La Pine.

35 Lavers suggests that 'Kxxxxx' could refer to Kitty Savile Clark, a professional beauty and a friend of Beardsley, who is a probable prototype of one of the figures in *The Bathers* (*On Dieppe Beach*, 1895); see Lavers, '*L'eau Savante*' (part II).

36 The French *salle á* [*sic*] *manger* means dining-room.

FIG. 1. *The Abbé* (1895, *CR* 999), reproduced from the *Savoy*, January 1896, p. 157.

Fig. 2. *The Toilet of Helen* (1895, *CR* 1000), reproduced from the *Savoy*, January 1896, p. 161.

FIG. 3. *The Fruit Bearers* (1895, *CR* 1001), reproduced from the *Savoy*, January 1896, p. 167.

FIG. 4. *The Ascension of Saint Rose of Lima* (1896, *CR* 1005), reproduced from the *Savoy*, April 1896, p. 189.

FIG. 5. *For the Third Tableau of Das Rheingold* (1896, *CR* 1006), reproduced from the *Savoy*, April 1896, p. 193.

CREATIVE EXPURGATION

'Chapter IV' for the *Savoy*

This chapter represents parts of the original manuscript that had to be significantly cut and rewritten to make publication in the *Savoy* (April 1896) possible. It notably includes an entirely fresh and important passage, not in the manuscript, of thoughts about Wagner's *Das Rheingold*. It still incorporates some fragments from the fourth chapter of the manuscript, as well as the first part of the Bacchanals of Fanfreluche from the third chapter, which became here the Bacchanals of Sporion. These are presented in the form of what Annette Lavers calls 'seemingly erudite footnotes' to the main text, in fact written by Beardsley himself. As Lavers observes, they may be regarded as 'a device Beardsley had probably come upon in that seventeenth- and eighteenth-century fiction he so relished'.[1] In his letter of 10 April 1896, Beardsley instructs Smithers: 'Don't let the footnotes get printed as anything but footnotes. As the Bacchanals purport to be nothing but a quotation from another book the asterisks can be left in without any offence'.[2] We also learn from the letters that Beardsley intended to illustrate the Bacchanals in the *Savoy* chapter in the style of 'the last century' and even ordered 'a copy of Hazlitt's essays' to complete the lettering, but this drawing was not finished.[3] Beardsley's footnotes, which he insisted on preserving as footnotes, are here numbered with Roman numerals in order to differentiate them from our annotations, which are presented as endnotes (numbered with Arabic numerals). Beardsley's footnotes are also italicized, as they appear in the *Savoy*. We do not repeat annotations for text that has been glossed in the annotated version above.

~

Under the Hill
A Romantic Story
Chapter IV

It is always delightful to wake up in a new bedroom. The fresh wall-paper, the strange pictures, the positions of doors and windows, imperfectly grasped the night before, are revealed with all the charm of surprise when we open our eyes the next morning.

It was about eight o'clock when Fanfreluche awoke, stretched himself deliciously in his great plumed four-post bed, murmured 'What a pretty room!' and freshened the frilled silk pillows behind him. Through the slim parting of the long flowered window curtains, he caught a peep of the sun-lit lawns outside, the silver fountains, the bright flowers, the gardeners at work, and beneath the shady trees some early breakfasters, dressed for a day's hunting in the distant wooded valleys.

'How sweet it all is', exclaimed the Abbé, yawning with infinite content. Then he lay back in his bed, stared at the curious patterned canopy above him and nursed his waking thoughts. He thought of the 'Romaunt de la Rose', beautiful, but all too brief.[4]

Of the Claude in Lady Delaware's[5] collection.[i]

Of a wonderful pair of blonde trousers he would get Madame Belleville to make for him.[6]

Of a mysterious park full of faint echoes and romantic sounds.

Of a great stagnant lake that must have held the subtlest frogs that ever were, and was surrounded with dark unreflected trees, and sleeping fleurs de luce.

Of Saint Rose, the well-known Peruvian virgin; how she vowed herself to perpetual virginity when she was four years old;[ii] how she was beloved by Mary, who from the pale fresco in the Church of Saint Dominic, would stretch out her arms to embrace her; how she built a little oratory at the end of the garden and prayed and sang hymns in it till all the beetles, spiders, snails and creeping things came round to listen; how she promised to marry Ferdinand de Flores, and on the bridal morning perfumed herself and painted her lips, and put on her wedding frock, and decked her hair with roses, and went up to a little hill not far without the walls of Lima;

---

[i] The chef d'oeuvre, *it seems to me, of an adorable and impeccable master, who more than any other landscape-painter puts us out of conceit with our cities, and makes us forget the country can be graceless and dull and tiresome. That he should ever have been compared unfavourably with Turner — the Wiertz of landscape-painting — seems almost incredible. Corot is Claude's only worthy rival, but he does not eclipse or supplant the earlier master. A painting of Corot's is like an exquisite lyric poem, full of love and truth; whilst one of Claude's recalls some noble eclogue glowing with rich concentrated thought.*

[ii] *'At an age', writes Dubonnet, 'when girls are for the most part well confirmed in all the hateful practices of coquetry, and attend with gusto, rather than with distaste, the hideous desires and terrible satisfactions of men'.*

All who would respire the perfumes of Saint Rose's sanctity, and enjoy the story of the adorable intimacy that subsisted between her and Our Lady, should read Mother Ursula's 'Ineffable and Miraculous Life of the Flower of Lima', published shortly after the canonization of Rose by Pope Clement X in 1671. 'Truly', exclaims the famous nun, 'to chronicle the girlhood of this holy virgin makes as delicate a task as to trace the forms of some slim, sensitive plant, whose lightness, sweetness, and simplicity defy and trouble the most cunning pencil'. Mother Ursula certainly acquits herself of the task with wonderful delicacy and taste. A cheap reprint of the biography has lately been brought out by Chaillot and Son.

how she knelt there some moments calling tenderly upon Our Lady's name, and how Saint Mary descended and kissed Rose upon the forehead and carried her up swiftly into heaven.[7]

He thought of the splendid opening of Racine's 'Britannicus'.[8]

Of a strange pamphlet he had round in Helen's library, called 'A Plea for the Domestication of the Unicorn'.[9]

Of the 'Bacchanals of Sporion'.[iii]

[iii] *A comedy ballet in one act by Philippe Savaral and Titurel de Schentefleur. The Marquis de Vandésir, who was present at the first performance, has left us a short impression of it in his* Mémoires.

[What follows is the first part of the Bacchanals of Fanfreluche from Chapter III, here renamed the Bacchanals of Sporion]

The curtain rose upon a scene of rare beauty, a remote Arcadian valley, a delicious scrap of Tempe, gracious with cool woods and watered with a little river as fresh and pastoral as a perfect fifth. It was early morning and the re-arisen sun, like the prince in the Sleeping Beauty, woke all the earth with his lips.

In that golden embrace the night dews were caught up and made splendid, the trees were awakened from their obscure dreams, the slumber of the birds was broken, and all the flowers of the valley rejoiced, forgetting their fear of the darkness. Suddenly to the music of pipe and horn a troop of satyrs stepped out from the recesses of the woods bearing in their hands nuts and green boughs and flowers and roots, and whatsoever the forest yielded, to heap upon the altar of the mysterious Pan that stood in the middle of the stage; and from the hills came down the shepherds and shepherdesses leading their flocks and carrying garlands upon their crooks. Then a rustic priest, white robed and venerable, came slowly across the valley followed by a choir of radiant children. The scene was admirably stage-managed and nothing could have been more varied yet harmonious than this Arcadian group. The service was quaint and simple, but with sufficient ritual to give the corps de ballet an opportunity of showing its dainty skill. The dancing of the satyrs was received with huge favour, and when the priest raised his hand in final blessing, the whole troop of worshippers made such an intricate and elegant exit, that it was generally agreed that Titurel had never before shown so fine an invention.

Scarcely had the stage been empty for a moment, when Sporion entered, followed by a brilliant rout of dandies and smart women. Sporion was a tall, slim, depraved young man with a slight stoop, a troubled walk, an oval impassable face with its olive skin drawn lightly over the bone, strong, scarlet lips, long Japanese eyes, and a great gilt toupet. Round his shoulders hung a high-collared satin cape of salmon pink with long black ribbands untied and floating about his body. His coat of sea green spotted muslin was caught in at the waist by a scarlet sash with scalloped edges and frilled out over the hips for about six inches. His trousers, loose and wrinkled, reached to the end of the calf, and were brocaded down the sides and ruched magnificently at the ankles. The stockings were of white kid with stalls for the toes, and had delicate red sandals strapped over them. But his little hands, peeping out from their frills, seemed quite the most insinuating things, such supple fingers tapering to the point with tiny nails stained pink, such unquenchable palms lined and mounted like Lord Fanny's in 'Love at all Hazards', and such blue-veined hairless backs! In his left hand he carried a small lace handkerchief broidered with a coronet.

As for his friends and followers, they made the most superb and insolent crowd imaginable, but to catalogue the clothes they had on would require a chapter as long as the famous tenth in Pénillière's 'History of Underlinen'. On the whole they looked a very distinguished chorus.

Sporion stepped forward and explained with swift and various gesture that he and his friends were tired of the amusements, wearied with the poor pleasures offered by the civil world, and had invaded the Arcadian valley hoping to experience a new frisson in the destruction of some shepherd's or some satyr's naivete and the infusion of their venom among the dwellers of the woods.

The chorus assented with languid but expressive movements.

Curious and not a little frightened at the arrival of the worldly company, the sylvans began to peep nervously at those subtle souls through the branches of the trees, and one or two fauns and a shepherd or so crept out warily. Sporion and all the ladies and gentlemen made enticing sounds and invited the rustic creatures with all the grace in the world to come and join them. By little batches they came, lured by the strange looks, by the scents and the drugs, and by the brilliant clothes, and some ventured quite near, timorously fingering the delicious textures of the stuffs. Then Sporion and each of his friends took a satyr or a shepherdess or something by the hand and made the preliminary steps of a courtly measure, for which the most admirable combinations had been invented and the most charming music written. The pastoral folk were entirely bewildered when they saw such restrained and graceful movements, and made the most grotesque and futile efforts to imitate them. Dio mio, a pretty sight! A charming effect too, was obtained by the intermixture of stockinged calf and hairy leg, of rich brocaded bodice and plain blouse, of tortured head-dress and loose untutored locks.

When the dance was ended the servants of Sporion brought on champagne, and with many pirouettes poured it magnificently into slender glasses, and tripped about plying those Arcadian mouths that had never before tasted such a royal drink.

* * * * * *

Then the curtain fell with a pudic rapidity.

Of Morales' Madonnas with their high egg-shaped creamy foreheads and well-crimped silken hair. Of Rossini's 'Stabat Mater' (that delightful *demodé* piece of decadence, with a quality in its music like the bloom upon wax fruit).

Of love, and of a hundred other things.

Then his half-closed eyes wandered among the prints that hung upon the rose-striped walls. Within the delicate curved frames lived the corrupt and gracious creatures of Dorat and his school, slender children in masque and domino smiling horribly, exquisite letchers leaning over the shoulders of smooth doll-like girls and doing nothing in particular, terrible little Pierrots posing as lady lovers and pointing at something outside the picture, and unearthly fops and huge bird-like women mingling in some rococo room, lighted mysteriously by the flicker of a dying fire that throws great shadows upon wall and ceiling. Fanfreluche had taken some books to bed with him. One was the witty, extravagant, 'Tuesday and Josephine', another was the score of 'The Rheingold'.[10] Making a pulpit of his knees he propped up the opera before him and turned over the pages with a loving hand, and found it delicious to attack Wagner's brilliant comedy with the cool head of the morning.[iv] Once more he was ravished with the beauty and wit of the opening scene;[11] the mystery of its prelude that seems to come up from the very mud of the Rhine, and to be as ancient, the abominable primitive wantonness of the music that follows the talk and movements of the Rhine-maidens, the black, hateful sounds of Alberic's love-making, and the flowing melody of the river of legends.[12]

But it was the third tableau that he applauded most that morning, the scene where Loge, like some flamboyant primeval Scapin, practises his cunning upon Alberic.[13] The feverish insistent ringing of the hammers at the forge, the dry staccato restlessness of Mime,[14] the ceaseless coming and going of the troup of Niblungs [*sic*], drawn hither and thither like a flock of terror-stricken and infernal sheep, Alberic's savage activity and metamorphoses, and Loge's rapid, flaming tongue-like movements, make the tableau the least reposeful, most troubled and confusing thing in the whole range of opera. How the Abbé rejoiced in the extravagant monstrous poetry, the heated melodrama, and splendid agitation of it all!

At eleven o'clock Fanfreluche got up and slipped off his dainty night-dress.

His bathroom was the largest and perhaps the most beautiful apartment in his splendid suite. The well-known engraving by Lorette that forms the frontispiece to Millevoye's 'Architecture du XVIIIme siècle' will give you a better idea than any words of mine of the construction and decoration of the room. Only in Lorette's engraving the bath sunk into the middle of the floor is a little too small. Fanfreluche stood for a moment like Narcissus gazing at his reflection in the still scented water, and then just ruffling its smooth surface with one foot, stepped elegantly into the cool basin and swam round it twice very gracefully.

However, it is not so much at the very bath itself as in the drying and delicious frictions that a bather finds his chiefest joys, and Helen had appointed her most tried attendants to wait upon Fanfreluche. He was more than satisfied with their attention, that aroused feelings within him almost amounting to gratitude, and when the rites were ended any touch of home-sickness he might have felt was utterly dispelled. After he had rested a little, and sipped his chocolate, he wandered into the dressing room, where, under the direction of the superb Dancourt, his toilet was completed.

As pleased as Lord Foppington with his appearance, the Abbé tripped off to bid good-morning to Helen.[15] He found her in a sweet white muslin frock, wandering upon the lawn, and plucking flowers to deck her breakfast table. He kissed her lightly upon the neck.

'I'm just going to feed Adolphe', she said, pointing to a little reticule of buns that hung from her arm. Adolphe was her pet unicorn. 'He is such a dear', she continued; 'milk-white all over excepting his black eyes, rose mouth & nostrils. *This* way'. The unicorn had a very pretty palace of its own made of green foliage and golden bars, a fitting home for such a delicate and dainty beast. Ah, it was a splendid thing to watch the white creature roaming

---

[iv] *It is a thousand pities that concerts should only be given either in the afternoon, when you are torpid, or in the evening, when you are nervous. Surely you should assist at fine music as you assist at the Mass — before noon — when your brain and heart are not too troubled and tired with the secular influences of the growing day.*

in its artful cage, proud and beautiful, knowing no mate, and coming to no hand except the queen's itself. As Fanfreluche and Helen approached, Adolphe began prancing and curvetting, pawing the soft turf with his ivory hoofs and flaunting his tail like a gonfalon. Helen raised the latch and entered.

'You mustn't come in with me, Adolphe is so jealous', she said, turning to the Abbe, who was following her, 'but you can stand outside and look on; Adolphe likes an audience'. Then in her delicious fingers she broke the spicy buns and with affectionate niceness breakfasted her snowy pet. When the last crumbs had been scattered, Helen brushed her hands together and pretended to leave the cage without taking any further notice of Adolphe. Adolphe snorted.

Notes

[1] Lavers, '"Aubrey Beardsley, Man of Letters"', p. 247.

[2] *Letters of Aubrey Beardsley*, p. 124. At the end of Beardsley's long note describing the Bacchanals is a line of asterisks, a common way of indicating the omission of potentially offensive material, and in fact they represent the orgy that is described at this point in Chapter III. Beardsley's comment on the 'pudic rapidity' of the curtain, combined with the asterisks, would have alerted readers of the *Savoy* to the fact that something unprintable had taken place.

[3] See Beardsley to Smithers, 8 and 10 April 1896, *Letters of Aubrey Beardsley*, pp. 123, 126. William Hazlitt was an English essayist and art critic. It is not entirely clear what Beardsley meant by this; perhaps he needed a quotation from Hazlitt to inscribe on the drawing.

[4] The *Romaunt* is famous for many things but not its brevity: the first part alone (by Guillaume de Lorris) runs for four thousand lines.

[5] 'Lady Delaware' might allude to the Countess De La Warr, wife of the 7th Earl De La Warr. We were unable to identify whether she owned works by Claude. In his own note here Beardsley discusses the relationship of Claude to Turner, bringing into play an understanding of the history of art. The French painter known as Claude was and remains revered as the founding father of landscape painting in the Western tradition. He was a key influence on the English landscapist Turner (Joseph Mallord William Turner) who in turn is revered as one of the greatest of all English painters. There may well have been commentators who saw Turner as surpassing Claude in some of his works. Turner's own attitude may be revealed in the bequest he made to the National Gallery, London, of two of his paintings to be hung alongside two specified paintings by Claude. His probable intention was to show that British artists could at least match the finest achievements of the Old Masters. Beardsley would have been able to see this group at the National Gallery and might have had it in mind when he wrote his comment. After a hiatus in the mid-twentieth century, the group once again hangs permanently in the National Gallery (Room 15), so visitors may judge for themselves. On the face of it, Beardsley's jibe that Turner was the 'Wiertz' of landscape painting is laughable, but it contains grains of truth that validate it as a witty and informed bon-mot. A complex and fascinating figure, the Belgian painter Anton Wiertz is now almost completely forgotten, although there is a museum of his work in his former studio in Brussels. He took to a final climactic extreme the then dominant concept of 'history painting' as the highest form of art, just before the advent of Impressionism swept it away. His gigantic, hugely overblown, moralising canvases of historical and Biblical subjects, intended for the education of the public, represent the diametric opposite of modern taste. The grain of truth in Beardsley's comparison of Wiertz with Turner lies in the facts that Turner achieved his enormous success partly by adapting to landscape the tradition of 'history', and that he was given to creating visual effects that were seen at the time as overblown. The French painter Jean-Baptiste Camille Corot is seen as a forerunner of Impressionism and Beardsley's comments on him, and his relationship to Claude, remain acute.

[6] *Belleville* means 'beautiful town' in French and is the name of a notorious working-class district of Paris, famous particularly for the role it played in both the Revolution of 1848 and the Paris Commune revolt of 1871.

[7] St Rose of Lima, the first saint of America, canonized in 1671. She took a vow of virginity and joined the Third Order of St Dominic. She was famous for her asceticism and extreme forms of self-inflicted suffering, undergone as a form of mortification before the mystical marriage with Christ. Described in detail in *The Life of Saint Rose of Lima* (1847), translated from French and edited by Frederic William Faber, her austerities scandalized English Catholics. *Dolman's Magazine* criticized Faber's decision to dwell on St Rose's 'extravagant modes of self-inflected torture', fearing that the account might inspire religious excesses. Nonetheless, the magazine quoted at length from the descriptions of St Rose's self-punishments and 'extraordinary miracles', including the following passage on her adoration of a statue of the Blessed Virgin: 'St. Rose spent some time every day in prayer before the altar on which this image was placed, with very great devotion, which increased more and more in her heart as she perceived that this inanimate statue cast towards her looks of tenderness, and made certain signs as if it wished to caress her, and manifest to her by these miraculous movements, the love which the Blessed Virgin, of whom it was but the copy, bore to her' ('The Saints and Servants of God', *Dolman's Magazine*, September 1848, pp. 175–83 (pp. 180, 181)). Beardsley's account of St Rose's devotion to the statue of the Virgin seems to draw on this sensual fragment, which he certainly knew, possibly in the original French, since he owned and was deeply attached to his two-volume folio edition of the *Lives of the Saints* in French; see *Letters of Aubrey Beardsley*, pp. 380, 432. Fletcher suggests that Beardsley's representation of St Rose's ascent was based on 'the

seventeenth-century accounts of her acts and miracles'; see Fletcher, 'Inventions for the Left Hand', p. 237. The effigy of St Rose of Lima is held in the Basilica of Santo Domingo, Lima, to which Beardsley alludes as the Church of Saint Dominic.

[8] *Britannicus* (first performed in 1669, published in 1670) is a tragedy in verse in five acts by Jean Racine. It tells the story of the first crime of the Roman emperor Nero. The trigger for this crime is his lust for Junie, the fiancée of his half-brother Britannicus. When Junie rejects his advances Nero blackmails her by threatening to kill Britannicus if she does not submit. She refuses, Nero poisons Britannicus, Julie flees to the safety of the temple of Vesta, and Nero's powerful mother, Agrippina, appalled by his behaviour, which she had opposed, curses him. An embittered and thwarted Nero turns from being a wise ruler to the notorious tyrant of history. In the opening scenes of the play Agrippina seeks to confront her son over his abduction of Junie. He refuses to see her. She goes to Britannicus, tells him what has happened and offers her support against Nero, thus setting in motion the tragedy.

[9] This fictitious pamphlet evokes the unpublishable passage in the manuscript treating the Queen's morning visit to her pet unicorn Adolphe.

[10] *The Rheingold* (*Das Rheingold*) is an opera in four scenes by Richard Wagner, composed in 1853–1854, first performed in 1869. It constitutes the Prologue or 'preliminary evening' (*Vorabend*) in his operatic cycle *The Ring* (*Der Ring des Nibelungen*). The tetralogy is based on the Scandinavian saga featuring gods and mortals.

[11] By defining Wagner's opera as a 'brilliant comedy' and underscoring its 'wit', Beardsley 'undercuts its mythic grandeur'; see Sutton, *Aubrey Beardsley and British Wagnerism*, p. 156. Beardsley planned to produce his own version of *Das Rheingold* 'in story form', subversively titled *The Comedy of the Rhinegold*; see Beardsley to Smithers, 16, 17, and 18 September in *Letters of Aubrey Beardsley*, pp. 164, 167. Although the project remained unrealized, a number of illustrations for it appeared in the *Savoy*. Thus, Chapter IV of 'Under the Hill' in the April issue included Beardsley's image of Loge, called *For the Third Tableau of 'Das Rheingold'*; Aubrey Beardsley, 'Under the Hill', *Savoy*, April 1896, pp. 187–96 (p. 193).

[12] Alberich is the Nibelung dwarf. He lustfully chases the Rhinemaidens until he sees the gold that they guard. From one of the daughters of the Rhine, Woglinde, he learns that whoever forges a ring from the gold will rule the world but will have to renounce love. Alberich curses love, steals the gold, and sets in motion Wagner's tetralogy.

[13] Loge is the God of Fire, distinguished by his cunning. Sutton suggests that Beardsley shared Loge's 'dispassionate amusement at the follies of the characters' and even identified with this hero who, like the consumptive author himself, burnt 'always with this hard, gem-like flame' (*Aubrey Beardsley and British Wagnerism*, p. 177, 181). Scapin is the title character of Moliere's *Scapin the Schemer* (*Les Fourberies de Scapin*, 1671), a trickster and a liar. According to Sutton, Beardsley's link to the French farcical comedy of intrigue again serves to undermine the serious effect of Wagner's opera (p. 137).

[14] Mime is the brother of Alberich and a skilful goldsmith. It is Mime who makes the Ring and a magical helmet from the Rhine's gold.

[15] Lord Foppington is a character in John Vanburgh's comedy *The Relapse* (1696), later adapted by Richard Brinsley Sheridan into a musical play *A Trip to Scarborough* (1777) with considerable modifications as well as added songs and music.

DIPLOMATIC TRANSCRIPTION

Symbols used in Transcription

[<] [>] Surround text inserted by Beardsley later into a line

< > Surround the original editors' marks in the manuscript

<X> The original editor's marginal mark indicating substitution of a word or name; occurs often in the chapters published in the *Savoy*. The word to be changed was underlined. These marks occur in both left and right margins of the pages and the position is indicated by the position of the mark in this text. These changes are tracked in our footnotes. If the change was not made there is no note.

[ ] Surround our comments

[?] Precedes a word that is difficult to decipher

<·x·> Beardsley's mark indicating an insertion of a textual fragment

See Note on the Texts above for a discussion of our editorial practices.

<1>

Under the Hill
A romantic novel
By
Aubrey Beardsley[1]
with his illustrations & ornaments
Chaps. I II III IV V[2]

< end 51 >[3]

<2>

La chaleur du brandon Venus
Le Roman de la Rose, v. 22051[4]

---

[1] The first three lines (excluding 'By') have numbers 1, 2, and 3 against them on the right but not in the margin.
[2] All pages of the manuscript are numbered in the top right corner, in Arabic numerals; the handwriting does not seem to belong to Beardsley and resembles that of Leonard Smithers.
[3] The title page appears on p. 151 in SV. The editorial mark indicates the end of the text on that page.
[4] Underlined for italics by the editor.

<3>

[top right corner, in mauve ink:]
<this page in small caps.>

To the most Eminent & Revered Prince
Giulio Poldo Pizzoli
Cardinal of the Holy Roman Church
Titular Bishop of S. Maria in Trastavere
Archbishop of Ostia & Velletri
Nuncio to The Holy See
in
Nicaragua & Patagonia
A father to the poor
A reformer of Ecclesiastical Discipline
A pattern of Learning
Wisdom & Holiness of life,
This book is dedicated with due reverence
by his humble servitor
a scrivener & limner of worldly things
who made this book
Aubrey Beardsley[1]
[?]M [?] D C[2]

[seven lines crossed out by Beardsley]

<4>

I[3]

[partly illegible mark on the margins in mauve ink:] <[ital]ic type [lower] case>[4]

Most Eminent Prince,

I know not by what mischance the writing of epistles dedicatory has fallen into disuse, whether through the vanity of authors or the humility of patrons. But the practice seems to me so very beautiful & becoming that I have ventured to make an essay in the modest art & lay with formalities

[1] The name is marked for capitalization by the editor.
[2] This could be the beginning of the date in Roman numerals (MDC).
[3] The five manuscript sheets containing the dedication are numbered with Roman numerals in the top right corner by Beardsley.
[4] In LS, the dedication page is headed by the capitalized lines 'To | the Most Eminent and Reverend Prince | Giulio Poldo Pezzoli'. That is, Smithers changed Beardsley's 'Pizzoli' to 'Pezzoli' (see p. 24, note 3).

<5>

II

my first book at your feet. I have it must be confessed many fears lest I shall be arraigned of presumption in choosing so exalted a name as your own to place at the beginning of [four words crossed out by Beardsley] [<]this history[>], but I hope that such a censure will not be too lightly passed upon me for if I am guilty, t'is but of a most natural pride that the accidents of my life should allow me to sail the little pinnace of my wit under your protection.[5]

But though I can clear myself of such a charge I am still minded to use the tongue of apology, for with what face can I offer you a book treating of so vain & fantastical a thing as love? I know that in the judgment of many the amorous passion is accounted a shameful thing & ridiculous, indeed it must be confessed that more blushes have risen for love's sake than for any other cause, & that lovers are an eternal laughing-stock. Still as the book will be found to contain matter of deeper import than mere venery, inasmuch as it treats of the great contrition of its chiefest character & of canonical things in certain pages I am not without hopes that your Eminence will pardon[6]

<6>

III

my writing of the <X> Hill of Venus, for which exposition let [<]my[>] youth excuse me.[7]

Then I must crave your forgiveness for addressing you in a language other than the Roman, but my small freedom in Latinity forbids me to wander beyond the idiom of my vernacular. I would not for the world that your delicate Southern ear should be offended by a barbarous assault of rude & gothic words, but methinks no language is rude that can boast polite writers, & not a few have flourished in this country in times past, bringing our common speech to very great perfection. In the present age, alas! our pens are ravished by unlettered authors & unmannered critics, that make a havoc rather than a building, a wilderness rather than a garden. But alack what boots it to drop tears upon the preterit?

T'is not of our own shortcomings though, but of your own great merits that I should speak, else I should be forgetful of the duties I have drawn upon myself in electing to address you in a dedication. T'is of your noble virtues (though all the world know of 'em), your

<7>

IV

taste & wit, your care for letters & very real regard for the arts, that I must be the proclaimer.

Though it be true that all men have sufficient wit to pass a judgment on this or that, & not a few sufficient impudence to print the same (these last being commonly accounted critics), I have ever held that the critical faculty is more rare than the inventive. T'is a faculty your Eminence possesses in so great a degree that your praise or blame is something oracular, your utterance infallible as great genius or as a beautiful woman. Your mind, I know, rejoicing in fine distinctions & subtle procedures of thought, beautifully discursive rather than hastily conclusive, has found in criticism its happiest exercise. T'is pity that so perfect a Mecaenas[8]<X> should

5 'this history' = 'these histories' (LS); 't'is' = 'it is' (in SV, JL here and below).

6 'in certain pages' = 'in its chapters' (SV, LS). JL follows the manuscript.

7 'writing of a loving Abbé' (SV, JL); 'exposition' = 'extravagance' (SV, JL).

8 The underlining for change was scribbled through and the change was not made.

have no Horace to befriend, no Georgics to accept; for the offices & function of patron or critic must of necessity be lessened in an age of little men & little work. In times past t'was nothing derogatory for great princes & men of State to extend their loves & favour to poets, for thereby they received as much honour as they conferred. Did not Prince

<8>

V

Festus with pride take the master-work of Julian into his protection, & was not the Aeneis a pretty thing to offer Caesar?

Learning without appreciation is a thing of nought, but I know not which is greatest in you, your love of the arts or your knowledge of 'em. What wonder, then, that I am studious to please you & desirous of your protection? How deeply thankful I am for your past affections, you know well, your great kindness & liberality having far outgone my slight merits & small accomplishment that seemed scarce to warrant any favour. Alas! T'is a slight offering I make you now, but, if after glancing into its pages (say of an evening upon your terrace) you should deem it worthy of the most remotest place in your princely library, the knowledge that it rested there would be reward sufficient for my labours & a crowning happiness to my pleasure in the writing of this slender book.

The humble & obedient servant of Your Eminence,
Aubrey Beardsley —

<9>

Under the Hill
Chapter I[9]

The Abbé ~~Aubrey~~ [<]Fanfreluche[>] having lighted off his horse, stood doubtfully for a moment beneath the ombre gateway of the Hill of Venus <X>, troubled with an exquisite fear lest a day's travel should have too cruelly undone the laboured niceness of his dress.[10] His hand slim & gracious as La Marquise du Deffand's in the drawing by Carmontelle, played nervously about the gold hair that fell upon his shoulders like a finely curled peruke, & from point to point of a precise toilet the fingers wandered, quelling the little mutinies of cravat & ruffle.

It was taper time; when the tired earth puts on its cloak of mists & shadows, when the enchanted woods are stirred with light footfalls & slender voices of the fairies, when all the air is full of delicate influences, & even the beaux, seated at their dressing tables, dream a little.

A delicious moment, thought ~~Aubrey~~ [<]Fanfreluche[>], to slip into exile.

---

[9] Underlining for italics (deleted), a mark for capitalization added. In LS, the chapter is titled 'How the Chevalier Tannhäuser Entered into the Hill of Venus'. The opening page was rewritten by Beardsley and inserted into the manuscript at a later stage. The margins here are wider than in other sheets and lined off in brown ink, while in the rest of the manuscript the lineation is purple.

[10] A large descending 'T' in Smithers's hand precedes the line (added in SV). 'Abbé Aubrey' = 'Abbé Fanfreluche' (SV, JL), 'Chevalier Tannhäuser' (LS); 'of Venus' is underlined and marked with an X in the margin. In SV, it is substituted with 'the mysterious Hill', which is transformed into the 'Venusberg' in LS.

<10>

The place ~~were~~ [<]where[>] he stood waved drowsily with strange flowers, heavy with perfume, dripping with odours.[11] Gloomy & nameless weeds, not to be found in Mentzelius. Huge moths so richly winged they must have banqueted upon tapestries & royal stuffs, slept on the pillars that flanked either side of the gateway, & the eyes of all the moths remained open, & were burning & bursting with a mesh of veins. The pillars were fashioned in some pale stone & rose up like hymns in the praise of Venus, for from cap to base each one was carved with loving sculptures showing such a cunning invention & such a curious knowledge that Tannhäuser <X> lingered not a little in reviewing them.[12] They surpassed all that Japan has ever pictured from her maisons vertes, all that was ever painted on the ~~infamous~~ [<]pretty[>] bathrooms of Cardinal La Motte & even outdid the astonishing illustrations to Jones' Sidelights on child life.[13] <X>

'A pretty portal', murmured the Knight, correcting his sash.[14]

As he spoke a faint sound of singing

<11>

was breathed out from the mountain, faint music as strange & distant as sea-legends that are heard in shells.

'The Vespers of <X> Venus, I take it', said <X> Tannhäuser & struck a few chords of accompaniment ever so lightly upon his little lute.[15] Softly across the spell-bound threshold the song floated & wreathed itself about the subtle columns till the moths were touched with passion & moved quaintly in their sleep. One of them was awakened by the intenser notes of the Chevalier's lute-strings & fluttered into his cave.[16] <X> Tannhäuser felt it was his cue for entry.[17]

'Adieu' he exclaimed with an inclusive gesture, & 'Good-bye Madonna', as the cold circle of the moon began to show, beautiful & full of enchantments. There was a shadow of sentiment in his voice as he spoke the words.

'Would to heaven' he sighed, 'I might receive the assurance of a looking glass before I make my début! However as she is a goddess I doubt not her eyes are a little sated with perfection & may not be displeased

<12>

to see it crowned with a tiny fault'.

A wild rose had caught upon the trimmings of his <X> muff, & in the first flush of displeasure he would have struck it brusquely away, & most severely punished the offending flower.[18] But the ruffled mood lasted only a moment, for there was something so deliciously incongruous in the hardy petal's invasion of so delicate a thing,

---

[11] The BE fragment starts with this sentence. The fragment is numbered with the Roman numeral I in the top left corner. In BE, the spelling mistake in 'where' is corrected, indicating that the fragment belongs to the rewriting of the original first chapter which was undertaken by Beardsley to prepare the manuscript for publication in SV and elude Lane by correcting the names of the chief characters. The paper is similar to the paper on which the first page of the first chapter of the Rosenbach manuscript is rewritten (see note 13). The margins on the right side of the BE fragment are wider (presumably, Beardsley cut the margins of the first page so that it could fit within his folder).

[12] 'Tannhäuser' = 'Aubrey' (BE).

[13] In BE, 'pretty' is crossed out, 'cool' is written on top in Beardsley's hand; 'pretty' is written in Smithers's hand on top of that; 'infamous bathrooms' = 'cool bath-rooms' (SV, JL); 'bathrooms' (LS). 'Sidelights on child life' = 'Nursery Numbers' (BE, SV, JL, LS).

[14] 'the Knight' = 'the Abbé' (BE, SV, JL), 'Chevalier' (LS). In BE, 'Cheval' is inscribed in pencil.

[15] 'Venus' = 'Helen' (JL, SV), 'Tannhäuser' = 'Fanfreluche' (SV, JL). In BE, Aubrey is crossed out and 'Fanfreluche' written on top of it in mauve ink. Next to it, 'Than' is written in pencil on the margins.

[16] 'Chevalier's' = 'the Abbé's' (BE, SV, JL). In BE, 'Chev' is written in pencil in the margin.

[17] 'Tannhäuser' = 'Fanfreluche' (SV, JL). In BE, 'Tannhäuser' = 'Aubrey', which is crossed out; 'Fanfreluche' is written in mauve ink on top of it; next to it, 'Than' is written in pencil.

[18] 'muff' = 'ruff' (SV, JL).

that <X> Tannhäuser witheld the finger of resentment & vowed that the wild rose should stay where it had clung, a passport, as it were, from the upper to the underworld.[19]

'The very excess & violence of the fault' he said 'will be its excuse', & undoing a tangle in the tassel of his stick, stepped into the shadowy corridor that ran into the bosom of the wan hill. Stepped with the admirable aplomb & unwrinkled suavity of Don John.[20]

<13>

II[21]

Before a toilet that shone like the altar of Nôtre Dame des Victoires, Venus <X> was seated in a little dressing gown of black & heliotrope.[22] The coiffeur Cosmé was caring for her scented chevelure, & with tiny silver tongs, warm from the caresses of the flame, made delicious intelligent curls that fell as lightly as a breath about her forehead & over her eyebrows, & clustered like tendrils about her neck. Her three favourite girls, Pappelarde, Blanchemains & Loreyne waited immediately upon her with perfume & powder in delicate flacons & frail cassolettes, & held in porcelain jars the ravishing paints prepared by Chateline for those cheeks & lips that had grown a little pale with anguish of exile. Her three favourite boys Claude, Clair, & Sarrasine stood amorously about with salver, fan & napkin. Millamant held a slight tray of slippers, Minette some tender gloves, La Popelinière, mistress of the robes, was ready with a frock of yellow & <X> yellow,[23] La Zambinella bore the jewels,

<14>

Florizel some flowers, Amadour a box of various pins & Vadius a box of sweets. Her doves ever in attendance walked about the room that was panelled with the gallant paintings of Paul <X> <?> <X>~~Chatouilleur De La Pine~~, & some dwarfs & doubtful creatures sat here & there lolling out their tongues ~~& behaving~~ <X> monstrously wise.[24] Sometimes Venus <X> <Helen> gave them little smiles.

As the toilet was in progress, [<] Mrs Marsuple [>] ~~Priapusa~~, the fat manicure & farded <X>, strode in & seated herself by the side of the dressing table, greeting ~~Venus~~ <Helen> with an intimate nod.[25] She wore a gown of white watered silk with gold lace trimmings, & a velvet necklet of <X> <false> vermilion. Her hair hung in bandeaux over her ears passing into a huge chignon at the back of her head; & the hat, wide-brimmed & hung with a vallance of pink muslin, was floral with red roses.

<X> Priapusa's <Marsuple> voice was full of salacious unction; she had terrible little gestures with the hands, strange movements with the shoulders, a short respiration that

---

[19] Beardsley misspells 'withheld'; the missing 'h' is added in BE in mauve ink. 'Tannhäuser' = 'Aubrey', which is crossed out; 'Fanfreluche' is written in mauve ink on top of it.

[20] The BE fragment of a page numbered III on the left side and 3 in the top right corner contains three lines identical to the Rosenbach manuscript, from 'corridor' to 'Don John'.

[21] In LS, the chapter is titled 'Of the Manner in Which Venus Was Coiffed and Prepared for Supper'. This is an evocative title which also suggests that Venus is to be 'consumed'.

[22] 'Venus' = 'Helen' (SV, JL).

[23] 'yellow and yellow' = 'yellow and white' (JL).

[24] 'of Paul' = 'of Jean Baptiste Dorat' (SV, JL, LS); 'their tongues' is followed by the phrase 'pinching each other, and behaving oddly enough' in SV, JL, LS.

[25] 'Priapusa' = 'Mrs Marsuple' (SV, JL); 'farded' = 'fardeuse' (SV, JL, LS).

<15>

made surprising wrinkles in her bodice, a corrupt skin, large horny eyes, a parrot's nose, a small loose mouth, great flaccid cheeks, & chin after chin. She was a wise person, & Venus loved her more than any of her other servants, & had a hundred pet names for her, such as, Dear Toad, Pretty Pol, cock robin, dearest lip, Touchstone, ~~figs faute de mieux~~, bijou, buttons, astiquelle, dear heart, dick-dock, ~~tête-bêche~~ Mrs Manly, little nipper, cochon de lait, naughty-naughty, blessèd thing, & ~~tup.~~ [<]trump[>].[26]

The talk that passed between <X> Priapusa <Mrs Marsuple>and her mistress was of that excellent kind that passes between old friends, a perfect understanding giving to scraps of phrases their full meaning, & to the merest reference, a point. Naturally <?> <X> Tannhäuser the new comer was discussed a little. ~~Venus~~ <X> <Helen> had not seen him yet, & asked a score of questions on his account that were delightfully to the point.

<?> Priapusa told the story of his sudden arrival, his curious wandering in the

<16>

gardens & calm satisfaction with all he saw there, his impromptu affection for a slender girl upon the first terrace & of the crowd of frocks that gathered round & pelted him with roses, of the graceful way he defended himself with his mask, & of the ~~little~~ [<]queer[>] ~~mock~~ reverence he made to the statue of ~~Priapus;~~ [<]God of all Gardens[>] [<]kissing the huge emblem with a pilgrim's devotion[>].[27] Just now he was at the baths & was creating a most favourable impression.[28]

The report & the coiffing were completed at the same moment.

<X> 'Cosmé' said Venus 'you have been quite sweet & quite brilliant, you have surpassed yourself to-night.'

'Madam flatters me' replied the antique old thing with a girlish giggle under his black satin mask, 'Gad Madam sometimes I believe I have no talent in the world, but tonight I must confess to a touch of the vain mood.'

It would pain me ~~to~~ horribly to tell you about the painting of her face, suffice it that the sorrowful work was accomplished, frankly, magnificently, & without a shadow of deception.

<17>

<X> Venus slipped away the dressing-gown & rose before the mirror in a flutter of frilled things. She was adorably tall & slender. Her neck & shoulders were so wonderfully drawn & the little malicious breasts were full of the irritation of loveliness that can never be entirely comprehended, or ever enjoyed to the utmost. Her arms & hands were loosely but delicately articulated & her legs were divinely long. From the hip to the knee twenty-two inches from the knee to the heel twenty-two inches as befitted a goddess.[29] I should like to speak more particularly about her, for generalities are not of the slightest service in a description. But I am afraid that an enforced silence ~~upon many points~~ would leave such numerous gaps in the picture that it had better not be begun at all than be left unfinished.[30]

<X> Priapusa grew quite lyric over the dear little lady & pecked at her arms with kisses.[31]

'Dear Tongue, you must really behave

---

[26] 'Little Cough Drop' is added after 'Touchstone' in SV, JL ('Cough-drop' in LS).

[27] 'kissing that deity with pilgrim's devotion' (LS).

[28] 'he' = 'Tannhäuser' (LS). The paragraph from 'Priapusa told' to 'favourable impression' was omitted from SV and JL.

[29] In SV, JL, and LS, the following text is added: 'Those who have seen Helen [LS: "only seen Venus"] in the Vatican, in the Louvre, in the Uffizi, or in the British Museum, can have no idea [LS: "of"] how very beautiful and sweet she looked. Not at all like the lady in "Lemprière"'.

[30] The text from 'I should like' to 'left unfinished' is enclosed in square brackets, marked with an undulated line and crossed out in the manuscript; there is also the inscription 'delete' in the margin. The marked text was omitted from SV and JL but published in LS; 'upon many points' = 'here and there' (LS).

[31] 'lady' = 'person' (SV, JL, LS).

<18>

yourself' said Venus, & called Millamant to bring her the slippers.

The tray was freighted with the most exquisite & shapely panto[<]u[>]fles, sufficient to make Cluny a place of naught. There were shoes of grey & black & brown suède, of white silk & rose satin & velvet of sarsinesshe, there were some of sea green sewn with cherry blossoms, some of red with willow & some of grey with bright winged birds.[32] There were heels of silver of ivory & of gilt, the~~ir~~[<]re[>] were buckles of very precious stones set in most strange & esoteric devices, there were ribbands tied & twisted into cunning forms, there were buttons so beautiful that the button-holes might have no pleasure till they closed upon them, there were soles of delicate leathers scented with maréchale, & linings of soft stuffs scented with the juice of July flowers.[33]

But [X] Venus finding none of them to her mind called for a discarded pair of blood red maroquin diapered with pearls. These looked very distinguished over her white silk stockings. <·x·>[34]

<19>

[<]Meantime[>] La Popelinière stepped forward with the frock.

'I shan't wear one tonight' said <X> Venus <Helen>. Then she slipped on her gloves.

When the toilet was at an end all her doves clustered round her feet, loving to frôler her ankles with their plumes, & the dwarfs clapped their hands & put their fingers between their lips & whistled. Never had Venus been so beautiful before.[35] Claude & Clair pale with pleasure stroked & touched her with their delicate hands, & wrinkled her stockings with their nervous lips, & smoothed them with their thin fingers; & Sarrasine undid her garters & kissed them inside & put them on again pressing her ~~legs~~ [<]thighs[>] with ~~kisses~~ his mouth.

There was almost a mêlée.

The dwarfs grew very daring & illustrated pages seventy two & seventy three of Delvau's Dictionary.

In the middle of it all, Pranzmungel announced that supper was ready upon the fifth terrace.[36]

'Ah' cried Venus 'I'm famished!'

<20>

III[37]

She was quite delighted with <X> Tannhäuser & of course he sat next her at supper. The terrace, made beautiful with a thousand vain & fantastical things, & set with a hundred tables & four hundred couches presented a truly splendid appearance.[38] In the middle was a huge bronze fountain with three basins. From the first rose a many-breasted dragon, & four little loves mounted upon swans, & each love was furnished with a bow & arrow. Two of them that faced the monster seemed to recoil in fear, two that were behind made bold enough to aim their shafts at him. From the verge of the second sprang a circle of slim golden columns that

---

[32] 'of sarsinesshe' = 'and sarcenet' (SV, JL, LS).

[33] 'ribbands' = 'ribbons' (SV, JL), 'ribands' (LS).

[34] <·x·> indicates the position for insertion of the following addition to the text, written by Beardsley on the unnumbered verso of p. 18: '<·x·> As the tray was being carried away Florizel snatched as usual a slipper [<]from it[>] & fitted the foot over his penis, [<]& made[>] the necessary movements. That was Florizel's little caprice'. The paragraph appears in LS but is understandably omitted from SV and JL.

[35] 'beautiful before' = 'radiant and compelling' (SV, JL, LS), followed by the sentence: 'Spiridion, in the corner, looked up from his game of Spellicans and trembled' (SV, JL, LS).

[36] 'In the middle of it all' = 'Just then' (SV, JL).

[37] In LS, the chapter is titled 'How Venus Supped and Thereafter Was Mightily Amused by The Curious Pranks of Her Entourage'.

[38] 'things' = 'devices' (LS).

supported silver doves with tails & wings spread out. The third, held by a group of grotesquely attenuated satyrs was centred with a thin pipe hung with masks & roses, & capped with children's heads.

From the mouths of the dragon & the loves, from the swan's eyes, from the

<21>

breasts of the doves, from the satyrs' horns & lips, from the masks at many points, & from the childrens' curls, the water played profusely, cutting strange arabesques & subtle figures.

The terrace was lit entirely by candles. There were four thousand of them not numbering those upon the tables. The candlesticks were of a countless variety & smiled with moulded cochonneries. Some were twenty feet high & bore single candles that flared like fragrant torches over the feast, & guttered till the wax stood round the tops in tall lances. Some hung with dainty petticoats of shining lustres, had a whole bevy of tapers upon them, devised in circles, in pyramids, in squares, in cuneiforms, in single lines regimentally & in crescents.

Then on quaint pedestals & terminal gods & gracious pilasters of every sort were shell-like vases of excessive fruits & flowers that hung about & burst over the edges & could never be restrained. The orange trees & myrtles looped with

<22>

vermilion sashes stood in frail porcelain pots & the rose-trees were wound & twisted with superb invention over trellis & standard. Upon one side of the terrace, a long gilded stage for the comedians was curtained off with [?] amphytrien tapestries, & in front of it the music stands were placed.[39] The tables arranged between the fountain & the flight of steps to the sixth terrace were all circular, covered with white damask & strewn with irises, roses, king-cups, colombines, daffodils, carnations & lilies, & the couches, high with soft cushions & spread with more stuffs than could be named, had fans thrown upon them & little ~~erotic~~ [<]amorous[>] surprise packets.[40]

Beyond the escalier stretched the gardens, which were designed so elaborately & with so much splendour that the architect of the Fêtes d'Armailhacq could have found in them no matter for cavil, & the still lakes strewn with profuse barges full of gay flowers & wax marionettes, the alleys of tall

<23>

trees, the arcades & cascades, the pavillions the grottos, & the garden-gods all took a strange tinge of revelry from the glare of the light that fell upon them from the feast.

The frockless <Helen> Venus & Tannhäuser, with Priapusa & Claude & Clair & Farcy the chief comedian sat at the same table. Tannhäuser who had doffed his travelling suit wore ~~nothing but some~~ long black silk stockings, a pair of pretty garters, a very elegant ~~chemise~~ [<]ruffled shirt[>], slippers & a wonderful dressing-gown. Claude & Clair wore nothing at all, delicious privilege of immaturity, & Farcy was in ordinary evening clothes.[41] As for the rest of the ~~amorous~~ company it boasted some very noticeable dresses & whole tables of quite delightful coiffures. There were spotted veils that seemed to stain the skin with some exquisite & august disease, fans with eye-slits in them through which their bearers peeped & peered, fans painted with <X> postures & covered with the sonnets of Sporion & the short stories of Scaramouche, & fans of big

[39] [?] 'amphytrien' = 'Pagonian' (SV, JL, LS).

[40] The underlined phrase was omitted from SV and JL.

[41] The underlined phrase was omitted from SV and JL.

<24>

living moths stuck upon mounts of silver sticks; [<]there were[>] masks of green velvet that make the face look trebly powdered; masks of the heads of birds, of apes, of serpents, of dolphins, of men & women, of little embryos & of cats, masks like the faces of gods masks of coloured glass, & masks of thin talc & of india-rubber. There were wigs of black & scarlet wools, of peacocks' feathers, of gold & silver threads, of swansdown, of the tendrils of the vine, & of human hairs; huge collars of stiff muslin rising high above the head; whole dresses of ostrich feathers curling inwards, tunics of panthers' skins that looked beautiful over pink tights, capotes of crimson satin trimmed with the wings of owls, sleeves cut into the shapes of apocryphal animals, drawers flounced down to the ankles & ~~broidered~~ [<]flecked[>] with tiny, red roses ~~that seemed like flecks of blood~~, stockings clocked with fêtes galantes & curious designs, & petticoats cut like artificial flowers. Some of the women had put on delightful little moustaches dyed in purples & bright

<25>

greens, twisted & waxed with absolute skill, & some wore great white beards [<]after the manner of Ste Wilgeforte[>].[42] Then <X> ~~De La Pine~~ had painted extraordinary grotesques & vignettes over their bodies here & there.[43] Upon a cheek, an old man scratching his horned head, upon a forehead, an old woman teased by an impudent amor, upon a shoulder, an amorous singerie, round a breast, a circlet of satyrs, about a wrist, a wreath of ~~unborn children~~ [<]babes[>], upon an elbow, a bouquet of spring flowers, across a back, some surprising scenes of adventure, at the corners of a mouth, tiny red spots, & upon a neck, a flight of birds, a caged parrot, a branch of fruit, a butterfly, a spider, a drunken dwarf or simply ~~her~~ [<]the bearer's[>] initials.[44] But most wonderful of all were the black silhouettes painted upon the legs, & which showed through a white silk stocking like a sumptuous bruise.[45]

The supper provided by [<]the ingenious[>] Rambouillet was quite beyond parallel. <·x·>[46]

~~Menu~~

~~Consommé~~ [two more words illegible, crossed out by Beardsley]

[42] The insertion is most likely by Smithers.

[43] 'De La Pine' = 'Dorat' (SV, JL, LS).

[44] 'babes' = 'pale, unconscious babes' (SV, JL, LS); 'the bearer's' = 'some' (SV, JL, LS).

[45] The underlined sentence was cut in SV and JL.

[46] <·x·> indicates the insertion of the following fragment written on the verso of p. 25 (the underlinings here are editorial instructions to the printer to set the French terms in italic):

'<·x·> Never had he created a more exquisite menu. The consommé impromptu alone would have been sufficient to establish the immortal reputation of any chef, what, then, can I say of the Dorade bouillie sauce ~~fouteuse~~, the ragoût aux langues de carpes, the ramereaux à la charnière, the ciboulette de gibier à l'espagnole, the paté de cuisses d'oie aux pois de Monsalvie, the dindon de la menagerie ~~à la peau de vièrge,~~ the queues d'agneau au clair de lune, ~~the vits des boeufs sauce naturelle~~, the rissolettes à la pine magistrale, the artichauts à la Grecque, the asperges sauce, ~~Lesbienne~~, the charlotte de Pommes à la Périnée, the bombes à la marée, and the glaces aux rayons d'or? A veritable tour de cuisine that surpassed even the famous little suppers given by the Marquis de Réchale at Passy, & which the Abbé Mirliton pronounced "impeccable, and too good to be eaten".

Ah! Pierre Antoine Berquin de Rambouillet, you are worthy of your divine mistress!'

<26>

[thirteen lines crossed out by Beardsley][47]

[inscription 'My own drawing' in Beardsley's hand in the margin, bottom right corner]

Mere hunger quickly gave place to those finer instincts of the pure gourmet, & the strange wines cooled in buckets of snow, unloosed all the décolleté spirits of astonishing conversation & atrocious laughter.[48] At first there was the fun with the surprise packets that contained myriads of ~~unmentionable~~ [<]astounding[>] things, then a general criticism of the decorations, everyone finding ~~their own peculiar~~ [<]a different[>] meaning in the fall of festoon, turn of twig, & twist of branch.[49] <X> ~~Suculex~~ as usual bore the palm for insight &

<27>

invention, & tonight he was more brilliant than ever.[50] He leant across the table and explained to the young page, Macfils de Martaga, what was intended by a certain arrangement of roses.[51] The young page smiled & hummed the refrain of 'La petite ~~burette~~'. ~~It was~~ [<]Sporion too, had delicate perceptions, & was greatly amused by[>] the disposition of the candelabra ~~that amused him most, & suddenly noticing that the change of one of them would produce an entirely new & amazing effect he sprang from his seat & made the improvement. All the tables round about raised a shout of delight~~.[52]

As the courses advanced the conversation became more personal.[53] The infidelities of Cérise, Sarmean's caprices ~~that morning~~ in the lily garden, Thorilliere's declining strength, ~~Vulva's~~ affection for Roseola, Falix's impossible member <·x·>, & a thousand amatory follies of the day were discussed.[54]

From harsh & shrill & clamant, the voices grew blurred & inarticulate. Bad sentences were helped out by worse gestures, & at one

<28>

table, Scabius could only express himself with his napkin, after the manner of Sir Jolly Jumble in the 'Soldier's Fortune' of Otway.[55] Basalissa & Lysistrata tried to pronounce each other's names & became very affectionate in the attempt, & Tala the tragedian robed in purple & wearing plume & buskin, rose to his feet & with swaying gestures began to recite one of his favourite parts.[56] He got no further than the first line but repeated it again &

---

[47] The menu of the Venusberg's supper first appears written out centred in the conventional form of a restaurant menu. Beardsley then scribbled it out, although it can just be seen that it was headed 'Menu' (bottom of p. 25). He then set it out in continuous narrative form in the inserted leaf preceding p. 26 (see Note on the Texts for a description of the MS).

[48] Chapter IV 'How the Court of Venus Behaved Strangely at Her Supper' starts here in LS.

[49] 'astounding' = 'amusing'; 'different' = 'delightful' (LS).

[50] 'Suculex' = 'Pulex' (LS).

[51] 'thing' inserted after 'what' (LS).

[52] 'greatly amused' = 'vastly entertained' (LS). The crossed-out passage did not appear in any edition.

[53] 'became more personal' = 'grew bustling and more personal' (SV, JL, LS).

[54] <·x·> indicates the insertion of a fragment from an unpaginated sheet which follows after p. 27: '<·x·> Cathelin's passion for Sulpilia's poodle, Sola's passion for herself, the nasty bite that Marisca gave Chloe, the epilation of Pulex, Cyril's diseases'. In LS, the line is completed with 'Butor's illness, Maryx's tiny cemetery, Lesbia's profound fourth letter, and a thousand amatory follies'. The fragment is censored in SV and JL, appearing as 'Pulex and Cyril, and Marisa and Cathelin, opened a fire of raillery, and a thousand amatory follies of the day were discussed'.

[55] 'with his napkin, after the manner of Sir Jolly Jumble in' = 'like the famous old knight in the first part of' (SV, JL).

[56] 'in purple' = 'in roomy purple' (SV, JL); 'in ample purple' (LS).

again with fresh accents & intonations each time, & was only silenced by the approach of the asparagus that was being served by satyrs costumed in white muslin.[57] <·x·>[58]

I wish I could be allowed to tell you what occurred round table 15 just at this moment, it would amuse you very much & would give you a capital idea of the habits of Venus' retinue. Indeed, for deplorable reasons, by far the greater part of what was said & done at this supper must remain unrecorded & even unsuggested.

Venus allowed most of the dishes to pass

<29>

untasted, she was so engaged with the beauty of Tannhäuser. She ~~hid~~ [<]laid[>] her head many times ~~under~~ [<]on[>] his robe kissing him passionately & his skin at once firm & yielding seemed to those exquisite little teeth of hers, the most incomparable pasture. Her upper lip curled & trembled with excitement, showing the gums. Tannhäuser on his side was no less devoted. He adored her all over & all the things she had on, & buried his face in the folds & flounces ~~of her linen~~ & ravished away a score of frills in his excess. He found her exasperating & crushed her in his arms & slaked his parched lips at her mouth. He caressed her eyelids softly with his finger tips & pushed aside the curls from her forehead & did a thousand gracious things, tuning her body as a violinist tunes his instrument before he plays upon it. <·x·>[59]

After the fruits & fresh wines had been brought in by a troop of woodland creatures decked with green leaves & all sorts of spring flowers, the candles in the

<30>

orchestra were lit, & in another moment the musicians bustled into their places. The wonderful Titurel de Schentefleur was the chef d'orchestre, & the most insidious of conductors. His bâton dived into a phrase & brought out the most magical & magnificent things, & seemed rather to play every instrument than to lead it.

---

57 'in white muslin' = 'in white' (SV, JL).

58 <·x·> indicates the insertion of a fragment from the verso of p. 28:
'<·x·> Clitor & Sodon had a violent struggle ~~over the beautiful Pella~~ & nearly upset a chandelier, Sophie became very intimate with an empty champagne bottle, swore it had made her enciente, & ended by having a mock accouchment on the top of the table, & Bellmour pretended to be a dog & pranced from couch to couch on all fours biting & barking ~~& licking~~, Mellefont crept about dropping ~~aphrodisiacs~~ [<]love philtres[>] into glasses, Juventus and Ruella ~~stripped &~~ put on each other's things, Spelto offered a prize for whoever should come first, & Spelto won it, and Aubrey [= Tannhäuser (LS)], just a little grisé, lay down on the cushions & let Julia do whatever she liked.'
This sentence ends Chapter III in SV and JL.

59 <·x·> indicates the insertion of a fragment from an unpaginated sheet which follows p. 29:
'<·x·> Priapusa snorted like an old war horse at the sniff of powder & tickled Tannhäuser & Venus by turns & slipped her tongue down their throats & refused to be quiet at all until she had had a mouthful of the Chevalier. Claude seizing his chance dived under the table & came up the other side just under the queen's couch & before she could say One! he was taking his coffee aux deux colonnes. Clair was furious at his friend's success & sulked for the rest of the evening.'

This fragment finishes Chapter IV in LS. It is followed by Chapter V 'Of the Ballet Danced by the Servants of Venus'. It opens with 'After the fruits' (p. 29 of the manuscript).

The next inserted sheet contains a fragment which was not used in SV, JL, or LS. The sheet is numbered '12' in Beardsley's hand; there is a number in a different ink on the top of the sheet: '25/[?]84'. An inscription in the top right corner reads: 'In the autograph of Aubrey Beardsley'. The text on the sheet is as follows: 'Kissing him passionately, & his skin at once firm & yielding seemed to those exquisite little teeth of hers, the most incomparable pasture. Her upper lip curled & trembled with excitement, showing the gums. Aubrey on his side was no less devoted. He adored her all over & all the things she had on, & buried his face in the folds & flounces of ~~his linen~~ her linen, & ravished away a score of frills in his excess. He found her exasperating & crushed her in his arms & slaked his parched lips at her mouth. He caressed her eyelids softly with his finger tips, & pushed aside the curls from her forehead & did a thousand gracious things.

– Bless you, my children! cried Mrs Marsuple.

Claude & Clair bit their lips & gazed at the loving two, & held each others hand.

To be continued.'

He could add a grace even to Scarlatti & a wonder to Beethoven. A delicate thin little man with thick lips & a nez retroussé, with long black hair & curled moustache, in the manner of Molière. What were his amatory tastes, no one in the Venusberg could tell; ~~&~~ he generally passed ~~for a virgin, [<]and Cathos had nicknamed him the Solitaire[>]~~ [<]as very chaste[>].

Tonight he appeared in a court suit of white silk, brilliant with decorations, his hair was curled into resplendent ringlets that trembled like springs at the merest gesture of his arm, & in his ears swung the diamonds given him by ~~Venus~~ [<]Helen[>]. [Two lines crossed out by Beardsley.] The orchestra was as usual in its uniform of red vest & breeches trimmed with gold

<31>

lace, white stockings & red shoes. Titurel had written a ballet for the evening's divertissement founded upon De Bergerac's comedy of 'Les Bacchanales de Fanfreluche', in which the action & dances were designed by him as well as the music.

[Nineteen lines crossed out by Beardsley][60]

31A

[top of the page:] <FOOTNOTE to face p[the sheet cut off]>[61]

[Eleven lines crossed out by Beardsley]

[<]The curtain rose upon a scene of rare beauty,[>] a remote arcadian valley, [several illegible words crossed out] & watered with a dear river as fresh & pastoral as a perfect fifth [eight lines crossed out] of this scrap of Tempe. It was early morning, & the re-arisen sun, like the prince in the Sleeping Beauty, woke all the earth with his lips.

<32>

[top left corner:] <footnote to p.3 [i.e. paragraph 3] of 195>[62]
<i. Ward.>[63]

In that golden embrace the night dews were caught up & made splendid, the trees were awakened from their obscure dreams, the slumber of the birds was broken & all the flowers of the valley rejoiced forgetting their fear of the darkness.

---

[60] Marked by Beardsley with a loose line down the right side of the text, with 'The curtain rose on a scene of rare beauty' written in the margin and an arrow pointing to the next page.

[61] In SV and JL, the 'footnote' is placed in Chapter IV, as a note to one of the items in the list of things Fanfreluche 'thought of' after awakening in Venusberg. See Creative Expurgation. In LS, the 'footnote' is divided into two parts, numbered with Roman numerals, and forms part of Chapter V.

[62] The mark is by Smithers and refers to the footnote's position in SV, where the text is placed at the third paragraph on p. 188 (the pagination evidently changed through the editorial process).

[63] 'Ward' appears to be a printer's instruction meaning to reserve. This is then followed by an opening square bracket, followed by an insertion which is a repetition, with some minor changes, of the passage from p. 31A running from 'The curtain' to 'his lips'. This insertion together with all the text following it, up to the end of p. 36, in fact formed an extended footnote in SV. The lower case 'i' preceding 'Ward' must refer to the number the note will have in SV, although this was not eventually adhered to. The changes as compared with the passage on p. 31A are as follows: 'Arcadian valley' is followed by 'a delicious scrap of Tempe'; 'a dear river' = 'a little river', 'of this scrap of Tempe' is deleted; edits are adopted in SV, JL, not in LS.

Suddenly to the music of pipe & horn, a troop of satyrs stepped out from the recesses of the woods, bearing in their hands nuts & green boughs & flowers & roots & whatsoever the forest yielded, to heap upon the altar of the mysterious Pan that stood in the middle of the stage; & from the hills came down the shepherds & shepherdesses leading their flocks & carrying garlands upon their crooks. Then a rustic priest, white-robed & venerable, came slowly across the valley followed by a choir of radiant children ~~whose delectable limbs, so tender & [illegible], utterly transported Tannhäuser~~.[64] The scene was admirably stage managed & nothing could have been more varied yet harmonious than this arcadian group. The service was quaint & simple, but

<33>

with sufficient ritual to give the corps de ballet an opportunity of showing its dainty skill. The dancing of the satyrs was received with huge favour & when the priest raised his hand in final blessing, the whole troop of worshippers made such an intricate & elegant exit that it was generally agreed that Titurel had never before shown ~~such a~~ [<]so[>]fine an invention.

Scarcely had the stage been empty for a moment, when ~~Fanfreluche~~ [<]Sporion[>] entered followed by a brilliant rout of dandies & smart women. ~~Fanfreluche~~ [<]Sporion[>] was a tall slim ~~deseased~~ [<]depraved[>] young man with a slight stoop, a troubled walk, an oval impassable face with its olive skin drawn tightly over the bone, strong, scarlet ~~painted~~ lips, long Japanese eyes, & a great gilt toupet. Round his shoulders hung a high-collared satin cape of salmon pink with long black ribands untied & floating about his body. His coat of sea-green spotted muslin was caught in at the waist by a scarlet sash with scalloped edges

<34>

& frilled out over the hips for about six inches. His trousers, loose & wrinkled, reached to the end of the calf, & were brocaded down the sides & ruched magnificently at the ankles. The stockings were of white kid with stalls for the toes, & had delicate red sandals strapped over them. But his little hands, peeping out from their frills seemed quite the most insinuating things, such supple fingers tapering to the point with tiny nails stained pink, such unquenchable palms, lined & mounted like Lord Fanny's in the [illegible, crossed out] [<]Love at all Hazards[>], & such blue-veined hairless backs! In his left hand he carried a small lace handkerchief broidered with a coronet.

As for his friends & followers they made the most superb & insolent crowd imaginable, [<]but to[>] ~~To~~ catalogue the clothes they had on would require a chapter as long as the famous tenth in Pénillière's history of underlinen. ~~Some of the things suggested secret diseases bursting in passionate scabs & pimples~~[65]

<34A>

On the whole they looked a very distinguished chorus.

~~Fanfreluche~~ [<]Sporion[>] stepped forward & explained with swift & various gesture that he & his friends were tired of the amusements, wearied with the poor pleasures offered by the civil world, & had invaded the arcadian

<35>

valley hoping to experience a new frisson in the destruction of some shepherd's or some satyr's naïveté, & the infusion of their venom among the dwellers of the woods.

The chorus assented with languid but expressive movements.

---

64 The bowdlerization is by Smithers, who also left it out in his edition.

65 The deletion is by Beardsley and is an authorial decision rather than a bowdlerization.

Curious & not a little frightened at the arrival of the worldly company, the sylvans began to peep nervously at those subtle souls through the branches of the trees & one or two fauns & a shepherd or so crept out warily. ~~Fanfreluche~~ [<]Sporion[>] & all the ladies & gentlemen made enticing sounds & invited the rustic creatures with all the grace in the world to come & join them. By little batches they came lured by the strange looks, by the scents & the drugs,[66] & by the brilliant clothes & some ventured quite near timorously fingering the delicious textures of the stuffs. Then ~~Fanfreluche~~ [<]Sporion[>] & each of his friends took a satyr or a shepherd or something by the hand & made the preliminary steps of a courtly measure for which the most admirable

<36>

combinations had been invented & the most charming music written. The pastoral folk were entirely bewildered when they saw such restrained & graceful movements, & made the most grotesque & futile efforts to imitate them. ~~To the huge & suppressed pleasure of Franfreluche, the satyrs grew very warm in the attempt & catered about the stage looking like the unappeased husbands of the Lysistrata of Aristophanes, though they were as innocent of offence as the very horses in Nanan's 'Amours catholiques.'~~

Dio mio, a pretty sight! A charming effect too, was obtained by the intermixture of stockinged calf & hairy leg, of rich brocaded bodice & plain blouse, of tortured head dress & loose untutored locks.

When the dance was ended, ~~Fanfreluche~~ the servants of ~~Fanfreluche~~ [<]Sporion[>] brought on champagne, and, with many pirouettes, poured it magnificently into slender glasses, & tripped about plying those arcadian mouths that had never before tasted such a royal drink.

[After a line of asterisks, in Smithers's hand:]
'Then the curtain fell with a pudic rapidity'.

<37>[67]

'Twas not long before the invaders began to enjoy the first fruits of their expedition plucking them in the most seductive manner with their smooth fingers, & feasting lip & tongue & tooth, whilst the shepherds & satyrs & shepherdesses fairly gasped under the new joys, for the pleasure they experienced was almost too keen & too profound for their simple & untilled natures. Fanfreluche & the rest of the rips & ladies tingled with excitement & frolicked like young lambs in a fresh meadow. Again & again the wine was danced round & the valley grew [<]as busy as a market day[>]. Attracted by the noise & merrymaking all those sweet infants I told you of, skipped suddenly on to the stage & began [<]clapping their hands, &[>] laughing immoderately at the passion & [<]the[>] disorder & commotion, & mimicking the nervous staccato movements [<]they saw[>] in their pretty childish way. In a flash Fanfreluche disentangled & sprang to his feet [<]gesticulating as if he would say[>] 'Ah, the little dears' 'Ah, the little ducks' 'Ah the rorty little things!', for he was so fond

<38>

of children.[68] Scarcely had he caught one by the thigh than a quick rush was made by everybody for the succulent limbs; & how they tousled them & mousled them! The children cried out I can tell you. Of course there were not enough for everybody, so some had to share, & some had simply to go on with what they were doing before. I must not by the way forget to mention the independent attitude taken by six or seven of the party, who sat & stood about with half-closed eyes inflated nostrils clenched teeth, & painful, parted lips, behaving like the Duc de Broglio when he watched the amours of the Regent Orléans.[69]

---

66 'the drugs' = 'the doings' (LS).
67 The passage from ''Twas not long' to 'uncanny tunes of Titurel' was omitted from SV and JL.
68 'disentangled' = 'disentangled himself' (LS).
69 'Orléans' = 'd'Orleans' (LS).

Now as Fanfreluche & his friends began to grow tired & exhausted with the new debauch, they cared no longer to take the initiative, but, relaxing every muscle abandoned themselves to passive joys yielding utterly to the ardent embraces of the [<]intoxicated[>] satyrs who waxed fast & furious & seemed

<39>

as if they would never come to the end of their strength. Full of the new tricks they had learnt that morning they played them passionately & roughly, making havoc of the cultured flesh, & tearing the splendid frocks & dresses into ribands. Duchesses & Maréchales, Marquises & Princesses, Dukes & Marshalls, Marquesses & Princes, were ravished & stretched & rumpled & crushed beneath the interminable vigour & hairy breasts of the inflamed woodlanders. They bit at the white thighs & nozzled wildly in the crevices, they sat astride the women's chests & consummated frantically with their bosoms, they caught their prey by the hips & held it over their heads, irrumating with prodigious gusto. It was the triumph of the valley. High up in the heavens the sun had mounted & filled all the air with generous warmth, whilst shadows grew shorter & sharper. Little light-winged papillons flitted across the stage, the bees made music on their flowery way, the birds were very gay & kept up a jargoning & refraining,

<40>

the lambs were bleating upon the hill side, & the orchestra kept playing, playing the uncanny tunes of Titurel.[70]

Venus & Tannhäuser had retired to the exquisite little boudoir or pavilion Le Con had designed for the queen on the first terrace, & which commanded the most delicious view of the parks & gardens. It was a sweet little place, all silk [<]curtains[>] & soft cushions. There were ~~six~~ [<]eight[>] sides to it, bright with mirrors & candelabra, & rich with pictured panels, & the ceiling, dome shaped & some ~~twenty~~ [<]thirty[>] feet above the head, shone obscurely with gilt mouldings, through the warm haze of candle light below. Tiny wax statuettes dressed theatrically & smiling with plump cheeks, quaint magots that looked as cruel as foreign gods, gilded monticules, pale celadon vases, clocks that said nothing, [<]ivory[>] boxes full of secrets, china figures playing whole scenes of plays, & a world of strange preciousness crowded the curious cabinets that stood against the walls. On one

<41>

side of the room there were six perfect little card tables, with quite the daintiest & most elegant chairs set primly round them; so, after all, there may be some truth in that line of Mr Theodore Watts, 'I played at piquet with the Queen of Love'.

Nothing in the pavilion was more beautiful than the folding screens painted by De La Pine with Claudian landscapes, the sort of things that fairly make one melt, things one can lie & look at for hours together & forget the country ~~is~~ [<]can ever be[>] dull & tiresome. There were four of them, delicate walls that hem in an amour so cosily & make room within room. The place was scented with huge branches of red roses, & with a faint amatory perfume breathed out from the couches & cushions, a perfume Chateline distilled in secret & called L'Eau Savante.[71]

Those who have only seen Venus at the Louvre or the British Museum, at Florence, at Naples, or at Rome, can have not the faintest idea how sweet & enticing & gracious, how really exquisitely beautiful

[70] This sentence marks the end of Chapter V in LS. Chapter VI is titled 'Of the Amorous Encounter which Took Place between Venus and Tannhäuser' (LS).

[71] 'L'Eau Savante' = 'L'Eau Lavante' (LS).

<42>

she looked lying with Tannhäuser, upon rose silk, in that pretty boudoir. Cosmé's precise curls & artful waves had been finely disarranged at supper, & strayed ringlets of the black hair fell loosely over her soft, delicious, tired, swollen eye-lids. Her frail chemise & dear little drawers were torn & moist & clung transparently about her, & all ~~her~~ [<]the[>] body was nervous & responsive.[72] <·x·>[73]

[seven lines crossed out by Beardsley]

Tannhäuser pale & speechless with excitement passed his gem-girt fingers brutally over the divine limbs tearing away smock & pantalon & stocking, & then stripping himself of his own few things, fell upon the splendid lady with a deep-drawn breath. [A line crossed out].

<43>

It is I know the custom of all romancers to paint heroes who can [<]give a lady[>] proof of their valliance [<]at least[>] twenty times a night. Now Tannhäuser had no such gargantuan facility, & was rather relieved when an hour later Priapusa & Doricourt & some others burst drunkenly into the room & claimed Venus for themselves. The pavilion soon filled with a noisy crowd that could scarcely keep its feet. Several of the actors were there, & Lesfesses who had played Fanfreluche so brilliantly & was still in his make-up, paid tremendous attention to Tannhäuser. But the Chevalier found him quite uninteresting off the stage & rose & crossed the room to where Venus & ~~Priapusa~~ [<]the manicure[>] were seated.

'How tired the dear baby looks', said ~~the manicure~~ [<]Priapusa[>], 'shall I put him in his little cot?'

'Well, if he's as sleepy as I am' yawned Venus, 'you can't do better.'

Priapusa lifted her mistress off the pillows

<44>

& carried her in her arms in a nice motherly way.

'Come along, children', said the fat old thing, 'come along, it's time you were both in bed.'

IV[74]

It is always delightful to wake up in a new bedroom. The fresh wallpaper, the strange pictures, the positions of doors & windows, imperfectly grasped the night before, are revealed with all the charm of surprise when we open our eyes the next morning.

It was about eleven o'clock when Tannhäuser awoke & stretched himself deliciously in his great plumed four-post bed, & nursed his waking thoughts & stared at the curious patterned canopy above him. He was very pleased with the room which certainly was chic & fascinating &

---

[72] 'finely disarranged' = 'finally disarranged' (LS); 'the body' = 'her body' (LS).

[73] <·x·> indicates the insertion of a fragment from an unpaginated sheet which follows p. 42: '<·x·> Her closed thighs seemed like a vast replica of the little bijou she held between them; the beautiful tétons du derrière were as firm as a plump virgin['s cheek (LS)] & promised a joy as profound as the mystery of the Rue Vend[ôme (LS)], & the minor chevelure, just profuse enough, curled as prettily as the hair upon a cherub's head.'

[74] Chapter IV of the manuscript is Chapter VII in LS, titled 'How Tannhäuser Awakened and Took His Morning Ablutions in the Venusberg'. The chapter was included in a censored and greatly changed form in the April issue of SV and in JL (see Creative Expurgation).

<45>

recalled the [<]voluptuous[>] interiors of the [<]elegant[>] amorous Baudouin.[75] Through the tiny parting of the long flowered window curtains the Chevalier caught a peep of the sun lit lawns outside, the silver fountains, the bright flowers, & the gardeners at work.

'Quite sweet', he murmured, & turned round to freshen the frilled silk pillows behind him, '& what delightful pictures,' he continued, wandering with his eyes from print to print that hung upon the rose striped walls. Within the delicate curved frames lived the corrupt & gracious creatures of Dorat & his school; slim children in masque & domino smiling horribly, exquisite letchers leaning over the shoulders of smooth doll-like ladies & doing nothing particular, terrible little Pierrots posing as mulierasts, or pointing at something outside the picture, & unearthly fops & strange women mingling in [<]some[>] rococo rooms lighted mysteriously by the flicker of a dying fire that throws huge shadows upon wall & ceiling. One of the prints showing

<46>

how an old marquis practised the five finger exercise whilst in front of him, his mistress offered her warm fesses to a panting poodle, made the Chevalier stroke himself a little.

After a while he got up & slipping off his dainty night-dress postured elegantly before a long mirror & made much of his body.[76] Now he would bend forward & admire the creases of his stomach, now he would stand ~~straight~~ [<]upright[>] & adore the contour of his loins & hips, now he would rest upon one leg & let the other hang loosely till he looked as if he might have been drawn by some early Italian master, & now he would lie upon the floor with his back to the glass & glance amorously over his shoulder.[77] Then with a white silk sash he draped himself in a hundred charming ways. So engrossed was [<]he[>] ~~Tannhäuser~~ with his mirrored shape that he had not noticed the entrance of a troop of serving boys, who stood admiringly but respectfully at a distance ready

<47>

to receive his waking orders. As soon as the chevalier observed them he smiled sweetly & bade them prepare the bath.

His bathroom was the largest & perhaps the most beautiful apartment in his splendid suite. The well-known engraving by Lorette that forms the frontispiece to Millevoye's 'Architecture du XVIIIme siècle' will give you a better idea than any words of mine of the construction & decoration of the room. Only in Lorette's engraving the bath sunk into the middle of the floor is a little too small.

Tannhäuser stood for a moment like Narcissus gazing at his reflection in the still scented water & then just ruffling its smooth surface with one foot, stepped elegantly into the cool basin & swam round it twice, very gracefully.

'Won't you join me?' he said turning to those beautiful boys who stood ready with warm towels & perfume. In a

[75] 'eleven o'clock' = 'eight o'clock'; passage from after 'four-post bed' to 'Baudouin' replaced with 'murmured "What a pretty room!" and freshened the frilled silk pillows behind him' (SV, JL).

[76] LS: 'After the chevalier got up, he slipped off his dainty night-dress, posturing elegantly before a long mirror, and made much of himself'.

[77] LS: 'admire the creases of his stomach' cut; '& now he would' = 'Anon he would'.

<48>

moment they were free of their light morning dress, & jumped into the water [<]& joined hands[>] & surrounded the Chevalier with a laughing chain.

'Splash me a little' he cried, & the boys teased him with water & quite excited him. He chased the prettiest of them & bit his fesses & kissed him upon the perineum till the dear fellow banded ~~like~~ [<]as freely[>] a Carmelite, & its little bald top-knot looked like a great pink pearl under the water. As the boy seemed anxious to take up the active attitude Tannhäuser graciously descended to the passive, a generous trait that won him the complete affections of his valets de bain, or pretty fish, as he called them, because they loved to swim between his legs.

However it is not so much at the very bath itself, as in the drying & delicious frictions that a bather finds his chiefest pleasures, & Tannhäuser was more than satisfied with the skill

<~~48~~-49>

his attendants displayed in the performance of those quasi amorous functions. The delicate attention they paid his loving parts ~~filled~~ aroused feelings within him that almost amounted to gratitude, & when the rites were ended, any touch of homesickness he might have felt before was utterly dispelled.

After he had rested a little & sipped his chocolate, he wandered into the dressing-room. Daucourt, his valet de chambre, Chenille, the perruquier & barber, & two charming young dressers, were awaiting him & ready with suggestions for the morning toilet. The shaving over, Daucourt commanded his underlings to step forward with the suite of suits from which he proposed Tannhäuser should make a choice. The [<]final[>] selection was a happy one. A dear little coat of pigeon rose silk that hung loosely about his hips & showed off the jut of his behind

<50>

to perfection, trousers of black lace in flounces, falling almost like a petticoat as far as the knee, & a delicate chemise of white muslin, spangled with gold, & profusely pleated.

The two dressers, under Daucourt's direction, did their work superbly, beautifully, leisurely, with an exquisite deference for the nude, & a [<]really[>] sensitive appreciation of Tannhäuser's scrumptious torso.

When all was said & done the Chevalier tripped off to bid good morning to Venus.[78] He found her wandering, in a sweet white muslin frock, upon the lawn outside, plucking flowers to deck her little déjeuner. He kissed her lightly upon the neck.

'I'm just going to feed Adolphe', she said, pointing to a little reticule of buns that hung from her arm.

Adolphe was her pet unicorn.

'He is such a dear' she continued, 'milk-white all over excepting his black eyes, rose mouth & nostrils, & scarlet john. This way.'

<51>

The unicorn had a very pretty palace of its own, made of green foliage & golden bars, a fitting home for such a delicate & dainty beast. Ah it was indeed a splendid thing to watch the white creature roaming in its artful cage, [<]proud & beautiful[>] & knowing no mate except the Queen herself.

As Venus & Tannhäuser approached the wicket Adolphe began prancing & curvetting, pawing the soft turf with his ivory hoofs, & flaunting his tail like a gonfalon. Venus raised the latch & entered.

[78] This sentence begins Chapter VIII 'The Ecstasy of Adolphe, and the Remarkable Manifestation Thereof' in LS.

'You mustn't come in with me, Adolphe is so jealous' she said turning to the Chevalier who was following her. 'But you can stand outside & look on; Adolphe likes an audience.' Then in her delicious fingers she broke the spicy buns & with affectionate niceness breakfasted her ardent pet. When the last crumbs had been scattered Venus brushed her hands together & pretended to leave the cage [<]without taking any more notice of Adolphe[>]. Every morning she went through this piece of play

<52>

& every morning the amorous unicorn was cheated into a distressing agony lest that day should have proved the last of Venus's love. Not for long though would she leave him in that doubtful [<]piteous[>] state but running back passionately to where he stood make adorable amends for her unkindness. Poor Adolphe! how happy he was touching the Queen's breasts with his quick tongue-tip. I have no doubt that the keener scent of animals must make women much more attractive to them than to men, [<]for[>] ~~That~~ [<]the[>] gorgeous odour that but faintly fills our nostrils must be revealed to the brute creation in divine fulness. Anyhow Adolphe sniffed as never a man did — around the skirts of Venus. After the first charming interchange of affectionate delicacies [<]was over[>], the unicorn lay down upon his side, and, closing his eyes, beat his stomach wildly with ~~his~~ [<]the[>] mark of manhood.

Venus caught that

<53>

stunning member in her hands & lay her cheek along it. But few touches were wanted to consummate the creature's pleasure. The Queen bared her left arm to the elbow & with the soft underneath of it made amazing movements horizontally upon the tight-strung instrument. When the melody began to flow, the unicorn offered up an astonishing vocal accompaniment. [<]Tannhäuser was amused to learn that the[>] etiquette of the Venusberg compelled everybody to await the outburst of these venereal sounds before they could sit down to déjeuner. [four lines crossed out by Beardsley]

Adolphe had been quite profuse that morning.

Venus knelt where it had fallen & lapped her little aperitif.

<54>

V[79]

The breakfasters were scattered over the gardens in têtes-à-têtes & tiny parties. Venus & Tannhäuser sat together upon the lawn that lay in front of the Casino, & made havoc of a ravishing déjeuner. The Chevalier was feeling very happy. Everything around him seemed so white & light & matinal, the floating frocks of the ladies, the scarce robed boys & satyrs stepping hither & thither elegantly, with meats & wines & fruits, the damask tablecloths, the delicate talk & laughter that rose everywhere; the flowers' colour & the flowers' scent, the shady trees, the wind's cool voice, & the sky above that was as fresh & pastoral as a perfect fifth. And Venus looked so beautiful. Not at all like the lady in Lempriere.

'You're such a dear' murmured Tannhäuser holding her hand.

At the further end of the lawn & a little hidden by a rose-tree a young man was breakfasting alone. [two lines crossed out]

---

79 Here in LS, Chapter IX 'How Venus and Tannhäuser Breakfasted and Then Drove through the Palace Gardens' begins.

<55>

He toyed nervously with his food now & then but for the most part leant back in his chair with unemployed hands, & gazed stupidly at Venus.

'That's Felix', said the ~~Queen~~ [<]goddess[>], in answer to an enquiry from the Chevalier, & she went on to explain his attitude. Felix always attended Venus upon her little [<]latrinal[>] excursions holding her serving her & making much of all she did. To undo her things, to lift her skirts, to wait & watch the coming, to dip a lip or finger in the royal output, to stain himself deliciously with it, to lie beneath her as the favours fell, [<]to carry off the crumpled crotted paper[>] these were the pleasures of that young man's life.

Truly there never was a Queen so beloved by her subjects as Venus. Everything she wore had its lover. Heavens[!] how her handkerchiefs were filched, her stockings stolen! [a line and a half crossed out] Daily, what intrigues, what countless ruses to possess her merest

<56>

frippery! [<]Every scrap of her body was adored.[>] Never for Savaral could her ear yield sufficient wax! Never for Pradon could she spit prodigally enough! And Saphius found a month an interminable time.

After breakfast was over & Felix's fears lest Tannhäuser should have robbed him of his capricious rights had been dispelled, Venus invited the Chevalier to take a more extensive view of the gardens, parks, pavilions, & ornamental waters. The carriage was ordered. It was a delicate shell-like affair with billowy cushions & a light canopy, & was drawn by ten satyrs, dressed as finely as the coachmen of the Empress Pauline the First.

The drive proved ~~charming~~ [<]interesting[>] & various, & Tännhauser was quite delighted with [<]almost[>] everything he saw.

And who is not pleased, when on either side of him rich lawns were are spread with lovely frocks & white limbs, & [<]upon flower beds[>] the dearest ladies

<57>

~~were~~ [<]are[>] implicated in a glory of underclothing, when he ~~could~~ [<]can[>] see in the deep cool shadows of the trees, warm boys entwined, here at the base, ~~now~~ [<]there[>] in the branch, when in the fountain's wave Love holds his court & the insistent water burrows in ~~delicious~~ [<]every delicious[>] crease & crevice?

A pretty sight too was [<]little[>] Rosalie perched like a postilion upon the painted phallus of the god of all gardens. Her eyes were closed & she was smiling as the carriage passed. [two lines crossed out] Round her neck & slender girlish shoulders there was a cloud of complex dress over which bulged [<]her wig-like flaxen tresses[>], her legs [<]& feet[>] were bare & ~~her~~ [<]the[>] toes twisted in an amorous style. At the foot of the statue lay her shoes & stockings & a few other things.

[five lines crossed out]

<58>

[six lines crossed out]

¬Tannhäuser [<]was singularly moved[>] & rose out of all proportion.[80] Venus slipped the fingers of comfort under ~~his~~ [<]the[>] lace flounces of his trousers saying 'Is it all mine? Is it all mine?' [<]& doing fascinating things[>]. In the end, the carriage was only prevented from being overturned by the happy interposition of Priapusa who stepped out from [<]somewhere or other[>] just in time to preserve its balance.

How the old lady's eye glistened as Tannhäuser withdrew his panting blade, & in her sincere admiration for fine things she quite forgot & forgave the shock she had received from ~~falling carriage~~ the falling of the gay

[80] LS: 'moved at this spectacle'.

equipage.[81] Venus & Tannhäuser were profuse with apology & thanks <·x·>.[82] The chevalier vowed he would never go in the carriage again, & was really quite upset about it. However after he had ~~received~~

<59>

had a little support from the smelling salts, he recovered his self-possession, & consented to drive on further.

The landscape grew rather mysterious. The park, no longer troubled & adorned with figures was full of [?]~~august~~ [<]grey[>] echoes, & mysterious sounds, the leaves whispered a little sadly, & there was a grotto that murmured like the voice that haunts the silence of a deserted oracle. Tannhäuser ~~grew~~ became a little triste. In the distance through the trees gleamed a still argent lake, a [<]reticent, romantic[>] water, that must have held the subtlest fish that ever were. Around its marge the trees & flags & fleurs de luce were unbreakably asleep.

The Chevalier fell into a strange mood as he looked at the lake, it seemed to him that the thing would speak, reveal some curious secret, say some beautiful word, if he should ~~break its silent~~ dare wrinkle its pale face with a pebble.

'I should be frightened to do that though' he said to himself.

Then he wondered what there might be upon the other side; other

<60>

gardens, other gods? <·x·>[83]

[<]When he woke up from his day-dream he noticed[>] that the carriage was on its way back to the palace.[84] They stopped at the Casino first & stepped out to join the players at petits chevaux. Tannhäuser preferred to watch the game rather than play himself & stood behind Venus who slipped into [<]a[>] vacant chair & cast gold pieces upon lucky numbers. The first thing that Tannhäuser noticed was the grace & charm, the gaiety & beauty of the croupiers. [<]They were quite adorable[>] even when they raked in one's little losings. Dressed in

---

[81] LS: 'his panting blade! In her sincere admiration'.

[82] <·x·> indicates the insertion of a fragment from an unpaginated sheet after p. 58: '<·x·> & quite a crowd of loving courtiers gathered round consoling & congratulating in a breath'.

[83] <·x·> indicates the insertion of a fragment from an unpaginated sheet after p. 60: '<·x·> A thousand drowsy fancies passed through his brain. Sometimes the lake took fantastic shapes, or grew to [<]twenty times[>] its size or shrunk into a miniature of itself, without ever once losing its unruffled calm, its deathly reserve. When the water increased the chevalier was very frightened, for he thought how huge the ~~toads~~ [<]frogs[>] must have become, he thought of their big eyes & monstrous wet feet, but when the water lessened he laughed to himself for the thought ~~of~~ how [= whilst thinking how (LS)] tiny the ~~toads~~ [<]frogs[>] must have grown, he thought of their legs that must ~~be~~ [<]look[>] thinner than spiders', & of their [<]dwindled[>] croaking that never could be heard. Perhaps the lake was only painted after all, he had seen things like it at the theatre. Anyhow it was a wonderful lake, [<]a beautiful lake,[>] & he would love to bathe in it, but he was sure he would be drowned if he did…'

JL includes this fragment as 'The Woods of Auffray', changing the narration to the first person and deleting the protagonist's direct speech. The fragment reads as follows:

'In the distance, through the trees, gleamed a still argent lake, a reticent water that must have held the subtlest fish that ever were. Around its marge the trees and flags and fleurs-de-luce were unbreakably asleep.

I fell into a strange mood as I looked at the lake, for it seemed to me that the thing would speak, reveal some curious secret, say some beautiful word, if I should dare to wrinkle its pale face with a pebble.

Then the lake took fantastic shapes, grew to twenty times its size, or shrank into a miniature of itself, without ever losing its unruffled calm and deathly reserve. When the waters increased I was very frightened, for I thought how huge the frogs must have become, I thought of their big eyes and monstrous wet feet; but when the water lessened I laughed to myself, for I thought how tiny the frogs must have grown, I thought of their legs that must look thinner than spiders', and of their dwindled croaking that never could be heard.

Perhaps the lake was only painted after all; I had seen things like it at the theatre. Anyhow it was a wonderful lake, a beautiful lake.'

(Beardsley, *Under the Hill and Other Essays in Prose and Verse*, p. 65.)

[84] Here Chapter X 'Of the Stabat Mater, Spiridion, and De La Pine' begins in LS.

black silk & wearing white kid gloves, [<]loose[>] yellow wigs, & feathered toques: with faces oval & young, bodies lithe & quick, voices silvery & affectionate, they made amends for all the hateful arrogance, disgusting aplomb, [<]& shameful ugliness[>] of the rest of their kind.

[four lines crossed out]

The dear fellow ~~was~~ who proclaimed the winner

<61>

was really quite delightful. He took a passionate interest in the horses & had licked all the paint off their balls.[85] You will ask me no doubt 'Is that all he did'? I will answer, 'Not quite', as the merest glance at their little posteriors would prove.[86]

[four lines crossed out]

In the afternoon light that came through the great silken-blinded windows of the Casino, all the gilded decorations, [<]all the gilded décor,[>] the chandeliers, the mirrors, ~~the gilded ornaments~~, the polished floor, the painted ceiling, [<]the horses galloping round their green meadow,[>] the [<]fat[>] rouleaux of gold & silver, [<]the ivory rakes,[>] the fanned & strange frocked crowd of dandy gamesters looked magnificently rich & warm. Tea was being served. It was so pretty to see some flushed little lady sipping ~~hurridly~~ nervously, ~~with her eyes~~ & keeping her eyes over the cup's edge intently upon the slackening horses. The more indifferent left the tables & took their tea in parties here & there.[87]

<62>

Tannhäuser found a great deal to amuse him at the Casino. Ponchon was the manager, & a person of extraordinary invention. Never a day but he was ready with a new show a novel attraction. A glance through the old Casino programmes would give you a very considerable idea of his talent. What countless ballets, comedies, comedy-ballets, concerts, masques, charades, proverbs, pantomimes, tableaux-magiques, ombres fantastiques, & peep-shows excentriques, what troupes of marionettes, what burlesques![88] ~~He~~ [<]Ponchon[>] had an astonishing flair for new talent, & many of the principal comedians & singers at the Queen's theatre and opera house had made their first appearance & reputation at the Casino.

This afternoon the pièce de resistance was a performance of Rossini's Stabat Mater & adorable masterpiece. It was given in the beautiful Salle des printemps parfumés. Ah! what a stunning rendering of the delicious demodé piece of decadence.[89] There is a subtle quality about the music, like

<63>

the unhealthy bloom upon wax fruit, ~~seen from under a glass~~, that both orchestra & singer contrived to emphasize with consummate delicacy.

The Virgin was sung by Spiridion that soft incomparable alto. A miraculous virgin too he made of her. ~~He dressed the rôle~~ To begin with he dressed the rôle most effectively. His plump legs up to ~~his~~ the feminine hips [<]of him[>] were in very white stockings clocked with a false pink, [<]he wore[>] brown kid boots buttoned to mid-calf, & his whorish thighs had thin scarlet garters round them. His jacket was cut like a jockey's, only the sleeves ended in manifold frills & round the neck & just upon the shoulders there was a black cape. His hair[<], dyed green,[>] was curled into ringlets such as the [<]smooth[>] Madonnas of Morales are made lovely

---

85 'balls' = 'petits couillons!' (LS).

86 'little posteriors' = 'petits derrières' (LS).

87 An unpaginated sheet follows containing eleven crossed-out lines and a sketch of a man's figure with his back to the reader.

88 'ombres fantastiques' omitted in LS.

89 'piece of decadence' = 'pièce de décadence' (LS).

with, & fell over his high egg-shaped [<]creamy[>] forehead & about his ears & cheeks & back. The alto's face was fearful & wonderful. A dream face. The eyes [<]were[>] full & black with puffy blue rimmed hemispheres under beneath them, the cheeks inclining to fatness were powdered & dimpled

<64>

the mouth was purple & ~~curled~~ curved painfully, the chin tiny & exquisitely modelled the expression cruel & womanish.

Heavens how splendid he looked & sounded. An exquisite piece of phrasing was accompanied with some curly gesture of the hand, some delightful undulation of the stomach, some nervous movement of the thigh or glorious rising of the bosom.

The performance provoked enthusiasm, thunders of applause. Claude & Clair pelted [<]the thing[>] ~~him~~ with roses & carried him off in triumph to the tables. His costume was declared ravishing. The men almost pulled him to bits, & mouthed at his great quivering bottom.[90] The little horses were quite forgotten for the moment. ~~The irresistible Sup penetrated.~~ ~~The penetrating Sup burst through~~ Sup the penetrating, burst through ~~Spiridion's~~ his silk fleshings, ~~& made a [? illegible]~~ & thrust in bravely up to the hilt whilst the alto's legs were feasted upon by Pudex, Cyril, Anquetin, & some others. Ballice, Corvo, Quadra, Senillé, Méllefont, Theodore, Levit,[91]

<65>

Le Vit, & Matta, all of the egoistic cult, stood & crouched round saturating the lovers with warm douches.

Later in the afternoon Venus & Tannhäuser paid a little visit to De La Pine's studio, as the Chevalier was very anxious to have his portrait painted. De La Pine's [<]glory[>] ~~reputation~~ as a painter was hugely increased by his reputation as a fouteur, for ladies that had pleasant memories of him looked with a biassed eye upon his fêtes galantes, merveilleuses, portraits & folies bergères. Yes, he was a bawdy [?]~~thing~~ creature & ~~his~~ the workshop a regular brothel. However his great talent stood in no need of such meretricious & phallic support, & he was every whit as strong & facile with his brush as with his tool.[92]

When Venus & the Chevalier entered his studio, he was standing amid a group of friends & connoisseurs who were liking his latest picture. It was a small canvas, one of his delightful morning pieces. Upon an Italian balcony stood a lady in a white

<66>

frock, reading a letter. She wore brown stockings, straw-coloured petticoats, white shoes, and a Leghorn hat. Her hair was red & in a chignon. At her ~~side~~ feet lay a tiny Japanese dog, painted from the Queen's favourite 'Fanny', & upon the ~~balcony~~ balustrade stood an open empty bird cage. The background was [<]a[>] stretch of Gallic country. Clusters of trees cresting the ridges of low hills, a bit of river, a chateau, & the morning sky.

De La Pine hastened to kiss the [<]moist & scented[>] hand of Venus. Tannhäuser bowed profoundly & begged to have some pictures shown him. The gracious painter took him round his studio.

~~The chevalier~~ Cosmé was one of the party, for De La Pine [<]just then[>] was painting his portrait, [<]a portrait[>] ~~which~~ by the way [<]which[>] promised to be a veritable chef d'oeuvre. [<]Cosmé was loved & admired by everybody.[>] To begin with, he was past master in his art, that fine relevant art of coiffing, then he was [<]really[>] modest & obliging & was only seen & heard when he was wanted. He was

---

[90] LS: 'bottom!'.

[91] Page 64 is followed by an unnumbered sheet containing two crossed-out lines.

[92] LS: 'tool!'.

<67>

useful, he was decorative in his white apron, black mask, & silver suit, he was discreet.

~~De la Pine~~ [<]The painter[>] was giving Venus & Tannhäuser a little dinner that evening & he insisted on Cosmé joining them. ~~Cosmé~~ [<]The Barber[>] vowed he would be de trop & required a world of pressing ~~to~~ [<]before he would[>] accept the invitation. Venus added her voice & he consented.

Ah I what a delightful little partie carré it turned out. The painter was in purple & full dress, all tassels & grand folds. His hair magnificently curled, his heavy eye-lids painted, his gestures large & romantic, he reminded one ~~something~~ a little of Maurel playing Wolfram in the [<]second act of the[>] opera of Wagner. Venus was in a ravishing toilet, a confection of Camilles[<], & looked like Kxxxxx[>]. Tannhäuser was dressed as a woman & looked like a ~~classic Venus~~ goddess. Cosmé sparkled with gold, bristled with ruffs, glittered with bright buttons, was painted, powdered, gorgeously bewigged, & looked like a marquis in a comic opera. The ~~dining room~~ salle á manger at de La Pine's was quite the prettiest that ever was. Upon

[Here the manuscript ends.]

REPRODUCTION OF THE MANUSCRIPT

"Under the Hill".

A romantic novel

by

Aubrey Beardsley

with his illustrations
& ornaments

Chaps I II III IV V

2

La chaleur du brandon Venus

Le Roman de la Rose, v. 22051

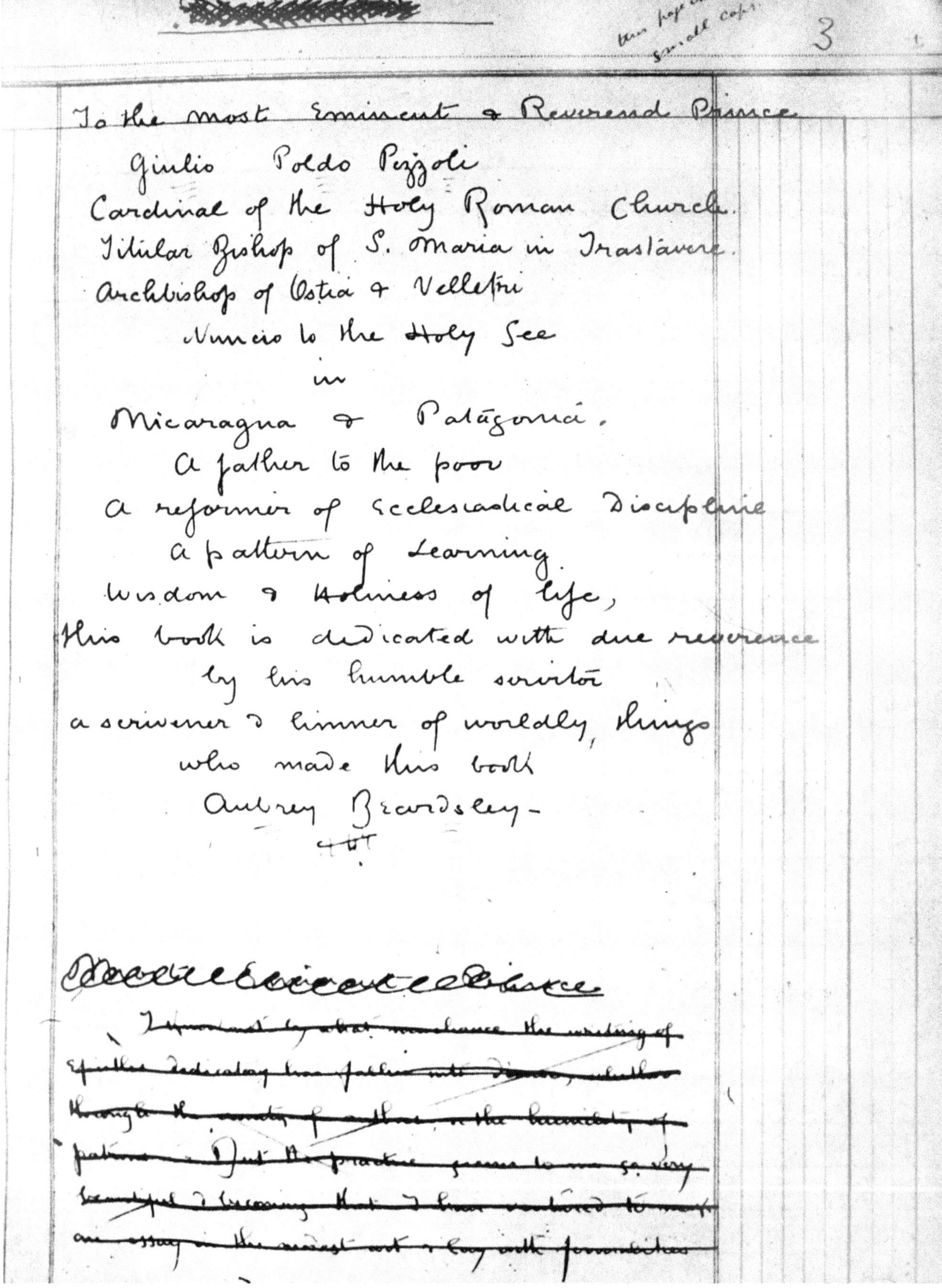

this page in small caps.

3

To the most Eminent & Reverend Prince
Giulio Poldo Pezzoli
Cardinal of the Holy Roman Church
Titular Bishop of S. Maria in Trastavere.
Archbishop of Ostia & Velletri
Nuncio to the Holy See
in
Nicaragua & Patagonia.
A father to the poor
A reformer of Ecclesiastical Discipline
A pattern of Learning
Wisdom & Holiness of life,
this book is dedicated with due reverence
by his humble servitor
a scrivener & limner of worldly things
who made this book
Aubrey Beardsley.

~~Most Eminent Prince~~

~~I know not by what mischance the writing of Epistles dedicatory has fallen into disuse, whether through the vanity of authors, or the humility of patrons. But the practice seems to me so very beautiful & becoming that I have ventured to make an essay in the modest art & lay with formalities~~

4

Most Eminent Prince

I know not by what mischance the writing of epistles dedicatory has fallen into disuse, whether through the vanity of authors or the humility of patrons. But the practice seems to me so very beautiful & becoming that I have ventured to make an essay in the modest art & lay with formalities

5 * 11

my first book at your feet. I have, it must be confessed many fears lest I shall be arraigned of presumption in choosing so exalted a name as your own to place at the beginning of this history, but I hope that such a censure will not be too lightly passed upon me for if I am guilty, 'tis but of a most natural pride that the accidents of my life should allow me to sail the little pinnace of my wit under your protection.

But though I can clear myself of such a charge I am still minded to use the tongue of apology, for with what face can I offer you a book treating of so vain & fantastical a thing as love? I know that in the judgment of many the amorous passion is accounted a shameful thing & ridiculous, indeed it must be confessed that more blushes have risen for love's sake than for any other cause, & that lovers are an eternal laughing stock. Still as the book will be found to contain matter of deeper import than mere venery, inasmuch as it treats of the great contrition of its chiefest character & of canonical things in certain pages I am not without hopes that your Eminence will pardon

6 III

my writing of The Hill of Venus for which exposition let my youth ~~[illegible]~~ excuse me.

Then I must crave your forgiveness for addressing you in a language other than the Roman, but my small freedom in Latinity forbids me to wander beyond the room of my vernacular. I would not for the world that your delicate southern ear should be offended by a barbarous assault of rude & gothic words, but methinks no language is rude that can boast polite writers, & not a few such have flourished in this country in times past, bringing our common speech to very great perfection. In the present age alas! our pens are ravished by unlettered authors & unmannered critics, that make a havoc rather than a building, a wilderness rather than a garden. But alack what boots it to drop tears upon the preterit?

T'is not of our own shortcomings though, but of your own great merits that I should speak, else I should be forgetful of the duties I have drawn upon myself in electing to address you in a dedication. T'is of your noble virtues (though all the world know of 'em), your

7 IX 4

taste & wit, your care for letters & very real regard for the arts that I must be the proclaimer.

Though it be true that all men have sufficient wit to pass a judgment on this or that, & not a few sufficient impudence to print the same (these last being commonly accounted critics) I have ever held that the critical faculty is more rare than the inventive. T'is a faculty your Eminence possesses in so great a degree that your praise or blame is something oracular, your utterance infallible as great genius or a beautiful woman. Your mind, I know, rejoicing in fine distinctions & subtle procedures of thought, beautifully discursive rather than hastily conclusive, has found in criticism its happiest exercise. T'is pity that so perfect a Mecaenas should have no Horace to befriend, no Georgics to accept; for the offices & function of patron or critic must of neccessity be lessened in an age of little men & little work. In times past t'was nothing derogatory for great princes & men of State to extend their loves & favour to poets, for thereby they received as much honour as they conferred. Did not Prince

Festus with pride take the masterwork of
Julian into his protection, & was not the
Aeneis a pretty thing to offer Caesar?
Learning without appreciation is a thing of 8
nought, but I know not which is greatest
in you, your love of the arts or your knowledge
of 'em. What wonder then that I am
studious to please you & desirous of your protection.
How deeply thankful I am for your past
affections you know well, your great kindness
& liberality leaving far outgone my slight
merits & small accomplishment that
seemed scarce to warrant any favour.
Alas 'tis a slight offering I make you
now, but if after glancing into its pages
(say of an evening upon your terrace) you
should deem it worthy of the most remotest
place in your princely library, the knowledge 9
that it rested there would be reward sufficient
for my labours & a crowning happiness to
my pleasure in the writing of ~~[illegible]~~
this slender book.

The humble & obedient servant of Your Eminence

Aubrey Beardsley

9

Under the Hill

Chapter I

The Abbé Fanfreluche Aubrey having lighted off his horse, stood doubtfully for a moment beneath the ombre gateway of the Hill of Venus, troubled with an exquisite fear lest a day's travel should have too cruelly undone the laboured niceness of his dress. His hand slim & gracious as La Marquise du Deffand's in the drawing by Carmontelle, played nervously about the gold hair that fell upon his shoulders like a finely curled peruke, & from point to point of a precise toilet the fingers wandered, quelling the little mutinies of cravat & ruffle.

It was taper time; when the tired earth puts on its cloak of mists & shadows, when the enchanted woods are stirred with light footfalls & slender voices of the fairies, when all the air is full of delicate influences, & even the beaux seated at their dressing tables, dream a little.

A delicious moment, thought Fanfreluche Aubrey, to slip into exile

The place where he stood waved drowsily
with strange flowers, heavy with perfume,
dripping with odours. Gloomy & nameless 10
weeds, not to be found in Mentzelius.
Huge moths so richly winged, they must
have banqueted upon tapestries & royal
stuffs, slept on the pillars that flanked
either side of the gateway, & the eyes of
all the moths remained open, & were burning
& bursting with a mesh of veins. The pillars
were fashioned in some pale stone &
rose up like hymns in the praise of Venus,
for from cap to base each one was carved
with loving sculptures showing such a
cunning invention & such a curious Knowledge
that Tannhauser lingered not a little
in reviewing them. They surpassed all
that Japan has ever pictured from her
maisons vertés, all that was ever painted
in the ~~infamous~~ pretty bath rooms of Cardinal La
Motte & even outdid the astonishing
illustrations to Jones' "Sidelights on child
life"
"A pretty portal," murmured the Knight
correcting his sash.
As he spoke a faint sound of singing

was breathed out from the mountain, faint music as strange & distant as sea legends that are heard in shells.

X "The vespers of Venus, I take it", said
X Tannhauser, & struck a few chords of accompaniment ever so lightly upon his little lute. Softly across the spell bound threshold the song floated & wreathed itself about the subtle columns till the moths were touched with passion & moved quaintly in their sleep. One of them was awakened by the intenser notes of the chevalier's lute strings & fluttered
X into the cave. Tannhauser felt it was his cue for entry

"Adieu" he exclaimed with an inclusive gesture, & "Goodbye Madonna", as the cold circle of the moon began to show, beautiful & full of enchantments. There was a shadow of sentiment in his voice as he spoke the words.

"Would to heaven" he sighed, "I might receive the assurance of a looking glass before I make my début!. However as she is a goddess I doubt not her eyes are a little sated with perfection & may not be displeased

to see it crowned with a tiny fault."
A wild rose had caught upon the trimmings
of his *muff*, & in the first flush of displeasure
he would have struck it brusquely away,
& most severely punished the offending
flower. But the ruffled mood lasted
only a moment, for there was something 12
so deliciously incongruous in the hardy
petals' invasion of so delicate a thing, that
Tannhauser withheld the finger of resentment
& vowed that the wild rose should stay
where it had clung, a passport, as it
were, from the upper to the underworld.
"The very excess & violence of the fault"
he said "will be its excuse", & undoing
a tangle in the tassel of his stick, stepped
into the shadowy corridor that ran into
the bosom of the wan hill. Stepped
with the admirable aplomb & unwrinkled
suavity of Don John.

II

13

Before a toilet that shone like the altar of Nôtre Dame des Victoires, Venus was seated in a little dressing gown of black & heliotrope. The coiffeur Cosmé was caring for her scented chevelure, & with tiny silver tongs, warm from the caresses of the flame made delicious intelligent curls. that fell as lightly as a breath about her forehead & over her eyebrows, & clustered like tendrils round her neck. Her three favorite girls, Pappelarde Blanchemains & Loreyne waited immediately upon her with perfume & powder in delicate flacons & frail cassolettes, & held in porcelaine jars the ravishing ~~paint~~ paints prepared by Chateline for those cheeks & lips that had grown a little pale with anguish of exile. Her three favorite boys Claude Clair & Sarrasine stood amorously about with salver, fan, & napkin. Millamant held a slight tray of slippers, Minette some tender gloves, La Popelinière, mistress of the robes, was ready with a frock of yellow & yellow, La Zambinella bore the jewels

Florizel some flowers, Amadour a box of various pins & Vadius a box of sweets. 14

Her doves ever in attendance walked about the room that was panelled with the galant paintings of Paul ~~Chateaulleur De La Porte~~, & some dwarfs & doubtful creatures sat here & there lolling out their tongues ~~& betraying~~ monstrously wise. Sometimes Venus gave them little smiles.

As the toilet was in progress Priapusa the fat manicure & farded, strode in & seated herself by the side of the dressing table, greeting ~~Venus~~ with an intimate nod. She wore a gown of white watered silk with gold lace trimmings & a velvet necklet of vermilion. Her hair hung in bandeaux over her ears ~~[illegible]~~ passing into a huge chignon at the back of her head; & the hat wide brimmed & hung with a vallance of pink muslin was floral with red roses.

Priapusa's voice was full of salacious unction; she had terrible little gestures with the hands, strange movements with the shoulders, a short respiration that

15

made surprising wrinkles in her bodice,
a corrupt skin, large horny eyes,
a parrots nose, a small loose mouth,
great flaccid cheeks, & chin after chin.
She was a wise person & Venus loved
her more than any other of her servants,
& had a hundred pet names for her
such as, Dear toad, pretty pol,
cock robin, dearest lip, touchstone, ~~figs~~
~~faute de mieux~~, ~~[illegible]~~ bijou, buttons,
astiquette, dear heart, dick-dock, ~~tête-bêche~~,
Mrs Manly, little nipper, cochon de
lait naughty-naughty, blessèd thing
& tup. trump
The talk that passed between Priapusa × Mrs Marsuple
& her mistress was of that excellent
kind that passes between old friends,
a perfect understanding giving to scraps
of phrases their full meaning, & to the
merest reference, a point. Naturally
× Tannhauser the new comer was discussed
a little. ~~Venus~~ had not seen him × Helen
yet & asked a score of questions on his
account that were delightfully to the point
Priapusa told the story of his sudden
arrival, his curious wandering in the

16

gardens & calm satisfaction with all he saw there, his impromptu affection for a slender girl upon the first terrace & of the crowd of frocks that gathered round & pelted him with roses, of the graceful way he defended himself with his mask, & of the ~~bottle~~ ~~mock~~ queer reverence he made to the statue of god of all gardens ~~Priapus; kissing the huge emblem~~ with a pilgrim's devotion. Just now he was at the baths & ~~[illegible]~~ was creating a most favourable impression.

The report & the coiffing were completed at the same moment.

"Cosmé" said Venus "you have been quite sweet & quite brilliant, you have surpassed yourself tonight".

"Madam flatters me" replied the antique old thing with a girlish giggle under his black satin mask, "Gad Madam sometimes I believe I have no talent in the world, but tonight I must confess to a touch of the vain mood."

It would pain me ~~to~~ horribly to tell you about the painting of her face, suffice it that the sorrowful work was accomplished; frankly, magnificently, & without ~~a~~ a shadow of deception.

Venus slipped away the dressing gown & rose before the mirror in a flutter of frilled things. She was adorably tall & slender. Her neck & shoulders were so wonderfully drawn & the little malicious breasts were full of the ~~—~~ irritation of loveliness that can never be entirely comprehended or ever enjoyed to the utmost. Her arms & hands were loosely but delicately articulated & her ~~—~~ legs were divinely long. From the hip to the knee twenty two inches from the knee to the heel twenty two inches as befitted a goddess. [I should like to speak more particularly about her, for generalities are not of the slightest service in a description. But I am afraid that an enforced silence upon many points would leave such numerous gaps in the picture that it had better not be begun at all than be left unfinished.]

17

Priapusa grew quite lyric over the dear little lady & pecked at her arms with kisses.

"Dear Tongue, you must really behave

yourself" said Venus, & called Millamant to bring her the slippers. 18

The tray was freighted with the most exquisite & shapely pantoffles, sufficient to make Cluny a place of naught. There were shoes of grey & black & brown suéde, of white silk & rose satin & velvet of sarsineoshe, there were some of sea green sewn with cherry blossoms, some of red with willow branches, & some of grey with bright winged birds. There were heels of silver of ivory & of gilt, their were buckles of very precious stones set in most strange & esoteric devices, there were rubbands tied & twisted into cunning forms, there were buttons so beautiful that the buttonholes might have no pleasure till they closed upon them there were soles of delicate leathers scented with maréchale, & linings of soft stuffs scented with the juice of July flowers.

But Venus finding none of them to her mind called for a discarded pair of blood red maroquin diapered with pearls. These looked very distinguished over her white silk stockings.

X

As the tray was being carried away Florizel as usual snatched a slipper from it & fitted the foot over his penis, & made the necessary movements. That was Florizel's little caprice.

meantime
La Popelinière stepped forward with the frock.
"I shant wear one tonight" said Venus. & Helen
Then she slipped on her gloves.
When the toilet was at an end all her doves clustered round her feet loving to frôler her ankles with their plumes, & the dwarfs clapped their hands & put their fingers between their lips & whistled. Never had Venus looked so beautiful before. Claude & Clair pale with pleasure stroked & touched her with their delicate hands, & wrinkled her stockings with their nervous lips, & smoothed them ~~again~~ with their thin fingers. & Sarrasine undid her garters & kissed them inside & put them on again pressing her ~~legs~~ thighs with ~~kisses~~ his mouth.
There was almost a mêlée.
The dwarfs grew very daring & illustrated pages seventy two & seventy three of Delvau's Dictionary.
In the middle of it all Pranzmungel announced that supper was ready upon the fifth terrace
Ah cried Venus I'm famished!

19

honi soit qui mal y pense

III

She was quite delighted with Tannhäuser & of course he sat next her at supper. The terrace, made beautiful with a thousand vain & fantastical things, & set with a hundred tables & four hundred couches presented a truly splendid appearance. In the middle was a huge bronze fountain with three basins. From the first rose a many breasted dragon, & four little Loves mounted upon swans, & each Love was furnished with a bow & arrow. Two of them that faced the monster seemed to recoil in fear, two that were behind made bold enough to aim their shafts at him. From the verge of the second sprang a circle of slim golden columns that supported silver doves with tails & wings spread out. The third, held by a group of grotesquely attenuated satyrs was centred with a thin pipe hung with masks & roses, & capped with children's heads.
From the mouths of the dragon & the Loves, from the swan's eyes, from the

breasts of the doves, from the satyrs horns 21
& lips, from the masks at many points
& from the children's curls the
water played profusely cutting strange
arabesques & subtle figures.
The terrace was lit entirely by candles.
There were four thousand of them not
numbering those upon the tables. The
candlesticks were of a countless variety
& smiled with moulded cochonneries.
Some were twenty feet high & bore
single candles that flared like
fragrant torches over the feast &
gutted till the wax stood round the tops
in tall lances. Some hung with
dainty petticoats of shining lustres, had
a whole bevy of tapers upon them, devised
in circles, in pyramids, in squares, in
cuneiforms, in single lines regimentally,
& in crescents.
Then on quaint pedestals & terminal
gods & gracious pilasters of every sort
were shell like vases of excessive fruits
& flowers that hung about & burst over
the edges & could never be restrained.
The orange trees & myrtles looped with

~~vases~~ vermilion sashes stood in frail porcelain pots & the rose trees were 22 wound & twisted with superb invention over trellis & standard. Upon one side of the terrace a long gilded stage for the comedians was curtained off with amphytrion tapestries, & in front of it the music stands were placed. The tables arranged between the fountain & the flight of steps to the sixth terrace were all circular, covered with white damask & strewn with irises, roses, King-cups, colombines, daffodils, carnations & lilies, & the couches high with soft cushions & spread with more stuffs than could be named had fans thrown upon them & little ~~erotic~~ amorous surprise packets.

Beyond the escalier stretched the venereal gardens that were designed so elaborately & with so much splendour that the architect of the Fêtes d'Armailhacq could have found in them no matter for cavil, & the still lakes strewn with profuse barges full of gay flowers & wax marionnettes, the alleys of tall

23

trees, the arcades & cascades, the
pavillions the grottos & the garden gods
all took a strange tinge of revelry from
the glare of the lights that fell upon
them from the feast.
The priceless Venus & Tannhäuser, with
Priapusa & Claude & Clair & Farcy
the chief comedian sat at the same table.
Tannhauser who had doffed his
travelling suit wore ~~nothing but some~~
long black silk stockings, a ~~pair~~ pair
of pretty garters, a very elegant ~~chemise~~ ruffled shirt,
slippers & a wonderful dressing gown. (Claude
& Clair wore nothing at all, delicious
privilege of immaturity, & Farcy was
in ordinary evening clothes. As for the
rest of the ~~[illegible]~~ company it boasted
some very noticeable dresses & whole
tables of quite delightful coiffures. There
were spotted veils that seemed to stain
the skin with some exquisite & august
desease, fans with eyeslits in them
through which the bearers peeped & peered,
fans painted with postures & covered
with the sonnets of Sporion & the short
stories of Scaramouch, & fans of big

living moths stuck upon mounts of silver 24
sticks; There were masks of green velvet that make
the face look trebly powdered, masks of
the heads of birds, of apes, of serpents, of
dolphins, of men & women, of little embryos
& of cats, masks like the faces of gods
masks of coloured glass, & masks of
thin talc & of india rubber. There
were wigs of black & scarlet wools, of
peacocks' feathers, & of gold & silver
threads, of swansdown, of the tendrils of
the vine, & of human hairs; huge collars
of stiff muslin rising high above the
head; whole dresses of ostrich feathers
curling inwards, tunics of panther's
skins that looked beautiful over pink
tights, capotes of crimson satin trimmed
with the wings of owls, sleeves cut into the
shapes of ~~apoce~~ apocryphal animals,
drawers flounced down to the ankles
& ~~broidered~~ flecked with tiny red roses, that seemed
like flecks of blood, stockings ~~cl~~ clocked
with fêtes galantes & curious designs,
& petticoats cut like artificial flowers.
Some of the women had put on delightful
little moustaches dyed in purples & bright

25

greens, twisted & waxed with absolute skill, & some were great white beards. Then ~~De~~ La Pine had painted extraordinary grotesques & vignettes over their bodies here & there. Upon a cheek, an old man scratching his horned head upon a forehead, an old woman teased by an impudent amor, upon a shoulder, an amorous singerie, round a breast, a circlet of satyrs, about a wrist, a wreath of ~~unborn~~ babies children upon an elbow a bouquet of spring flowers, across a back, some surprising scenes of adventure, at the corners of a mouth, tiny red spots, & upon a neck, a flight of birds, a caged parrot, a branch of fruit, a butterfly, a spider, a drunken dwarf or simply her initials. But most wonderful of all were the black silhouettes painted upon the legs, & which showed through a white stocking like a sumptuous bruise.

The supper provided by the ingenious Rambouillet was quite beyond parallel.

after the manner of the Wilgaforte

*/ Never had he created a more exquisite menu. The consommé impromptu alone would have been sufficient to establish the immortal reputation of any chef, what then can I say of the Dorade bouillie sauce, ~~fouteuse~~, the ragoût aux langues de carpes, the ramereaux à la charnière, the ciboulette de gibier à l'espagnole, ~~the~~ poussins aux accidents féminins, the pâté de cuisses d'oie aux pois de Monsalvi, the dindon de la menagerie ~~à la peau~~ de vièrge, the queues d'agneau au clair de lune, the vits ~~des boeufs sauce naturelle~~ the rissolettes à la ~~pine~~ magistrale the artichauts à la grecque, the asperges sauce Lestrenne, the charlotte de Pommes à la Pérınée the bombes à la marée & the glaces aux rayons d'or? A veritable tour de cuisine that surpassed even the famous ~~ale [illegible]~~ little suppers given by the Marquis de Réchale at Passy, & which the Abbé Mirliton pronounced "impeccable & too good to be eaten". Ah Pierre Antoine Berquin de Rambouillet you are worthy of your divine mistress!

26

Mere hunger quickly gave place to those finer instincts of the pure gourmet & the strange wines cooled in buckets of snow, unloosed all the décolleté spirits of astonishing conversation & atrocious laughter. At first there was the fun with the surprise packets that contained myriads of unmentionable things, then a general criticism of the decorations everyone finding their own peculiar meaning in the fall of festoon turn of twig & twist of branch. Suculex as usual bore the palm for insight &

invention, & to-night he was more brilliant
than ever. He leant across the table
& explained to the young page Macfils 27
de Martaga what was intended by a
certain arrangement of roses. The
young page smiled & hummed the
refrain of "La Petite, ~~Lurette~~." Sporion too, had delicate perceptions
~~[illegible]~~
and was greatly amused by
It was the disposition of the candelabra
that amused him most, & suddenly
noticing that the change of one of them would
produce an entirely new & amazing effect
he sprang from his seat & made the
improvement. All the tables round
about raised a shout of delight.)
As the courses advanced the conversation
became more personal. {The infidelities
of Cérise, Sarmean's caprices ~~that morning~~
in the lily garden, Thorilliere's declining
strength, Vutva's affection for Roscola,
Falix's impossible member#, & a thousand
amatory follies of the day were discussed.
From harsh & shrill & clamant, the
voices grew blurred & ~~[illegible]~~
inarticulate. Bad sentences were
helped out by worse gestures. & at one

x/ Cathelin's passion for Suepitia's poodle, Sola's passion for herself, the nasty bite that Marisca gave Chloe, the epilation of Pulex, Cyril's deseases,

table, Scabius could only express himself with his napkin after the manner of Sir Jolly Jumble in the "Soldiers Fortune" of Otway. Bassalissa & Lysistrata tried to pronounce each others names & became very affectionate in the attempt, & Tala the tragedian robed in purple & wearing plume & buskin, rose to his feet & with swaying gestures began to recite one of his favorite parts. He got no further than the first line but repeated it again & again with fresh accents & intonations each time, & was only silenced by the approach of the asparagus that was being served by satyrs costumed in white muslin. ✝/

28

[I wish I could be allowed to tell you what occurred round table 15 just at this moment, it would amuse you very much & would give you a capital idea of the habits of Venus' retinue. ~~Ind~~ Indeed, for deplorable reasons, by far the greater part of what was said & done at this supper must remain unrecorded & even unsuggested.

Venus allowed most of the dishes to pass

†/ Clitor & Sodon had a violent struggle ~~over the beautiful Pella~~ & nearly upset a chandelier, Sophie became very intimate with an empty ~~crafty~~ champagne bottle, swore it had made her enceinte, & ended by having 'a mock accouchement on the top of the table, Bellmour pretended to be a dog & pranced from couch to ~~coa~~ couch on all fours biting & barking & licking, Mellefont crept about dropping ~~aphadeacaa~~ aphrodisiacs into glasses, Juventus & Ruella ~~stripped & put~~ on each other's things, ~~Epesto~~ Spelto offered a prize for whoever should come first & Spelto won it, and Aubrey, just a little grisé, lay down on the cushions & let Julia do whatever she liked.

29

untasted, she was so engaged with the lad beauty of Tannhäuser. She hid her head many times on his robe kissing him passionately & his skin at once firm & yielding seemed to those exquisite little teeth of hers, the most incomparable pasture. Her upper lip curled & trembled with excitement showing the gums. Tannhauser on his side was no less devoted. He adored her all over & all the things she had on, & buried his face in the folds & flounces ~~of her linen~~ & ravished away a score of frills in his excess. He found her exasperating & crushed her in his arms & slaked his parched lips at her mouth. He caressed her eyelids softly with his finger tips & pushed aside the curls from her forehead & did a thousand gracious things tuning her body as a violinist tunes his instrument before he plays upon it. ✕

After the fruits & fresh wines had been brought in by a troop of woodland creatures decked with green leaves & all sorts of spring flowers, the candles in the

*/ Priapusa snorted like an old war horse at the sniff of powder & licked Tannhäuser & Venus by turns & slipped her tongue down their throats & refused to be quiet at all till she had had a mouthful of the Chevalier. Claude seizing his chance dived under the table & came up the other side just under the queen's couch & before she could say, one! he was taking his coffee aux deux colonnes. Clair was furious at his friend's success & sulked for the rest of the evening.

12

kissing him passionately, & his skin at once firm & yielding seemed to those exquisite little teeth of hers the most incomparable pasture. Her upper lip curled & trembled with excitement showing the gums. Aubrey on his side was no less devoted. He adored her all over & all the things she had on, & buried his face in the folds & flounces of her linen, & ravished away a score of frills in his excess. He found her exasperating & crushed her in his arms & slaked his parched lips at her mouth. He caressed her eyelids softly with his finger tips, & pushed aside the curls from her forehead & did a thousand gracious things.

"Bless you my children" cried Mrs Marsuple. Claude & Clair bit their lips & gazed deeply at the loving two, & held each others hand.]

Ku

To be continued.

orchestra were lit, & in another moment the musicians bustled into their places. 30 The wonderful Titurel de Schentefleur was the chief d'orchestre, & the most insidious of conductors. His bâton dived into a phrase & brought out the most magical & magnificent things, & seemed rather to play every ~~into~~ instrument than to lead it. He could add a grace even to Scarlatti & a wonder to Beethoven. A delicate thin little man with thick lips & a nez retroussé, with long black hair & curled moustache in the manner of Molière. (What were his amatory tastes no one in the Venusberg could tell; & he generally passed for a virgin, & Cathos had nicknamed him the Solitaire.) To night he appeared in a court suit of white silk, brilliant with decorations, his hair was curled into resplendent ringlets that trembled like springs at the merest gesture of his arm, & in his ears swung the diamonds given him by Venus. ~~[illegible]~~ The orchestra was as usual in its uniform of red vest & breeches trimmed with gold

lace, white stockings & red shoes.
Titurel had written a ballet for 31
the evenings divertissement founded
upon De Bergerac's comedy of "Les
Bacchanales de Fanfreluche," in which
the action & dances were designed by him
as well as the music.

[illegible]

This was followed by

[illegible]

FOOTNOTE to face p

31 A

The curtain rose upon a scene of rare beauty, a remote arcadian valley, & watered with a clear river as fresh & pastoral as a perfect fifth.

of this scrap of Tempe. It was early morning & the re-arisen sun, like the prince in the sleeping beauty, woke all the earth with his lips. In

footnote to p. 3 of MS

1. Ward

The curtain rose upon a scene of rare beauty, a remote arcadian valley, a delicious scrap of Tempe, gracious with ~~cool~~ cool woods & watered with a little river as fresh & pastoral as a perfect fifth. It was early morning & the re-arisen sun like the Prince in the Sleeping Beauty woke all the earth with his lips.

In that golden embrace the night dews were caught up & made splendid, the trees were wakened from their obscure dreams, the slumber of the birds was broken & all the flowers of the valley rejoiced forgetting their fear of the darkness.

32

Suddenly to the music of pipe & horn a troop of satyrs stepped out from the recesses of the woods bearing in their hands nuts & green boughs & flowers & roots & whatsoever the forest yielded, to heap upon the altar of the mysterious Pan that stood in the middle of the stage; & from the hills came down the shepherds & shepherdesses leading their flocks & carrying garlands upon their crooks. Then a rustic priest, white robed & venerable, came slowly across the valley followed by a choir of radiant children. ~~whose delectable limbs, so tender & ... utterly ...~~. The ~~[illegible]~~ scene was admirably stage managed & nothing could have been more varied yet harmonious ~~[illegible]~~ than this arcadian group. The service was quaint & simple, but

(1)

with sufficient ritual to give the corps de ballet an opportunity of showing its dainty skill. The dancing of the satyrs was received with huge favour & when the priest raised his hand in jovial blessing, the whole troop of worshippers made such an intricate & elegant exit, that it was generally agreed that Titurel had never before shown ~~such~~ so a fine an invention.

Scarcely had the stage been empty for a moment, when ~~[illegible]~~ Sporion entered followed by a brilliant rout of dandies & smart women. ~~[illegible]~~ Sporion was a tall slim ~~[illegible]~~ depraved young man with a slight stoop, a troubled ~~[illegible]~~ walk, an oval impassable face with its olive skin drawn tightly over the bone, strong, scarlet ~~painted~~ lips, long japanese eyes, & a great gilt toupet. Round his shoulders hung a high collared satin cape of salmon pink with long black ribbands untied & floating about his body. His coat of sea green spotted muslin was caught in at the waist by a scarlet sash with scalloped edges

& frilled out over the hips for about six inches. His trousers, loose & wrinkled reached to the end of the calf, & were brocaded down the sides & ruched magnificently at the ankles. The stockings were of white kid with stalls for the toes, & tiny delicate red sandals strapped over them. 34

But his little hands, peeping out from their frills seemed quite the most insinuating things, such supple fingers tapering to the point with tiny nails stained pink, such unquenchable palms lined & mounted like Lord Fanny's in "Love at all hazards" & such blue veined hairless backs. In his left hand he carried a small lace handkerchief broidered with a coronet.

As for his friends & followers they made the most superb & insolent crowd imaginable, but to catalogue the clothes they had on would require a chapter as long as the famous tenth in Penillière's history of underlinen.

On

the whole they looked a very distinguished chorus.

~~[illegible]~~ Sporion stepped forward & explained 34 A.
with swift & various gesture that he & his
friends were tired of the amusements, wearied
with the poor pleasures offered by the ~~world~~
civil world, & had invaded the arcadian

35

valley hoping to experience a new frisson in the destruction of some shepherd's or some satyr's naiveté, & the infusion of their venom among the dwellers of the woods.

The chorus assented with languid, but expressive ~~[illegible]~~ movements.

Curious & not a little frightened at the arrival of ~~[illegible]~~ the worldly company, the sylvans began to peep nervously at those subtle souls through the branches of the trees & one or two fauns & a shepherd or so crept out warily.

Sporion ~~[illegible]~~ & all the ladies & gentlemen made enticing sounds & invited the rustic creatures with all the grace in the world to come & join them. By little batches they came lured by the strange looks ~~[illegible]~~ by the scents & by the brilliant clothes & the drugs, & some ventured quite near timorously fingering the delicious textures of the stuffs. Then Sporion ~~[illegible]~~ & each of his friends took a satyr or a shepherdess or something by the hand & made the preliminary steps of a courtly measure for which the most admirable

5

combinations had been invented & the
most charming music written. The
pastoral folk were entirely bewildered
when they saw such restrained & graceful
movements & made the most grotesque
& futile efforts to imitate them. ~~To
the huge & suppressed pleasure of Tarefaluchi
the [illegible] great [illegible] in the
attempt to caper about the stage
[illegible] husbands are
in the "Lysistrata" of Aristophanes, though they were
as innocent of offence as the very horses
in Nanan's "Amours catholiques"~~
Dio mio, a pretty sight! A charming
effect too, was obtained by the intermixture
of stockinged calf & hairy leg, of rich
brocaded bodice & plain blouse, of
tortured head dress & loose untutored
locks.

When the dance was ended ~~Tarefaluchi~~
the servants of ~~[illegible]~~ Sporion brought on
champagne & with many pirouettes
poured it magnificently into ~~[illegible]~~ slender glasses,
& tripped about plying those arcadian
mouths that had never before tasted
such a royal drink.

* * * * * * * * * *

"Then the curtain fell with a pudic rapidity."

T'was not long before the invaders began
to enjoy the first fruits of their expedition
plucking them in the most seductive 37
manner with their smooth fingers, &
feasting lip & tongue & tooth, whilst the
shepherds & satyrs & shepherdesses fairly
gasped under ~~on~~ the new joys, for the
pleasure they experienced was almost
too keen & too profound for their simple &
untilled natures. Fanfreluche &
the rest of the rips & ladies tingled
with excitement & frolicked like young
lambs in a fresh meadow. Again
& again the wine was danced round
& the valley grew as busy as a market day. ~~[illegible]~~ ~~[illegible]~~.
Attracted by the noise of merrymaking
all those sweet infants I told you of
skipped suddenly on to the stage & began clapping their hands,
& laughing immoderately ~~[illegible]~~ at the
passion & the disorder & commotion, ~~clapping their hands~~
& mimicking the nervous staccato movements they saw
in their pretty childish way. In
a flash Fanfreluche disentangled
& sprang to his feet gesticulating as if the world away ~~[illegible]~~ Ah the
little dears Ah the little ducks Ah
the rorty little things!, for he was so fond

of children. Scarcely had he caught one by the thigh than a quick rush was made by everybody for the succulent limbs; & how they tousled them & mousled them. The children cried out I can tell you. Of course there were not enough for everybody so some had to share, & some had simply to go on with what they were doing before. I must not by the way forget to mention the independent attitude taken by six or seven of the party, who sat & stood about with half closed eyes inflated nostrils clenched teeth. & painful parted lips, behaving like the Duc de Broglio when he watched the amours of the Regent Orleans. 38

Now as Fanfreluche & his friends began to grow tired & exhausted with the new debauch, they cared no longer to take the initiative, but relaxing every muscle abandoned themselves to passive joys yielding utterly to the ardent embraces of the ~~[illegible]~~ intoxicated satyrs who waxed fast & furious & seemed

as if they would never come to the
end of their strength. Full of the new
tricks they had learnt that morning 39
they played them passionately & roughly,
making havoc ~~with~~ of the cultured flesh
& tearing the splendid frocks & dresses
into ribbands. Duchesses & Maréchales,
Marquises & Princesses, Dukes & marshalls
Marquesses & Princes, were ravished & stretched
& rumpled & crushed beneath the
interminable vigour & hairy breasts
of the inflamed woodlanders. They
bit at the white thighs & nozzled wildly
in the crevices, they sat astride the
women's chests & consummated frantically
with their bosoms, they caught their
prey by the lips & held it over their
heads ruminating ~~[illegible]~~ with prodigious gusto.
It was the triumph of the valley. High
up in the heavens the sun had mounted
& filled all the air with a generous warmth,
whilst shadows grew shorter & sharper.
Little light winged papillons flitted
across the stage, the bees made music
on their flowery way, the birds were very
gay & kept up a jargoning & refraining,

the lambs were bleating upon the hill side
& the orchestra kept playing, playing
the uncanny tunes of Titurel. 40
Venus & Tannhäuser had retired to the
exquisite little boudoir or pavillion
Le Con had designed for the Queen
upon the first terrace & that commanded
the most delicious view of the parks &
gardens. It was a sweet little place
all silk curtains & soft cushions. There were
eight sides to it bright with mirrors &
candelabra, & rich with pictured
panels, & the ceiling, dome shaped &
some thirty feet above the head,
shone obscurely, with gilt mouldings, through the warm haze
of candle light below. Tiny wax
statuettes dressed theatrically & smiling
with plump cheeks,
quaint magots
that looked as cruel as foreign gods,
gilded monticules, pale celadon vases,
clocks that said nothing, ivory boxes full of
secrets, china figures playing whole scenes
of plays, & a world of strange
preciousness crowded the curious cabinets
that stood against the walls. On one

side of the room there were six perfect
little card tables, with quite the daintiest
& most elegant chairs set primly round 41
them, so after all there may be some
truth in that line of Mr Theodore Watts
"*I played at piquet with the Queen of Love*".
Nothing in the pavilion was more beautiful
than the folding screens painted by
De La Pine with Claudian landscapes,
the sort of things that fairly make one melt,
things one can lie & look at for hours
together & forget the country can ever be dull
& tiresome. There were four of them,
delicate walls that hem in an amour
so cosily & make room within room.
The place was scented with huge branches
of red roses, & with a faint amatory
perfume breathed out from the couches
& cushions, a perfume Chateline
distilled in secret & had called *L'Eau
Savante*.

Those who have only seen Venus at the
Louvre or the British Museum, at Florence,
at Naples, or at Rome, can have not
the faintest idea how sweet & enticing
& gracious, how really exquisitely beautiful

she looked, lying with Tannhäuser,
upon rose silk, in that pretty boudoir. 42
Cosmé's precise curls & artful waves had
been finely disarranged at supper,
& strayed ringlets of the black hair
fell loosely over her soft delicious
~~[illegible]~~
lived swollen eyelids. Her frail
chemise & dear little drawers were
torn & moist & clung transparently
about her, & all the body was nervous
~~[illegible]~~ & responsive. ~~[illegible]~~
~~[illegible]~~
~~[illegible]~~
~~[illegible]~~
~~[illegible]~~
~~[illegible]~~
~~[illegible]~~
Tannhauser pale & speechless with
excitement passed his gem girt fingers
brutally over the divine limbs tearing
away smock & pantalon & stocking,
& then stripping himself of his own
few things, fell upon the splendid lady
with a deep drawn breath. ~~[illegible]~~
~~[illegible]~~

-X-/

/ Her closed thighs seemed like a vast ~~[illegible]~~ replica of the little bijou she held between them; ~~that~~ the beautiful tétons du derrière, were as ~~[illegible]~~ firm as a plump virgi[n's] & promised a joy as profound as the mystery of the Rue Veni ~~[illegible]~~, & the minor chevelure, just profuse enough, curled as ~~[illegible]~~ prettily as the hair upon a cherub's head.

It is I know the custom of all romancers
to paint heros who can give a lady proof of
their valliance at least twenty times a night. 43
Now Tannhäuser had no such
gargantuan facility, & was rather
relieved when an hour later Priapusa
& Doricourt & some others burst drunkenly
into the room & claimed Venus for
themselves. The pavillion was soon
filled with a noisy crowd that could
scarcely keep its feet. Several of the
actors were there, & Lesfesses who had
played Fanfreluche so brilliantly &
was still in his make up paid
tremendous attention to Tannhäuser.
But the chevalier found
him quite uninteresting off the stage
& rose & crossed the room to where
Venus & the manicure were seated.
"How tired the dear baby looks," said
Priapusa, "shall I put him
in his little cot?"
"Well if he's as sleepy as I am" yawned
Venus you can't do better.
Priapusa lifted her mistress off the pillows

& carried her in her arms in a nice motherly way. 44

"Come along children" said the fat old thing, "come along, its time you were both in bed."

IV

It is always delightful to wake up in a new bedroom. The fresh wallpaper, the strange pictures, the positions of doors & windows, imperfectly grasped the night before, are revealed with all the charm of surprise when we open our eyes the next morning.

It was about eleven o'clock when Tannhauser awoke & stretched himself deliciously in his great plumed four post bed, & nursed his walking thoughts. ~~[illegible]~~ ~~[illegible]~~ & stared at the curious ~~[illegible]~~ patterned canopy above him. He was very pleased with the room which certainly was chic & fascinating &

& recalled the voluptuous interiors of the elegant amorous Baudouin. Through the tiny parting of the long flowered window curtains the chevalier caught a peep of the sun lit lawns outside, the silver fountains, the bright flowers & the gardeners at work. "Quite sweet," he murmured, & turned round to freshen the frilled silk pillows behind him, & what delightful pictures he continued wandering with his eyes from print to print that hung upon the rose striped walls. Within the delicate curved frames lived the corrupt & gracious creatures of Dorat & his school; slim children in masque & domino smiling horribly, exquisite lechers leaning over the shoulders of smooth doll like ladies & doing nothing particular, terrible little Pierrots posing as mulierasts, or pointing at something outside the picture, & unearthly fops & strange women mingling in some rococo rooms lighted mysteriously by the flicker of a dying fire that throws huge shadows upon wall & ceiling. One of the prints showing

45

how an old marquis practised the five
finger exercise whilst in front of him, his
mistress offered her warm fesses to a panting 46
poodle, made the chevalier stroke
himself a little.
After a while he got up & slipping
off his dainty night dress postured
elegantly before a long mirror & made
much of his body. Now he would
bend forward & admire the creases of
his stomach, now he would stand upright
& adore the contour of his loins & hips,
now he would rest upon one leg &
let the other hang loosely till he
looked as if he might have been drawn
by some early Italian master, &
now he would lie upon the floor
with his back to the glass & glance
amorously over his shoulder. Then
with a white silk sash he draped
himself in a hundred charming ways.
So engrossed was he with
his mirrored shape that he had
not noticed the entrance of a troop of
serving boys who stood admiringly
but respectfully at a distance ready

to receive his walking orders. As soon as the Chevalier observed them he smiled sweetly & bade them prepare the bath.

His bathroom was the largest & perhaps the most beautiful apartment in his splendid suite. The well known engraving by Lorette that forms the frontispiece to Millevoye's ~~history~~ "Architecture du XVIIIme siècle" will give you a better idea than any words of mine, of the ~~[illegible]~~ construction & decoration of the room. Only in Lorette's engraving the bath sunk into the middle of the floor is a little ~~[illegible]~~ too small.

Tannhäuser stood for a moment like Narcissus ~~Narcissus~~ gazing at his reflection in the still scented water, & then just ruffling it's smooth surface with one foot, stepped elegantly into the cool basin & swam round it twice very gracefully.

"Wont you join me?" he said turning to those beautiful boys who stood ready with warm towels & perfume. In a moment they were free of their light morning dress, & jumped into the water, & joined hands & surrounded the chevalier with a laughing chain. 48

"Splash me a little" he cried, & the boys teased him with water, & quite excited him. He chased the prettiest of them & bit his fesses & kissed him upon the perineum till the dear fellow banded as freely as a carmelite & it's little bald topknot looked like a great pink pearl under the water. As the boy seemed anxious to take up the active attitude Tannhauser graciously descended to the passive, a generous trait that won him the complete affections of his valets de bain, or pretty fish as he called them, because they loved to swim between his legs.

However it is not so much in the very bath itself, as in the drying & delicious frictions that a bather finds his chiefest pleasures, & Tannhauser was more than satisfied with the skill his ~~[illegible]~~ attendants displayed in the performance of those quasi amorous functions. The delicate attention they paid his loving parts ~~[illegible]~~ aroused feelings within him that almost amounted to gratitude, & when the rites were ended ~~[illegible]~~ any touch of home sickness he might have felt before was utterly dispelled.

48

49.

After ~~[illegible]~~ he had rested a little & sipped his ~~[illegible]~~ chocolate, he wandered into the dressing room. Dancourt, his valet de chambre, Chenille ~~[illegible]~~ the perruquier & barber, & two charming young dressers were awaiting him, & ready with suggestions for the morning's toilet. The shaving over, Dancourt commanded his underlings to step forward with the suite of ~~[illegible]~~ suits from which he proposed Tannhauser should make a choice. The final selection was a happy one. A dear little coat of pigeon rose silk that hung loosely about his hips & showed off the jut of his behind to perfection, trousers of black lace in flounces, falling almost like a ~~skirt~~ petticoat as far as the knee, & a delicate chemise of white muslin spangled with gold, & profusely pleated. The two dressers, under Daucourt's direction, did their work superbly, beautifully, leisurely, & with an exquisite deference for the nude, ~~and with~~ & a really sensitive appreciation of Tannhäuser's ~~[illegible]~~ scrumptious torso.

When all was said & done the Chevalier tripped off to bid good morning to Venus. He found her wandering in a sweet white muslin frock upon the lawn outside plucking flowers to deck her little dejeuner. He kissed her lightly upon the neck.

"I'm just going to feed Adolphe ~~[illegible]~~" she said, pointing to a little reticule of buns that hung from her arm.

~~[illegible]~~ Adolphe ~~[illegible]~~ was her pet unicorn.

"He is such a dear" she continued, ~~[illegible]~~ "milk white all over excepting his black eyes, rose mouth & nostrils, & scarlet john*. ~~[illegible]~~ ~~[illegible]~~. This way"!

50

The unicorn had a very pretty palace
of its own made of green foliage &
golden bars, a fitting home for such
a delicate & dainty beast. Ah
it was indeed a splendid thing to
watch the white creature roaming in
its artful cage, ^proud & beautiful & knowing no mate
except the Queen herself.

As Venus & Tannhauser approached
the wicket Adolphe began prancing
& curvetting, pawing the soft turf
with his ivory hoofs, & flaunting his
~~tail~~ tail like a gonfalon. Venus
raised the latch & entered.

"You mus'nt come in with me, Adolphe
is so jealous" she said turning to
the chevalier who was following her.
"But you can stand outside & look on,
Adolphe likes an audience".

Then ~~with~~ ^in her delicious fingers she
broke the spicy buns & with affectionate
niceness breakfasted her ardent pet.

When the last crumbs had been scattered
Venus brushed her hands together &
pretended to leave the cage ^without taking any more notice of Adolphe. Every
morning she went through this piece of play

every morning the amorous unicorn was cheated into ~~[illegible]~~ a distressing agony lest that day should have proved the last of Venus' love. Not ~~[illegible]~~ for long though would she leave him in that doubtful piteous state but running back passionately to where he stood make adorable amends for her unkindness. Poor Adolphe! how happy he was touching the ~~queen's~~ Queen's breast with his quick tongue tip! ~~I have no doubt that the keener scent~~ I have no doubt that the keener scent of ~~[illegible]~~ animals must make women much more attractive to them than to men, ~~[illegible]~~ for ~~that~~ the gorgeous odour that but faintly fills our nostrils must be revealed to the brute creation in divine fulness. Anyhow Adolphe sniffed as never a man did—around the skirts of Venus. After the first charming interchange of affectionate delicacies was over, ~~he~~ the unicorn lay down upon his side & closing his eyes beat his stomach wildly with ~~his~~ the mark of manhood. Venus caught that

52

[illegible] in her hands & lay her cheek along it. But few touches were wanted to consummate the creature's pleasure. The Queen bared her left arm to the elbow & with the soft underneath of it made amazing movements horizontally upon the tight strung instrument. When the melody began to flow the unicorn offered up an astonishing vocal accompaniment. Tannhauser was amused to learn that the etiquette of the Venusberg compelled everybody to wait the outburst of these venereal sounds before they could sit down to dejeuner.

Adolphe had been quite profuse that morning.

Venus knelt where it had fallen & lapped her little aperitif.

VI.

The breakfasters were scattered over the gardens in têtes a têtes & tiny parties. 54

Venus & Tannhauser sat together upon the lawn that lay in front of the Casino, & made havoc of a ravishing dejeuner. The chevalier was feeling very happy. Everything around him seemed so ~~bright~~ white & light & matinal, the floating frocks of the ladies, the scarce robed boys & satyrs stepping hither & thither elegantly with meats & wines & fruit, the damask table cloths, the delicate talk & laughter that rose everywhere the flowers' colour & the flowers' scent, the shady trees, the wind's cool voice, & the sky above that was as fresh & pastoral as a perfect fifth. And Venus looked so beautiful. Not at all like the lady in Lempriere.

You're such a dear murmurred Tannhauser holding her hand.

At the further end of the lawn & a little hidden by a rose tree a young man was breakfasting alone. ~~[illegible]~~

He toyed nervously with his food now
& then but for the most part leant
back in his chair with
& unemployed hands, & gazed stupidly 55
at Venus.
"That's Felix" said the goddess, in answer
to an enquiry from the Chevalier; &
she went on to explain his attitude.
Felix always attended Venus upon
her little Latrinal excursions holding her
serving her & making much of all she
did. To undo her things, to lift her
skirts, to wait & watch the coming, to
dip lip & finger in the royal output,
to stain himself deliciously with it to
lie beneath her as the favours fell, to carry off the crumpled crotted paper
these were the pleasures of that young
man's life.
Truly there never was a Queen so beloved
by her subjects as Venus. Everything
she wore had its lover.
Heavens how
her handkerchiefs were filched, her stockings
stolen!
Daily, what intrigues,
what countless ruses to possess her merest

~~Every scrap of her body was adored.~~
frippery! . Never for Savaral could her ear yield sufficient wax! Never for Pradon could she spit prodigally enough! And Saphius found a month ~~an~~ an interminable time.

After breakfast was over & Felix' fears lest Tannhauser should have robbed him of his capricious rights, had been dispelled; Venus invited the Chevalier to take a more extensive ~~[illegible]~~ view of the gardens parks pavilions & ornamental waters. The carriage ~~[illegible]~~ ~~[illegible]~~ was ordered. It was a delicate shell like affair with billowy cushions & a light canopy, & was drawn by ten satyrs dressed as finely as the coachmen of the Empress Pauline the first.

~~[illegible]~~

The drive proved ~~[illegible]~~ interesting & various, & Tannhauser was quite delighted with almost everything he saw.

And who ~~[illegible]~~ is not pleased, when on either side of him rich lawns ~~[illegible]~~ are spread with lovely frocks & white limbs, ~~[illegible]~~ ~~[illegible]~~ & upon flower beds the dearest ladies are implicated in a glory of underclothing when he can see in deep cool shadows of the trees, warm boys entwined, here at the base, there in the branch, when in the fountain's wave Love holds his court & the insistent water burrows in very delicious crease & crevice?

A pretty sight too was little Rosalie perched like a postillion upon the painted phallus of the god of all gardens. Her eyes were closed & she was smiling as the carriage passed. Round her neck & slender girlish shoulders there was a cloud of complex dress over which bulged two long like flaxen tresses, her legs & feet were bare & the toes twisted in an amorous style. At the foot of the statue lay her shoes & stockings & a few other things.

Tannhauser was singularly moved & rose out of all proportion. Venus slipped the fingers of comfort under the lace flounces of his trousers saying "Is it all mine, Is it all mine?" & doing fascinating things. In the end the carriage was only prevented from being overturned by the happy interposition of Priapusa who stepped out from somewhere or other just in time to preserve its balance.

How the old lady's eye glistened as Tannhauser withdrew his panting blade, & in her sincere admiration for fine things she quite forgot & forgave the shock she had received from the falling of the gay equipage.

Venus & Tannhauser were profuse with apology & thanks, & the chevalier vowed he would never go in the carriage again & was really quite upset about it. However after he had

x. & quite a crowd of loving courtiers
gathered round condoling & congratulating
in a breath.

had a little support from the smelling
salts he recovered his self possession &
consented to drive on further. 59
The landscape grew rather mysterious.
The park, no longer troubled & adorned with
figures was full of ~~argent~~ grey echoes, & mysterious
sounds, the leaves whispered a little sadly
& there was a grotto that murmured like the
~~a~~ voice that haunts the silence of a deserted
oracle. Tannhäuser ~~grew~~ became a little triste.
In the distance through the trees gleamed
a still urgent lake, a ~~[illegible]~~ reticent romantic
water, that must have held the subtlest
fish that ever were,. ~~&~~ ~~Around~~ around its marge
the trees & flags & fleurs de luce ~~[illegible]~~ were
unbreakably asleep.
The chevalier fell into a strange mood
as he looked at the lake, it seemed to
him that the thing would speak, reveal
some curious secret, say some beautiful
word, if he should ~~break its calm~~ dare to
wrinkle its pale face with a pebble.
"I should be frightened to do that though"
he said to himself.
Then he wondered what there might ~~be~~
be ~~[illegible]~~ upon the other side; other

gardens other gods? when he woke up from his day dream he noticed that the carriage was on its way back to the palace. 60

They stopped at the Casino first & stepped out to join the players at petits chevaux. Tannhauser preferred to watch the game rather than play himself & stood behind Venus who stepped into a vacant chair & cast gold pieces upon lucky numbers. The first thing that Tannhauser noticed was the grace & charm, the gaiety & beauty of the croupiers. They were quite adorable even when they raked in one's little coins. Dressed in black silk & wearing white kid gloves, cerise yellow wigs, & feathered toques: with faces oval & young, limbs lithe & quick, voices silvery & affectionate, they made amends for all the hateful arrogance, disgusting & contemptible ugliness & aplomb of the rest of their kind. The dear fellow who proclaimed the winner,

~~His imagination deepened~~ * & a thousand drowsy fancies passed through his brain. Sometimes the lake took fantastic shapes, or grew to ~~twice~~ twenty times its size or shrunk into a miniature of itself, ~~without~~ without ever once loosing its ~~&~~ unruffled calm it's deathly reserve. When the water increased the chevalier was very frightened for he thought ~~of~~ how huge the ~~toads~~ frogs must have become, he thought of their big eyes & monstrous wet feet, but when the water lessened he laughed to himself for he thought ~~of~~ how tiny the ~~toads~~ frogs ~~must~~ must have grown he thought of their legs that must ~~be~~ look ~~so~~ thinner than spiders', ~~&~~ & of their dwindled croaking that never could be heard. ~~[illegible]~~ Perhaps the lake was only painted after all, he had seen things like it at the theatre. Anyhow it was a wonderful lake, a beautiful lake, & he would love to bathe in it, ~~[illegible]~~ ~~[illegible]~~ but he was sure he would be drowned if he did.

67

was really quite delightful. He took a passionate interest in the horses & had licked all the paint off their balls. You will ask me no doubt "Is that all he did?" I will answer "not ~~quite~~ quite", as the merest glance at their little posteriors would prove.

~~The room around the tables was amusing enough. Rows of sweet little women [illegible] before the cages crouched [illegible] of delicious [illegible]~~

In the afternoon light that ~~came~~ came through the great silken blinded windows of the casino all the gilded decor the chandeliers, the mirrors, ~~the gilded ornaments~~ the polished floor the painted ceiling ~~the tables~~ the horses galloping round their green meadow the ivory rakes the fat rouleaux of gold & silver the fanned & strange frocked crowd of dainty gamesters looked magnificently rich & warm. Tea was being served. It was so pretty to see some frivolous little lady sipping ~~nervously~~ nervously with ~~her eyes~~ & keeping her eyes over the cups edge intently upon the slackening horses. The more indifferent left the tables & took their tea in parties here & there.

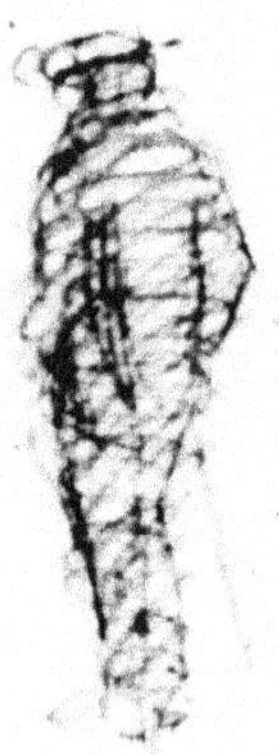

Tannhauser found a great deal to amuse him at the Casino. Ponchon was the manager, & a person of extraordinary invention. Never a day but he was ready with a new show a novel attraction. A glance through the old Casino programmes ~~would~~ would give you a very considerable idea of his talent. What countless ballets, comedies, comedy-ballets concerts, masques, charades, proverbs, pantomimes, tableaux magiques, ombres fantastiques, & peep shows excentriques, what troupes of marionettes, what burlesques!. Ponchon ~~He~~, had an astonishing flair for new talent & many of the principal comedians & singers at the Queens theatre & opera house had ~~[illegible]~~ ~~[illegible]~~ made their first appearance & reputation at the Casino.

This afternoon the piece de resistance was a performance of Rossini's Stabat Mater & adorable masterpiece. It was given in the beautiful Salle des printemps parfumes. Ah what a stunning rendering of the delicious demode piece of decadence. There is a subtle quality about the music, like the unhealthy bloom upon wax fruit, ~~[illegible]~~, that both orchestra & singer contrived to emphasize with consummate ~~tact~~ delicacy. 63

The Virgin was sung by Spiridion that soft incomparable alto. A miraculous virgin too he made of her. ~~[illegible]~~ ~~[illegible]~~ To begin with he dressed the rôle most effectively. His plump legs up to ~~[illegible]~~ the feminine hips, of him, were in very white stockings clocked with a false pink, he wore brown kid ~~[illegible]~~ boots buttoned to mid calf, & ~~[illegible]~~ his whorish thighs had thin scarlet garters round them. His jacket was cut like a jockey's, only the sleeves ended in manifold frills & round the neck & just upon the shoulders there was a black cape. His hair, dyed green, was curled into ringlets such as the smooth madonnas of Morales are made lovely with, & fell over his high egg shaped creamy, forehead & about his ~~[illegible]~~ ears & cheeks & back. The alto's face was fearful & wonderful. A dream face. The eyes, were full & black with puffy ~~[illegible]~~ blue rimmed hemispheres beneath ~~[illegible]~~ them, – the cheeks inclining to fatness were powdered & dimpled

, the mouth was purple & curved painfully,
the chin tiny & exquisitely modelled
the expression cruel & womanish.
Heavens how splendid he looked & sounded!
An exquisite piece of phrasing was accompanied
with some curly gesture of the hand, some
delightful undulation of the
stomach, some nervous movement of the
thigh, or glorious rising of the bosom. The
performance provoked enthusiasm, thunders
of applause. Claude & Clair pelted the thing
with roses & carried him off
in triumph to the tables. His
costume was declared ravishing. The men
almost pulled him to bits, & mouthed at
his great quivering bottom. The little
horses were quite forgotten for the moment.
The irresistible Sup.
Sup.
the penetrating [illegible] through [illegible]
silk fleshings [illegible] &
cutting thrust [illegible] craving up to the hilt
whilst the other's legs were feasted upon
by Pudex, Cyril, Anquetin & some
others. Balbus, Corvo, Quadra,
Smith, Millefont, Theodore,

64

[illegible]

[illegible]

Le Vit & Matta, all of the egoistic cult, stood & crouched round saturating the lovers with warm douches.
Later in the afternoon Venus & Tannhauser paid a little visit to De La Pine's studio, as the chevalier was very anxious to have his portrait painted. De La Pine's glory as a painter was hugely increased by his reputation as a fouteur, for ladies that had pleasant memories of him looked with a biassed eye upon his fêtes galantes merveilleuses, portraits & folies bergeres. Yes he was a bawdy creature & the workshop a regular brothel. However his great talent stood in no need of such meretricious & phallic support, & he was every whit as strong & facile with his brush as with his tool.
When Venus & the chevalier entered his studio, he was standing amid a group of friends & connoisseurs who were liking his latest picture. It was a small canvas, one of his delightful morning pieces. Upon an Italian balcony stood a lady in a white

66

frock reading a letter. She wore brown stockings straw coloured petticoats white shoes and a Leghorn hat, Her hair was red & in a chignon. At her ~~side~~ feet lay a tiny japanese dog painted from the Queen's favorite "Fanny", & upon the ~~balcony~~ balustrade stood an open empty bird cage. The background was a stretch of ~~[illegible]~~ gallic country. Clusters of ~~[illegible]~~ trees cresting the ridges of low hills, a bit of river a chateau & ~~a~~ the morning sky.

~~[illegible]~~ De La Pine hastened to kiss the moist & scented hand of Venus. Tannhauser bowed profoundly & begged to have some pictures shown him. The gracious painter ~~[illegible]~~ took him round his studio.

~~[illegible]~~ Cosmé was one of the party, for ~~[illegible]~~ De La Pine just then was painting his portrait, a portrait ~~[illegible]~~ by the way which promised to be ~~[illegible]~~ a veritable chef d'oeuvre. ~~[illegible]~~ (Cosmé was loved & admired by Everybody) ~~[illegible]~~, To begin with he was past master in his art, that fine relevant art of coiffing, then he was ~~[illegible]~~ really modest & obliging & was only seen & heard when he was wanted. He was

useful he was ~~decorative~~ decorative in his
white apron black mask & silver suit,
he was discreet.
~~[illegible]~~ The painter was giving Venus & Tannhäuser
a little dinner that evening & he
insisted on Cosme joining them. ~~Cosme~~ The Barber
vowed he would be de trop & required a
world of pressing before he would ~~to~~ accept the invitation.
Venus aided her voice & he consented.
Oh what a delightful little partie carré
it turned out. The painter was in purple
& full dress, all tassels & grand folds.
His hair magnificently curled, his heavy
eyelids painted his gestures large &
romantic he reminded one ~~something~~ a little
of Maurel playing Wolfram in the second act of the
opera of Wagner. Venus was in a
ravishing toilet, a confection of Camille's, & looked like
Tannhauser was dressed ~~like~~ as a woman
& looked like a ~~[illegible]~~ goddess.
Cosme sparkled with gold, bristled
with ruffs, glittered with bright buttons,
was painted powdered gorgeously be-wigged,
& looked like a marquis in a comic opera.
The ~~[illegible]~~ salle a manger at ~~De la Pine~~ De La Pine's
was quite the prettiest that ever was. Upon

CHECKLIST OF BEARDSLEY'S LETTERS MENTIONING *UNDER THE HILL*

Aubrey Beardsley's letters listed below contain mentions of *Under the Hill* and thus provide a chronology of his work on the manuscript. Page references are to Henry Maas, J. L. Duncan, and W. G. Good, eds, *The Letters of Aubrey Beardsley* (London: Cassell, 1970).

To F. H. Evans — 27 June 1894, pp. 71–72

To F. H. Evans — 20 August 1894, p. 73

To F. H. Evans — early October 1894, p. 75

To W. Palmer (an Old Boy of Brighton Grammar School) — 2–3 October 1894, pp. 76–77

To F. H. Evans — November 1894, pp. 78–79

To M.-A. Raffalovich — 28 May 1895, pp. 88–89

To L. Smithers — 19 August 1895, pp. 97–98

To J. Pollitt — October 1895, p. 102

To L. Smithers — 7 November 1895, p. 103

To J. H. Ashworth — November 1895, pp. 104–105

To L. Smithers — November 1895, p. 105

To L. Smithers — 21 November 1895, p. 106

To M.-A. Raffalovich — 28 November 1895, p. 107

To L. Smithers — 27 March 1896, pp. 120–21

To L. Smithers — 6 April 1896, p. 122

To L. Smithers — 8 April 1896, pp. 122–23

To L. Smithers — 10 April 1896, pp. 124–25

To L. Smithers — 26 April 1896, p. 126

To L. Smithers — late May 1896, pp. 133–35

APPENDIX A
POETRY AND ESSAYS

'The Three Musicians'

'The Three Musicians' was published in the January 1896 issue of the *Savoy*. It focuses on a cosmopolitan trio of musicians — a Polish pianist, a 'gracious boy' dreaming of international fame, and a soprano. They wander in the woods until the pianist drops behind and the other two then enjoy a hinted-at erotic experience until interrupted by a recognizably British tourist. In a letter to Leonard Smithers of 28 April 1896, Beardsley notes that the German pianist Sophie Menter is 'the heroine' of the poem, presumably the soprano.[1] Stanley Weintraub identifies the 'gracious boy' as Edouard Dujardin, a French novelist who sported the same Regency style as the boy in Beardsley's illustrations for the poem.[2] Matthew Sturgis notes that the 'image of the Polish pianist conducting an orchestra of flowers seems to have been inspired by an account of Liszt doing exactly that'.[3] 'The Three Musicians' was favourably received by the press. According to the *Daily Chronicle*, it possesses 'a certain light elegance of its own and faithfully works up to a hinted impropriety'.[4] Fletcher points out that the 'golden world of pastoral France', dreamed up in 'The Three Musicians', is the 'closest spot on earth to the Venusberg'.[5] Jennifer Higgins argues that French references carry 'a cultural capital of sophistication and sexual freedom that the tourist does not possess'.[6] Linda Zatlin has shown that the poem is filled with sexual codes.[7]

Beardsley made three illustrations for his poem, the first of which was suppressed (Fig. 86). It felicitously represents the lines about the 'cantatrice' who 'fans herself, half shuts her eyes, and smoothes the frock about her knees. | The gracious boy is at her feet, | And weighs his courage with his chance; | His fears soon melt in noon-day heat'. The second drawing (Fig. 87) represents an earlier moment in the poem, the couple strolling purposefully into the woods. The third (Fig. 88) is a V-shaped tailpiece showing a young boy with a scythe who stares seductively at the viewer from a flower bed. Musical instruments are arranged at his feet and an erection is hinted at by the folds of his trousers. Zatlin points out that the imagery 'alludes to illustrations in seventeenth-century texts', employing 'the emblematic tradition to create in this drawing a storyline both seemingly innocent and at the same time sexual'.[8] Like the tailpiece for 'The Ballad of a Barber', this drawing foregrounds the themes of love and death.

The Three Musicians

Along the path that skirts the wood,
    The three musicians wend their way,
Pleased with their thoughts, each other's mood,
    Franz Himmel's latest roundelay,[9]
The morning's work, a new-found theme, their breakfast and the summer day.

---

[1] *Letters of Aubrey Beardsley*, p. 127.
[2] Stanley Weintraub, *Aubrey Beardsley: Imp of the Perverse* (London: Pennsylvania State University Press, 1976), p. 249.
[3] *Aubrey Beardsley: Poems*, ed. by Matthew Sturgis, Occasional Series, 6 (London: Privately Printed for The Eighteen Nineties Society, 1998), p. 43.
[4] 25 January 1896, p. 3, quoted in Zatlin, *CR* II, p. 251.
[5] Fletcher, 'Inventions for the Left Hand', p. 254.
[6] Jennifer Higgins, 'Unfamiliar Places: France and the Grotesque in Aubrey Beardsley's Poetry and Prose', *Modern Language Review*, 106.1 (2011), 63–85 (p. 74).
[7] Linda Gertner Zatlin, *Aubrey Beardsley and Victorian Sexual Politics* (Oxford: Clarendon, 1990), pp. 151–54.
[8] Zatlin, *CR* II, pp. 251, 252.
[9] A roundelay is a short, simple song, with a refrain.

One's a soprano, lightly frocked
In cool, white muslin that just shows
Her brown silk stockings gaily clocked,[10]
Plump arms and elbows tipped with rose,
And frills of petticoats and things, and outlines as the warm wind blows.

Beside her a slim, gracious boy
Hastens to mend her tresses' fall,
And dies her favour to enjoy,
And dies for *réclame*[11] and recall
At Paris and St. Petersburg, Vienna and St. James's Hall.[12]

The third's a Polish Pianist
With big engagements everywhere,
A light heart and an iron wrist,
And shocks and shoals of yellow hair,
And fingers that can trill on sixths and fill beginners with despair.

The three musicians stroll along
And pluck the ears of ripened corn,
Break into odds and ends of song,
And mock the woods with Siegfried's horn,[13]
And fill the air with Gluck,[14] and fill the tweeded[15] tourist's soul with scorn.

The Polish genius lags behind,
And, with some poppies in his hand,
Picks out the strings and wood and wind
Of an imaginary band,
Enchanted that for once his men obey his beat and understand.

The charming cantatrice[16] reclines
And rests a moment where she sees
Her château's[17] roof that hotly shines
Amid the dusky summer trees,
And fans herself, half shuts her eyes, and smoothes the frock about her knees.

---

[10] A clocked stocking is one with a decorative design on the outer side, usually just above the ankle.

[11] *Réclame* is the French word for publicity.

[12] London's main concert hall from its opening in 1858 to its demolition in 1905. A spectacular neo-Gothic building, it stood on the corner of Regent Street and Piccadilly.

[13] Siegfried is the young hero of Wagner's opera of the same name. He has a silver hunting horn which plays a significant role in the opera. It awakens the dragon Fafner in his lair in the forest and enables Siegfried to kill him, splashing his hand with the dragon's blood in the process. He sucks the blood off and is enabled to understand the language of the birds, who then give him vital information. Beardsley made one of his most important early drawings of this scene (*Siegfried, Act II, c.* 1892–1893). He might also have been thinking of it when he made his later drawing of Salome dipping her finger in the blood of John the Baptist (*The Dancer's Reward*, 1893).

[14] Christoph Willibald Gluck was an eighteenth-century German composer of opera who revolutionized the form by making it more dramatic, and radically reducing length.

[15] Tweeded means wearing clothing made of tweed, a heavy, hard-wearing woollen cloth, typically brown in colour, flecked with muted greens and reds, and made in Scotland. It was and still is much beloved of the English upper and middle classes for leisurewear, particularly for shooting or travelling. Beardsley's reference to it here is loaded with social and cultural connotations. It identifies the tourist as a conventional middle-class Englishman.

[16] *Cantatrice* is the French word for a female singer, particularly an opera singer.

[17] *Château* is the French word for castle, or any grand house.

The gracious boy is at her feet,
And weighs his courage with his chance;
His fears soon melt in noon-day heat.
The tourist gives a furious glance,
Red as his guide-book grows,[18] moves on, and offers up a prayer for France.

'The Ballad of a Barber'

'The Ballad of a Barber' was published in the July 1896 issue of the *Savoy*. The facsimile reproduction of the manuscript by R. A. Walker shows that the poem was initially conceived of as the ninth chapter of *Under the Hill*. Beardsley refers to it as such in a letter to Smithers of 27 March 1896.[19] The manuscript provides an alternative ending which is reproduced here after the final version of the poem as it was printed in the *Savoy*.

When Leonard Smithers reported to Beardsley that Arthur Symons disliked 'The Ballad of a Barber', Beardsley responded in the tone of mocking self-flagellation:

> I am horrified at what you tell me about 'The Ballad'. I had no idea it was 'poor'. For goodness' sake print the poem under a pseudonym and separately from Under the Hill. What do you think of 'Symons' as a nom de plume? Seriously the thing must not be printed under my name. Any signature will do. Make it Arthur Malyon.* [...]
> * However I reserve my private judgement and think my poem is rather interesting.[20]

In the end, the poem was published separately from *Under the Hill* and under Beardsley's own name. John Gray's Decadent poem 'The Barber' (1894) is among the sources for 'The Ballad', alongside Alexander Pope's *The Rape of the Lock* (1712), which Beardsley 'embroidered' in 1896.[21] According to Fletcher, the 'barber is a species of poet who kills "the thing he loves" in order to preserve it forever at a perfect moment'.[22] Zatlin argues that the barber's skills connote his sexual prowess, while Chris Snodgrass points out that the name of the character 'reinforces the pun' because Carrousel 'means "joust", yet another conventional term for intercourse'.[23] Karl Beckson notes the Decadent qualities of the poem: 'the Baudelairean use of cosmetics as a means of transcending nature through artifice, the barber's disastrous loss of artistic control, the sudden bizarre violence'.[24] Beardsley planned to write a rather morbid 'sequel' to the poem, as is testified by his letter to Smithers of 29 June 1896: 'Sequel to the "Barber" nearly finished. The first ten verses give a very spirited description of the post mortem examination of the princess'.[25] These verses have vanished. Carrousel's address in 'Meridian Street' suggests that Beardsley might be imagining the setting as the Royal Palace of Greenwich, which lies on the Prime Meridian. Oddly perhaps, there is not, or no longer, a Meridian Street in Greenwich.

Beardsley made two illustrations for the poem, *The Coiffing* (Fig. 89) and *Cul-de-lampe* (Fig. 90), the latter offering, according to Ian Fletcher, 'the old pun that connects figuratively and literally love and death': the amalgamation is realized in 'the figure of an amorino bearing in place of quivers and arrows the noose and the gallows that await Carrousel'.[26]

---

[18] A reference to popular Baedeker guides, which were recognizable by their red covers; here it is used as a shorthand for middle-class respectability.
[19] Walker, pp. 109–10; *Letters of Aubrey Beardsley*, pp. 120–21.
[20] *Letters of Aubrey Beardsley*, p. 122.
[21] Alexander Pope, *The Rape of the Lock: Embroidered with Nine Drawings by Aubrey Beardsley* (London: Smithers, 1896).
[22] Fletcher, 'Inventions for the Left Hand', p. 254.
[23] Zatlin, *Aubrey Beardsley and Victorian Sexual Politics*, p. 154; Snodgrass, *Aubrey Beardsley, Dandy of the Grotesque*, p. 73.
[24] Karl Beckson, '"Aubrey Beardsley: Poems" Matthew Sturgis, Ed. [Book Review]', *English Literature in Transition, 1880–1920*, 42.2 (1999), 192–94 (p. 194).
[25] *Letters of Aubrey Beardsley*, p. 139.
[26] Fletcher, 'Inventions for the Left Hand', p. 258.

The Ballad of a Barber

Here is the tale of Carrousel,
The barber of Meridian Street.
He cut, and coiffed, and shaved so well,
That all the world was at his feet.

The King, the Queen, and all the Court,
To no one else would trust their hair,
And reigning belles of every sort
Owed their successes to his care.

With carriage and with cabriolet[27]
Daily Meridian Street was blocked,
Like bees about a bright bouquet
The beaux about his doorway flocked.

Such was his art he could with ease
Curl wit into the dullest face;
Or to a goddess of old Greece
Add a new wonder and a grace.

All powders, paints, and subtle dyes,
And costliest scents that men distil,
And rare pomades, forgot their price
And marvelled at his splendid skill.

The curling irons in his hand
Almost grew quick enough to speak,
The razor was a magic wand
That understood the softest cheek.

Yet with no pride his heart was moved;
He was so modest in his ways!
His daily task was all he loved,
And now and then a little praise.

An equal care he would bestow
On problems simple or complex;
And nobody had seen him show
A preference for either sex.

How came it then one summer day,
Coiffing the daughter of the King,
He lengthened out the least delay
And loitered in his hairdressing?

The Princess was a pretty child,
Thirteen years old, or thereabout.
She was as joyous and as wild
As spring flowers when the sun is out.

[27] A cabriolet is a two-wheeled vehicle drawn by a single horse, with a folding hood.

Her gold hair fell down to her feet
And hung about her pretty eyes;
She was as lyrical and sweet
As one of Schubert's melodies.[28]

Three times the barber curled a lock,
And thrice he straightened it again;
And twice the irons scorched her frock,
And twice he stumbled in her train.

His fingers lost their cunning quite,
His ivory combs obeyed no more;
Something or other dimmed his sight,
And moved mysteriously the floor.

He leant upon the toilet table,
His fingers fumbled in his breast;
He felt as foolish as a fable,
And feeble as a pointless jest.

He snatched a bottle of Cologne,
And broke the neck between his hands;
He felt as if he was alone,
And mighty as a king's commands.

The Princess gave a little scream,
Carrousel's cut was sharp and deep;
He left her softly as a dream
That leaves a sleeper to his sleep.

He left the room on pointed feet;
Smiling that things had gone so well.
They hanged him in Meridian Street.
You pray in vain for Carrousel.[29]

---

[28] Franz Schubert was an early nineteenth-century Austrian composer famous for writing more than 600 songs to the lyrics of such poets as Shakespeare, Goethe, and Schiller. These songs are considered the height of Romanticism. Schubert also composed chamber music, including his acclaimed *String Quintet* (1828).

[29] The crossed-out concluding stanzas in the manuscript read as follows:

The flowers on the toilet table
He plucked & stuck them in her breast,
He felt as foolish as a fable,
And feeble as a pointless jest.

He snatched a flacon of cologne
And broke the neck between his hands,
He felt as if he was alone,
And mighty as a King's commands.

The Princess gave a little scream,
Her maids of honour hurried in,
And laughed like people in a dream,
And wiped the red off from her chin.

Ah Carrousel the indiscreet!
What you have done I may not tell.
They hanged him in Meridian Street.
You pray in vain for Carrousel!

(cont.)

'Carmen CI'

Beardsley's translation of Catullus's poem 'Carmen CI' (Song 101) was published in the November 1896 issue of the *Savoy*. Gaius Valerius Catullus (*c.* 84–*c.* 54 BC) was a Roman poet, part of the 'neoterics' group, who rejected traditional Roman values in favour of Hellenistic Greek culture. As Julia H. Gaisser notes, 'Catullus' poetry is set in a social world appropriate to the unsettled period: sophisticated, pleasure loving, and more interested in private concerns (*otium*) than in public responsibility (*negotium*)'.[30] His output was diverse, ranging from obscene erotica to heroic epic poetry and confessional lyrics.

According to Sturgis, Beardsley's 'version of *Carmen CI* owed much to the literal-translation provided by Leonard Smithers in the 1894 edition of *The Carmina of Catullus*, which Smithers co-edited with Sir Richard Burton', the famous Victorian traveller and Arabist who published translations of the *Arabian Nights* and the *Kama Sutra*.[31] Beardsley seems to have been satisfied with his 'Carmen CI' to the extent that he inquired (through Smithers) about Symons's opinion, despite the animosity between the literary editor and the chief artist of the *Savoy*.[32] After it was printed, John Gray wrote to Beardsley with 'great congratulations' on his poem.[33] Fletcher considers it 'his best and indeed one of the better lyrics of the English *fin de siècle*'.[34] Beardsley created an elegant and sombre illustration for 'Carmen CI', inscribed 'Ave atque Vale', 'Hail and Farewell' (Fig. 91).

Discussing required revisions in a letter to Smithers, Beardsley writes:

> I think the last verse of 'Ballad' must have yet another alteration. The line will read as if something in the room was left behind that could convict him of the crime. Let the verse go thus:
>
> He left the room on pointed feet,
> Smiling that things had gone so well.
> They hanged him etc.
>
> I hope this is not too late.

See Beardsley to Smithers, 16 June 1896, in *Letters of Aubrey Beardsley*, pp. 136–37. The manuscript also includes the following stanza:

Equal respect alike he paid
A courtier in or out of place,
Priest, poet, dandy, or old maid,
A cook, or mistress in disgrace.

It was changed to the following version:

Equal respect alike he paid
To courtiers in favour or disgrace.
He never called a spade a spade
And always seemed to know his place.

Neither version of the stanza was used in the published variant of the poem.

30 Julia H. Gaisser, 'Catullus (1), Gaius Valerius', in *The Oxford Classical Dictionary* (Oxford: Oxford University Press, 2012) in *Oxford Reference* <https://www.oxfordreference.com/view/10.1093/acref/9780199545568.001.0001/acref-9780199545568-e-1443> [accessed 17 January 2021].

31 Sturgis, *Aubrey Beardsley: Poems*, p. 46.

32 Beardsley to Smithers, 29 September 1896, in *Letters of Aubrey Beardsley*, p. 173.

33 Beardsley to Smithers, 15 November 1896, in *Letters of Aubrey Beardsley*, p. 203.

34 Fletcher, 'Inventions for the Left Hand', p. 258.

Catullus
Carmen CI
A Verse Translation from the Latin by Aubrey Beardsley

By ways remote and distant waters sped,
Brother, to thy sad grave-side am I come,
That I may give the last gifts to the dead,
And vainly parley with thine ashes dumb:
Since she who now bestows and now denies
Hath ta'en thee, hapless brother, from mine eyes.

But lo! these gifts, the heirlooms of past years,
Are made sad things to grace thy coffin shell,
Take them, all drenchèd with a brother's tears,
And, brother, for all time, hail and farewell!

'The Ivory Piece'

'The Ivory Piece' is a fragment of a poem started by Beardsley at Menton in January 1898. This 'poetic reverie', in Sturgis's words, remained unfinished.[35] A facsimile reproduction of the manuscript is provided in Walker's miscellany.[36] Calloway and Colvin observe that although 'both theme and context' of this draft 'remain tantalisingly obscure', it 'gives an intriguing glimpse into the elliptic flights of Beardsley's imagination'.[37]

The Ivory Piece

Carelessly coiffed, with sash half slipping down
Cravat mis-tied, and tassels left to stream,
I walked haphazard through the early town,
Teased with the memory of a charming dream.

I recollected a great room. The day,
Half dead, lit faintly on the walls the pale
And sudden eyes that showed the formal play
Of woven actors in some curious tale.

In fabulous gardens, where romantic trees
Perched on the branches birds without a name.

[35] Matthew Sturgis, *Aubrey Beardsley: A Biography* (London: HarperCollins, 1998), p. 349.
[36] Walker, p. 116.
[37] Aubrey Beardsley, *In Black and White*, p. 172.

FIG. 86. *The Three Musicians*, first version (1895, *CR* 994), reproduced from *A Book of Fifty Drawings* (1897), p. 167.

Fig. 87. *The Three Musicians*, second version (1895, *CR* 995), reproduced from the *Savoy*, January 1896, p. 64.

FIG. 88. Tailpiece for 'The Three Musicians' (1895, *CR* 996), reproduced from the *Savoy*, January 1896, p. 64.

FIG. 89. *The Coiffing* (1896, *CR* 1009), reproduced from the *Savoy*, April 1896, p. 90.

FIG. 90. Cul-de-lampe for 'The Ballad of a Barber' (1896, *CR* 1010), reproduced from the *Savoy*, April 1896, p. 93.

Fig. 91. *Ave Atque Vale* (1896, *CR* 1017), reproduced from *The Later Work of Aubrey Beardsley* (London: John Lane, 1900), plate 128.

'The Art of the Hoarding'

Beardsley's short and snappy essay 'The Art of the Hoarding', published in July 1894 in the *New Review*, tapped into the style of the polemical, personality-centred New Journalism of the 1880s and 1890s. His piece was published next to articles by two other popular poster artists of the day, Jules Chéret (1836–1932) and Dudley Hardy (1867–1922), and illustrated with two of Beardsley's samples: his poster design for the *Yellow Book* (1894) and one for the publisher William Heinemann (1863–1920), made to advertise Cecil Raynor's novel *The Spinster's Scrip* (1894).

Beardsley attacks the established genres and institutions, i.e. oil painting and the Royal Academy, and praises, somewhat controversially, the poster as a new art form. Walker claims that Beardsley imitates Whistler's 'habit of jeering at the critics', in particular, in his book *The Gentle Art of Making Enemies* (1890).[1] Although self-promotion was certainly among the aims of Beardsley's publication (at which the first sentence of his piece hints, as Sturgis points out),[2] the essay is also carefully thought through and replete with illuminating observations such as the comparison of a weather-beaten poster to 'an old fresco over an Italian church door'.

The Art of the Hoarding

> Advertisement is an absolute necessity of modern life, and if it can be made beautiful as well as obvious, so much the better for the makers of soap and the public who are likely to wash.
>
> The popular idea of a picture is something told in oil or writ in water[3] to be hung on a room's wall or in a picture gallery to perplex an artless public. No one expects it to serve a useful purpose or take a part in everyday existence. Our modern painter has merely to give a picture a good name and hang it.
>
> Now the poster first of all justified its existence on the grounds of utility, and should it further aspire to beauty of line and colour, may not our hoardings claim kinship with the galleries, and the designers of affiches[4] pose as proudly in the public eye as the masters of Holland Road or Bond Street Barbizon (and, recollect, no gate money, no catalogue)?[5]
>
> Still there is a general feeling that the artist who puts his art into the poster is déclassé — on the streets — and consequently of light character. The critics can discover no brush work to prate of, the painter looks

[1] Walker, p. 91.

[2] Sturgis, *Aubrey Beardsley: A Biography*, p. 212.

[3] Beardsley uses the phrase as a poetic way of describing the artistic medium of watercolour. However, in this paragraph he is also playing a teasing game with ideas about art, and popular attitudes to it. To say that a painting in oil or watercolour is something 'told' or 'writ', implying that it tells a story, would have infuriated a modernist artist such as James McNeill Whistler, a founder of one of the fundamental doctrines of modernist art, that it should be purely visual, without narrative. Indeed, this teasing may have been aimed at Whistler, as in 1893 he had badly upset Beardsley, who then caricatured him a number of times. The last sentence of the paragraph, with its 'modern painter' who 'has merely to give a picture a good name and hang it', may again reference Whistler and his system of titling his paintings as 'arrangements' or 'harmonies'. In addition, Beardsley is here referencing the famous words that the poet John Keats asked to be put on his anonymous grave in the Protestant Cemetery in Rome, where he died: 'Here lies one whose name was writ in water'. It was a defiant last word to the critics who had dismissed his work as ephemeral. He died of tuberculosis at the age of 26, and Beardsley, apart from his admiration for Keats's poetry, must have felt a strong affinity with him as a fellow sufferer of that terrible disease, from which he was to die even younger than Keats. Beardsley also plays on the meaning of 'hang' as a method of execution, and puns on the popular saying 'give a dog a bad name and hang it', to imply that the modern painting, in the popular view, deserves death by hanging. He then goes on to point out another characteristic of modern paintings, that they 'perplex the public', and sets out what was then another relatively new and controversial doctrine of modernist art, that it does not 'serve a useful purpose or take part in everyday existence'.

[4] *Affiche* is the French word for poster.

[5] Beardsley here refers to the early nineteenth-century Barbizon School of French landscape painters, named after the village of Barbizon in the Forest of Fontainebleau, just to the south of Paris. They pioneered a focus on landscape as a significant subject, and on the practice of painting it out of doors, both of which formed a basis for the development of Impressionism. By the end of the century, however, their avant-garde status had been eclipsed by Impressionism and they had become a safe buy for wealthy people. This trade was catered for by expensive art galleries in London's Bond Street, and in Holland Road — an area lived in by successful artists and their patrons. Bond Street exhibitions of the major figures of Barbizon painting such as Théodore Rousseau and Jean-François Millet often had an admission fee as well as a pricey catalogue. Beardsley's suggestion that poster designers were equal to these admired and expensive artists (and, furthermore, free) was provocative.

askance upon a thing that achieves publicity without a frame, and beauty without modelling, and the public find it hard to take seriously a poor printed thing left to the mercy of sunshine, soot, and shower, like any old fresco over an Italian church door.

What view the bill-sticker and sandwich man[6] take of the subject I have yet to learn. The first is, at least, no bad substitute for a hanging committee, and the clothes of the second are better company than somebody else's picture, and less obtrusive than a background of stamped magenta paper.[7]

Happy, then, those artists who thus escape the injustice of juries and the shuffling of dealers, and choose to keep that distance that lends enchantment to the private view, and avoid the world of worries that attends on those who elect to make an exhibition of themselves.

London will soon be resplendent with advertisements, and, against a leaden sky, sky-signs will trace their formal arabesque.[8] Beauty has laid siege to the city, and telegraph wires shall no longer be the sole joy of our aesthetic perceptions.

Now, as to the technicalities of the art, I have nothing to say. To generalise upon any subject is to fall foul of the particular, and 'twere futile to lay down any rules for the making of posters. One's ears are weary of the voice of the art teacher who sits like the parrot on his perch, learning the jargon of the studios, making but poor copy and calling it criticism. We have had enough of their omniscience, their parade of technical knowledge, and their predilection for the wrong end of the stick. But if there be any who desire to know — not how posters are made — but how they should be, I doubt not that I could give them the addresses of one or two gentlemen who, having taken art under their wing, would give all necessary information.

Volpone Prospectus

An edition of Ben Jonson's *Volpone* was Beardsley's last project. Twenty-four 'illustrative and decorative' drawings for the play were planned; only eight were completed by the time of his death.[9] His first mention of the project occurs in a letter to his friend, the art collector Herbert Charles (Jerome) Pollitt of 6 November 1897, in which Beardsley enquires about Swinburne's study of the subject (to be cited in his notes).[10] Beardsley felt acutely that *Volpone* was his final work, the one that would define, or even redefine, his legacy. While his health was dwindling, the artist willed the drawings to be 'full of force both in conception and treatment', 'really forcible and contain some ideas'.[11] His letters are saturated with deep anxiety and urgency about the success of this 'important book', for which he reported having 'left behind' all his 'former methods'.[12] *Volpone* thus acquired a personal significance comparable only with that of *Under the Hill*. On 11 December 1897, Beardsley wrote to Pollitt, 'I carry *Volpone* about with me from dawn to dawn, and dream of nothing else', and asked his friend: 'If you have a Catholic church in your part of the world do put up a candle or two for a successful illustration of the *Fox*'.[13] The next day, he also begged his sister Mabel to 'put up prayers and candles whenever [she] like[d] to its success'.[14] Beardsley's slow but steady work continued throughout January 1898, but finish his illustrations

[6] A man who walked city streets wearing large boards carrying advertisements on his front and back — hence he was the filling in a sandwich. Also known as a 'sandwich board man'.

[7] The colour known as magenta is an aniline dye first synthesized by chemists in both France and England about 1859. It is a shade of purple which became very popular. In writing 'stamped', Beardsley is adapting the French word *estampe* which means an artistic print of any kind — engraving, etching, lithographic poster — and derives from the fact that all such things are created in a press which 'stamps' the image onto the paper. Here, Beardsley's comment perhaps implies that he found the colour garish, but at about the same time as this interview, he had chosen it as the dominant colour in his design for the publisher T. Fisher Unwin's poster for children's books (1894), which was nicknamed in the press the 'Purple Lady'. He may even have had his own poster in mind in writing this.

[8] A curved line. See note 3, p. 34.

[9] Beardsley to Smithers, 14 December 1897, in *Letters of Aubrey Beardsley*, p. 407.

[10] *Letters of Aubrey Beardsley*, p. 387.

[11] Beardsley to Smithers, 29 November 1897, in *Letters of Aubrey Beardsley*, p. 399.

[12] Beardsley to Smithers, 19 December 1897, in *Letters of Aubrey Beardsley*, p. 409.

[13] Beardsley to Pollitt, 11 December 1897, in *Letters of Aubrey Beardsley*, p. 405. *Volpone* is 'sly fox' in Italian.

[14] Beardsley to Mabel Beardsley, 12 December 1897, in *Letters of Aubrey Beardsley*, p. 406.

he could not. On 22 February, he confessed to Pollitt that he had 'had a vile attack of congestion of the lungs, and spent three weeks in bed'. Agonising over his inability to work, Beardsley added: 'Such splendid things I had planned out too'.[15] This incident marked the final collapse of his health.

His notes for *Volpone* were intended as a preparatory stage, and he encouraged Smithers to 'improve, amplify and glorify to any extent' his remarks.[16] Sturgis suggests that there was an 'echo of Smithers' about Beardsley's notes, particularly with respect to the treatment of Volpone's morality.[17] The posthumous publication of *Volpone* was accompanied by the Prospectus in which Smithers printed Beardsley's critical piece. It was issued on 'art paper and in a larger format than the book, with the splendid design of Volpone and his Treasure'.[18] Zatlin describes Beardsley's text as 'keen in its analysis of character, acute in its awareness of history and cultural context'.[19]

Volpone Prospectus

Mr. Smithers has pleasure in reproducing here some notes on Volpone written by Mr. Beardsley shortly before his regretted death;

Volpone was first brought out at the Globe Theatre in 1605, and printed in quarto in 1607, after having been acted with great applause at both Universities and was republished by Jonson in 1616 without alterations or additions. *Volpone* is undoubtedly the finest comedy in the English language outside the works of Shakespeare. Daring and forcible in conception, brilliant and faultless in execution, its extraordinary merits have excited the enthusiasm of all critics. The great French historian of English literature, Henri Taine, has devoted to it some of the most splendid pages of his famous work.[20] 'Volpone', he exclaims, 'oeuvre sublime, la plus vive peinture des mœurs du siècle, où s'étale la pleine beauté des convoitises méchantes, où la luxure, la cruauté, l'amour de l'or, l'impudeur de vice, déploient une poésie sinistre et splendide, digne d'une bacchanale du Titien'.[21]

In none other of his plays, not even in *The Alchemist*, in *Bartholomew Fair*, or in *The Silent Woman*,[22] is Ben Jonson's prodigious intellect and ardent satirical genius so perfectly revealed as in *Volpone*. The whole of Juvenal's satires[23] are not more full of scorn and indignation than this one play, and the portraits which the Latin poet has given us of the letchers [*sic*], dotards, pimps and parasites of Rome, are not drawn with a more passionate virulence than the English dramatist has displayed in the portrayal of the Venetian magnifico,[24] his creatures and his gulls. Like *Le Misanthrope*, *Le Festin de Pierre*, like *L'Avare*, *Volpone* might more fitly be styled a tragedy, for the pitiless unmasking of the fox at the conclusion of the play is terrible rather than sufficient.[25]

---

[15] Beardsley to Pollitt, in *Letters of Aubrey Beardsley*, p. 436.

[16] Beardsley to Smithers, 9 December 1897, in *Letters of Aubrey Beardsley*, pp. 403–04.

[17] Sturgis, *Aubrey Beardsley: A Biography*, p. 345.

[18] Walker, p. 85.

[19] Zatlin, *CR* II, p. 396.

[20] The critic Beardsley cites is Hippolyte, not Henri, Taine. Beardsley incorrectly surmised the first name from the initial 'H'. Hippolyte Taine was a French philosopher and a leading exponent of positivism. In his highly influential *History of English Literature* (*Histoire de la littérature anglaise*, 1863–1864, translated into English by Henry Van Laun in 1872), he argued that *race, milieu, moment* (race, social milieu, historical moment) determined the character of a national literature.

[21] 'a sublime work, the sharpest picture of the manners of the age, in which is displayed the full brightness of evil lusts, in which lewdness, cruelty, love of gold, shamelessness of vice, display a sinister yet splendid poetry, worthy of one of Titian's bacchanals'; see Hippolyte Taine, *History of English Literature*, trans. by Henri Van Laun, 3 vols (New York: The Colonial Press), I, p. 334. We are grateful to Martin Lohrer for sourcing the translation.

[22] *The Alchemist* was first performed in 1610; *Bartholomew Fair* in 1614; *Epicene, or The Silent Woman* in 1609.

[23] The Roman poet Juvenal belonged to the phase of Roman literature regarded in the nineteenth century as 'decadent' (see more on this in the Introduction). Juvenal's sixteen satires attacked the vice and folly of Roman society, and especially Roman women. Beardsley produced two illustrations for Juvenal's *Sixth Satire* depicting the promiscuous Roman empress Valeria Messalina: *Messalina and Her Companion* (1894) and *Messalina Returning from Bath* (1896). Beardsley also created a frontispiece for the *Sixth Satire* entitled *Juvenal Scourging a Woman* (1896).

[24] A borrowing from Italian meaning a person of high rank or position.

[25] Beardsley lists comedies by Molière: *Le Misanthrope* (*The Misanthrope*), first performed in 1666; *Dom Juan ou le Festin de pierre* (*Don Juan or The Feast of the Stone*), performed in 1665; *L'Avare* (*The Miser*) first performed in 1668.

Volpone is a splendid sinner and compels our admiration by the fineness and very excess of his wickedness. We are scarcely shocked by his lust, so magnificent is the vehemence of his passion, and we marvel and are aghast rather than disgusted at his cunning and audacity. As Mr. Swinburne observes, 'there is something throughout of the lion as well as the fox in this original and incomparable figure'.[26] Volpone's capacity for pleasure is even greater than his capacity for crime, and Ben Jonson has added to these two salient characteristics a third, which is equally dominant in the Italian — the passion for the theatre. Disguise, costume, and the attitude have an irresistible attraction for him, the blood of the mime is in his veins. To be effective, to be imposing, to play a part magnificently, are as much a joy to him as the consciousness of the most real qualities and powers; and how perfectly Volpone acts, how marvellously he improvises! He takes up a rôle with as much gusto and sureness as a finished comedian for whom the stage has not yet lost its glamour, and each new part gives him the huge pleasure of developing and accentuating some characteristic of his inexhaustibly rich nature, and of exercising his immensely fertile brain.

One of the most striking features in Elizabethan and Jacobean drama is the wonderful knowledge which our poets possess of the Italian nature, but it is generally upon the more gloomy side of that nature that they have dwelt with the greatest success. In *Volpone* we find the beau-idéal[27] of manhood as the seventeenth century in Italy conceived it. 'Faire de l'homme un être fort, muni de génie, d'audace, de presence d'ésprit, de fine politique, de dissimulation, de patience, et tourner toute cette puissance à la recherche de tous les plaisirs, de luxe, des arts, des lettres, de l'autorité, c'est-à-dire, fermer et déchaîner un animal admirable et redoutable', such, in the words of Taine, was the aim of polite education in the days of Benvenuto Cellini.[28]

The qualities which the Latin nations admire most are beauty, strength, cunning and versatility, and Volpone is Latin to the finger tips. He is as perfect an epitome of the Southern races as Hamlet is of the Northern.

---

[26] Beardsley cites Algernon Charles Swinburne, *A Study of Ben Jonson* (London: Chatto & Windus, 1889), p. 42.

[27] The ideal Beautiful; the highest conceivable type of beauty or excellence of any kind.

[28] 'To make man a strong being, endowed with genius, audacity, presence of mind, astute policy, dissimulation, patience, and to turn all this power to the acquisition of every kind of pleasure, pleasures of the body, of luxury, arts, literature, authority; that is, to form and to set free an admirable and formidable animal'; Taine, *History of English Literature*, II, p. 6. Benvenuto Cellini was a sculptor and goldsmith of the Italian Renaissance and the author of one of the most celebrated autobiographies in the history of art. Begun in 1558, it was first published in 1728; translated into German by Goethe in 1798, the account became central to the Romantic ideal of the artist. It was translated into English by Thomas Roscoe in 1822 and by John Addington Symonds in 1888; see *The Life of Benvenuto Cellini*, trans. by John Addington Symonds, 2 vols (London: John C. Nimmo, 1888). Symonds was an important art critic and translator attracted to the Hellenic ideal of male beauty and Platonic love. The sexologist Havelock Ellis included excerpts from Symonds's clandestinely printed pamphlets *A Problem in Greek Ethics* (1883) and *A Problem in Modern Ethics* (1891) in his influential *Studies in the Psychology of Sex: Sexual Inversion* (London: Wilson and Macmillan, 1897).

APPENDIX B
CRITICAL CONTEXTS

'Mr. Aubrey Beardsley and His Work':An interview for *The Idler* (1897)

Published in *The Idler* in March 1897, a year before Beardsley's death, this interview provides valuable insights with respect to Beardsley's artistic methods and, most revealingly, his methods of self-fashioning. There is evidence in one of Beardsley's letters to Raffalovich that he may have penned the interview himself: 'This afternoon I have spent interviewing myself for the *Idler* and hope I have not said too many foolish things'.[1]

Mr. Aubrey Beardsley and His Work
By Arthur H. Lawrence

There are widely divergent views entertained by the noble army of art critics as to the value of Mr. Aubrey Beardsley's black-and-white work. 'L'Art decadent, c'est moi' is somewhere stated to have been Mr. Beardsley's own idea on the matter; but whether that utterance is to be taken as a proud boast, or a humble confession, there is no evidence to show. I have heard genial art critics boldly confess that they considered Mr. Beardsley's work represented no more than the spoiling of paper; on the other hand, Mr. Beardsley has had a number of enthusiastic admirers, amongst them being Sir Edward Burne-Jones and Mr. Joseph Pennell, both of them men who are generally credited with knowing something about the art which they practise and criticise.[2] It was on the advice of the former that Mr. Beardsley ventured to submit his work to the public.

Although, according to medical opinion, he has not long to live, Mr. Aubrey Beardsley is yet but twenty-three years of age, and it is doubtful whether in such a short period of time as five years any artist has ever succeeded in obtaining so much public attention. Whether the public be a good, bad, or indifferent judge is a debateable matter, but certain it is that in no series of articles dealing with the black-and-white work of the past half-dozen years could Mr. Aubrey Beardsley's work be safely ignored. When an artist succeeds in an amazingly short space of time in catching the public eye, he is reckoned as having achieved something; and it may be safely assumed with regard to Mr. Beardsley's work that, even if it does not represent genius, it at least represents something more than the spoiling of paper; while if it be true that imitation is the sincerest form of flattery, a walk down the street and a glance at the hoardings, or a cursory inspection of the illustrated periodical press will serve to convince one that however unfortunate it may seem to us — Mr. Beardsley has founded a school, and has been blessed for some time by that superlative form of flattery which unoriginal artists are ever ready to supply.

Mr. Aubrey Beardsley is, at present, staying — his mother with him — at a south of England seaside resort. He has the young man's natural preference for life in London or Paris; but the air of these cities is not considered by the faculty as being conducive to the cure of haemorrhage of the lungs in an advanced stage, and in Mr. Beardsley's case medical orders are strict. Accordingly, it was on a cold and wet winter's afternoon that I presented myself at his house, and, after a tiring journey by train, I must admit that, even though an optimistic interviewer, I felt inclined to look on the bad side of everything. Questions of art did not appeal to

[1] Beardsley to Raffalovich, 20 December 1896, in *Letters of Aubrey Beardsley*, p. 229.

[2] Edward Burne-Jones was a painter, illustrator, and designer of stained glass and tapestries, who belonged to the second Pre-Raphaelite generation that gathered around Rossetti in the late 1850s. When Beardsley was 18, he visited Burne-Jones's studio with sister Mabel. Upon seeing Beardsley's drawings, Burne-Jones exclaimed, 'Nature has given you every gift which is necessary to become a great artist. I *seldom* or *never* advise anyone to take up art as a profession, but in *your* case I *can do nothing else*' (according to Beardsley's report). The meeting is described in detail in Beardsley's letter to A. W. King, 13 July 1891, in *Letters of Aubrey Beardsley*, pp. 21–23 (p. 22).

Joseph Pennell was an acclaimed printmaker, illustrator, and art writer. When the first issue of the influential art periodical *Studio* was published, he helped to boost Beardsley's professional reputation with a laudatory critical article; see Joseph Pennell, 'A New Illustrator: Aubrey Beardsley', *Studio*, 1 (1893), 14–19.

me; and grotesque art, or decadent art, least of all. When, however, I found myself sitting and chatting with the invalid in his combined sitting and work-room my spirits gradually rose, for although he looked haggard and pale as victims of consumption generally do, I found in Mr. Beardsley an excellent talker, concise and to the point, interested in everything, listening eagerly, and, although his slight stoop and frail physique betrayed the invalid, entering into every point with considerable keenness.

Mr. Beardsley, when I saw him, was faultlessly dressed; and I suddenly remembered that a candid friend of his had told me that 'Beardsley had two grand passions in life. One was for Wagner's music, and the other', which he thought surpassed in intensity his love for music, 'was for fine raiment'. His charming study overlooks the sea. Before we commence chatting I glance at his library, with its rare copies of last century *livres à vignettes*,[3] and various presentation copies of valuable books, and he points, with considerable pride, to his numerous pictures, engravings from Watteau, Lancret, Pater, Prudhon, and so on.[4]

'Yes, this is my studio', Mr. Beardsley explains. 'It is made up of a table and those two Empire ormolu[5] candlesticks. Without those two candlesticks I never work, and they go with me everywhere'.

'But is it true that you always work by candlelight?'

'I suppose I ought to express some apology for its being the truth; but I admit that I can't work by daylight. I am happiest when the lamps of the town have been lit, and I am so used to working by artificial light that if I want to work in the daytime I have to pull the blind down and get my candles in order before I begin'.

'No, I had no idea of going in for black-and-white work professionally when I began studying the subject. It was on the recommendation of Sir Edward Burne-Jones, whose work has no more ardent admirer than myself, and of M. Puvis de Chavannes[6] that I did so. That was five years ago, and since then I have turned out about a thousand sketches, drawings, posters, illustrations for various books, and the like.

'I was not twenty-one when Dent and Co. gave me a contract.[7] Then, when my work had been appearing for some little time John Lane took me in hand. I made about three hundred illustrations for Malory's *Morte Darthur*, and several other sketches while with Dent. Then the next thing, I believe, was my work for the *Pall Mall Budget*, which principally consisted of theatrical sketches.[8] I designed also the wrapper for *The Studio*, a design which they also used for their poster.[9] Then I illustrated the "Key-note Series" for Mr. John Lane.[10] When the *Yellow Book* came out two years ago I became its art editor, and after about a year of it I joined Mr. Leonard Smithers, who has an exclusive contract with me for all the work I do, and together we got up the *Savoy*. You may have noticed that, in the eighth and last number of the *Savoy*, Symonds[11] has done all the

---

[3] *Livres à vignettes* translates as 'vignette books'. The French word *vignette* is also used in English and describes a small illustration in a book that is on the page, not a separate plate. Typically, a vignette appears as a heading at the beginning of a chapter or in the lower part of the page at the end of a chapter. Books of a relatively modest size and price, illustrated in this manner, became popular in the eighteenth and nineteenth centuries. Beardsley would have had an obvious interest in such things. In his *Bon-Mots* series (1893–1894), for example, he developed the idea of the *livre à vignettes*, in a novel and unusual way.

[4] Nicolas Lancret was a French painter who studied under Claude Gillot, the same artist who taught Watteau. Lancret became Watteau's admirer and imitator. Jean-Baptiste Pater was another imitator of Watteau. Pierre-Paul Prud'hon was a French portrait and historical painter, a favourite of two Empresses, Josephine and Marie Louise.

[5] From French <*or moulu*, literally 'moulded gold'; refers to cast gilded bronze decoration on French furniture, and to decorative objects in gilded bronze such as candlesticks.

[6] Pierre Puvis de Chavannes was a French mural painter of the second half of the nineteenth century whose art influenced many artists of the younger generation, including Henri de Toulouse-Lautrec, Georges Seurat, and Paul Gauguin. Beardsley met him in Paris in 1893. He showed Puvis de Chavannes his 'mad and a little indecent' new drawings and 'got great encouragement'; see Beardsley to G. F. Scotson-Clark, 15 February 1893, in *Letters of Aubrey Beardsley*, pp. 43–45 (p. 43).

[7] J. M. Dent was a London publisher who gave Beardsley his first large-scale art commission, illustrations for *Le Morte Darthur* in 1892.

[8] Beardsley produced a handful of theatrical sketches for the London weekly *Pall Mall Budget* in 1893.

[9] In early 1893, Beardsley designed the prospectus for the art journal *The Studio*. The design, which depicted stylized vegetation, was used as the cover for Volumes I, II, and part of III. The original drawing was censored: the figure of a faun with a curl of fur suggestive of a phallus was expurgated.

[10] The publisher of *Salome* and the *Yellow Book* John Lane also issued a series of books of contemporary fiction under the imprint the Keynotes Series. Beardsley made cover designs for twenty-two books. He also designed decorative keys printed on the spines which included ornamental monographs of the authors' initials.

[11] This is a typo mixing the editor of the *Savoy* Arthur Symons with John Addington Symonds, the art critic and writer on 'sexual inversion' (homosexuality) (see note 28, p. 191).

letterpress and I have done all the sketches. Smithers tells me that it is almost a record for such a volume to consist entirely of the work of two men; but he is a good friend, as well as a publisher', Mr. Beardsley adds with a smile, 'and I believe he will say anything to please me. I have ventured to illustrate several of Wagner's operas', Mr. Beardsley continues, 'I would do anything and go anywhere — if I could — to hear Wagner's music decently rendered'.

'I don't really know', remarks Mr. Beardsley, in reply to another question, 'whether I am a quick worker or not. I have got through as many as twenty chapter headings in one afternoon, but this particular sketch', showing me a drawing with a great deal of fine work in it, 'took me nearly a fortnight to do'.

'This interviewing is a wonderful and terrible business', my host exclaims suddenly, 'and I suppose I ought to make something in the nature of a confession. Well, I think I am about equally fond of good books, good furniture, and good claret. By-the-way, I have got hold of a claret which you must sample, and I think you will act on my advice and lay down a few dozen of it while there is a chance of getting hold of it', Mr. Beardsley interjects with a childlike heedlessness of the fact that interviewers do not, as a rule, receive princely salaries from publishers, while very often their credit is none of the best. But Mr. Beardsley is not to be denied on these matters, and refuses to say anything more about himself until I have sufficiently admired a goodly collection of Chippendale furniture[12] — two rare old settees in particular, which he assures me are almost priceless — while he rapidly goes over the titles and dates of some of his rare editions, making up a collection sufficient to cause a bibliophile's eyes to bulge with envy.

'My opinion on my own work?' my host exclaims, as I bring him back to the main point of our chat. 'Well, I don't know in what sort of way you want me to answer a question so inane — I mean so comprehensive. Of course, I think it's marvellously good; but, if you won't think me beating about the bush, I may claim it as a proud boast that, although I have had to earn my bread and cheese by my work' — ('together with the Château Latour of 1865', I murmured)[13] 'I have always done my sketches, as people would say, for the fun of the thing'. No one has prescribed the lines on which I should work, or set any sort of limits on what I should do. I have worked to amuse myself, and if it has amused the public as well, so much the better for me! Of course, I have one aim — the grotesque. If I am not grotesque I am nothing. Apart from the grotesque I suppose I may say that people like my decorative work, and that I may claim to have some command of line. I try to get as much as possible out of a single curve or straight line'.

Then Mr. Beardsley goes on to tell me, amongst other things, how much he loves the big cities, and smilingly points out, that when a year ago his doctor ordered him to the Ardennes, he had obeyed his directions by going over to Brussels, following his stay there by a sojourn in Paris. 'How can a man die better than by doing just what he wants to do most!' he adds with a laugh. 'It is bad enough to be an invalid, but to be a slave to one's lungs and to be found wintering in some unearthly place and sniffing sea-breezes or pine-breezes, with the mistaken idea that it will prolong one's threatened existence, seems to me utter foolishness'.

A well-known publisher having described Mr. Beardsley as 'the most widely-read man' he had ever met, I question my host on the subject. 'I am an omnivorous reader', he replies modestly, 'but I have no respect for the classics, as classics. My reading has been mainly confined to English, French, and Latin literature. I am very interested just now in the works of French Catholic divines, and have just received a copy of Bourdaloue's sermons from my publisher.[14] I suppose my favourite authors are Balzac, Voltaire,[15] and Beardsley. By the way', he continues, 'the goody-goody taste of the British public is somewhat peculiar. The very work that they expect from a French artist or author will only excite indignation if it emanates from the pencil or pen of an Englishman'.

'But in matters of taste we go to extremes', I suggest.

'Yes, you are right', my host replies. 'We first of all reach the high-water mark of narrow-minded bigotry, and then follows the reaction. Rabid Puritanism comes in like a high wave and is immediately followed by a

---

[12] Thomas Chippendale was a cabinet maker and designer. He authored *The Gentleman and Cabinet Maker's Director* (1754), which became influential in Europe and America. The term 'Chippendale' is usually used for English Rococo furniture, inspired by the *Director*.

[13] Château Latour is a historic French wine estate that produces highly regarded and costly red wine.

[14] Louis Bourdaloue was a very popular French Jesuit preacher.

[15] Voltaire is the pseudonym of François Marie Arouet, a leading figure of the eighteenth-century French Enlightenment, poet, playwright, and encyclopaedist.

steady ebb-tide of brutal coarseness. This again is succeeded by the finnicking censorship of the present day, which I hope will be followed by a little more tolerance and breadth of opinion. Of course', Mr. Beardsley says with a smile, 'the easiest thing to write, if I may believe my informants, is abuse; and there is a certain type of art critic who trades in it. He never praises anything except that work which he knows no one else will condemn. The stuff such a man writes is easily written, but I should imagine it has little effect on the public but to amuse it'.

Then we chat of many things. *Apropos* to his love for music, he tells me that his illness was the reason he could not attend the Bayreuth Festival this year,[16] and further that he was originally brought up for the musical profession. He laughs at the mention of the word 'impressionism' and exclaims, 'How many of our young English impressionists know the difference between a palette and a picture, save and except Walter Sickert.[17] Do you know, I think that the attempts of modern artists to go back to the methods and formulae of the primitive workmen are as foolish as would be the attempts of a fully-matured man to go back to the dress, manner, and infantine conversation of his babyhood. To my mind', Mr. Beardsley remarks confidentially, 'there is nothing so depressing as a Gothic cathedral. I hate to have the sun shut out by the saints'.

'By-the-way, are you any relation to the Miss Mabel Beardsley who played in *The Chili Widow* at the Royalty Theatre?'[18] I interject, catching sight of a portrait which serves to bring to my recollection the pleasure I derived from that frolicsome piece.

'Well, yes; as a matter of fact I am her brother. That is her latest photograph'. And, by permission, I forthwith promptly appropriate it.

Speaking of literary matters, Mr. Beardsley says: 'When an Englishman has expressed his belief in the supremacy of Shakespeare amongst all the poets, he feels himself excused from the general study of literature. He also feels himself entirely excused from the particular study of Shakespeare'.

To my intense horror, my host remarks of Turner that 'he is only a rhetorician in paint. That is why Ruskin understood and liked him'.[19] 'I love decorative work', Mr. Beardsley tells me, as I glance at the hour indicated by a Louis Quatorze[20] clock on the mantelpiece and determine to wind up my merciless interrogatories; 'and wherever I have gone I have always brought away some little decorative scheme with me. In fact, I think you could always guess where I am working from the work in my sketches. But have you never noticed that it is the realism of one age which becomes the decorative work of the next?'

'And what is your next work?' I enquire. 'Well, I am just engaged on a series of illustrations and decorations for a translation Mr. Dawson is making of *Les Liasons Dangereuses*.[21] My pictures will be in no way "Galants" [*sic*], but severe and reticent'.[22]

---

[16] Bayreuth is a town in northern Bavaria, Germany, where in 1876 Richard Wagner established an annual festival dedicated to his operas.

[17] Walter Sickert was a British painter, printmaker, and critic, associated with British Impressionism. He painted a portrait of Beardsley in 1894.

[18] Mabel Beardsley played an important role in her brother's life. In *Aubrey Beardsley and the Dying Lady*, Easton called the siblings 'twin souls' (p. 153). Mabel became a professional actor and died prematurely, probably of cancer. *The Chili Widow*, an adaptation by A. Bourchier of a French farce *Monsieur le Directeur* by Alexandre Bisson and Fabrice Carré (1895), opened at the Royalty Theatre in London on 7 September 1895. Its success led to a North American tour with Mabel Beardsley as one of the company. When the female lead fell ill, Mabel took over the title role of a beautiful young widow from Chile.

[19] J. M. W. Turner was the English painter considered one of the greatest artists in the history of landscape painting. He was often inspired by modern poetry. Shown at the Royal Academy exhibitions, his paintings were often accompanied by verses in the catalogue. In the 1830–40s, he was the subject of ridicule and hostility in the press. The art critic John Ruskin was Turner's champion. Encyclopaedic in range, Ruskin's five-volume work *Modern Painters* (1843–1860) was started as a defence of Turner.

[20] Louis Quatorze is the style of French Baroque and Classical architecture of the reign of King Louis XIV, beginning in the 1660s.

[21] Designs for Smithers's edition of *Les Liaisons dangereuses* (*Dangerous Affairs*, 1782) by Choderlos de Laclos were among Beardsley's many unfinished projects. He 'planned to write an essay on the book and to make 170 initials, one for each of the letters in this epistolary novel; ten full-page illustrations; plus a different frontispiece for each of two volumes'; Zatlin, *CR* II, p. 301. The only drawing Beardsley completed is the portrait of the protagonist, Count Valmont, which was published in the eighth issue of the *Savoy* (1896). The surname of the Decadent poet and translator of French literature Ernest Dowson is misspelled. Dowson translated *Les Liaisons dangereuses* for Smithers's beautiful two-volume edition (1898), but the illustrations were by the eighteenth-century French artist Jean-Honoré Fragonard.

[22] By 'Galants' Beardsley means depicting the kind of flirtatious behaviour that gave its name to the category of painting in the

And then I take my leave of certainly the youngest, and, perhaps, in many ways the most original of our latter-day geniuses, and one who has succeeded — whether as a master of line work or as the apostle of the grotesque — in making for himself a lasting name, while his work, with its originality and cleverness, is bound to have an abiding and, one may boldly add, a beneficent influence on the art world.

Arthur Symons, 'Beardsley as a Man of Letters' (1904)

This article was published by Arthur Symons in response to the publication of *Under the Hill and Other Essays in Prose and Verse* by John Lane in 1904. It is discussed in the Introduction to this volume.

Beardsley as a Man of Letters

The republication by Mr. Lane, the publisher of *The Yellow Book*, of Beardsley's contributions in prose and verse to the *Savoy*, its 'rival', as Mr. Lane correctly calls it, with the illustrations which there accompanied them, reopens a little, busy chapter in contemporary history. It is the history of yesterday, and it seems already at the distance of half a century. Then, what brave petulant outbursts of poets and artists, what comic rivalries and reluctances of publishers, what droll conflicts of art and morality, what thunders of the trumpets of the press! The press is silent now, or admiring; the publishers have changed places, and all rivalries are handsomely buried, with laudatory inscriptions on their tombstones. The situation has its irony, which would have appealed most to the actor most conspicuously absent from the scene.

Beardsley was very anxious to be a writer, and his force of mind, his energy and persistence were so great that he could not have failed to write something remarkable, if he had continued to work at the art of literature. He began with music, and played the piano in drawing-rooms when he was a child, as a sort of infant prodigy; and he had a taste for music not less fine than his taste for literature. He planned many books, a book on Rousseau,[23] a book or an essay on George Sand,[24] besides stories and verses. The fragment which ran through a few numbers of the *Savoy*, and is now reprinted under the title which was there given to it, 'Under the Hill', was to be a legend of Venus and Tannhäuser, and at least one drawing was done for the book under its projected form. But some complication between publishers made it impossible for Beardsley to carry out this idea as he had intended, and Helen was put in the place of Venus and the Abbé Fanfreluche (who was to be the Abbé Aubrey) in the place of Tannhäuser. No definite version of the legend, nor indeed any plot whatever, was decided upon, and when the writing was actually begun, Beardsley had only decided on one point: that it was to be quite the most 'decadent' thing that had ever been written. He bought some wonderful old manuscript paper that had belonged to some royal person, and he used to sit for hours every day in the tiny close reading-room in the Casino at Dieppe, or on the benches of the concert-room when there was a band, writing in ink or pencil, in his neat, clerk-like handwriting, on this heavy, widely-ruled paper. He worked desperately, and he learnt how to write through sheer determination to learn. Nothing came easily to him, and he was seriously concerned at the difficulty of making one paragraph end and another begin. But a sense of form was inherent in him, and he acquired his own way of writing, as he had acquired his own way of drawing; taking freely from every source, and combining things which had never been combined before, in a new, astonishing way.

It was at the same time that he began to write verse, and for the writing of verse he had no natural impulse whatever. He decided that he would write verse, and he wrote verse; it is not poetry, but, technically, it is very

---

eighteenth century invented by Antoine Watteau (who was greatly admired by Beardsley), known as *fête galante*; see also our annotation to Chapter III, note 16 (p. 35).

[23] Jean-Jacques Rousseau was an eminent French philosopher, known for his elevation of nature over culture and corrupted human society. His key works include an influential political philosophical work *The Social Contract* (1762) and an educational treatise *Émile* (1762).

[24] George Sand is the pseudonym of Aurore Dupin, baroness Dudevant, a prolific French novelist. Her Romantic novels such as *Lélia* (1833) and *Mauprat* (1837) advocate for women's emancipation. Beardsley's 'Table Talk' includes an aphorism entitled 'George Sand etc.', which reads as follows: 'After all the Muses are women, and you must be a man to possess them — properly'; see Aubrey Beardsley, *Under the Hill and Other Essays in Prose and Verse* (London: Bodley Head, 1904), p. 63. This sexist epigram also possibly alludes to the rumours of Sand's lesbianism.

clever verse of a kind. I remember that day on the ruined walls of Arques-la-Bataille,[25] when he laboured at 'The Three Musicians' from early morning to sunset, forcing his brain to think in metre, and forcing it to an absolute metrical precision. The piece is without merit except that it is a thing done to order, to one's own order, and done without any flaw in the logic. Nothing he did, I think, ever gave him more satisfaction.

In the prose there is a much finer quality, and this fragment of an unachieved and unplanned romance has a savour of its own. It is the work, not of a craftsman, but of an amateur, and in this it may be compared with the prose of Whistler, so great an artist in his own art and so brilliant an amateur in the art of literature. Beardsley too was something of a wit, and in his prose one sees hard intellect, untinged with sentiment, employed on the work of fancy. He wrote and he saw, unimaginatively, and without passion, but with a fierce sensitive precision; and he saw by preference things elaborately perverse, full of fantastic detail, unlikely and possible things, brought together from the four corners of the universe. All those descriptions in 'Under the Hill' are the equivalent of his drawings, and they are of especial interest in showing how definitely he saw things, and with what calm minuteness he could translate what seemed a feverish drawing into oddly rational words. Listen, for instance, to this garden-picture: 'In the middle was a huge bronze fountain with three basins. From the first rose a many-breasted dragon and four little loves mounted upon swans, and each love was furnished with a bow and arrow. Two of them that faced the monster seemed to recoil in fear, two that were behind made bold enough to aim their shafts at him. From the verge of the second sprang a circle of slim golden columns that supported silver doves with tails and wings spread out. The third, held by a group of grotesquely attenuated satyrs, is centred with a thin pipe hung with masks and roses and capped with children's heads'. The picture was never drawn, but does it want more than the drawing?

The prose of 'Under the Hill' does not arrive at being really good prose, but it has felicities that astonish, those felicities by which the amateur astonishes the craftsman. The imaginary dedication is the best, the most sustained, piece of writing in it, but there is wit everywhere, subtly intermingled with fancy, and there are touches of colour such as this: 'Huge moths, so richly winged that they must have banqueted upon tapestries and royal stuffs, slept on the pillars that flanked either side of the gate-way, and the eyes of all the moths remained open and were burning and bursting with a mesh of veins'. Here and there is a thought or a mental sensation like that of 'the irritation of loveliness that can never be entirely comprehended, or ever enjoyed to the utmost'. There are many affectations, some copied from Oscar Wilde, others personal enough, such as the use of French words instead of English ones: 'chevelure' for hair, and 'pantoufles' for slippers. I do not think Beardsley finally found a place for the word which he had adapted from the French, 'papillions', instead of *papillons* or butterflies; the word would have come amusingly, and it was one of his pet words. But his whole conception of writing was that of a game with words; some obsolete game with a quaint name, like that other favourite word of his, 'spellicans',[26] for which he did find a place in the story.

Taken literally, this fragment is hardly more than a piece of nonsense, and was hardly meant to be more than that. Yet, beyond the curiosity and ingenuity of the writing, how much there is of real skill in the evocation of a certain impossible but quite credible atmosphere! Its icy artificiality is indeed one of its qualities, and produces, by mere negation, an emotional effect. Beardsley did not believe in his own enchantments, was never haunted by his own terrors, and, in his queer sympathy and familiarity with evil, had none of the ardours of a lost soul. In the place of Faust[27] he would have kept the devil at his due distance by a polite incredulity, openly expressed, as to the very existence of his interlocutor. He found it so easy never to see except on paper.

The publication of this volume of literary remains can but be welcomed by all who are interested in the work and genius of Beardsley. It contains, as far as I know, everything in prose and verse that he left, and the prose and verse will be found accompanied by the illustrations which he did for them. But it should have been explained, in reprinting 'Under the Hill', that it was a fragment, that its continuation was more than once announced in the *Savoy*, and that Beardsley did not deliberately leave it in the unfinished state in which it

---

[25] A commune with a famous castle in the Normandy region of France.

[26] Spellican (or spillikin) is a game played with a heap of small rods of wood, bone, or the like, the object being to pull off each by means of a hook without disturbing the rest. Not in the MS, the word was introduced into the SV version.

[27] Dr Faust or Faustus is the legendary figure immortalized in various literary and operatic works, including Christopher Marlowe's *The Tragical History of Dr Faustus* (1588) and Goethe's poetic drama *Faust* (1808/1832). According to the legend, Faust sold his soul to the Devil in exchange for magical powers and omniscience in his earthly life.

remains. Its basis, or at least point of departure, in the legend of Venus and Tannhäuser should also have been explained. Some misprints have crept into the text, and in Mr. Lane's preface both my name and the name of Mr. P. G. Hamerton are misspelt; mine only once, Mr. Hamerton's three times. In the advertisement at the end it is stated that of Beardsley's literary work 'Under the Hill' and 'a poem' appeared in the *Savoy*. 'A poem' should read 'three poems', the three poems now reprinted. Among the illustrations the two hitherto unpublished were really not worth publishing. It is not the least among the misfortunes of death that that accident should be thought to confer value on what is valueless in itself, merely because it can no longer be corrected or repeated.

E. F. Benson, Excerpt from *As We Were: A Victorian Peep-Show* (1930)

Edward Frederic Benson was a popular novelist whose first commercial success came with the publication of the novel *Dodo* (1894). He knew Oscar Wilde and Alfred Douglas well, and based the protagonist of his novel *The Babe, B.A.* (1896) on Beardsley's friend Jerome Pollitt. The hero of the novel decorates his rooms at Cambridge with Beardsley's pictures from the *Yellow Book* and expresses a wish to 'look as if Aubrey Beardsley had drawn' him.[28] *As We Were: A Victorian Peep-Show* is Benson's book of anecdotes and reminiscences.

Excerpt from *As We Were: A Victorian Peep-Show*

Before the dawn even of the nineties, the old idols had been quite toppled over, and the attempt to demonstrate that there was now marching out of the premises of the Bodley Head under the flying flag of *The Yellow Book* a band of April-eyed young brothers singing revolutionary ditties and bent on iconoclasm is disastrous to any clear conception of what was actually going on. Aubrey Beardsley, we are told, the greatest of them all, was the artist of the corps of rebels, Oscar Wilde was its dramatist, Arthur Symons, Ernest Dowson, Lionel Johnson, Richard Le Gallienne its poets, Max Beerbohm and Hubert Crackenthorpe [*sic*] its prose writers.[29] Arthur Symons was also its critic and Aubrey Beardsley was not only its typical and supreme artist, but poet and prose-writer in the same ranks. The banner of *The Yellow Book* went on before.

Now the confusions and misconceptions resulting from such a classified arrangement are numerous and profound. For, to begin with, if these rebels (of a rising already successfully accomplished) were marching under the flag of *The Yellow Book*, they marched under false colours, for *The Yellow Book*, an interesting illustrated quarterly the first number of which appeared in April 1894, so far from being a revolutionary gazette was a respectable, almost high-brow organ, and its contributors (leaving Aubrey Beardsley aside for the moment) were for the most part persons of recognized standing and were no more rebels against Victorian conventions than the Queen herself. In the first four numbers, which, as we shall see, were the only ones which counted, there were pictures by Walter Crane, Wilson Steer, John Sargent, Charles Furse, Joseph Pennell, and above all, Sir Frederick Leighton, President of the Royal Academy, who, incidentally, had the greatest admiration for Beardsley's work.[30] In the letter-press there were two most substantial stories by Henry James,

---

[28] E. F. Benson, *The Babe, B.A.: Being the Uneventful History of a Young Gentleman at Cambridge University* (New York: G. P. Putnam's Sons, 1896), pp. 38, 101.

[29] The poet Richard Le Gallienne was a member of the famous 1890s Rhymers Club which met at the Cheshire Cheese pub in London. From 1892, he was the first official reader of The Bodley Head, the publishing house of John Lane and Elkin Mathews. Le Gallienne's works were published in all but four volumes of the *Yellow Book*. Hubert Crackanthorpe was a fiction writer and contributor to the *Yellow Book*. Being charged with the transmission of venereal disease to his spouse, Crackanthorpe killed himself at the age of 26. At the time of death, he was the author of two collections of short stories, *Wreckage* (1893) and *Vignettes: A Miniature Journal of Whim and Sentiment* (1896). See *Hubert Crackanthorpe: Selected Writings*, ed. by William Greenslade and Emanuela Ettorre (Cambridge: MHRA, 2020).

[30] These artists may be seen as more rebellious than Benson suggests. Walter Crane was a pioneer socialist and put his art at the service of the cause in designing posters and pamphlets. His colour printed illustrated children's books of the 1870s and 1880s are important contributions to the revolution in book illustration and design of the period, in which Beardsley was to play such a central role in the 1890s. In the 1880s, Philip Wilson Steer was the first English painter to adopt a full Impressionist style. John Singer Sargent created a scandal in Paris with his profoundly unconventional portrait *Madame X* (1884), before moving to England where he developed a personal form of Impressionism as well as painting society portraits which, while immensely glamorous, often have disturbing undercurrents. Charles Furse was a more conventional artist who nevertheless exhibited with

namely 'The Death of the Lion', which opened the first number, and 'The Coxon Fund', while Miss Hepworth Dixon, Dr Richard Garnett, George Saintsbury, John Oliver Hobbes (with George Moore as her collaborator) contributed stories, articles, and dramatic sketches, José Maria de Heredia (of the French Academy), Edmund Gosse, William Watson, Theo Marzials,[31] dear to the heart of all true Victorians by reason of his song 'The Summer Shower', were among its bards; but as for Oscar Wilde who has been gazetted as the official dramatist of the group, it is sufficient to state that he never published a single line of verse or prose in *The Yellow Book* at all, nor was he in any sense a revolutionary dramatist, but of the Sheridan school. Apart from a poem by Arthur Symons called 'Stella Maris', which Mr Philip Hamerton found very grievous and profane,[32] it is really impossible to find in these first four numbers of the magazine a single piece that could possibly shock the moral or artistic susceptibilities of that or any other day, or a single sign that these distinguished contributors intended to do so. Max Beerbohm, it is true, wrote in the first number 'A Defence of Cosmetics'[33] which earned him some startling maledictions, but he explained in the second number that it was not meant to be taken seriously and pointed out the joke. Most of these authors had wit and graceful diction, but there was not one bubble of revolutionary ferment among them all.

But then there was Aubrey Beardsley, and his work remains to this day as individual and apart from that of all subsequent artists as it was then from those of his period. Instead of being the principal figure in a group of the like minded, he was unallied to any of the contributors to *The Yellow Book*, and, after four numbers of it had appeared, the editor and publisher showed how little they were prepared to risk for the one feature of the magazine which indeed was startlingly novel. The editor was Henry Harland, best known as the author of an excellently written romantic sentimentality called 'The Cardinal's Snuff Box',[34] and the publisher was John

---

the New English Art Club when it was still seen as anti-establishment, and whose wife Katharine (née Symonds), became the first Director of the Women's Royal Naval Service. Joseph Pennell was a friend, artistic follower, and biographer of Whistler, and an important figure in the developments in illustration and printmaking of the period. Sir Frederick Leighton (later Lord Leighton) was a deeply establishment figure who nevertheless produced several enigmatic masterpieces of Symbolist painting, and was himself a solitary and enigmatic figure, living in the highly exotic surroundings of his house in Kensington, London, now a museum. In 1894, he bought a drawing by Beardsley, although which one is not known, and wrote a warm letter of appreciation to the artist (Zatlin, *CR* I, p. 146).

[31] Ella Hepworth Dixon is most famous for her feminist novel *The Story of a Modern Woman* (1894). She published one story in the *Yellow Book*, 'The Sweet o' the Year' (April 1896). John Oliver Hobbes was the pseudonym of the novelist and playwright Pearl Mary Teresa Richards. She collaborated with the Irish writer George Moore on her play *The Fool's Hour* (its first act was published in the first volume of the *Yellow Book*, 1894). The writer Edmund Gosse was a contributor to the *Yellow Book*, and a friend of Beardsley and the periodical's literary editor Henry Harland. His poem 'Alere Flammam', published in the first volume of the *Yellow Book* (April 1894), was dedicated to Benson. William Watson was the publisher John Lane's author who led the campaign to remove Beardsley from the *Yellow Book* after Oscar Wilde's downfall in 1895. Théophile-Jules-Henri 'Theo' Marzials was a composer, songwriter, and poet, and friend of Gosse and other luminaries of the 1890s.

[32] Arthur Symons's poem 'Stella Maris' is a hymn to a street prostitute whose title is provocatively taken from a Christian hymn to the Virgin Mary 'Ave, maris stella' ('Hail, star of the sea'). Symons describes her as 'the Juliet of a night', equating her, again provocatively, with Shakespeare's celebrated and tragic heroine. Symons also writes lyrically, and for the time remarkably explicitly, of the pleasure of making love with her, including the moment of orgasm. Unsurprisingly, the poem upset conventionally minded readers, including the writer on art Philip Gilbert Hamerton, whose criticisms the publisher John Lane included in the second issue of the *Yellow Book* as a means of stoking controversy and increasing sales. Concluding with the exasperated rhetorical question, 'why should poetic art be employed to celebrate common fornication?', Hamerton's account of the poem certainly would have done that.

[33] This essay in defence of artificiality by Beardsley's close friend and almost exact contemporary, Max Beerbohm, caused a storm of protest in the press, which Beerbohm answered in a letter to the editor published in the second issue of the *Yellow Book*. This cites various criticisms of his essay including it being 'the rarest and most nauseous thing in all literature', and that 'a short Act of Parliament should be passed to make this kind of thing illegal'. As *Under the Hill* demonstrates, Beardsley took artificiality extremely seriously, and it is of course the central theme of the keynote work of Decadent literature, *À Rebours* (*Against Nature*, 1884) by J.-K. Huysmans.

[34] Beardsley and the writer Henry Harland first discussed the idea of an avant-garde periodical where literature and visual works would be published on artistic merit and independently from each other on 1 January 1894. They pitched the idea to John Lane, whose firm The Bodley Head would produce the first volume of the *Yellow Book* in April 1894. 'With fourteen realistic short stories or sentimental romances to his credit, as well as three satirical essays under the pen name "The Yellow Dwarf," Harland was the only author who contributed at least one story or article to each volume of *The Yellow Book*'; Barbara Schmidt, 'Henry

Lane, whose enterprise on behalf of new and startling talent was tempered with sound business instincts: he had no objection, that is to say, to thin ice, provided he felt reasonably sure that it would not let him through. William Watson, one of *The Yellow Book* bards, and of high reputation in the nineties, now sent these two an ultimatum, and told them that his poems should not appear between the same covers as those which carried and contained Beardsley's designs. It was up to them to choose, and after consultation they chose Watson and safety. The fifth number of *The Yellow Book* containing more of Beardsley's work was already in the press, but it was withdrawn and Beardsley's connection with it was severed. Arthur Symons left it also, and in the next year he started a new magazine called the *Savoy* of which eight numbers were issued. He himself, Ernest Dowson, George Moore, and Bernard Shaw[35] were among those who contributed to it, and these are very distinguished names. But as regards the *Savoy*, none of them really counted at all, in spite of the excellence of their work. the *Savoy* was admittedly Beardsley's organ.

Admirable stuff appeared in it, for Symons had a very fine critical taste, and the *Savoy* represented a definite point of view which was his, whereas *The Yellow Book* had no point of view at all. But it was only significant because of Beardsley's work, and the public subscribed to it (though very meagrely as soon appeared) for that reason. There were published in it not only his drawings, but poems by him and two long and wholly amazing instalments of a story from his pen called 'Under the Hill' which he also illustrated. Of this it may be said that no prose-writer of that day or perhaps of any other could have written a letterpress to which the drawings were so completely appropriate and no artist but he could have illustrated the story. Picture and press echo each other like the voices of a fugue, and both reek of that fascinating and evil suggestiveness of which the nineties considered him so skilled an exponent. He wrote further chapters of it, but his health was already far gone in its final decline, and for that reason, as well as perhaps for others, no further instalment of it appeared in the six subsequent issues of the *Savoy* which from that time was published monthly and then, from want of support, expired. His poems with accompanying illustrations by him were 'The Three Musicians' (only to be described as 'naughty') and 'The Ballad of the Barber': there was also a masterly translation of Catullus's ode 'Ave atque vale'. Without seeking to depreciate in any degree the value of the rest of the contents of the *Savoy*, of which the last number was entirely written by Arthur Symons and entirely illustrated by Beardsley, there was nothing very distinctive about them. In this last number the editor promised a future revival of the magazine, but nothing further appeared, for Beardsley died, and the sap of it was gone. He had been the *clou*[36] of *The Yellow Book*, for after he ceased to draw for it, it turned grey, as was remarked at the time, in a single night, though it lingered on, feeble and quite respectable, for nine issues more, and the *Savoy* died with him. In a word he had been the life of them both.

These two magazines have since then been taken as having constituted the organs of the 'literary movement' of the nineties, but for the foregoing reasons I think this is an entirely mistaken view. Moreover, their contents disclose no evidence of the existence of any kind of concerted movement, like that of the pre-Raphaelites, nor were those who are now classed as a school, bound together, as the pre-Raphaelites were, by the common aim of revolt against convention. Those painters, with affiliated members of identical aims in other arts, like William Morris and Swinburne, were consciously fighting conventions as definitely stated in their creed, but this literary movement had no such foes to contend against, for Victorianism was already dead and buried, and nobody was concerned to meddle with what was already decaying so nicely. The movement had neither crusading aspirations nor an inspiring aim, and at the time nobody thought of it as a school or even a movement. The interest in the two magazines (and that a very limited one) was due to the fact that Beardsley's drawings appeared in them.

Harland (1861–1905)', *Y90s Biographies* (2012), in *Yellow Nineties 2.0*, ed. by Lorraine Janzen Kooistra (2019) <https://www.1890s.ca/harland_bio/> [accessed 20 October 2021]. *The Cardinal's Snuff Box* (London: John Lane, 1900) was Harland's first book to achieve a success.

35 George Bernard Shaw was an Irish dramatist famous for his socially conscious comedies such as *Pygmalion* (1913).

36 The French word *clou* means a nail. Benson is suggesting he was the nail on which the *Yellow Book* hung, or its kingpin.

SELECT BIBLIOGRAPHY

Works by Aubrey Beardsley
In chronological order

'The Valiant', *Past and Present*, June 1885, pp. 45–46

'The Art of the Hoarding', *New Review*, 11.62 (1894), 47–55

'The Three Musicians', *Savoy*, January 1896, pp. 65–66

'The Ballad of a Barber', *Savoy*, July 1896, pp. 91–93

Catullus, 'Carmen CI', trans. by Aubrey Beardsley, *Savoy*, November 1896, p. 52

Under the Hill and Other Essays in Prose and Verse (London: Bodley Head, 1904)

Last Letters of Aubrey Beardsley, ed. by John Gray (London: Longmans, Green, 1904)

The Story of Venus and Tannhäuser (London: [Smithers], 1907)

Letters from Aubrey Beardsley to Leonard Smithers, ed. by R. A. Walker (London: First Edition Club, 1937)

'Volpone Prospectus', in *A Beardsley Miscellany*, ed. by R. A. Walker (London: Bodley Head, 1949), pp. 85–89

'The Ivory Piece', in *A Beardsley Miscellany*, ed. by R. A. Walker (London: Bodley Head, 1949), p. 116

Beardsley, Aubrey, and John Glassco, *Under the Hill; or, The Story of Venus and Tannhäuser [...] Now Completed by John Glassco* (Paris: Olympia Press, 1959)

Maas, Henry, J. L. Duncan, and W. G. Good, eds, *The Letters of Aubrey Beardsley* (London: Cassell, 1970)

Poems, ed. by Matthew Sturgis, Occasional Series, 6 (London: Privately Printed for The Eighteen Nineties Society, 1998)

In Black and White: The Literary Remains of Aubrey Beardsley, ed. by Stephen Calloway and David Colvin (London: Cypher, 1998)

Translations of Beardsley's Writings
In chronological order

Beardsley, Aubrey, *Unter dem Hügel: Eine Romantische Novelle*, trans. by R. A. Schröder (Leipzig: W. Drugulin, 1905)

'Pod Kholmom', *Vesy*, 11 (1905), 30–49

'Zastol′naia boltovnia', *Vesy*, 11 (1905), 50–52

Briefe [an Leonard Smithers]: Kalendernotizen u. die vier Zeichnungen zu E. A. Poe (Munich: Verlag Hans von Weber, 1908)

Sous la colline et d'autres essais en prose et en vers: précédé d'une préface par Jacques-E. Blanche, trans. by A.-H. Cornette (Paris: H. Floury, 1908)

Aubrey Beardsleys letzte Briefe, trans. by Karl Moorburg (Leipzig: Insel-Verlag, 1910)

Likiardopulo, M., ed., *Obri Berdslei: Risunki, povesti, stikhi, aforizmy, pis′ma, monografii i stat′i o Berdslee*, trans. by Mikhail Likiardopulo and Mikhail Kuzmin (Moscow: Skorpion, 1912)

Beardsley, Aubrey, and Franz Blei, *Venus und Tannhäuser, eine romantische Novelle*, trans. by Prokop Templin (Hannover: Steegemann, 1920)

Venuše a Tannhäuser, trans. by Arnošt Vaněček (Prague: M. D. N., 1930)

Biographical and Critical Writings

Aristophanes, *The Lysistrata of Aristophanes* (London: [Smithers], 1896)

Armour, Margaret, 'Aubrey Beardsley and the Decadents', *Magazine of Art*, January 1897, pp. 9–12

Berlant, Lauren, and Michael Warner, 'Sex in Public', *Critical Inquiry*, 24.2 (1998), 547–66

Bizzotto, Elisa, 'Blurring the Confines of Art and Gender: Aubrey Beardsley's *Legend of Venus and Tannhäuser*, "The Fragment of a Story"', in *Strange Sisters: Literature and Aesthetics in the Nineteenth Century*, ed. by Francesca Orestano and Francesca Frigerio (Bern: Peter Lang, 2009), pp. 213–32

BLANCHE, JACQUES-EMILE, 'Aubrey Beardsley', *Antée*, 1 April 1907, pp. 1103–22

BLEI, FRANZ, 'Aubrey Beardsley', *Pan*, 5.4 (1899), 256–60

BURDETT, OSBERT, *The Beardsley Period: An Essay in Perspective* (London: John Lane, 1925)

CALLOWAY, STEPHEN, *Aubrey Beardsley* (London: V & A Publications, 1998)

DELVAU, ALFRED, *Dictionnaire érotique moderne* (Bale: Karl Schmidt, 1864)

DESMARAIS, JANE, *The Beardsley Industry: The Critical Reception in England and France 1893 to 1914* (Aldershot: Ashgate, 1998)

DESMARAIS, JANE, and CHRIS BALDICK, eds, *Decadence: An Annotated Anthology* (Manchester: Manchester University Press, 2012)

DOWLING, LINDA, '"Venus and Tannhäuser": Beardsley's Satire of Decadence', *Journal of Narrative Technique*, 8.1 (1978), 26–41

EASTON, MALCOLM, *Aubrey and the Dying Lady: A Beardsley Riddle* (Boston: Godine, 1972)

EELLS, EMILY, 'Du Côté de Dieppe: Jacques-Émile Blanche and the "Not Quite Conventional" English', *Forum for Modern Language Studies*, 53.3 (2017), 291–302

ELLIS, HAVELOCK, 'A Note on Paul Bourget', in *Views and Reviews: A Selection of Uncollected Articles, 1884–1932. First Series: 1884–1919* (London: Desmond Harmsworth, 1932), pp. 48–60

FLETCHER, IAN, *Aubrey Beardsley* (Boston: Twayne Publishers, 1987)

—— 'Inventions for the Left Hand: Beardsley in Verse and Prose', in *Reconsidering Aubrey Beardsley*, ed. by Robert Langenfeld (Ann Arbor: UMI Research Press, 1989)

FLUHR, NICOLE, '"Queer Reverence": Aubrey Beardsley's Venus and Tannhäuser', *Cahiers Victoriens et Édouardiens*, 90, 2019 <https://doi.org/10.4000/cve.6482>

GRAY, JOHN, 'Aubrey Beardsley', *La Revue Blanche*, May 1898, pp. 68–70

HANSON, ELLIS, *Decadence and Catholicism* (Cambridge, MA: Harvard University Press, 1997)

HEYD, MILLY, *Aubrey Beardsley: Symbol, Mask, and Self-Irony* (New York: Peter Lang, 1986)

HIGGINS, JENNIFER, 'Unfamiliar Places: France and the Grotesque in Aubrey Beardsley's Poetry and Prose', *Modern Language Review*, 106.1 (2011), 63–85

JACKSON, HOLBROOK, 'Aubrey Beardsley', in *The Eighteen Nineties: A Review of Art and Ideas at the Close of the Nineteenth Century* (London: G. Richards, 1913), pp. 109–25

LAVERS, ANNETTE, '"Aubrey Beardsley, Man of Letters"', in *Romantic Mythologies*, ed. by Ian Fletcher (London: Routledge, 1967), pp. 243–70

—— '*L'eau Savante*: Aspects of Erotic Writing in Aubrey Beardsley: Part I' [1998], in *AB 2020: The Aubrey Beardsley Society* <https://ab2020.org/leau-savante-aspects-of-erotic-writing-in-aubrey-beardsley/>

—— '*L'eau Savante*: Aspects of Erotic Writing in Aubrey Beardsley: Part II' [1998], in *AB 2020: The Aubrey Beardsley Society* <https://ab2020.org/leau-savante-aspects-of-erotic-writing-in-aubrey-beardsley-2/>

LAWRENCE, ARTHUR H., 'Mr. Aubrey Beardsley and His Work', *Idler*, March 1897, pp. 188–202

MACKIE, GREGORIE, 'Aubrey Beardsley, H. S. Nichols, and the Decadent Archive', *Volupté: Interdisciplinary Journal of Decadence Studies*, 3.1 (2020), 49–74

MCWEBB, CHRISTINE, ed., *Debating the Roman de La Rose: A Critical Anthology* (New York: Routledge, 2007)

MEIER-GRAEFE, JULIUS, *Modern Art: A Contribution to a New System of Aesthetics*, trans. by Florence Simmonds and George William Chrystal, 3 vols (London: W. Heinemann, 1908)

NELSON, JAMES G., *Publisher to the Decadents: Leonard Smithers in the Careers of Beardsley, Wilde, Dowson* (University Park: Pennsylvania State University Press, 2000)

PENNELL, JOSEPH, 'A New Illustrator: Aubrey Beardsley', *Studio*, 1 (1893), 14–19

POPE, ALEXANDER, *The Rape of the Lock: Embroidered with Nine Drawings by Aubrey Beardsley* (London: Smithers, 1896)

POTOLSKY, MATTHEW, *The Decadent Republic of Letters: Taste, Politics, and Cosmopolitan Community from Baudelaire to Beardsley* (Philadelphia: University of Pennsylvania Press, 2013)

ROSS, ROBERT, *Aubrey Beardsley* (London: John Lane, 1909)

ROTHENSTEIN, WILLIAM, *Men and Memories: Recollections of William Rothenstein, 1872–1900*, 2 vols (London: Faber and Faber, 1931)

SNODGRASS, CHRIS, *Aubrey Beardsley, Dandy of the Grotesque* (New York: Oxford University Press, 1995)

—— 'Decadent Mythmaking: Arthur Symons on Aubrey Beardsley and Salome', *Victorian Poetry*, 28.3/4 (1990), 61–109

Sontag, Susan, 'Notes on "Camp"', in *Against Interpretation and Other Essays* (London: Vintage, 2009), pp. 275–92

Sturgis, Matthew, *Aubrey Beardsley: A Biography* (London: HarperCollins, 1998)

Sutton, Emma, *Aubrey Beardsley and British Wagnerism in the 1890s* (Oxford: Oxford University Press, 2002)

Symons, Arthur, 'Aubrey Beardsley', *Fortnightly Review*, 63 (May 1898), 752–61

—— *Aubrey Beardsley* (London: At the Sign of the Unicorn, 1898)

—— 'Beardsley as a Man of Letters', *Saturday Review*, 9 January 1904, pp. 41–42

—— 'The Decadent Movement in Literature', *Harper's Magazine*, 87.522 (November 1893), 858–67

Timpano, Nathan J., '"His Wretched Hand": Aubrey Beardsley, the Grotesque Body, and Viennese Modern Art', *Art History*, 40.3 (2016), 554–81

Upstone, Robert, 'Sado-Masochism and Synaesthesia: Aubrey Beardsley's "Frontispiece to Chopin's Third Ballade"', *Burlington Magazine*, 145.1204 (2003), 510–15

Walker, R. A., ed., *A Beardsley Miscellany* (London: Bodley Head, 1949)

Weintraub, Stanley, *Aubrey Beardsley: Imp of the Perverse* (London: Pennsylvania State University Press, 1976)

Yeats, W. B., *Autobiographies: Reveries over Childhood and Youth and The Trembling of the Veil* (London: Macmillan, 1926)

Zatlin, Linda Gertner, *Aubrey Beardsley: A Catalogue Raisonné*, 2 vols (New Haven: Yale University Press, 2016)

—— *Aubrey Beardsley and Victorian Sexual Politics* (Oxford: Clarendon, 1990)

MHRA Critical Texts

Jewelled Tortoise

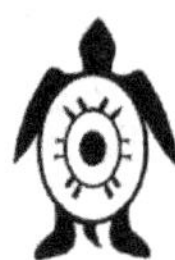

The 'Jewelled Tortoise', named after J. K. Huysmans's iconic image of Decadent taste in *A Rebours* (1884), is a series dedicated to Aesthetic and Decadent literature. Its scholarly editions, complete with critical introductions and accompanying materials, aim to make available to students and scholars alike works of literature and criticism which embody the intellectual daring, formal innovation, and cultural diversity of the British and European *fin de siècle*. The 'Jewelled Tortoise' is under the joint general editorship of Stefano Evangelista and Catherine Maxwell.

For a full listing of titles available in the series and details of how to order please visit our website at www.tortoise.mhra.org.uk

www.ingramcontent.com/pod-product-compliance
Lightning Source LLC
Chambersburg PA
CBHW080012040726
47505CB00016B/2246